Contents

Moll Flanders

Daniel Defoe

ALMA CLASSICS

ALMA CLASSICS
an imprint of

ALMA BOOKS LTD
3 Castle Yard
Richmond
Surrey TW10 6TF
United Kingdom
www.almaclassics.com

Moll Flanders first published in 1722
This edition first published by Alma Classics in 2019

Cover design by Will Dady

Edited text and notes © Alma Books Ltd

Printed in Great Britain by CPI Group (UK) Ltd, Croydon CR0 4YY

MIX
Paper from
responsible sources
FSC® C020471

ISBN: 978-1-84749-809-0

Moll Flanders

The Preface

THE WORLD IS SO TAKEN UP of late with novels and romances that it will be hard for a private history to be taken for genuine where the names and other circumstances of the person are concealed, and on this account we must be content to leave the reader to pass his own opinion upon the ensuing sheets, and take it just as he pleases.

The author is here supposed to be writing her own history, and in the very beginning of her account she gives the reasons why she thinks fit to conceal her true name, after which there is no occasion to say any more about that.

It is true that the original of this story is put into new words, and the style of the famous lady we here speak of is a little altered – particularly she is made to tell her own tale in modester words than she told it at first, the copy which came first to hand having been written in language more like one still in Newgate* than one grown penitent and humble, as she afterwards pretends to be.

The pen employed in finishing her story and making it what you now see it to be has had no little difficulty to put it into a dress fit to be seen, and to make it speak language fit to be read. When a woman debauched from her youth – nay, even being the offspring of debauchery and vice – comes to give an account of all her vicious practices, and even to descend to the particular occasions and circumstances by which she first became wicked, and of all the progression of crime which she run through in threescore year, an author must be hard put to it to wrap it up so clean as not to give room, especially for vicious readers, to turn it to his disadvantage.

All possible care, however, has been taken to give no lewd ideas, no immodest turns in the new dressing up this story – no, not to the worst parts of her expressions. To this purpose some of the vicious part of her life, which could not be modestly told, is quite left out, and several other parts are very much shortened. What is left 'tis hoped will not offend the chastest reader, or the modestest hearer, and as the best use is made even of the worst story, the moral 'tis hoped will keep the reader serious even where the story might incline him to be otherwise. To give the history of a wicked life repented of necessarily requires that the wicked part should be made as wicked as the real history of it will bear, to illustrate and give a beauty to the penitent part, which is certainly the best and brightest, if related with equal spirit and life.

It is suggested there cannot be the same life, the same brightness and beauty, in relating the penitent part as is in the criminal part. If there is any truth in that suggestion, I must be allowed to say 'tis because there is not the same taste and relish in the reading, and indeed it is too true that the difference lies not in the real worth of the subject so much as in the gust* and palate of the reader.

But as this work is chiefly recommended to those who know how to read it and how to make the good uses of it, which the story all along recommends to them, so it is to be hoped that such readers will be much more pleased with the moral than the fable, with the application than with the relation, and with the end of the writer than with the life of the person written of.

There is in this story abundance of delightful incidents, and all of them usefully applied. There is an agreeable turn artfully given them in the relating that naturally instructs the reader, either one way or other. The first part of her lewd life with the young gentleman at Colchester has so many happy turns given it to expose the crime and warn all whose circumstances are adapted to it of the ruinous end of such things, and the foolish thoughtless and abhorred conduct of both the parties, that it abundantly atones for all the lively description she gives of her folly and wickedness.

The repentance of her lover at the Bath, and how brought by the just alarm of his fit of sickness to abandon her, the just caution given there against even the lawful intimacies of the dearest friends, and how unable they are to preserve the most solemn resolutions of virtue without divine assistance – these are parts which to a just discernment will appear to have more real beauty in them than all the amorous chain of story which introduces it.

In a word, as the whole relation is carefully garbled* of all the levity and looseness that was in it, so it is all applied, and with the utmost care, to virtuous and religious uses. None can without being guilty of manifest injustice cast any reproach upon it, or upon our design in publishing it.

The advocates for the stage have in all ages made this the great argument to persuade people that their plays are useful, and that they ought to be allowed in the most civilized and in the most religious government – namely, that they are applied to virtuous purposes, and that by the most lively representations they fail not to recommend virtue and generous principles, and to discourage and expose all sorts of vice and corruption of manners. And were it true that they did so, and that they constantly adhered to that rule, as the test of their acting on the theatre, much might be said in their favour.

Throughout the infinite variety of this book, this fundamental is most strictly adhered to: there is not a wicked action in any part of it but is first and last rendered unhappy and unfortunate; there is not a superlative villain brought upon the stage but either he is brought to an unhappy end or brought to be a penitent; there is not an ill thing mentioned but it is condemned, even in the relation, nor a virtuous just thing but it carries its praise along with it. What can more exactly answer the rule laid down, to recommend even those representations of things which have so many other just objections lying against them – namely, of example, of bad company, obscene language and the like?

Upon this foundation this book is recommended to the reader as a work from every part of which something may be learnt, and some just and religious inference is drawn by which the reader will have something of instruction, if he pleases to make use of it.

All the exploits of this lady of fame, in her depredations upon mankind, stand as so many warnings to honest people to beware of them, intimating to them by what methods innocent people are drawn in, plundered and robbed, and by consequence how to avoid them. Her robbing a little innocent child, dressed fine by the vanity of the mother to go to the dancing school, is a good memento to such people hereafter, as is likewise her picking the gold watch from the young lady's side in the park.

Her getting a parcel from a hare-brained wench at the coaches in St John Street, her booty made at the fire, and again at Harwich – all give us excellent warnings in such cases to be more present to ourselves in sudden surprises of every sort.

Her application to a sober life, and industrious management at last in Virginia, with her transported spouse, is a story fruitful of instruction to all the unfortunate creatures who are obliged to seek their re-establishment abroad, whether by the misery of transportation or other disaster – letting them know that diligence and application have their due encouragement, even in the remotest parts of the world, and that no case can be so low, so despicable or so empty of prospect but that an unwearied industry will go a great way to deliver us from it, will in time raise the meanest creature to appear again in the world and give him a new cast for his life.

These are a few of the serious inferences which we are led by the hand to in this book, and these are fully sufficient to justify any man in recommending it to the world, and much more to justify the publication of it.

There are two of the most beautiful parts still behind which this story gives some idea of, and lets us into the parts of them, but they are either of them too long to be brought into the same volume, and indeed are, as I may call them, whole volumes of themselves, viz. 1. the life of her governess, as she calls her, who had run through, it seems, in a few years, all the eminent degrees of a gentlewoman, a whore and a bawd, a midwife and a midwife-keeper,* as they are called, a pawnbroker, a child-taker, a receiver of thieves and of thieves' purchase – that is to say, of stolen goods – and, in a word, herself a thief, a breeder up of thieves and the like, and yet at last a penitent.

The second is the life of her transported husband, a highwayman, who, it seems, lived a twelve years' life of successful villainy upon the road, and even at last came off so well as to be a volunteer transport, not a convict, and in whose life there is an incredible variety.

But, as I have said, these are things too long to bring in here, so neither can I make a promise of their coming out by themselves.*

We cannot say, indeed, that this history is carried on quite to the end of the life of this famous Moll Flanders, as she calls herself, for nobody can write their own life to the full end of it unless they can write it after they are dead. But her husband's life, being written by a third hand, gives a full account of them both, how long they lived together in that country and how they came both to England again after about eight year, in which time they were grown very rich, and where she lived, it seems, to be very old, but was not so extraordinary a penitent, as she was at first – it seems only that indeed she always spoke with abhorrence of her former life, and of every part of it.

In her last scene at Maryland and Virginia, many pleasant things happened, which makes that part of her life very agreeable, but they are not told with the same elegancy as those accounted for by herself – so it is still to the more advantage that we break off here.

THE

FORTUNES

AND

MISFORTUNES

OF THE FAMOUS

MOLL FLANDERS,

ETC.

M Y TRUE NAME IS SO WELL KNOWN in the records or registers at Newgate, and in the Old Bailey,* and there are some things of such consequence still depending there relating to my particular conduct that it is not to be expected I should set my name or the account of my family to this work. Perhaps after my death it may be better known – at present it would not be proper – no, not though a general pardon should be issued, even without exceptions and reserve of persons or crimes.

It is enough to tell you that, as some of my worst comrades, who are out of the way of doing me harm, having gone out of the world by the steps and the string, as I often expected to go, knew me by the name of Moll Flanders – so you may give me leave to speak of myself under that name till I dare own who I have been, as well as who I am.

I have been told that in one of our neighbour nations, whether it be in France or where else I know not, they have an order from the King that when any criminal is condemned either to die or to the galleys,* or to be transported, if they leave any children, as such are generally unprovided for, by the poverty or forfeiture of their parents, so they are immediately taken into the care of the government and put into an hospital called "the house of orphans", where they are bred up, clothed, fed, taught, and when fit to go out are placed out to trades, or to services, so as to be well able to provide for themselves by an honest industrious behaviour.

Had this been the custom in our country, I had not been left a poor desolate girl without friends, without clothes, without help or helper in the world, as was my fate – and by which I was not only exposed to very great distresses, even before I was capable either of understanding my case or how to amend it, nor brought into a course of life which was not only scandalous in itself, but which in its ordinary course tended to the swift destruction both of soul and body.

But the case was otherwise here. My mother was convicted of felony for a certain petty theft, scarce worth naming – viz. having an opportunity of borrowing three pieces of fine holland* of a certain draper in Cheapside.* The circumstances are too long to repeat, and I have heard them related so many ways that I can scarce be certain which is the right account.

However it was, this they all agree in: that my mother pleaded her belly,* and being found quick with child, she was respited for about seven months, in which time having brought me into the world, and being about again, she was called down, as they term it, to her former judgement, but obtained the favour of being transported to the plantations, and left me about half a year old – and in bad hands you may be sure.

This is too near the first hours of my life for me to relate anything of myself, but by hearsay 'tis enough to mention that as I was born in such an unhappy place I had no parish* to have recourse to for my nourishment in my infancy, nor can I give the least account how I was kept alive, other than that, as I have been told, some relation of my mother's took me away for a while as a nurse, but at whose expense or by whose direction I know nothing at all of it.

The first account that I can recollect, or could ever learn of myself, was that I had wandered among a crew of those people they call Gypsies, or Egyptians,* but I believe it was but a very little while that I had been among them, for I had not had my skin discoloured or blackened, as they do very young to all the children they carry about with them, nor can I tell how I came among them, or how I got from them.

It was at Colchester in Essex that those people left me, and I have a notion in my head that I left them there (that is, that I hid myself and would not go any farther with them), but I am not able to be particular in that account. Only this I remember: that being taken up by some of the parish officers of Colchester, I gave an account that I came into the town with the Gypsies, but that I would not go any farther with them, and that so they had left me, but whither they were gone that I knew not, nor could they expect it of me, for though they sent round the country to enquire after them, it seems they could not be found.

I was now in a way to be provided for, for though I was not a parish charge upon this or that part of the town by law, yet as my case came to be known, and that I was too young to do any work, being not above three years old, compassion moved the magistrates of the town to order some care to be taken of me, and I became one of their own as much as if I had been born in the place.

In the provision they made for me, it was my good hap to be put to nurse, as they call it, to a woman who was indeed poor, but had been in better circumstances, and who got a little livelihood by taking such as I was supposed to be, and keeping them with all necessaries till they were at a certain age, in which it might be supposed they might go to service or get their own bread.

This woman had also a little school, which she kept to teach children to read and to work – and having, as I have said, lived before that in good fashion, she bred up the children she took with a great deal of art, as well as with a great deal of care.

But that which was worth all the rest, she bred them up very religiously, being herself a very sober pious woman, (2.) very housewifely and clean, and (3.) very mannerly and with good behaviour, so that, in a word, excepting a plain diet, coarse lodging and mean cloths, we were brought up as mannerly and as genteelly as if we had been at the dancing school.

I was continued here till I was eight years old, when I was terrified with news that the magistrates, as I think they called them, had ordered that I should go to service. I was able to do but very little service wherever I was to go, except it was to run of errands and be a drudge to some cook maid; and this they told me of often, which put me into a great fright, for I had a thorough aversion to going to service, as they called it – that is, to be a servant – though I was so young; and I told my nurse, as we called her, that I believed I could get my living without going to service if she pleased to let me, for she had taught me to work with my needle and spin worsted, which is the chief trade of that city – and I told her that if she would keep me, I would work for her, and I would work very hard.

I talked to her almost every day of working hard, and, in short, I did nothing but work and cry all day, which grieved the good kind woman so much that at last she began to be concerned for me, for she loved me very well.

One day after this, as she came into the room where all we poor children were at work, she sat down just over against me, not in her usual place as mistress, but as if she set herself on purpose to observe me and see me work. I was doing something she had set me to – as I remember, it was marking some shirts, which she had taken to make – and after a while she began to talk to me: "Thou foolish child," says she, "thou art always crying" (for I was crying then). "Prithee, what doest cry for?" "Because they will take me away," says I, "and put me to service, and I can't work housework." "Well, child," says she, "but though you can't work housework, as you call it, you will learn it in time, and they won't put you to hard things at first." "Yes, they will," says I, "and if I can't do it, they will beat me, and the maids will beat me to make me do great work, and I am but a little girl, and I can't do it" – and then I cried again till I could not speak any more to her.

This moved my good motherly nurse, so that she from that time resolved I should not go to service yet, so she bid me not cry, and she would speak to Mr Mayor, and I should not go to service till I was bigger.

Well, this did not satisfy me, for to think of going to service was such a frightful thing to me that if she had assured me I should not have gone till I was twenty years old, it would have been the same to me – I should have cried, I believe, all the time, with the very apprehension of its being to be so at last.

When she saw that I was not pacified yet, she began to be angry with me. "And what would you have?" says she. "Don't I tell you that you shall not go to service till you are bigger?" "Ay," says I, "but then I must go at last." "Why, what?" said she. "Is the girl mad? What, would you be a gentlewoman?" "Yes," says I, and cried heartily till I roared out again.

This set the old gentlewoman a-laughing at me, as you may be sure it would. "Well, madam, forsooth," says she, gibing at me, "you would be a gentlewoman – and pray how will you come to be a gentlewoman? What, will you do it by your fingers' ends?"

"Yes," says I again, very innocently.

"Why, what can you earn?" says she. "What can you get at your work?"

"Three pence," said I, "when I spin, and 4*d*.* when I work plain work."*

"Alas, poor gentlewoman!" said she again, laughing. "What will that do for thee?"

"It will keep me," says I, "if you will let me live with you" – and this I said in such a poor, petitioning tone that it made the poor woman's heart yearn to me, as she told me afterwards.

"But," says she, "that will not keep you, and buy you clothes too – and who must buy the little gentlewoman clothes?" says she, and smiled all the while at me.

"I will work harder, then," says I, "and you shall have it all."

"Poor child! It won't keep you," says she. "It will hardly keep you in victuals."

"Then I will have no victuals," says I, again very innocently. "Let me but live with you."

"Why, can you live without victuals?" says she.

"Yes," again says I, very much like a child, you may be sure, and still I cried heartily.

I had no policy in all this – you may easily see it was all nature – but it was joined with so much innocence and so much passion that, in short, it set the good motherly creature a-weeping too, and she cried at last as fast as I did, and then took me and led me out of the teaching room. "Come," says she, "you shan't go to service – you shall live with me" – and this pacified me for the present.

Some time after this, she going to wait on the mayor and talking of such things as belonged to her business, at last my story came up, and my good nurse told Mr Mayor the whole tale. He was so pleased with it that he would call his lady and his two daughters to hear it, and it made mirth enough among them, you may be sure.

However, not a week had passed over but on a sudden comes Mrs Mayoress and her two daughters to the house to see my old nurse, and to see her school and the children. When they had looked about them a little: "Well, Mrs ——," says the mayoress to my nurse, "and pray which is the little lass that intends to be a gentlewoman?" I heard her, and I was terrible frighted at first, though I did not know why neither, but Mrs Mayoress comes up to me: "Well, miss," says she, "and what are you at work upon?" The word "miss" was a language that had hardly been heard of in our school, and I wondered what sad name it was she called me. However, I stood up, made a curtsy, and she took my work out of my hand, looked on it and said it was very well. Then she took up one of my hands. "Nay," says she, "the child may come to be a gentlewoman for ought anybody knows – she has a gentlewoman's hand," says she. This pleased me mightily, you may be sure, but Mrs Mayoress did not stop there, but, giving me my work again, she put her hand in her pocket, gave me a shilling and bid me mind my work, and learn to work well, and I might be a gentlewoman for ought she knew.

Now, all this while my good old nurse, Mrs Mayoress and all the rest of them did not understand me at all, for they meant one sort of thing by the word "gentlewoman", and I meant quite another. For, alas, all I understood by being a gentlewoman was to be able to work for myself and get enough to keep me without that terrible bugbear, going to service, whereas they meant to live great, rich and high, and I know not what.

Well, after Mrs Mayoress was gone, her two daughters came in, and they called for the gentlewoman too, and they talked a long while to me, and I answered them in my innocent way – but always if they asked me whether I resolved to be a gentlewoman, I answered yes. At last one of them asked me what a gentlewoman was. That puzzled me much, but, however, I explained myself negatively that it was one that did not go to service, to do housework. They were pleased to be familiar with me, and liked my little prattle to them, which it seems was agreeable enough to them, and they gave me money too.

As for my money, I gave it all to my mistress nurse, as I called her, and told her she should have all I got for myself when I was a gentlewoman, as well as now. By this and some other of my talk, my old tutress began to understand me about what I meant by being a gentlewoman, and that I understood by it no more than to be able to get my bread by my own work, and at last she asked me whether it was not so.

I told her yes, and insisted on it that to do so was to be a gentlewoman. "For," says I, "there is such a one" – naming a woman that mended lace and washed the ladies' laced heads.* "She," says I, "is a gentlewoman, and they call her madam."

"Poor child," says my good old nurse, "you may soon be such a gentlewoman as that, for she is a person of ill fame, and has had two or three bastards."

I did not understand anything of that, but I answered: "I am sure they call her madam, and she does not go to service, nor do housework" – and therefore I insisted that she was a gentlewoman, and I would be such a gentlewoman as that.

The ladies were told all this again, to be sure, and they made themselves merry with it, and every now and then the young ladies, Mr Mayor's daughters, would come and see me, and ask where the little gentlewoman was, which made me not a little proud of myself.

This held a great while, and I was often visited by these young ladies, and sometimes they brought others with them, so that I was known by it almost all over the town.

I was now about ten years old, and began to look a little womanish, for I was mighty grave and humble, very mannerly, and, as I had often heard the ladies say I was pretty and would be a very handsome woman, so you may be sure that hearing them say so made me not a little proud. However, that pride had no ill effect upon me yet – only, as they often gave me money, and I gave it my old nurse, she, honest woman, was so just to me as to lay it all out again for me, and gave me headdresses, and linen, and gloves and ribbons, and I went very neat, and always clean – for that I would do, and if I had rags on, I would always be clean, or else I would dabble them in water myself. But, I say, my good nurse, when I had money given me, very honestly laid it out for me, and would always tell the ladies this or that was bought with their money, and this made them oftentimes give me more, till at last I was indeed called upon by the magistrates, as I understood it, to go out to service. But then I was come to be so good a workwoman myself, and the ladies were so kind to me, that it was plain I could maintain myself – that is to say, I could earn as much for my nurse as she was able by it to keep me – so she told them that if they would give her leave, she would keep the gentlewoman, as she called me, to be her assistant, and teach the children, which I was very well able to do, for I was very nimble at my work, and had a good hand with my needle, though I was yet very young.

But the kindness of the ladies of the town did not end here, for when they came to understand that I was no more maintained by the public allowance as before, they gave me money oftener than formerly, and as I grew up, they brought me work to do for them, such as linen to make and laces to mend, and heads to dress up, and not only paid me for doing them, but even taught me how to do them, so that now I was a gentlewoman indeed – as I understood that word and as I desired to be, for by that time I was twelve years old: I not only found myself clothes* and paid my nurse for my keeping, but got money in my pocket too beforehand.

The ladies also gave me clothes frequently of their own, or their children's – some stockings, some petticoats, some gowns, some one thing, some another – and these my old woman managed for me like a mere* mother, and kept them for me, obliged me to mend them and turn them* and twist them to the best advantage, for she was a rare housewife.

At last one of the ladies took so much fancy to me that she would have me home to her house for a month, she said, to be among her daughters.

Now, though this was exceeding kind in her, yet, as my old good woman said to her, unless she resolved to keep me for good and all, she would do the little gentlewoman more harm than good. "Well," says the lady, "that's true, and therefore I'll only take her home for a week, then, that I may see how my daughters and she agree together, and how I like her temper, and then I'll tell you more. And in the mean time, if anybody comes to see her as they used to do, you may only tell them you have sent her out to my house."

This was prudently managed enough, and I went to the lady's house, but I was so pleased there with the young ladies, and they so pleased with me, that I had enough to do to come away, and they were as unwilling to part with me.

However, I did come away, and lived almost a year more with my honest old woman, and began now to be very helpful to her – for I was almost fourteen years old, was tall of my age and looked a little womanish. But I had such a taste of genteel living at the lady's house that I was not so easy in my old quarters as I used to be, and I thought it was fine to be a gentlewoman indeed, for I had quite other notions of a gentlewoman now than I had before – and as I thought, I say, that it was fine to be a gentlewoman, so I loved to be among gentlewomen, and therefore I longed to be there again.

About the time that I was fourteen years and a quarter old, my good old nurse – mother, I ought rather to call her – fell sick and died. I was then in a sad condition indeed, for as there is no great bustle in putting an end to a poor body's family, when once they are carried to the grave, so the poor good woman being buried, the parish children she kept were immediately removed by the churchwardens; the school was at an end, and the children of it had no more to do but just stay at home till they were sent somewhere else – and as for what she left, her daughter, a married woman with six or seven children, came and swept it all away at once, and, removing the goods, they had no more to say to me than to jest with me and tell me that the little gentlewoman might set up for herself if she pleased.

I was frighted out of my wits almost, and knew not what to do, for I was, as it were, turned out of doors to the wide world, and that which was still worse, the old honest woman had two-and-twenty shillings of mine in her hand, which was all the estate the little gentlewoman had in the world – and when I asked the daughter for it, she huffed me and laughed at me, and told me she had nothing to do with it.

It was true the good poor woman had told her daughter of it, and that it lay in such a place, that it was the child's money, and had called once or twice for me, to give it me, but I was unhappily out of the way, somewhere or other, and when I came back she was past being in a condition to speak of it. However, the daughter was so honest afterwards as to give it me, though at first she used me cruelly about it.

Now was I a poor gentlewoman indeed, and I was just that very night to be turned into the wide world, for the daughter removed all the goods, and I had not so much as a lodging to go to, or a bit of bread to eat. But it seems some of the neighbours who had known my circumstances took so much compassion of me as to acquaint the lady in whose family I had been a week, as I mentioned above, and immediately she sent her maid to fetch me away, and two of her daughters came with the maid, though unsent. So I went with them bag and baggage, and with a glad heart, you may be sure – the fright of my condition had made such an impression upon me that I did not want now to be a gentlewoman, but was very willing to be a servant, and that any kind of servant they thought fit to have me be.

But my new generous mistress had better thoughts for me. I call her generous, for she exceeded the good woman I was with before in everything, as well as in the matter of estate – I say in everything except honesty, and for that, though this was a lady most exactly just, yet I must not forget to say on all occasions that the first, though poor, was as uprightly honest as it was possible for anyone to be.

I was no sooner carried away as I have said by this good gentle-woman but the first lady – that is to say, the mayoress that was – sent her two daughters to take care of me, and another family which had taken notice of me when I was the little gentlewoman, and had given me work to do, sent for me after her, so that I was mightily made of, as we say – nay, and they were not a little angry, especially madam the mayoress, that her friend had taken me away from her, as she called it. For, as she said, I was hers by right, she having been the first that took any notice of me. But they that had me would not part with me – and as for me, though I should have been very well treated with any of the other, yet I could not be better than where I was.

Here I continued till I was between seventeen and eighteen years old, and here I had all the advantages for my education that could be imagined: the lady had masters home to the house to teach her daughters to dance, and to speak French, and to write, and others to teach them music, and as I was always with them, I learnt as fast as they, and though the masters were not appointed to teach me, yet I learnt by imitation and enquiry all that they learnt by instruction and direction. So that, in short, I learnt to dance and speak French as well as any of them, and to sing much better, for I had a better voice than any of them. I could not so readily come at playing on the harpsichord or spinet, because I had no instrument of my own to practise on, and could only come at theirs in the intervals when they left it, which was uncertain, but yet I learnt tolerably well too, and the young ladies at length got two instru-ments – that is to say, a harpsichord and a spinet too – and then they taught me themselves. But as to dancing, they could hardly help my learning country dances, because they always wanted me to make up even number, and, on the other hand, they were as heartily willing to learn me everything that they had been taught themselves as I could be to take the learning.

By this means I had, as I have said above, all the advantages of education that I could have had if I had been as much a gentlewoman as they were with whom I lived – and in some things I had the advantage of my ladies, though they were my superiors. But they were all the gifts of nature, and which all their fortunes could not furnish. First, I was apparently handsomer than any of them. Secondly, I was better shaped, and, thirdly, I sang better, by which I mean I had a better voice – in all which you will, I hope, allow me to say, I do not speak my own conceit of myself, but the opinion of all that knew the family.

I had with all these the common vanity of my sex, viz. that being really taken for very handsome, or if you please for a great beauty, I very well knew it, and had as good an opinion of myself as anybody else could have of me – and particularly I loved to hear anybody speak of it, which could not but happen to me sometimes, and was a great satisfaction to me.

Thus far I have had a smooth story to tell of myself, and in all this part of my life I not only had the reputation of living in a very good family – and a family noted and respected everywhere for virtue and sobriety, and for every valuable thing – but I had the character too of a very sober, modest and virtuous young woman, and such I had always been. Neither had I yet any occasion to think of anything else, or to know what a temptation to wickedness meant.

But that which I was too vain of was my ruin, or rather my vanity was the cause of it. The lady in the house where I was had two sons, young gentlemen of very promising parts and of extraordinary behaviour, and it was my misfortune to be very well with them both – but they managed themselves with me in a quite different manner.

The eldest: a gay gentleman that knew the town as well as the country, and though he had levity enough to do an ill-natured thing, yet had too much judgement of things to pay too dear for his pleasures; he began with that unhappy snare to all women, viz. taking notice upon all occasions how pretty I was, as he called it, how agreeable, how well carriaged* and the like, and this he contrived so subtly as if he had known as well how to catch a woman in his net as a partridge when he went a-setting, for he would contrive to be talking this to his sisters when, though I was not by, yet when he knew I was not so far off, but that I should be sure to hear him. His sisters would return softly to him, "Hush brother, she will hear you – she is but in the next room." Then he would put it off and talk softlier, as if he had not known it, and begin to acknowledge he was wrong; and then, as if he had forgot himself, he would speak aloud again, and I that was so well pleased to hear it was sure to listen for it upon all occasions.

After he had thus baited his hook and found easily enough the method how to lay it in my way, he played an opener game, and one day, going by his sister's chamber when I was there, doing something about dressing her, he comes in with an air of gaiety. "Oh, Mrs Betty!" said he to me. "How do you do, Mrs Betty? Don't your cheeks burn, Mrs Betty?" I made a curtsy and blushed, but said nothing. "What makes you talk so, brother?" says the lady. "Why," says he, "we have been talking of her below stairs this half-hour." "Well," says his sister, "you can say no harm of her, that I am sure, so 'tis no matter what you have been talking about." "Nay," says he, "'tis so far from talking harm of her that we have been talking a great deal of good, and a great many fine things have been said of Mrs Betty, I assure you – and particularly that she is the handsomest young woman in Colchester, and, in short, they begin to toast her health in the town."

"I wonder at you, brother," says the sister. "Betty wants but one thing, but she had as good want everything, for the market is against our sex just now, and if a young woman have beauty, birth, breeding, wit, sense, manners, modesty, and all these to an extreme, yet if she have not money she's nobody – she had as good want them all, for nothing but money now recommends a woman. The men play the game all into their own hands."

Her younger brother, who was by, cried, "Hold, sister, you run too fast – I am an exception to your rule. I assure you, if I find a woman so accomplished as you talk of, I say, I assure you I would not trouble myself about the money."

"Oh," says the sister, "but you will take care not to fancy one, then, without the money."

"You don't know that neither," says the brother.

"But why, sister," says the elder brother, "why do you exclaim so at the men for aiming so much at the fortune? You are none of them that want a fortune, whatever else you want."

"I understand you, brother," replies the lady very smartly. "You suppose I have the money and want the beauty, but as times go now, the first will do without the last, so I have the better of my neighbours."

"Well," says the younger brother, "but your neighbours, as you call them, may be even with you, for beauty will steal a husband sometimes in spite of money, and when the maid chances to be handsomer than the mistress, she oftentimes makes as good a market, and rides in a coach before her."

I thought it was time for me to withdraw and leave them, and I did so – but not so far but that I heard all their discourse, in which I heard abundance of fine things said of myself which served to prompt my vanity, but, as I soon found, was not the way to increase my interest in the family, for the sister and the younger brother fell grievously out about it, and as he said some very disobliging things to her upon my account, so I could easily see that she resented them by her future conduct to me – which indeed was very unjust to me, for I had never had the least thought of what she suspected as to her younger brother. Indeed, the elder brother, in his distant, remote way, had said a great many things as in jest which I had the folly to believe were in earnest, or to flatter myself with the hopes of what I ought to have supposed he never intended, and perhaps never thought of.

It happened one day that he came running upstairs towards the room where his sisters used to sit and work, as he often used to do, and calling to them before he came in, as was his way too, I being there alone, stepped to the door and said, "Sir, the ladies are not here – they are walked down the garden." As I stepped forward to say this towards the door, he was just got to the door, and, clasping me in his arms, as if it had been by chance: "Oh, Mrs Betty!" says he. "Are you here? That's better still – I want to speak with you more than I do with them" – and then, having me in his arms, he kissed me three or four times.

I struggled to get away, and yet did it but faintly neither, and he held me fast, and still kissed me, till he was almost out of breath, and then, sitting down, says, "Dear Betty, I am in love with you."

His words I must confess fired my blood – all my spirits flew about my heart and put me into disorder enough, which he might easily have seen in my face. He repeated it afterwards several times, that he was in love with me, and my heart spoke as plain as a voice that I liked it. Nay, whenever he said "I am in love with you", my blushes plainly replied, "Would you were, sir."

However, nothing else passed at that time. It was but a surprise, and when he was gone, I soon recovered myself again. He had stayed longer with me, but he happened to look out at the window and see his sisters coming up the garden, so he took his leave, kissed me again, told me he was very serious and I should hear more of him very quickly, and away he went, leaving me infinitely pleased, though surprised – and had there not been one misfortune in it, I had been in the right, but the mistake lay here: that Mrs Betty was in earnest and the gentleman was not.

From this time my head ran upon strange things, and I may truly say I was not myself. To have such a gentleman talk to me of being in love with me, and of my being such a charming creature, as he told me I was – these were things I knew not how to bear; my vanity was elevated to the last degree. It is true I had my head full of pride, but knowing nothing of the wickedness of the times I had not one thought of my own safety, or of my virtue about me, and had my young master offered it at first sight, he might have taken any liberty he thought fit with me. But he did not see his advantage, which was my happiness for that time.

After this attack, it was not long but he found an opportunity to catch me again, and almost in the same posture – indeed, it had more of design in it on his part, though not on my part. It was thus: the young ladies were all gone a-visiting with their mother; his brother was out of town; and as for his father, he had been at London for a week before. He had so well watched me that he knew where I was, though I did not so much as know that he was in the house, and he briskly comes up the stairs, and seeing me at work comes into the room to me directly, and began just as he did before with taking me in his arms and kissing me for almost a quarter of an hour together.

It was his younger sister's chamber that I was in, and as there was nobody in the house but the maids below stairs, he was, it may be, the ruder. In short, he began to be in earnest with me indeed – perhaps he found me a little too easy, for God knows I made no resistance to him while he only held me in his arms and kissed me. Indeed, I was too well pleased with it to resist him much.

However, as it were, tired with that kind of work, we sat down, and there he talked with me a great while. He said he was charmed with me, and that he could not rest night or day till he had told me how he was in love with me, and if I was able to love him again, and would make him happy, I should be the saving of his life – and many such fine things. I said little to him again, but easily discovered that I was a fool, and that I did not in the least perceive what he meant.

Then he walked about the room, and, taking me by the hand, I walked with him, and by and by, taking his advantage, he threw me down upon the bed, and kissed me there most violently, but to give him his due, offered no manner of rudeness to me, only kissed me a great while. After this he thought he had heard somebody come upstairs, so he got off from the bed, lifted me up, profess-ing a great deal of love for me, but told me it was all an honest affection, and that he meant no ill to me, and with that he put five guineas into my hand and went away downstairs.

I was more confounded with the money than I was before with the love, and began to be so elevated that I scarce knew the ground I stood on. I am the more particular in this part, that if my story comes to be read by any innocent young body, they may learn from it to guard themselves against the mischiefs which attend an early knowledge of their own beauty. If a young woman once thinks herself handsome, she never doubts the truth of any man that tells her he is in love with her, for if she believes herself charming enough to captivate him, 'tis natural to expect the effects of it.

This young gentleman had fired his inclination as much as he had my vanity, and as if he had found that he had an opportunity, and was sorry he did not take hold of it, he comes up again in half an hour or thereabouts, and falls to work with me again as before, only with a little less introduction.

And, first, when he entered the room, he turned about and shut the door. "Mrs Betty," said he, "I fancied before somebody was coming upstairs, but it was not so. However," adds he, "if they find me in the room with you, they shan't catch me a-kissing of you." I told him I did not know who should be coming upstairs, for I believed there was nobody in the house but the cook and the other maid, and they never came up those stairs. "Well, my dear," says he, "'tis good to be sure, however" – and so he sits down and we began to talk. And now, though I was still all on fire with his first visit and said little, he did as it were put words in my mouth, telling me how passionately he loved me, and that though he could not mention such a thing till he came to his estate, yet he was resolved to make me happy then, and himself too – that is to say, to marry me – and abundance of such fine things, which I, poor fool, did not understand the drift of, but acted as if there was no such thing as any kind of love but that which tended to matrimony; and if he had spoke of that, I had no room, as well as no power, to have said no, but we were not come that length yet.

We had not sat long but he got up and, stopping my very breath with kisses, threw me upon the bed again – but then, being both well warmed, he went farther with me than decency permits me to mention, nor had it been in my power to have denied him at that moment had he offered much more than he did.

However, though he took these freedoms with me, it did not go to that which they call the last favour – which, to do him justice, he did not attempt, and he made that self-denial of his a plea for all his freedoms with me upon other occasions after this. When this was over, he stayed but a little while, but he put almost a handful of gold in my hand, and left me, making a thousand protestations of his passion for me, and of his loving me above all the women in the world.

It will not be strange if I now began to think, but – alas! – it was but with very little solid reflection: I had a most unbounded stock of vanity and pride, and but a very little stock of virtue. I did indeed cast* sometimes with myself what my young master aimed at, but thought of nothing but the fine words and the gold – whether he intended to marry me or not to marry me seemed a matter of no great consequence to me, nor did my thoughts so much as suggest to me the necessity of making any capitulation* for myself, till he came to make a kind of formal proposal to me, as you shall hear presently.

Thus I gave up myself to a readiness of being ruined without the least concern, and am a fair memento to all young women whose vanity prevails over their virtue. Nothing was ever so stupid on both sides. Had I acted as became me and resisted as virtue and honour required, this gentleman had either desisted his attacks, finding no room to expect the accomplishment of his design, or had made fair and honourable proposals of marriage – in which case, whoever had blamed him, nobody could have blamed me. In short, if he had known me, and how easy the trifle he aimed at was to be had, he would have troubled his head no further, but have given me four or five guineas and have lain with me the next time he had come at me. And if I had known his thoughts, and how hard he thought I would be to be gained, I might have made my own terms with him, and if I had not capitulated for an immediate marriage, I might for a maintenance till marriage, and might have had what I would, for he was already rich to excess, besides what he had in expectation. But I seemed wholly to have abandoned all such thoughts as these, and was taken up only with the pride of my beauty, and of being beloved by such a gentleman. As for the gold, I spent whole hours in looking upon it – I told the guineas over and over a thousand times a day. Never poor vain creature was so wrapped up with every part of the story as I was, not considering what was before me, and how near my ruin was at the door. Indeed, I think I rather wished for that ruin than studied to avoid it.

In the mean time, however, I was cunning enough not to give the least room to any in the family to suspect me, or to imagine that I had the least correspondence with this young gentleman. I scarce ever looked towards him in public, or answered if he spoke to me if anybody was near us. But for all that, we had every now and then a little encounter where we had room for a word or two, and now and then a kiss, but no fair opportunity for the mischief intended; and especially considering that he made more circumlocution than, if he had known my thoughts, he had occasion for, and the work appearing difficult to him, he really made it so.

But as the Devil is an unwearied tempter, so he never fails to find opportunity for that wickedness he invites to. It was one evening that I was in the garden with his two younger sisters and himself, and all very innocently merry, when he found means to convey a note into my hand by which he directed me to understand that he would tomorrow desire me publicly to go of an errand for him into the town, and that I should see him somewhere by the way.

Accordingly, after dinner he very gravely says to me, his sisters being all by, "Mrs Betty, I must ask a favour of you." "What's that?" says his second sister. "Nay, sister," says he very gravely. "If you can't spare Mrs Betty today, any other time will do." Yes, they said, they could spare her well enough, and the sister begged pardon for asking, which she did but of mere course, without any meaning. "Well, but brother," says the eldest sister, "you must tell Mrs Betty what it is. If it be any private business that we must not hear, you may call her out, there she is." "Why, sister," says the gentleman very gravely, "what do you mean? I only desire her to go into the high street" (and then he pulls out a turnover)* "to such a shop," and then he tells them a long story of two fine neckcloths he had bid money for, and he wanted to have me go and make an errand to buy a neck* to the turnover that he showed, to see if they would take my money for the neckcloths – to bid a shilling more and haggle with them. And then he made more errands, and so continued to have such petty business to do that I should be sure to stay a good while.

When he had given me my errands, he told them a long story of a visit he was going to make to a family they all knew, and where was to be such and such gentlemen, and how merry they were to be, and very formally asks his sisters to go with him, and they as formally excused themselves, because of company that they had notice was to come and visit them that afternoon, which by the way he had contrived on purpose.

He had scarce done speaking to them and giving me my errand, but his man came up to tell him that Sir W—— H——'s coach stopped at the door. So he runs down and comes up again immediately. "Alas!" says he, aloud. "There's all my mirth spoilt at once: Sir W—— has sent his coach for me, and desires to speak with me upon some earnest business." It seems this Sir W—— was a gentleman who lived about three miles out of town, to whom he had spoken on purpose the day before to lend him his chariot for a particular occasion, and had appointed it to call for him, as it did, about three o'clock.

Immediately he calls for his best wig, hat and sword, and ordering his man to go to the other place to make his excuse – that was to say, he made an excuse to send his man away – he prepares to go into the coach. As he was going, he stopped a while, and speaks mighty earnestly to me about his business, and finds an opportunity to say very softly to me, "Come away, my dear, as soon as ever you can." I said nothing, but made a curtsy, as if I had done so to what he said in public. In about a quarter of an hour I went out too. I had no dress,* other than before, except that I had a hood, a mask, a fan and a pair of gloves in my pocket, so that there was not the least suspicion in the house. He waited for me in the coach in a back lane, which he knew I must pass by, and had directed the coachman whither to go, which was to a certain place called Mile End,* where lived a confidant of his, where we went in, and where was all the convenience in the world to be as wicked as we pleased.

When we were together, he began to talk very gravely to me, and to tell me he did not bring me there to betray me, that his passion for me would not suffer him to abuse me, that he resolved to marry me as soon as he came to his estate, that in the mean time, if I would grant his request, he would maintain me very honourably, and made me a thousand protestations of his sincerity and of his affection to me, and that he would never abandon me – and, as I may say, made a thousand more preambles than he need to have done.

However, as he pressed me to speak, I told him I had no reason to question the sincerity of his love to me, after so many protestations, but... And there I stopped, as if I left him to guess the rest. "But what, my dear?" says he. "I guess what you mean: what if you should be with child – is not that it? Why then," says he, "I'll take care of you, and provide for you, and the child too, and that you may see I am not in jest," says he, "here's an earnest* for you" – and with that he pulls out a silk purse with an hundred guineas in it, and gave it me. "And I'll give you such another," says he, "every year till I marry you."

My colour came and went at the sight of the purse, and with the fire of his proposal together, so that I could not say a word, and he easily perceived it. So, putting the purse into my bosom, I made no more resistance to him, but let him do just what he pleased, and as often as he pleased, and thus I finished my own destruction at once, for from this day, being forsaken of my virtue and my modesty, I had nothing of value left to recommend me, either to God's blessing or man's assistance.

But things did not end here. I went back to the town, did the business he publicly directed me to, and was at home before anybody thought me long. As for my gentleman, he stayed out, as he told me he would, till late at night, and there was not the least suspicion in the family either on his account or on mine.

We had, after this, frequent opportunities to repeat our crime, chiefly by his contrivance – especially at home, when his mother and the young ladies went abroad a-visiting, which he watched so narrowly as never to miss, knowing always beforehand when they went out, and then failed not to catch me all alone, and securely enough, so that we took our fill of our wicked pleasure for near half a year. And yet, which was the most to my satisfaction, I was not with child.

But before this half-year was expired, his younger brother, of whom I have made some mention in the beginning of the story, falls to work with me – and he, finding me alone in the garden one evening, begins a story of the same kind to me, made good honest professions of being in love with me, and, in short, proposes fairly and honourably to marry me, and that before he made any other offer to me at all.

I was now confounded and driven to such an extremity as the like was never known – at least not to me. I resisted the proposal with obstinacy, and now I began to arm myself with arguments: I laid before him the inequality of the match, the treatment I should meet with in the family, the ingratitude it would be to his good father and mother, who had taken me into their house upon such generous principles, and when I was in such a low condition – and, in short, I said everything to dissuade him from his design that I could imagine, except telling him the truth, which would indeed have put an end to it all, but that I durst not think of mentioning.

But here happened a circumstance that I did not expect, indeed, which put me to my shifts,* for this young gentleman, as he was plain and honest, so he pretended to nothing with me but what was so too, and knowing his own innocence he was not so careful to make his having a kindness for Mrs Betty a secret in the house, as his brother was, and though he did not let them know that he had talked to me about it, yet he said enough to let his sisters perceive he loved me, and his mother saw it too – which, though they took no notice of it to me, yet they did to him, and immediately I found their carriage to me altered, more than ever before.

I saw the cloud, though I did not foresee the storm. It was easy, I say, to see that their carriage to me was altered, and that it grew worse and worse every day, till at last I got information among the servants that I should, in a very little while, be desired to remove.

I was not alarmed at the news, having a full satisfaction that I should be otherwise provided for, and especially considering that I had reason every day to expect I should be with child, and that then I should be obliged to remove without any pretences for it.

After some time, the younger gentleman took an opportunity to tell me that the kindness he had for me had got vent in the family. He did not charge me with it, he said, for he knew well enough which way it came out – he told me his plain way of talking had been the occasion of it, for that he did not make his respect for me so much a secret as he might have done, and the reason was that he was at a point, that if I would consent to have him, he would tell them all openly that he loved me, and that he intended to marry me – that it was true his father and mother might resent it and be unkind, but that he was now in a way to live, being bred to the law, and he did not fear maintaining me, agreeable to what I should expect, and that, in short, as he believed I would not be ashamed of him, so he was resolved not to be ashamed of me, and that he scorned to be afraid to own me now, who he resolved to own after I was his wife, and therefore I had nothing to do but to give him my hand, and he would answer for all the rest.

I was now in a dreadful condition indeed, and now I repented heartily my easiness with the eldest brother, not from any reflection of conscience, but from a view of the happiness I might have enjoyed and had now made impossible – for though I had no great scruples of conscience, as I have said, to struggle with, yet I could not think of being a whore to one brother and a wife to the other. But then it came into my thoughts that the first brother had promised to make me his wife when he came to his estate, but I presently remembered what I had often thought of: that he had never spoken a word of having me for a wife after he had conquered me for a mistress – and indeed, till now, though I said I thought of it often, yet it gave me no disturbance at all, for as he did not seem in the least to lessen his affection to me, so neither did he lessen his bounty, though he had the discretion himself to desire me not to lay out a penny of what he gave me in clothes, or to make the least show extraordinary, because it would necessarily give jealousy in the family, since everybody knew I could come at such things no manner of ordinary way, but by some private friendship, which they would presently have suspected.

But I was now in a great strait, and really knew not what to do. The main difficulty was this: the younger brother not only laid close siege to me, but suffered it to be seen. He would come into his sister's room, and his mother's room, and sit down, and talk a thousand kind things of me, and to me, even before their faces, and when they were all there. This grew so public that the whole house talked of it, and his mother reproved him for it, and their carriage to me appeared quite altered. In short, his mother had let fall some speeches as if she intended to put me out of the family – that is, in English, to turn me out of doors. Now, I was sure this could not be a secret to his brother, only, that he might not think, as indeed nobody else yet did, that the youngest brother had made any proposal to me about it, but as I easily could see that it would go further, so I saw likewise there was an absolute necessity to speak of it to him, or that he would speak of it to me, and which to do first I knew not – that is, whether I should break it to him or let it alone till he should break it to me.

Upon serious consideration – for indeed now I began to consider things very seriously, and never till now – I say, upon serious consideration, I resolved to tell him of it first, and it was not long before I had an opportunity, for the very next day his brother went to London upon some business, and, the family being out a-visiting, just as it had happened before, and as indeed was often the case, he came according to his custom to spend an hour or two with Mrs Betty.

When he came and had sat down a while, he easily perceived there was an alteration in my countenance – that I was not so free and pleasant with him as I used to be, and particularly that I had been a-crying. He was not long before he took notice of it, and asked me in very kind terms what was the matter, and if anything troubled me. I would have put it off if I could, but it was not to be concealed, so after suffering many importunities to draw that out of me, which I longed as much as possible to disclose, I told him that it was true, something did trouble me, and something of such a nature that I could not conceal from him, and yet that I could not tell how to tell him of it neither – that it was a thing that not only surprised me but greatly perplexed me, and that I knew not what course to take, unless he would direct me. He told me with great tenderness that, let it be what it would, I should not let it trouble me, for he would protect me from all the world.

I then began at a distance, and told him I was afraid the ladies had got some secret information of our correspondence, for that it was easy to see that their conduct was very much changed towards me for a great while, and that now it was come to that pass that they frequently found fault with me, and sometimes fell quite out with me, though I never gave them the least occasion – that whereas I used always to lie with the eldest sister, I was lately put to lie by myself, or with one of the maids, and that I had overheard them several times talking very unkindly about me; but that which confirmed it all was that one of the servants had told me that she had heard I was to be turned out, and that it was not safe for the family that I should be any longer in the house.

He smiled when he heard all this, and I asked him how he could make so light of it, when he must needs know that if there was any discovery I was undone for ever – and that even it would hurt him, though not ruin him as it would me. I upbraided him that he was like all the rest of the sex – that when they had the character and honour of a woman at their mercy, oftentimes made it their jest, and at least looked upon it as a trifle, and counted the ruin of those they had had their will of as a thing of no value.

He saw me warm and serious, and he changed his style immediately. He told me he was sorry I should have such a thought of him – that he had never given me the least occasion for it, but had been as tender of my reputation as he could be of his own, that he was sure our correspondence had been managed with so much address that not one creature in the family had so much as a suspicion of it, that if he smiled when I told him my thoughts, it was at the assurance he lately received that our understanding one another was not so much as known or guessed at, and that when he had told me how much reason he had to be easy, I should smile as he did, for he was very certain it would give me a full satisfaction.

"This is a mystery I cannot understand," says I, "or how it should be to my satisfaction that I am to be turned out of doors, for if our correspondence is not discovered, I know not what else I have done to change the countenances of the whole family to me, or to have them treat me as they do now who formerly used me with so much tenderness, as if I had been one of their own children."

"Why, look you, child," says he, "that they are uneasy about you, that is true. But that they have the least suspicion of the case as it is, and as it respects you and I, is so far from being true that they suspect my brother Robin – and, in short, they are fully persuaded he makes love to you. Nay, the fool has put it into their heads too himself, for he is continually bantering them about it, and making a jest of himself. I confess, I think he is wrong to do so, because he cannot but see it vexes them, and makes them unkind to you, but 'tis a satisfaction to me, because of the assurance it gives me that they do not suspect me in the least, and I hope this will be to your satisfaction too."

"So it is," says I, "one way, but this does not reach my case at all, nor is this the chief thing that troubles me, though I have been concerned about that too." "What is it then?" says he. With which I fell into tears, and could say nothing to him at all. He strove to pacify me all he could, but began at last to be very pressing upon me to tell what it was. At last I answered that I thought I ought to tell him too, and that he had some right to know it – besides, that I wanted his direction in the case, for I was in such perplexity that I knew not what course to take, and then I related the whole affair to him. I told him how imprudently his brother had managed himself in making himself so public, for that if he had kept it a secret, as such a thing ought to have been, I could but have denied him positively without giving any reason for it, and he would in time have ceased his solicitations; but that he had the vanity, first, to depend upon it that I would not deny him, and then had taken the freedom to tell his resolution of having me to the whole house.

I told him how far I had resisted him, and told him how sincere and honourable his offers were. "But," says I, "my case will be doubly hard, for as they carry it ill to me now, because he desires to have me, they'll carry it worse when they shall find I have denied him, and they will presently say there's something else in it, and then out it comes that I am married already to somebody else, or else that I would never refuse a match so much above me as this was."

This discourse surprised him indeed very much. He told me that it was a critical point indeed for me to manage, and he did not see which way I should get out of it, but he would consider of it, and let me know next time we met what resolution he was come to about it, and in the mean time desired I would not give my consent to his brother, nor yet give him a flat denial, but that I would hold him in suspense awhile.

I seemed to start at his saying I should not give him my consent. I told him he knew very well I had no consent to give, that he had engaged himself to marry me, and that my consent was at the same time engaged to him – that he had all along told me I was his wife, and I looked upon myself as effectually so, as if the ceremony had passed,* and that it was from his own mouth that I did so, he having all along persuaded me to call myself his wife.

"Well, my dear," says he, "don't be concerned at that now. If I am not your husband, I'll be as good as a husband to you, and do not let those things trouble you now, but let me look a little further into this affair, and I shall be able to say more next time we meet."

He pacified me as well as he could with this, but I found he was very thoughtful, and that though he was very kind to me and kissed me a thousand times, and more I believe, and gave me money too, yet he offered no more all the while we were together, which was above two hours, and which I much wondered at indeed at that time, considering how it used to be and what opportunity we had.

His brother did not come from London for five or six days, and it was two days more before he got an opportunity to talk with him, but then, getting him by himself, he began to talk very close to him about it, and the same evening got an opportunity (for we had a long conference together) to repeat all their discourse to me – which, as near as I can remember, was to the purpose following. He told him he heard strange news of him since he went, viz. that he made love to Mrs Betty. "Well," says his brother, a little angrily, "and so I do, and what then? What has anybody to do with that?" "Nay," says his brother, "don't be angry, Robin. I don't pretend to have anything to do with it. Nor do I pretend to be angry with you about it. But I find they do concern themselves about it, and that they have used the poor girl ill about it, which I should take as done to myself." "Who do you mean by *they*?" says Robin. "I mean my mother and the girls," says the elder brother.

"But hark ye," says his brother, "are you in earnest? Do you really love the girl? You may be free with me, you know." "Why then," says Robin, "I will be free with you. I do love her above all the women in the world, and I will have her, let them say and do what they will. I believe the girl will not deny me."

It stuck me to the heart when he told me this, for though it was most rational to think I would not deny him, yet I knew in my own conscience I must deny him, and I saw my ruin in my being obliged to do so. But I knew it was my business to talk otherwise then, so I interrupted him in his story thus:

"Ay!" said I. "Does he think I cannot deny him? But he shall find I can deny him for all that."

"Well, my dear," says he, "but let me give you the whole story as it went on between us, and then say what you will."

Then he went on and told me that he replied thus: "But brother, you know she has nothing, and you may have several ladies with good fortunes." "'Tis no matter for that," said Robin. "I love the girl, and I will never please my pocket in marrying, and not please my fancy." "And so, my dear," adds he, "there is no opposing him."

"Yes, yes," says I, "you shall see I can oppose him. I have learnt to say no now, though I had not learnt it before. If the best lord in the land offered me marriage now, I could very cheerfully say no to him."

"Well, but, my dear," says he, "what can you say to him? You know, as you said when we talked of it before, he will ask you many questions about it, and all the house will wonder what the meaning of it should be."

"Why," says I, smiling, "I can stop all their mouths at one clap by telling him and them too that I am married already to his elder brother."

He smiled a little too at the word, but I could see it startled him, and he could not hide the disorder it put him into. However, he returned, "Why, though that may be true in some sense, yet I suppose you are but in jest when you talk of giving such an answer as that. It may not be convenient on many accounts."

"No, no," says I pleasantly, "I am not so fond of letting that secret come out without your consent."

"But what then can you say to him, or to them," says he, "when they find you positive against a match which would be apparently so much to your advantage?"

"Why," says I, "should I be at a loss? First of all, I am not obliged to give them any reason at all. On the other hand, I may tell them I am married already and stop there, and that will be a full stop too to him, for he can have no reason to ask one question after it."

"Ay," says he, "but the whole house will tease you about that, even to Father and Mother – and if you deny them positively, they will be disobliged at you, and suspicious besides."

"Why," says I, "what can I do? What would you have me do? I was in strait enough before, and, as I told you, I was in perplexity before, and acquainted you with the circumstances, that I might have your advice."

"My dear," says he, "I have been considering very much upon it, you may be sure, and though it is a piece of advice that has a great many mortifications in it to me and may at first seem strange to you, yet all things considered I see no better way for you than to let him go on, and if you find him hearty and in earnest, marry him."

I gave him a look full of horror at those words, and, turning pale as death, was at the very point of sinking down out of the chair I sat in, when, giving a start, "My dear," says he aloud, "what's the matter with you? Where are you a going?" – and a great many such things; and with jogging* and calling to me fetched me a little to myself, though it was a good while before I fully recovered my senses, and was not able to speak for several minutes more.

When I was fully recovered he began again. "My dear," says he, "what made you so surprised at what I said? I would have you consider seriously of it. You may see plainly how the family stand in this case, and they would be stark mad if it was my case, as it is my brother's, and for ought I see it would be my ruin and yours too."

"Ay!" says I, still speaking angrily. "Are all your protestations and vows to be shaken by the dislike of the family? Did I not always object that to you, and you made a light thing of it, as what you were above, and would not value? And is it come to this now?" said I. "Is this your faith and honour, your love, and the solidity of your promises?"

He continued perfectly calm, notwithstanding all my reproaches, and I was not sparing of them at all, but he replied at last, "My dear, I have not broken one promise with you yet. I did tell you I would marry you when I was come to my estate, but you see my father is a hale, healthy man, and may live these thirty years still, and not be older than several are round us in the town – and you never proposed my marrying you sooner, because you know it might be my ruin. And as to all the rest, I have not failed you in anything: you have wanted for nothing."

I could not deny a word of this, and had nothing to say to it in general. "But why, then," says I, "can you persuade me to such a horrid step as leaving you, since you have not left me? Will you allow no affection, no love on my side, where there has been so much on your side? Have I made you no returns? Have I given no testimony of my sincerity and of my passion? Are the sacrifices I have made of honour and modesty to you no proof of my being tied to you in bonds too strong to be broken?"

"But here, my dear," says he, "you may come into a safe station, and appear with honour and with splendour at once, and the remembrance of what we have done may be wrapped up in an eternal silence, as if it had never happened. You shall always have my respect and my sincere affection, only then it shall be honest, and perfectly just to my brother. You shall be my dear sister, as now you are my dear—" And there he stopped.

"Your dear whore," says I, "you would have said, if you had gone on. And you might as well have said it – but I understand you. However, I desire you to remember the long discourses you have had with me, and the many hours' pains you have taken to persuade me to believe myself an honest woman – that I was your wife intentionally, though not in the eye of the world, and that it was as effectual a marriage that had passed between us as if we had been publicly wedded by the parson of the parish. You know and cannot but remember that these have been your own words to me."

I found this was a little too close upon him, but I made it up in what follows. He stood stock-still for a while and said nothing, and I went on thus: "You cannot," says I, "without the highest injustice, believe that I yielded upon all these persuasions without a love not to be questioned, not to be shaken again by anything that could happen afterwards. If you have such dishonourable thoughts of me, I must ask you what foundation in any of my behaviour have I given for such a suggestion.

"If then I have yielded to the importunities of my affection, and if I have been persuaded to believe that I am really, and in the essence of the thing, your wife, shall I now give the lie to all those arguments and call myself your whore, or mistress, which is the same thing? And will you transfer me to your brother? Can you transfer my affection? Can you bid me cease loving you, and bid me love him? Is it in my power, think you, to make such a change at demand? No sir," said I. "Depend upon it, 'tis impossible, and whatever the change of your side may be, I will ever be true. And I had much rather, since it is come that unhappy length, be your whore than your brother's wife."

He appeared pleased, and touched with the impression of this last discourse, and told me that he stood where he did before – that he had not been unfaithful to me in any one promise he had ever made yet, but that there were so many terrible things presented themselves to his view in the affair before me, and that on my account in particular, that he had thought of the other as a remedy so effectual as nothing could come up to it; that he thought this would not be an entire parting us, but we might love as friends all our days, and perhaps with more satisfaction than we should in the station we were now in, as things might happen; that, he durst say, I could not apprehend anything from him as to betraying a secret which could not but be the destruction of us both, if it came out; that he had but one question to ask of me that could lie in the way of it, and if that question was answered in the negative, he could not but think still it was the only step I could take.

I guessed at his question presently – namely, whether I was sure I was not with child. As to that, I told him he need not be concerned about it, for I was not with child. "Why then, my dear," says he, "we have no time to talk further now. Consider of it, and think closely about it – I cannot but be of the opinion still that it will be the best course you can take" – and with this he took his leave, and the more hastily too, his mother and sisters ringing at the gate just at the moment that he had risen up to go.

He left me in the utmost confusion of thought, and he easily perceived it the next day, and all the rest of the week, for it was but Tuesday evening when we talked. But he had no opportunity to come at me all that week, till the Sunday after, when I, being indisposed, did not go to church, and he, making some excuse for the like, stayed at home.

And now he had me an hour and a half again by myself, and we fell into the same arguments all over again, or at least so near the same as it would be to no purpose to repeat them. At last, I asked him warmly what opinion he must have of my modesty that he could suppose I should so much as entertain a thought of lying with two brothers, and assured him it could never be. I added if he was to tell me that he would never see me more, than which nothing but death could be more terrible – yet I could never entertain a thought so dishonourable to myself, and so base to him. And therefore I entreated him, if he had one grain of respect or affection left for me, that he would speak no more of it to me, or that he would pull his sword out and kill me. He appeared surprised at my obstinacy, as he called it, told me I was unkind to myself and unkind to him in it, that it was a crisis unlooked for upon us both, and impossible for either of us to foresee, but that he did not see any other way to save us both from ruin, and therefore he thought it the more unkind – but that if he must say no more of it to me, he added with an unusual coldness that he did not know anything else we had to talk of. And so he rose up to take his leave – I rose up too, as if with the same indifference, but when he came to give me as it were a parting kiss, I burst out into such a passion of crying that though I would have spoke, I could not, and only pressing his hand seemed to give him the adieu, but cried vehemently.

He was sensibly moved with this, so he sat down again and said a great many kind things to me to abate the excess of my passion, but still urged the necessity of what he had proposed, all the while insisting that if I did refuse he would notwithstanding provide for me, but letting me plainly see that he would decline me in the main point – nay, even as a mistress, making it a point of honour not to lie with the woman that, for ought he knew, might come to be his brother's wife.

The bare loss of him as a gallant was not so much my afflic-tion as the loss of his person, whom indeed I loved to distrac-tion, and the loss of all the expectations I had, and which I always had built my hopes upon, of having him one day for my husband. These things oppressed my mind so much that in short I fell very ill – the agonies of my mind, in a word, threw me into a high fever, and long it was that none in the family expected my life.*

I was reduced very low indeed, and was often delirious and light-headed, but nothing lay so near me as the fear that when I was light-headed I should say something or other to his prejudice. I was distressed in my mind also to see him, and so he was to see me, for he really loved me most passionately – but it could not be. There was not the least room to desire it on one side or other, or so much as to make it decent.

It was near five weeks that I kept my bed, and though the violence of my fever abated in three weeks, yet it several times returned, and the physicians said two or three times they could do no more for me, but that they must leave nature and the distemper to fight it out, only strengthening the first with cor-dials to maintain the struggle. After the end of five weeks I grew better, but was so weak, so altered, so melancholy, and recovered so slowly, that the physicians apprehended I should go into a consumption – and, which vexed me most, they gave it as their opinion that my mind was oppressed, that something troubled me, and, in short, that I was in love. Upon this the whole house was set upon me to examine me, and to press me to tell whether I was in love or not, and with whom. But, as I well might, I denied my being in love at all.

They had on this occasion a squabble one day about me at table that had like to have put the whole family in an uproar, and for some time did so. They happened to be all at table but the father – as for me, I was ill and in my chamber. At the beginning of the talk, which was just as they had finished their dinner, the old gentlewoman, who had sent me somewhat to eat, called her maid to go up and ask me if I would have any more, but the maid brought down word I had not eaten half what she had sent me already.

"Alas," says the old lady, "that poor girl. I am afraid she will never be well."

"Well!" says the elder brother. "How should Mrs Betty be well? They say she is in love."

"I believe nothing of it," says the old gentlewoman.

"I don't know," says the eldest sister, "what to say to it. They have made such a rout about her being so handsome and so charming, and I know not what, and that in her hearing too, that has turned the creature's head, I believe – and who knows what possessions* may follow such doings? For my part, I don't know what to make of it."

"Why, sister, you must acknowledge she is very handsome," says the elder brother.

"Ay, and a great deal handsomer than you, sister," says Robin, "and that's your mortification."

"Well, well, that is not the question," says his sister. "The girl is well enough, and she knows it well enough. She need not be told of it to make her vain."

"We are not a-talking of her being vain," says the elder brother, "but of her being in love. It may be she is in love with herself – it seems my sisters think so."

"I would she was in love with me," says Robin. "I'd quickly put her out of her pain."

"What d'ye mean by that, son?" says the old lady. "How can you talk so?"

"Why, madam," says Robin again, very honestly, "do you think I'd let the poor girl die for love, and of one that is near at hand to be had too?"

"Fie, brother," says the second sister, "how can you talk so? Would you take a creature that has not a groat in the world?"

"Prithee, child," says Robin, "beauty's a portion, and good humour with it is a double portion. I wish thou hadst half her stock of both for thy portion." So there was her mouth stopped.

"I find," says the eldest sister, "if Betty is not in love, my brother is. I wonder he has not broke his mind to Betty – I warrant she won't say no."

"They that yield when they're asked," says Robin, "are one step before them that were never asked to yield, sister, and two steps before them that yield before they are asked – and that's an answer to you, sister."

This fired the sister, and she flew into a passion and said things were come to that pass that it was time the wench, meaning me, was out of the family, and but that she was not fit to be turned out, she hoped her father and mother would consider of it as soon as she could be removed.

Robin replied that was business for the master and mistress of the family, who were not to be taught by one that had so little judgement as his eldest sister.

It run up a great deal further: the sister scolded, Robin rallied* and bantered, but poor Betty lost ground by it extremely in the family. I heard of it, and I cried heartily, and the old lady came up to me, somebody having told her that I was so much concerned about it. I complained to her that it was very hard the doctors should pass such a censure upon me for which they had no ground, and that it was still harder, considering the circumstances I was under in the family, that I hoped I had done nothing to lessen her esteem for me, or given any occasion for the bickering between her sons and daughters – and I had more need to think of a coffin than of being in love, and begged she would not let me suffer in her opinion for anybody's mistakes but my own.

She was sensible of the justice of what I said, but told me, since there had been such a clamour among them, and that her younger son talked after such a rattling way as he did, she desired I would be so faithful to her as to answer her but one question sincerely. I told her I would with all my heart, and with the utmost plainness and sincerity. Why then, the question was whether there was anything between her son Robert and me. I told her with all the protestations of sincerity that I was able to make, and as I might well do, that there was not, nor ever had been. I told her that Mr Robert had rattled and jested, as she knew it was his way, and that I took it always, as I supposed he meant it, to be a wild airy way of discourse that had no signification in it, and again assured her that there was not the least tittle* of what she understood by it between us, and that those who had suggested it had done me a great deal of wrong, and Mr Robert no service at all.

The old lady was fully satisfied, and kissed me, spoke cheerfully to me and bid me take care of my health and want for nothing, and so took her leave. But when she came down she found the brother and all his sisters together by the ears* – they were angry even to passion at his upbraiding them with their being homely and having never had any sweetheart, never having been asked the question, and their being so forward as almost to ask first. He rallied them upon the subject of Mrs Betty – how pretty, how good-humoured, how she sung better than they did and danced better, and how much handsomer she was. And in doing this he omitted no ill-natured thing that could vex them, and indeed pushed too hard upon them. The old lady came down in the height of it, and to put a stop to it told them all the discourse she had had with me, and how I answered that there was nothing between Mr Robert and I.

"She's wrong there," says Robin, "for if there was not a great deal between us, we should be closer together than we are. I told her I loved her hugely," says he, "but I could never make the jade believe I was in earnest." "I do not know how you should," says his mother. "Nobody in their senses could believe you were in earnest to talk so to a poor girl whose circumstances you know so well.

"But prithee, son," adds she, "since you tell me that you could not make her believe you were in earnest, what must we believe about it? For you ramble so in your discourse that nobody knows whether you are in earnest or in jest. But as I find the girl by your own confession has answered truly, I wish you would do so too and tell me seriously, so that I may depend upon it: is there anything in it or no? Are you in earnest or no? Are you distracted indeed, or are you not? 'Tis a weighty question, and I wish you would make us easy about it."

"By my faith, madam," says Robin, "'tis in vain to mince the matter or tell any more lies about it. I am in earnest, as much as a man is that's going to be hanged. If Mrs Betty would say she loved me, and that she would marry me, I'd have her tomorrow morning fasting, and say 'To have and to hold' instead of eating my breakfast."

"Well," says the mother, "then there's one son lost" – and she said it in a very mournful tone, as one greatly concerned at it.

"I hope not, madam," says Robin. "No man is lost when a good wife has found him."

"Why, but child," says the old lady, "she is a beggar."

"Why, then, madam, she has the more need of charity," says Robin. "I'll take her off of the hands of the parish, and she and I'll beg together."

"It's bad jesting with such things," says the mother.

"I don't jest, madam," says Robin. "We'll come and beg your pardon, madam – and your blessing, madam, and my father's."

"This is all out of the way, son," says the mother. "If you are in earnest, you are undone."

"I am afraid not," says he, "for I am really afraid she won't have me. After all my sister's huffing and blustering, I believe I shall never be able to persuade her to it."

"That's a fine tale indeed. She is not so far out of her senses neither – Mrs Betty is no fool," says the youngest sister. "Do you think she has learnt to say no any more than other people?"

"No, Mrs Mirth-Wit," says Robin. "Mrs Betty's no fool – but Mrs Betty may be engaged some other way, and what then?"

"Nay," says the eldest sister, "we can say nothing to that. Who must it be to then? She is never out of the doors – it must be between you."

"I have nothing to say to that," says Robin. "I have been examined enough. There's my brother – if it must be between us, go to work with him."

This stung the elder brother to the quick, and he concluded that Robin had discovered something. However, he kept himself from appearing disturbed. "Prithee," says he, "don't go to sham your stories off upon me – I tell you, I deal in no such ware. I have nothing to say to Mrs Betty, nor to any of the Miss Bettys in the parish." And with that he rose up and brushed off.

"No," says the eldest sister, "I dare answer for my brother – he knows the world better."

Thus the discourse ended, but it left the elder brother quite confounded. He concluded his brother had made a full discovery, and he began to doubt whether I had been concerned in it or not. But with all his management he could not bring it about to get at me. At last, he was so perplexed that he was quite desperate and resolved he would come into my chamber and see me, whatever came of it. In order to this, he contrived it so: that one day after dinner, watching his eldest sister till he could see her go upstairs, he runs after her. "Hark ye, sister," says he. "Where is this sick woman? May not a body see her?" "Yes," says the sister, "I believe you may, but let me go first a little, and I'll tell you." So she ran up to the door and gave me notice, and presently called to him again: "Brother," says she, "you may come if you please." So in he came, just in the same kind of rant. "Well," says he at the door as he came in, "where is this sick body that's in love? How do ye do, Mrs Betty?" I would have got up out of my chair, but was so weak I could not for a good while, and he saw it and his sister too, and she said, "Come, do not strive to stand up. My brother desires no ceremony, especially, now you are so weak." "No, no,

Mrs Betty, pray sit still," says he, and so sits himself down in a chair over-against me, and appeared as if he was mighty merry.

He talked a deal of rambling stuff to his sister, and to me, sometimes of one thing, sometimes of another, on purpose to amuse his sister, and every now and then would turn it upon the old story, directing it to me. "Poor Mrs Betty," says he. "It is a sad thing to be in love – why, it has reduced you sadly." At last I spoke a little: "I am glad to see you so merry, sir," says I, "but I think the doctor might have found something better to do than to make his game at his patients. If I had been ill of no other distemper, I know the proverb too well to have let him come to me." "What proverb?" says he. "Oh, I remember it now. What,

"where love is the case,
the doctor's an ass.

"Is not that it, Mrs Betty?" I smiled, and said nothing. "Nay," says he, "I think the effect has proved it to be love, for it seems the doctor has been able to do you but little service – you mend very slowly, they say. I doubt there's somewhat in it, Mrs Betty – I doubt you are sick of the incurables, and that is love." I smiled and said, "No, indeed, sir, that's none of my distemper."

We had a deal of such discourse, and sometimes others that signified as little. By and by he asked me to sing them a song, at which I smiled and said my singing days were over. At last he asked me if he should play upon his flute to me. His sister said she believed it would hurt me, and that my head could not bear it. I bowed and said no, it would not hurt me. "And pray, madam," said I, "do not hinder it. I love the music of the flute very much." Then his sister said, "Well, do then, brother." With that he pulled out the key of his closet. "Dear sister," says he, "I am very lazy – do step to my closet and fetch my flute. It lies in such a drawer" – naming a place where he was sure it was not, that she might be a little while a-looking for it.

As soon as she was gone, he related the whole story to me of the discourse his brother had about me, and of his pushing it at him, and his concern about it, which was the reason of his contriving this visit to me. I assured him I had never opened my mouth either to his brother or to anybody else. I told him the dreadful exigence I was in – that my love to him, and his offering to have me forget that affection and remove it to another, had thrown me down, and that I had a thousand times wished I might die rather than recover, and to have the same circumstances to struggle with as I had before, and that this backwardness to life had been the great reason of the slowness of my recovering. I added that I foresaw that as soon as I was well I must quit the family, and that as for marrying his brother, I abhorred the thoughts of it after what had been my case with him, and that he might depend upon it I would never see his brother again upon that subject – that if he would break all his vows and oaths and engagements with me, be that between his conscience and his honour and himself. But he should never be able to say that I, who he had persuaded to call myself his wife and who had given him the liberty to use me as a wife, was not as faithful to him as a wife ought to be, whatever he might be to me.

He was going to reply, and had said that he was sorry I could not be persuaded, and was a-going to say more, but he heard his sister a-coming, and so did I – and yet I forced out these few words as a reply: that I could never be persuaded to love one brother and marry another. He shook his head and said, "Then I am ruined" – meaning himself, and that moment his sister entered the room and told him she could not find the flute. "Well," says he merrily, "this laziness won't do." So he gets up and goes himself to go to look for it, but comes back without too – not but that he could have found it, but because his mind was a little disturbed, and he had no mind to play. And besides, the errand he sent his sister on was answered another way, for he only wanted an opportunity to speak to me – which he gained, though not much to his satisfaction.

I had, however, a great deal of satisfaction in having spoken my mind to him with freedom, and with such an honest plainness, as

I have related, and though it did not at all work the way I desired – that is to say, to oblige the person to me the more – yet it took from him all possibility of quitting me but by a downright breach of honour and giving up all the faith of a gentleman to me, which he had so often engaged by, never to abandon me, but to make me his wife as soon as he came to his estate.

It was not many weeks after this before I was about the house again and began to grow well, but I continued melancholy, silent, dull and retired, which amazed the whole family – except he that knew the reason of it. Yet it was a great while before he took any notice of it, and I – as backward to speak as he – carried respectfully to him, but never offered to speak a word to him that was particular of any kind whatsoever, and this continued for sixteen or seventeen weeks, so that as I expected every day to be dismissed the family, on account of what distaste they had taken another way, in which I had no guilt, so I expected to hear no more of this gentleman, after all his solemn vows and protestations, but to be ruined and abandoned.

At last I broke the way myself in the family for my removing, for, being talking seriously with the old lady one day – about my own circumstances in the world, and how my distemper had left a heaviness upon my spirits that I was not the same thing I was before – the old lady said, "I am afraid, Betty, what I have said to you about my son has had some influence upon you, and that you are melancholy on his account. Pray will you let me know how the matter stands with you both? If it may not be improper, for as for Robin, he does nothing but rally and banter when I speak of it to him." "Why, truly madam," said I, "that matter stands as I wish it did not, and I shall be very sincere with you in it, whatever befalls me for it. Mr Robert has several times proposed marriage to me, which is what I had no reason to expect, my poor circumstances considered. But I have always resisted him, and that perhaps in terms more positive than became me, considering the regard that I ought to have for every branch of your family. But," said I, "madam, I could never so far forget my obligations to you, and all your house, to offer to consent to a thing which I know must needs be disobliging to you – and this I have made my argument to him, and have positively told him that I would never entertain a thought of that kind unless I had your consent, and his father's also, to whom I was bound by so many invincible obligations."

"And is this possible, Mrs Betty?" says the old lady. "Then you have been much juster to us than we have been to you, for we have all looked upon you as a kind of a snare to my son, and I had a proposal to make to you for your removing, for fear of it. But I had not yet mentioned it to you because I thought you were not thorough well, and I was afraid of grieving you too much, lest it should throw you down again, for we have all a respect for you still, though not so much as to have it be the ruin of my son. But if it be as you say, we have all wronged you very much."

"As to the truth of what I say, madam," said I, "I refer you to your son himself – if he will do me any justice, he must tell you the story just as I have told it."

Away goes the old lady to her daughters, and tells them the whole story just as I had told it her, and they were surprised at it, you may be sure, as I believed they would be. One said she could never have thought it; another said Robin was a fool; a third said she would not believe a word of it, and she would warrant that Robin would tell the story another way. But the old gentlewoman, who was resolved to go to the bottom of it before I could have the least opportunity of acquainting her son with what had passed, resolved too that she would talk with her son immediately, and to that purpose sent for him, for he was gone but to a lawyer's house in the town upon some petty business of his own – and upon her sending he returned immediately.

Upon his coming up to them, for they were all still together, "Sit down, Robin," says the old lady. "I must have some talk with you." "With all my heart, madam," says Robin, looking very merry. "I hope it is about a good wife, for I am at a great loss in that affair." "How can that be?" says his mother. "Did not you say you resolved to have Mrs Betty?" "Ay, madam," says Robin, "but there is one has forbid the banns." "Forbid the banns!" says his mother. "Who can that be?" "Even Mrs Betty herself," says Robin. "How so?" says his mother. "Have you asked her the question, then?" "Yes, indeed, madam," says Robin. "I have attacked her in form* five times since she was sick, and am beaten off. The jade is so stout she won't capitulate, nor yield upon any terms except such as I cannot effectually grant." "Explain yourself," says the mother, "for I am surprised – I do not understand you. I hope you are not in earnest."

"Why, madam," says he, "the case is plain enough upon me – it explains itself. She won't have me, she says – is not that plain enough? I think 'tis plain and pretty rough too." "Well, but," says the mother, "you talk of conditions that you cannot grant – what, does she want a settlement? Her jointure* ought to be according to her portion, but what fortune does she bring you?" "Nay, as to fortune," says Robin, "she is rich enough – I am satisfied in that point. But 'tis I that am not able to come up to her terms, and she is positive she will not have me without."

Here the sisters put in. "Madam," says the second sister, "'tis impossible to be serious with him. He will never give a direct answer to anything. You had better let him alone, and talk no more of it to him. You know how to dispose of her out of his way if you thought there was anything in it." Robin was a little warmed with his sister's rudeness, but he was even with her, and yet with good manners too. "There are two sorts of people, madam," says he, turning to his mother, "that there is no contending with: that is, a wise body and a fool – 'tis a little hard I should engage with both of them together."

The younger sister then put in, "We must be fools indeed," says she, "in my brother's opinion, that he should think we can believe he has seriously asked Mrs Betty to marry him and that she has refused him."

"Answer, and answer not, says Solomon,"* replied her brother. "When your brother had said to your mother that he had asked her no less than five times, and that it was so, that she positively denied him, methinks a younger sister need not question the truth of it, when her mother did not." "My mother, you see, did not understand it," says the second sister. "There's some difference," says Robin, "between desiring me to explain it and telling me she did not believe it."

"Well, but, son," says the old lady, "if you are disposed to let us into the mystery of it, what were these hard conditions?" "Yes, madam," says Robin, "I had done it before now if the teasers here had not worried me by way of interruption. The conditions are that I bring my father and you to consent to it, and without that she protests she will never see me more upon that head. And these conditions, as I said, I suppose I shall never be able to grant. I hope my warm sisters will be answered now, and blush a little – if not, I have no more to say till I hear further."

This answer was surprising to them all, though less to the mother because of what I had said to her. As to the daughters, they stood mute a great while, but the mother said with some passion, "Well, I had heard this before, but I could not believe it. But if it is so, then we have all done Betty wrong, and she has behaved better than I ever expected." "Nay, says the eldest sister, if it is so, she has acted handsomely indeed." "I confess," says the mother, "it was none of her fault if he was fool enough to take a fancy to her, but to give such an answer to him shows more respect to your father and me than I can tell how to express. I shall value the girl the better for it as long as I know her." "But I shall not," says Robin, "unless you will give your consent." "I'll consider of that awhile," says the mother. "I assure you, if there were not some other objections in the way, this conduct of hers would go a great way to bring me to consent." "I wish it would go quite through with it," says Robin. "If you had as much thought about making me easy as you have about making me rich, you would soon consent to it."

"Why, Robin," says the mother again, "are you really in earnest? Would you so fain have her as you pretend?" "Really, madam," says Robin, "I think 'tis hard you should question me upon that head after all I have said. I won't say that I will have her – how can I resolve that point when you see I cannot have her without your consent? Besides, I am not bound to marry at all. But this I will say I am in earnest in: that I will never have anybody else if I can help it. So you may determine for me – Betty or nobody is the word, and the question which of the two shall be in your breast to decide, madam, provided only that my good-humoured sisters here may have no vote in it."

All this was dreadful to me, for the mother began to yield, and Robin pressed her home in it. On the other hand, she advised with the eldest son, and he used all the arguments in the world to persuade her to consent, alleging his brother's passionate love for me and my generous regard to the family in refusing my own advantages upon such a nice point of honour, and a thousand such things. And as to the father, he was a man in a hurry of public affairs and getting money, seldom at home, thoughtful of the main chance,* but left all those things to his wife.

You may easily believe that when the plot was thus, as they thought, broke out, and that everyone thought they knew how things were carried, it was not so difficult or so dangerous for the elder brother, who nobody suspected of anything, to have a freer access to me than before. Nay, the mother, which was just as he wished, proposed it to him to talk with Mrs Betty. "For it may be, son," said she, "you may see farther into the thing than I, and see if you think she has been so positive as Robin says she has been, or no." This was as well as he could wish, and he as it were yielding to talk with me at his mother's request, she brought me to him into her own chamber, told me her son had some business with me at her request, and desired me to be very sincere with him, and then she left us together, and he went and shut the door after her.

He came back to me and took me in his arms and kissed me very tenderly, but told me he had a long discourse to hold with me, and it was now come to that crisis that I should make myself happy or miserable as long as I lived – that the thing was now gone so far that if I could not comply with his desire we should be both ruined. Then he told me the whole story between Robin, as he called him, and his mother, and sisters, and himself – as it is above. "And now, dear child," says he, "consider what it will be to marry a gentleman of a good family, in good circumstances, and with the consent of the whole house, and to enjoy all that the world can give you – and what, on the other hand, to be sunk into the dark circumstances of a woman that has lost her reputation. And that though I shall be a private friend to you while I live, yet, as I shall be suspected always, so you will be afraid to see me, and I shall be afraid to own you."

He gave me no time to reply, but went on with me thus: "What has happened between us, child, so long as we both agree to do so, may be buried and forgotten. I shall always be your sincere friend, without any inclination to nearer intimacy, when you become my sister, and we shall have all the honest part of conversation without any reproaches between us of having done amiss. I beg of you to consider it, and do not stand in the way of your own safety and prosperity. And to satisfy you that I am sincere," added he, "I here offer you 500*l.* in money to make you some amends for the freedoms I have taken with you, which we shall look upon as some of the follies of our lives, which 'tis hoped we may repent of."

He spoke this in so much more moving terms than it is possible for me to express, and with so much greater force of argument than I can repeat, that I only recommend it to those who read the story to suppose that as he held me above an hour and half in that discourse, so he answered all my objections and fortified his discourse with all the arguments that humane wit and art could devise.

I cannot say, however, that anything he said made impression enough upon me so as to give me any thought of the matter, till he told me at last very plainly that, if I refused, he was sorry to add that he could never go on with me in that station as we stood before – that though he loved me as well as ever, and that I was as agreeable to him as ever, yet sense of virtue had not so far forsaken him as to suffer him to lie with a woman that his brother courted to make his wife. And if he took his leave of me with a denial in this affair, whatever he might do for me in the point of support, grounded on his first engagement of maintaining me, yet he would not have me be surprised that he was obliged to tell me he could not allow himself to see me any more, and that indeed I could not expect it of him.

I received this last part with some tokens of surprise and disorder, and had much ado to avoid sinking down, for indeed I loved him to an extravagance not easy to imagine. But he perceived my disorder – he entreated me to consider seriously of it, assured me that it was the only way to preserve our mutual affection, that in this station we might love as friends, with the utmost passion, and with a love of relation untainted, free from our just reproaches, and free from other people's suspicions; that he should ever acknowledge his happiness owing to me; that he would be debtor to me as long as he lived, and would be paying that debt as long as he had breath. Thus he wrought me up, in short, to a kind of hesitation in the matter, having the dangers on one side represented in lively figures, and indeed heightened by my imagination of being turned out to the wide world, a mere cast-off whore, for it was no less, and perhaps exposed as such, with little to provide for myself, with no friend, no acquaintance in the whole world, out of that town, and there I could not pretend to stay – all this terrified me to the last degree, and he took care upon all occasions to lay it home to me in the worst colours that it could be possible to be drawn in. On the other hand, he failed not to set forth the easy prosperous life which I was going to live.

He answered all that I could object from affection, and from former engagements, with telling me the necessity that was before us of taking other measures now. And as to his promises of marriage, the nature of things, he said, had put an end to that by the probability of my being his brother's wife before the time to which his promises all referred.

Thus, in a word, I may say, he reasoned me out of my reason. He conquered all my arguments, and I began to see a danger that I was in, which I had not considered of before, and that was of being dropped by both of them and left alone in the world to shift for myself.

This, and his persuasion, at length prevailed with me to consent, though with so much reluctance that it was easy to see I should go to church like a bear to the stake.* I had some little apprehensions about me, too, lest my new spouse, who by the way I had not the least affection for, should be skilful enough to challenge me on another account, upon our first coming to bed together. But whether he did it with design or not, I know not, but his elder brother took care to make him very much fuddled before he went to bed, so that I had the satisfaction of a drunken bedfellow the first night. How he did it I know not, but I concluded that he certainly contrived it that his brother might be able to make no judgement of the difference between a maid and a married woman – nor did he ever entertain any notions of it or disturb his thoughts about it.

I should go back a little here to where I left off. The elder brother having thus managed me, his next business was to manage his mother, and he never left till he had brought her to acquiesce and be passive in the thing, even without acquainting the father other than by post letters, so that she consented to our marrying privately, and leaving her to manage the father afterwards.

Then he cajoled with his brother, and persuaded him what service he had done him, and how he had brought his mother to consent – which, though true, was not indeed done to serve him but to serve himself. But thus diligently did he cheat him, and had the thanks of a faithful friend for shifting off his whore into his brother's arms for a wife. So certainly does interest banish all manner of affection, and so naturally do men give up honour and justice, humanity, and even Christianity, to secure themselves.

I must now come back to brother Robin, as we always called him, who, having got his mother's consent as above, came big with the news to me, and told me the whole story of it, with a sincerity so visible that I must confess it grieved me that I must be the instrument to abuse so honest a gentleman. But there was no remedy: he would have me, and I was not obliged to tell him that

I was his brother's whore, though I had no other way to put him off. So I came gradually into it, to his satisfaction – and behold, we were married.

Modesty forbids me to reveal the secrets of the marriage bed, but nothing could have happened more suitable to my circumstances than that, as above, my husband was so fuddled when he came to bed that he could not remember in the morning whether he had had any conversation* with me or no, and I was obliged to tell him he had, though in reality he had not, that I might be sure he could make no enquiry about anything else.

It concerns the story in hand very little to enter into the further particulars of the family, or of myself, for the five years that I lived with this husband – only to observe that I had two children by him, and that at the end of five years he died. He had been really a very good husband to me, and we lived very agreeably together, but as he had not received much from them, and had in the little time he lived acquired no great matters, so my circumstances were not great, nor was I much mended by the match. Indeed, I had preserved the elder brother's bonds to me, to pay me 500*l.*, which he offered me for my consent to marry his brother, and this with what I had saved of the money he formerly gave me, and about as much more by my husband, left me a widow with about 1,200*l.* in my pocket.

My two children were indeed taken happily off of my hands by my husband's father and mother, and that by the way was all they got by Mrs Betty.

I confess I was not suitably affected with the loss of my husband, nor indeed can I say that I ever loved him as I ought to have done, or as was proportionable to the good usage I had from him, for he was a tender, kind, good-humoured man as any woman could desire, but his brother, being so always in my sight – at least, while we were in the country – was a continual snare to me, and I never was in bed with my husband but I wished myself in the arms of his brother. And though his brother never offered me the least kindness that way after our marriage, but carried it just as a brother ought to do, yet it was impossible for me to do so to him – in short, I committed adultery and incest with him every day in my desires, which without doubt was as effectually criminal in the nature of the guilt as if I had actually done it.

Before my husband died, his elder brother was married, and we being then removed to London were written to by the old lady to come and be at the wedding. My husband went, but I pretended indisposition and that I could not possibly travel, so I stayed behind – for, in short, I could not bear the sight of his being given to another woman, though I knew I was never to have him myself.

I was now, as above, left loose to the world, and being still young and handsome, as everybody said of me – and I assure you, I thought myself so – and with a tolerable fortune in my pocket, I put no small value upon myself. I was courted by several very considerable tradesmen – and, particularly, very warmly by one, a linen draper, at whose house after my husband's death I took a lodging, his sister being my acquaintance. Here I had all the liberty and all the opportunity to be gay and appear in company that I could desire, my landlord's sister being one of the maddest, gayest things alive, and not so much mistress of her virtue as I thought at first she had been. She brought me into a world of wild company, and even brought home several persons – such as she liked well enough to gratify – to see her pretty widow, so she was pleased to call me, and that name I got in a little time in public. Now, as fame and fools make an assembly, I was here wonderfully caressed, had abundance of admirers, and such as called themselves lovers, but I found not one fair proposal among them all. As for their common design, that I understood too well to be drawn into any more snares of that kind. The case was altered with me: I had money in my pocket and had nothing to say to them. I had been tricked once by that cheat called Love, but the game was over – I was resolved now to be married or nothing, and to be well married or not at all.

I loved the company indeed of men of mirth and wit, men of gallantry and figure, and was often entertained with such, as I was also with others. But I found by just observation that the brightest men came upon the dullest errand – that is to say, the dullest as to what I aimed at. On the other hand, those who came with the best proposals were the dullest and most disagreeable part of the world. I was not averse to a tradesman, but then I would have a tradesman, forsooth, that was something of a gentleman too – that when my husband had a mind to carry me to the court, or to the play, he might become a sword and look as like a gentleman as another man, and not be one that had the mark of his apron strings upon his coat, or the mark of his hat upon his periwig;* that should look as if he was set onto his sword when his sword was put onto him, and that carried his trade in his countenance.

Well, at last I found this amphibious creature, this land-water thing called a "gentleman tradesman", and as a just plague upon my folly I was catched in the very snare which, as I might say, I laid for myself – I say laid for myself, for I was not trepanned,* I confess, but I betrayed myself.

This was a draper too, for though my comrade would have brought me to a bargain with her brother, yet when it came to the point, it was it seems for a mistress, not a wife, and I kept true to this notion: that a woman should never be kept for a mistress that had money to keep herself.

Thus my pride, not my principle, my money, not my virtue, kept me honest – though, as it proved, I found I had much better have been sold by my she-comrade to her brother than have sold myself as I did to a tradesman that was rake, gentleman, shopkeeper and beggar all together.

But I was hurried on (by my fancy to a gentleman) to ruin myself in the grossest manner that ever woman did, for my new husband, coming to a lump of money at once, fell into such a profusion of expense that all I had, and all he had before, if he had anything worth mentioning, would not have held it out above one year.

He was very fond of me for about a quarter of a year, and what I got by that was that I had the pleasure of seeing a great deal of my money spent upon myself – and, as I may say, had some of the spending it too. "Come, my dear," says he to me one day, "shall we go and take a turn into the country for about a week?" "Ay, my dear," says I. "Whither would you go?" "I care not whither," says he, "but I have a mind to look like quality for a week. We'll go to Oxford," says he. "How," says I, "shall we go? I am no horse woman, and 'tis too far for a coach." "Too far!" says he. "No place is too far for a coach and six.* If I carry you out, you shall travel like a duchess." "Hum," says I, "my dear, 'tis a frolic, but if you have a mind to it, I don't care." Well, the time was appointed; we had a rich coach, very good horses, a coachman, postilion and two footmen in very good liveries, a gentleman on horseback and a page with a feather in his hat upon another horse. The servants all called him "My Lord", and the innkeepers you may be sure did the like, and I was "Her Honour, the countess". And thus we travelled to Oxford, and a very pleasant journey we had, for, give him his due, not a beggar alive knew better how to be a lord than my husband. We saw all the rarities at Oxford, talked with two or three fellows of colleges about putting out a young nephew that was left to His Lordship's care to the university, and of their being his tutors. We diverted ourselves with bantering several other poor scholars with hopes of being at least His Lordship's chaplains and putting on a scarf. And thus having lived like quality indeed, as to expense, we went away for Northampton, and, in a word, in about twelve days' ramble came home again, to the tune of about 93l. expense.

Vanity is the perfection of a fop. My husband had this excellence: that he valued nothing of expense, and as his history, you may be sure, has very little weight in it, 'tis enough to tell you that in about two years and a quarter he broke, and was not so happy to get over into the Mint, but got into a sponging house,* being arrested in an action too heavy for him to give bail to, so he sent for me to come to him.

It was no surprise to me, for I had foreseen some time that all was going to wreck, and had been taking care to reserve something if I could, though it was not much for myself. But when he sent for me he behaved much better than I expected, and told me plainly he had played the fool and suffered himself to be surprised, which he might have prevented – that now he foresaw he could not stand it, and therefore he would have me go home, and in the night take away everything I had in the house of any value and secure it. And after that, he told me, that if I could get away 100*l*. or 200*l*. in goods out of the shop, I should do it – "Only," says he, "let me know nothing of it, neither what you take or whither you carry it, for as for me," says he, "I am resolved to get out of this house and be gone, and if you never hear of me more, my dear," says he, "I wish you well. I am only sorry for the injury I have done you." He said some very handsome things to me indeed at parting, for I told you he was a gentleman, and that was all the benefit I had of his being so: that he used me very handsomely and with good manners upon all occasions, even to the last, only spent all I had and left me to rob the creditors for something to subsist on.

However, I did as he bade me, that you may be sure, and having thus taken my leave of him, I never saw him more, for he found means to break out of the bailiff's house that night, or the next, and got over into France – and for the rest, the creditors scrambled for it as well as they could. How I knew not, for I could come at no knowledge of anything more than this: that he came home about three o'clock in the morning, caused the rest of his goods to be removed into the Mint and the shop to be shut up, and having raised what money he could get together, he got over as I said to France, from whence I had one or two letters from him, and no more.

I did not see him when he came home, for he having given me such instructions as above, and I having made the best of my time, I had no more business back again at the house, not knowing but I might have been stopped there by the creditors. For a commission of bankrupt being soon after issued, they might have stopped me by orders from the commissioners, but my husband having so dextrously got out of the bailiff's house by letting himself down in a most desperate manner from almost the top of the house to the top of another building, and leaping from thence – which was almost two storeys, and which was enough indeed to have broken his neck – he came home and got away his goods before the creditors could come to seize, that is to say, before they could get out the commission and be ready to send their officers to take possession.

My husband was so civil to me – for still I say he was much of a gentleman – that in the first letter he wrote me from France he let me know where he had pawned twenty pieces of fine holland for 30*l*. which were really worth above 90*l*., and enclosed me the token and an order for the taking them up, paying the money, which I did, and made in time above 100*l*. of them, having leisure to cut them and sell them, some and some, to private families, as opportunity offered.

However, with all this, and all that I had secured before, I found, upon casting things up, my case was very much altered, and my fortune much lessened, for including the hollands and a parcel of fine muslins, which I carried off before, and some plate and other things, I found I could hardly muster up 500*l*. And my condition was very odd, for though I had no child (I had had one by my gentleman draper, but it was buried), yet I was a widow bewitched; I had a husband and no husband, and I could not pretend to marry again, though I knew well enough my husband would never see England any more if he lived fifty years. Thus, I say, I was limited from marriage, what offer soever might be made me, and I had not one friend to advise with in the condition I was in – at least not one I durst trust the secret of my circumstances to, for if the commissioners were to have been informed where I was, I should have been fetched up and examined upon oath, and all I had saved be taken away from me.

Upon these apprehensions the first thing I did was to go quite out of my knowledge, and go by another name. This I did effectually, for I went into the Mint too, took lodgings in a very private place, dressed me up in the habit of a widow and called myself Mrs Flanders.

Here, however I concealed myself, and though my new acquaintances knew nothing of me, yet I soon got a great deal of company about me, and whether it be that women are scarce among the sorts of people that generally are to be found there, or that some consolation in the miseries of the place are more requisite than on other occasions, I soon found an agreeable woman was exceedingly valuable among the sons of affliction there, and that those that wanted money to pay half a crown in the pound to their creditors, and that run in debt at the sign of the Bull* for their dinners, would yet find money for a supper if they liked the woman.

However, I kept myself safe yet, though I began – like My Lord Rochester's mistress, that loved his company but would not admit him further – to have the scandal of a whore without the joy,* and upon this score, tired with the place, and indeed with the company too, I began to think of removing.

It was indeed a subject of strange reflection to me to see men who were overwhelmed in perplexed circumstances, who were reduced some degrees below being ruined, whose families were objects of their own terror and other people's charity, yet while a penny lasted – nay, even beyond it – endeavouring to drown their sorrow in their wickedness, heaping up more guilt upon themselves, labouring to forget former things which now it was the proper time to remember, making more work for repentance, and sinning on as a remedy for sin past.

But it is none of my talent to preach. These men were too wicked even for me. There was something horrid and absurd in their way of sinning, for it was all a force even upon themselves. They did not only act against conscience, but against nature. They put a rape upon* their temper to drown the reflections which their circumstances continually gave them, and nothing was more easy than to see how sighs would interrupt their songs, and paleness and anguish sit upon their brows, in spite of the forced smiles they put on. Nay, sometimes it would break out at their very mouths, when they had parted with their money for a lewd treat or a wicked embrace. I have heard them, turning about, fetch a deep sigh and cry, "What a dog am I! Well, Betty, my dear, I'll drink thy health though" – meaning the honest wife, that perhaps had not a half-crown for herself, and three or four children. The next morning they are at their penitentials again, and perhaps the poor weeping wife comes over to him, either brings him some account of what his creditors are doing, and how she and the children are turned out of doors, or some other dreadful news, and this adds to his self-reproaches. But when he has thought and pored on it till he is almost mad, having no principles to support him, nothing within him or above him to comfort him, but finding it all darkness on every side, he flies to the same relief again, viz. to drink it away, debauch it away, and, falling into company of men in just the same condition with himself, he repeats the crime, and thus he goes every day one step onward of his way to destruction.

I was not wicked enough for such fellows as these yet. On the contrary, I began to consider here very seriously what I had to do, how things stood with me and what course I ought to take. I knew I had no friends (no, not one friend or relation in the world), and that little I had left apparently wasted – which, when it was gone, I saw nothing but misery and starving was before me. Upon these considerations, I say, and filled with horror at the place I was in and the dreadful objects which I had always before me, I resolved to be gone.

I had made an acquaintance with a very sober, good sort of a woman, who was a widow too like me, but in better circumstances. Her husband had been a captain of a merchant ship, and having had the misfortune to be cast away coming home on a voyage from the West Indies, which would have been very profitable if he had come safe, was so reduced by the loss that though he had saved his life then, it broke his heart, and killed him afterwards, and his widow being pursued by the creditors was forced to take shelter in the Mint. She soon made things up with the help of friends, and was at liberty again, and finding that I rather was there to be concealed than by any particular prosecutions, and finding also that I agreed with her, or rather she with me in a just abhorrence of the place and of the company, she invited me to go home with her, till I could put myself in some posture of settling in the world to my mind – withal telling me that it was ten to one but some good captain of a ship might take a fancy to me and court me in that part of the town where she lived.

I accepted her offer, and was with her half a year, and should have been longer, but in that interval what she proposed to me happened to herself, and she married very much to her advantage. But whose fortune soever was upon the increase, mine seemed to be upon the wane, and I found nothing present except two or three boatswains, or such fellows, but as for the commanders they were generally of two sorts: 1. such as, having good business – that is to say, a good ship – resolved not to marry but with advantage – that is, with a good fortune; 2. such as, being out of employ, wanted a wife to help them to a ship. I mean (1.) a wife who, having some money, could enable them to hold, as they call it, a good part of a ship themselves, so to encourage owners to come in; or (2.) a wife who, if she had not money, had friends who were concerned in shipping and so could help to put the young man into a good ship, which to them is as good as a portion – and neither of these was my case, so I looked like one that was to lie on hand.*

This knowledge I soon learnt by experience, viz. that the state of things was altered as to matrimony, and that I was not to expect at London what I had found in the country – that marriages were here the consequences of politic schemes for forming interests and carrying on business, and that love had no share, or but very little, in the matter.

That, as my sister-in-law at Colchester had said, beauty, wit, manners, sense, good humour, good behaviour, education, virtue, piety or any other qualification, whether of body or mind, had no power to recommend. That money only made a woman agreeable. That men chose mistresses indeed by the gust of their affection, and it was requisite to a whore to be handsome, well shaped, have a good mien and a graceful behaviour. But that for a wife, no deformity would shock the fancy, no ill qualities, the judgement – the money was the thing. The portion was neither crooked or monstrous, but the money was always agreeable, whatever the wife was.

On the other hand, as the market ran very unhappily on the men's side, I found the women had lost the privilege of saying no – that it was a favour now for a woman to have the question asked, and if any young lady had so much arrogance as to counterfeit a negative, she never had the opportunity given her of denying twice, much less of recovering that false step and accepting what she had, but seemed to decline. The men had such choice everywhere that the case of the women was very unhappy, for they seemed to ply at every door, and if the man was by great chance refused at one house, he was sure to be received at the next.

Besides this, I observed that the men made no scruple to set themselves out and to go a-fortune-hunting, as they call it, when they had really no fortune themselves to demand it or merit to deserve it, and that they carried it so high that a woman was scarce allowed to enquire after the character or estate of the person that pretended to her. This I had an example of in a young lady at the next house to me, and with whom I had contracted an intimacy. She was courted by a young captain, and though she had near 2,000l. to her fortune, she did but enquire of some of his neighbours about his character, his morals or substance, and he took occasion at the next visit to let her know, truly, that he took it very ill, and that he should not give her the trouble of his visits any more. I heard of it, and as I had begun my acquaintance with her, I went to see her upon it. She entered into a close conversation with me about it, and unbosomed herself very freely. I perceived presently that though she thought herself very ill-used, yet she had no power to resent it, and was exceedingly piqued that she had lost him, and particularly that another of less fortune had gained him.

I fortified her mind against such a meanness, as I called it. I told her that as low as I was in the world, I would have despised a man that should think I ought to take him upon his own recommendation only, without having the liberty to inform myself of his fortune and of his character. Also I told her that as she had a good fortune, she had no need to stoop to the disaster of the times; that it was enough that the men could insult us that had but little money to recommend us, but if she suffered such an affront to pass upon her without resenting it, she would be rendered low-prized upon all occasions, and would be the contempt of all the women in that part of the town; that a woman can never want an opportunity to be revenged of a man that has used her ill, and that there were ways enough to humble such a fellow as that, or else certainly women were the most unhappy creatures in the world.

I found she was very well pleased with the discourse, and she told me seriously that she would be very glad to make him sensible of her just resentment, and either to bring him on again or have the satisfaction of her revenge being as public as possible.

I told her that if she would take my advice I would tell her how she should obtain her wishes in both those things, and that I would engage I would bring the man to her door again and make him beg to be let in. She smiled at that, and soon let me see that if he came to her door, her resentment was not so great as to give her leave to let him stand long there.

However, she listened very willingly to my offer of advice, so I told her that the first thing she ought to do was a piece of justice to herself, namely that whereas she had been told by several people that he had reported among the ladies that he had left her and pretended to give the advantage of the negative to himself, she should take care to have it well spread among the women – which she could not fail of an opportunity to do in a neighbourhood so addicted to family news as that she lived in was – that she had enquired into his circumstances and found he was not the man as to estate he pretended to be. "Let them be told, madam," said I, "that you had been well informed that he was not the man that you expected, and that you thought it was not safe to meddle with him – that you heard he was of an ill temper, and that he boasted how he had used the women ill upon many occasions, and that particularly he was debauched in his morals, etc." – the last of which indeed had some truth in it, but at the same time I did not find that she seemed to like him much the worse for that part.

As I had put this into her head, she came most readily into it. Immediately she went to work to find instruments, and she had very little difficulty in the search, for telling her story in general to a couple of gossips in the neighbourhood, it was the chat of the tea table all over that part of the town, and I met with it wherever I visited. Also, as it was known that I was acquainted with the young lady herself, my opinion was asked very often, and I confirmed it with all the necessary aggravations, and set out his character in the blackest colours. But then, as a piece of secret intelligence, I added what the other gossips knew nothing of, viz. that I had heard he was in very bad circumstances, that he was under a necessity of a fortune to support his interest with the owners of the ship he commanded, that his own part was not paid for, and if it was not paid quickly his owners would put him out of the ship, and his chief mate was likely to command it, who offered to buy that part which the captain had promised to take.

I added, for I confess I was heartily piqued at the rogue, as I called him, that I had heard a rumour, too, that he had a wife alive at Plymouth, and another in the West Indies, a thing which they all knew was not very uncommon for such kind of gentlemen.

This worked as we both desired it, for presently the young lady at next door, who had a father and mother that governed both her and her fortune, was shut up, and her father forbid him the house. Also, in one place more where he went, the woman had the courage, however strange it was, to say no, and he could try nowhere but he was reproached with his pride, and that he pretended not to give the women leave to enquire into his character, and the like.

Well, by this time he began to be sensible of his mistake, and having alarmed all the women on that side the water, he went over to Ratcliff* and got access to some of the ladies there. But though the young women there too were, according to the fate of the day, pretty willing to be asked, yet such was his ill luck that his character followed him over the water, and his good name was much the same there as it was on our side, so that though he might have had wives enough, yet it did not happen among the women that had good fortunes, which was what he wanted.

But this was not all. She very ingeniously managed another thing herself, for she got a young gentleman, who was a relation, and was indeed a married man, to come and visit her two or three times a week in a very fine chariot and good liveries, and her two agents and I also presently spread a report all over that this gentleman came to court her, that he was a gentleman of a thousand pounds a year, and that he was fallen in love with her, and that she was going to her aunt's in the City because it was inconvenient for the gentleman to come to her with his coach in Redriff,* the streets being so narrow and difficult.

This took immediately. The captain was laughed at in all companies, and was ready to hang himself. He tried all the ways possible to come at her again, and wrote the most passionate letters to her in the world, excusing his former rashness, and, in short, by great application obtained leave to wait on her again, as he said, to clear his reputation.

At this meeting she had her full revenge of him, for she told him she wondered what he took her to be that she should admit any man to a treaty of so much consequence as that of marriage without enquiring very well into his circumstances, that if he thought she was to be huffed* into wedlock, and that she was in the same circumstances which her neighbours might be in, viz. to take up with the first good Christian that came, he was mistaken – that, in a word, his character was really bad, or he was very ill beholding to his neighbours, and that unless he could clear up some points in which she had justly been prejudiced, she had no more to say to him, but to do herself justice, and give him the satisfaction of knowing that she was not afraid to say no, either to him or any man else.

With that she told him what she had heard, or rather raised herself by my means, of his character: his not having paid for the part he pretended to own of the ship he commanded; of the resolution of his owners to put him out of the command and to put his mate in his stead; and of the scandal raised on his morals, his having been reproached with such and such women, and his having a wife at Plymouth and in the West Indies, and the like. And she asked him whether he could deny that she had good reason, if these things were not cleared up, to refuse him, and in the mean time to insist upon having satisfaction in points so significant as they were.

He was so confounded at her discourse that he could not answer a word, and she almost began to believe that all was true by his disorder, though at the same time she knew that she had been the raiser of all those reports herself.

After some time he recovered himself a little, and from that time became the most humble, the most modest and the most importunate man alive in his courtship.

She carried her jest on a great way. She asked him if he thought she was so at her last shift that she could or ought to bear such treatment, and if he did not see that she did not want those who thought it worth their while to come farther to her than he did, meaning the gentleman who she had brought to visit her by way of sham.

She brought him by these tricks to submit to all possible measures to satisfy her, as well of his circumstances as of his behaviour. He brought her undeniable evidence of his having paid for his part of the ship; he brought her certificates from his owners that the report of their intending to remove him from the command of the ship and put his chief mate in was false and groundless – in short, he was quite the reverse of what he was before.

Thus I convinced her that if the men made their advantage of our sex in the affair of marriage upon the supposition of there being such choice to be had and of the women being so easy, it was only owing to this: that the women wanted courage to maintain their ground and to play their part, and that according to My Lord Rochester,

A woman's ne'er so ruined but she can
Revenge herself on her undoer, man.*

After these things, this young lady played her part so well that though she resolved to have him, and that indeed having him was the main bent of her design, yet she made his obtaining her be to him the most difficult thing in the world, and this she did not by a haughty reserved carriage, but by a just policy, turning the tables upon him and playing back upon him his own game. For as he pretended by a kind of lofty carriage to place himself above the occasion of a character and to make enquiring into his character a kind of an affront to him, she broke with him upon that subject, and at the same time that she made him submit to all possible enquiry after his affairs, she apparently shut the door against his looking into her own.

It was enough to him to obtain her for a wife. As to what she had, she told him plainly that as he knew her circumstances, it was but just she should know his, and though at the same time he had only known her circumstances by common fame, yet he had made so many protestations of his passion for her that he could ask no more but her hand to his grand request, and the like ramble according to the custom of lovers. In short, he left himself no room to ask any more questions about her estate, and she took the advantage of it like a prudent woman, for she placed part of her fortune so in trustees, without letting him know anything of it, that it was quite out of his reach, and made him be very well content with the rest.

It is true she was pretty well besides – that is to say, she had about 1,400*l*. in money, which she gave him. And the other, after some time, she brought to light, as a perquisite to herself, which he was to accept as a mighty favour – seeing, though it was not to be his, it might ease him in the article of her particular expenses. And I must add that by this conduct the gentleman himself became not only the more humble in his applications to her to obtain her, but also was much the more an obliging husband to her when he had her. I cannot but remind the ladies here how much they place themselves below the common station of a wife (which, if I may be allowed not to be partial, is low enough already) – I say they place themselves below their common station and prepare their own mortifications by their submitting so to be insulted by the men beforehand, which I confess I see no necessity of.

This relation may serve therefore to let the ladies see that the advantage is not so much on the other side as the men think it is, and though it may be true that the men have but too much choice among us, and that some women may be found who will dishonour themselves, be cheap and easy to come at and will scarce wait to be asked, yet if they will have women, as I may say, worth having, they may find them as uncome-at-able as ever, and that those that are otherwise are a sort of people that have such deficiencies, when had, as rather recommend the ladies that are difficult than encourage the men to go on with their easy courtship and expect wives equally valuable that will come at first call.

Nothing is more certain than that the ladies always gain of the men by keeping their ground and letting their pretended lovers see they can resent being slighted, and that they are not afraid of saying no. They, I observe, insult us mightily with telling us of the number of women – that the wars and the sea, and trade, and other incidents have carried the men so much away that there is no proportion between the numbers of the sexes, and therefore the women have the disadvantage. But I am far from granting that the number of the women is so great, or the number of the men so small; but if they will have me tell the truth, the disadvantage of the women is a terrible scandal upon the men, and it lies here, and here only – namely, that the age is so wicked, and the sex so debauched, that in short the number of such men as an honest woman ought to meddle with is small indeed, and it is but here and there that a man is to be found who is fit for a woman to venture upon.

But the consequence even of that, too, amounts to no more than this: that women ought to be the more nice.* For how do we know the just character of the man that makes the offer? To say that the woman should be the more easy on this occasion is to say we

75

should be the forwarder to venture, because of the greatness of the danger, which in my way of reasoning is very absurd.

On the contrary, the women have ten thousand times the more reason to be wary and backward, by how much the hazard of being betrayed is the greater – and would the ladies consider this and act the wary part, they would discover every cheat that offered. For, in short, the lives of very few men nowadays will bear a character, and if the ladies do but make a little enquiry, they will soon be able to distinguish the men and deliver themselves. As for women that do not think their own safety worth their thought – that, impatient of their present state, resolve as they call it to take the first good Christian that comes, that run into matrimony as a horse rushes into the battle* – I can say nothing to them but this: that they are a sort of ladies that are to be prayed for among the rest of distempered people, and to me they look like people that venture their whole estates in a lottery where there is a hundred thousand blanks to one prize.

No man of common sense will value a woman the less for not giving up herself at the first attack, or for not accepting his proposal without enquiring into his person or character. On the contrary, he must think her the weakest of all creatures in the world, as the rate of men now goes. In short, he must have a very contemptible opinion of her capacities – nay, even of her understanding – that, having but one cast for her life, shall cast that life away at once, and make matrimony, like death, be a leap in the dark.

I would fain have the conduct of my sex a little regulated in this particular – which is the thing in which of all the parts of life I think at this time we suffer most in. 'Tis nothing but lack of courage, the fear of not being married at all, and of that frightful state of life called an old maid – of which I have a story to tell by itself. This, I say, is the woman's snare, but would the ladies once but get above that fear and manage rightly, they would more certainly avoid it by standing their ground, in a case so absolutely necessary to their felicity, than by exposing themselves as they do.

And if they did not marry so soon as they may do otherwise, they would make themselves amends by marrying safer. She is always married too soon who gets a bad husband, and she is never married too late who gets a good one. In a word, there is no woman – deformity or lost reputation excepted – but if she manages well may be married safely one time or other; but if she precipitates herself, it is ten thousand to one but she is undone.

But I come now to my own case, in which there was at this time no little nicety. The circumstances I was in made the offer of a good husband the most necessary thing in the world to me, but I found soon that to be made cheap and easy was not the way. It soon began to be found that the widow had no fortune, and to say this was to say all that was ill of me, for I began to be dropped in all the discourses of matrimony. Being well bred, handsome, witty, modest and agreeable – all which I had allowed to my character, whether justly or no is not to the purpose – I say, all these would not do without the dross, which was now become more valuable than virtue itself. In short, the widow, they said, had no money.

I resolved, therefore, as to the state of my present circumstances, that it was absolutely necessary to change my station, and make a new appearance in some other place where I was not known, and even to pass by another name if I found occasion.

I communicated my thoughts to my intimate friend, the captain's lady, who I had so faithfully served in her case with the captain, and who was as ready to serve me in the same kind as I could desire. I made no scruple to lay my circumstances open to her: my stock was but low, for I had made but about 540*l*. at the close of my last affair, and I had wasted some of that. However, I had about 460*l*. left, a great many very rich clothes, a gold watch and some jewels, though of no extraordinary value, and about 30 or 40*l*. left in linen not disposed of.

My dear and faithful friend, the captain's wife, was so sensible of the service I had done her in the affair above that she was not only a steady friend to me, but, knowing my circumstances, she frequently made me presents as money came into her hands such as fully amounted to a maintenance, so that I spent none of my own. And at last she made this unhappy proposal to me, viz. that as we had observed, as above, how the men made no scruple to set themselves out as persons meriting a woman of fortune, when they had really no fortune of their own, it was but just to deal with them in their own way, and if it was possible, to deceive the deceiver.

The captain's lady, in short, put this project into my head, and told me if I would be ruled by her I should certainly get a husband of fortune, without leaving him any room to reproach me with want of my own. I told her, as I had reason to do, that I would give up myself wholly to her directions, and that I would have neither tongue to speak or feet to step in that affair but as she should direct me, depending that she would extricate me out of every difficulty that she brought me into, which she said she would answer for.

The first step she put me upon was to call her cousin, and go to a relation's house of hers in the country, where she directed me, and where she brought her husband to visit me, and, calling me cousin, she worked matters so about that her husband and she together invited me most passionately to come to town and be with them, for they now lived in a quite different place from where they were before. In the next place she tells her husband that I had at least 1,500*l*. fortune, and that after some of my relations I was like to have a great deal more.

It was enough to tell her husband this – there needed nothing on my side. I was but to sit still and wait the event, for it presently went all over the neighbourhood that the young widow at Captain ——'s was a fortune, that she had at least 1,500*l*. and perhaps a great deal more, and that the captain said so. And if the captain was asked at any time about me, he made no scruple to affirm it, though he knew not one word of the matter other than that his wife had told him so, and in this he thought no harm, for he really believed it to be so, because he had it from his wife – so slender a foundation will those fellows build upon if they do but think there is a fortune in the game. With the reputation of this fortune, I presently found myself blessed with admirers enough, and that I had my choice of men, as scarce as they said they were, which by the way confirms what I was saying before. This being my case, I who had a subtle game to play had nothing now to do but to single out from them all the properest man that might be for my purpose – that is to say, the man who was most likely to depend upon the hearsay of a fortune and not enquire too far into the particulars, and unless I did this, I did nothing, for my case would not bear much enquiry.

I picked out my man without much difficulty, by the judgement I made of his way of courting me. I had let him run on with his protestations and oaths that he loved me above all the world, that if I would make him happy, that was enough – all which I knew was upon supposition, nay, it was upon a full satisfaction, that I was very rich, though I never told him a word of it myself.

This was my man, but I was to try him to the bottom, and indeed in that consisted my safety, for if he baulked, I knew I was undone as surely as he was undone if he took me, and if I did not make some scruple about his fortune, it was the way to lead him to raise some about mine. And first, therefore, I pretended on all occasions to doubt his sincerity, and told him perhaps he only courted me for my fortune. He stopped my mouth in that part with the thunder of his protestations, as above, but still I pretended to doubt.

One morning he pulls off his diamond ring and writes upon the glass of the sash in my chamber this line:

You I love, and you alone.

I read it, and asked him to lend me his ring, with which I wrote under it thus:

And so in love says everyone.

He takes his ring again, and writes another line thus:

Virtue alone is an estate.

I borrowed it again, and I wrote under it:

But money's virtue; gold is fate.

He coloured as red as fire to see me turn so quick upon him, and in a kind of a rage told me he would conquer me, and writes again thus:

I scorn your gold, and yet I love.

I ventured all upon the last cast of poetry, as you'll see, for I wrote boldly under his last:

I'm poor: let's see how kind you'll prove.

This was a sad truth to me. Whether he believed me or no I could not tell – I supposed then that he did not. However, he flew to me, took me in his arms and, kissing me very eagerly and with the greatest passion imaginable, he held me fast till he called for a pen and ink, and then told me he could not wait the tedious writing on the glass, but, pulling out a piece of paper, he began and wrote again:

Be mine, with all your poverty.

I took his pen and followed him immediately thus:

Yet secretly you hope I lie.

He told me that was unkind, because it was not just, and that I put him upon contradicting me, which did not consist with good manners any more than with his affection. And therefore since I had insensibly drawn him into this poetical scribble, he begged I would not oblige him to break it off – so he writes again:

Let love alone be our debate.

I wrote again:

She loves enough that does not hate.

This he took for a favour, and so laid down the cudgels – that is to say, the pen. I say he took it for a favour, and a mighty one it was if he had known all. However, he took it as I meant it – that is, to let him think I was inclined to go on with him, as indeed I had all the reason in the world to do, for he was the best-humoured, merry sort of a fellow that I ever met with, and I often reflected on myself how doubly criminal it was to deceive such a man, but that necessity, which pressed me to a settlement suitable to my condition, was my authority for it. And certainly his affection to me, and the goodness of his temper, however they might argue against using him ill, yet they strongly argued to me that he would better take the disappointment than some fiery-tempered wretch who might have nothing to recommend him but those passions which would serve only to make a woman miserable all her days.

Besides, though I had jested with him, as he supposed it, so often about my poverty, yet, when he found it to be true, he had foreclosed all manner of objection, seeing – whether he was in jest or in earnest – he had declared he took me without any regard to my portion, and – whether I was in jest or in earnest – I had declared myself to be very poor. So that, in a word, I had him fast both ways, and though he might say afterwards he was cheated, yet he could never say that I had cheated him.

He pursued me close after this, and, as I saw there was no need to fear losing him, I played the indifferent part with him longer than prudence might otherwise have dictated to me. But

I considered how much this caution and indifference would give me the advantage over him when I should come to be under the necessity of owning my own circumstances to him, and I managed it the more warily because I found he inferred from thence, as indeed he ought to do, that I either had the more money or the more judgement, and would not venture at all.

I took the freedom one day, after we had talked pretty close to the subject, to tell him that it was true I had received the compliment of a lover from him – namely, that he would take me without enquiring into my fortune, and I would make him a suitable return in this, viz. that I would make as little enquiry into his as consisted with reason, but I hoped he would allow me to ask a few questions, which he should answer or not as he thought fit, and that I would not be offended if he did not answer me at all. One of these questions related to our manner of living, and the place where, because I had heard he had a great plantation in Virginia, and that he had talked of going to live there, and I told him I did not care to be transported.*

He began from this discourse to let me voluntarily into all his affairs, and to tell me in a frank open way all his circumstances, by which I found he was very well to pass in the world, but that great part of his estate consisted of three plantations which he had in Virginia, which brought him in a very good income, generally speaking, to the tune of 300*l.* a year, but that if he was to live upon them, would bring him in four times as much. "Very well," thought I, "you shall carry me thither as soon as you please, though I won't tell you so beforehand."

I jested with him extremely about the figure he would make in Virginia, but I found he would do anything I desired, though he did not seem glad to have me undervalue his plantations, so I turned my tale. I told him I had good reason not to desire to go there to live, because if his plantations were worth so much there, I had not a fortune suitable to a gentleman of 1,200*l.* a year, as he said his estate would be.

He replied generously: he did not ask what my fortune was – he had told me from the beginning he would not, and he would be as good as his word. But whatever it was, he assured me he would never desire me to go to Virginia with him, or go thither himself without me, unless I was perfectly willing and made it my choice.

All this, you may be sure, was as I wished, and indeed nothing could have happened more perfectly agreeable. I carried it on as far as this with a sort of indifferency that he often wondered at, more than at first, but which was the only support of his courtship; and I mention it the rather to intimate again to the ladies that nothing but want of courage for such an indifferency makes our sex so cheap and prepares them to be ill-used as they are. Would they venture the loss of a pretending fop now and then who carries it high upon the point of his own merit, they would certainly be slighted less and courted more. Had I discovered really and truly what my great fortune was, and that in all I had not full 500*l.* when he expected 1,500*l.*, yet I had hooked him so fast, and played him so long, that I was satisfied he would have had me in my worst circumstances. And indeed it was less a surprise to him when he learnt the truth than it would have been, because having not the least blame to lay on me, who had carried it with an air of indifference to the last, he could not say one word except that indeed he thought it had been more, but that if it had been less he did not repent his bargain, only that he should not be able to maintain me so well as he intended.

In short, we were married, and very happily married on my side, I assure you, as to the man, for he was the best-humoured man that ever woman had, but his circumstances were not so good as I imagined, as, on the other hand, he had not bettered himself by marrying so much as he expected.

When we were married I was shrewdly put to it to bring him that little stock I had, and to let him see it was no more. But there was a necessity for it, so I took my opportunity one day when we were alone to enter into a short dialogue with him about it. "My dear," said I, "we have been married a fortnight. Is it not time to let you know whether you have got a wife with something or with nothing?" "Your own time for that, my dear," says he. "I am satisfied that I have got the wife I love. I have not troubled you much," says he, "with my enquiry after it."

"That's true," said I, "but I have a great difficulty upon me about it, which I scarce know how to manage."

"What's that, my dear?" says he.

"Why," says I, "'tis a little hard upon me, and 'tis harder upon you. I am told that Captain ———" (meaning my friend's husband) "has told you I had a great deal more money than I ever pretended to have, and I am sure I never employed him to do so."

"Well," says he, "Captain ——— may have told me so, but what then? If you have not so much, that may lie at his door, but you never told me what you had, so I have no reason to blame you if you have nothing at all."

"That is so just," said I, "and so generous that it makes my having but a little a double affliction to me."

"The less you have, my dear," says he, "the worse for us both. But I hope your affliction you speak of is not caused for fear I should be unkind to you for want of a portion. No, no – if you have nothing, tell me plainly and at once. I may perhaps tell the captain he has cheated me, but I can never say you have cheated me, for did you not give it under your hand that you were poor? And so I ought to expect you to be."

"Well," said I, "my dear, I am glad I have not been concerned in deceiving you before marriage. If I deceive you since, 'tis ne'er the worse; that I am poor is too true, but not so poor as to have nothing neither." So I pulled out some bank bills and gave him about a hundred and sixty pounds. "There's something, my dear," says I, "and not quite all neither."

I had brought him so near to expecting nothing by what I had said before that the money, though the sum was small in itself, was doubly welcome to him. He owned it was more than he looked for, and that he did not question by my discourse to him, but that my fine clothes, gold watch and a diamond ring or two had been all my fortune.

I let him please himself with that 160*l.* two or three days, and then, having been abroad that day, and as if I had been to fetch it, I brought him a hundred pounds more home in gold, and told him there was a little more portion for him – and, in short, in about a week more I brought him 180*l.* more, and about 60*l.* in linen, which I made him believe I had been obliged to take with the 100*l.* which I gave him in gold, as a composition* for a debt of 600*l.*, being little more than five shilling in the pound, and overvalued too.

"And now, my dear," says I to him, "I am very sorry to tell you that there is all, and that I have given you my whole fortune." I added that if the person who had my 600*l.* had not abused me, I had been worth a thousand pound to him, but that as it was I had been faithful to him and reserved nothing to myself, but if it had been more he should have had it.

He was so obliged by the manner and so pleased with the sum, for he had been in a terrible fright least it had been nothing at all, that he accepted it very thankfully. And thus I got over the fraud of passing for a fortune without money, and cheating a man into marrying me on pretence of a fortune – which, by the way, I take to be one of the most dangerous steps a woman can take, and in which she runs the most hazard of being ill-used afterwards.

My husband, to give him his due, was a man of infinite good nature, but he was no fool, and finding his income not suited to the manner of living which he had intended if I had brought him what he expected, and being under a disappointment in his return of his plantations in Virginia, he discovered many times his inclination of going over to Virginia to live upon his own, and often would be magnifying the way of living there – how cheap, how plentiful, how pleasant, and the like.

I began presently to understand his meaning, and I took him up very plainly one morning, and told him that I did so, that I found his estate turned to no account at this distance, compared to what it would do if he lived upon the spot, and that I found he had a mind to go and live there – and I added that I was sensible he had been disappointed in a wife, and that, finding his expectations not answered that way, I could do no less to make him amends than tell him that I was very willing to go over to Virginia with him and live there.

He said a thousand kind things to me upon the subject of my making such a proposal to him. He told me that however he was disappointed in his expectations of a fortune, he was not disappointed in a wife, and that I was all to him that a wife could be, and he was more than satisfied in the whole when the particulars were put together – but that this offer was so kind that it was more than he could express.

To bring the story short, we agreed to go. He told me that he had a very good house there, that it was well furnished, that his mother was alive and lived in it, and one sister, which was all the relations he had, that as soon as he came there his mother would remove to another house, which was her own for life and his after her decease, so that I should have all the house to myself – and I found all this to be exactly as he had said.

To make this part of the story short, we put on board the ship which we went in a large quantity of good furniture for our house, with stores of linen and other necessaries, and a good cargo for sale, and away we went.

To give an account of the manner of our voyage, which was long and full of dangers, is out of my way. I kept no journal; neither did my husband. All that I can say is that after a terrible passage, frighted twice with dreadful storms – and once with what was still more terrible, I mean a pirate, who came on board and took away almost all our provisions, and, which would have been beyond all to me, they had once taken my husband to go along with them, but by entreaties were prevailed with to leave him – I say, after all these terrible things, we arrived in York River in Virginia, and coming to our plantation we were received with all the demonstrations of tenderness and affection (by my husband's mother) that were possible to be expressed.

We lived here all together, my mother-in-law, at my entreaty, continuing in the house, for she was too kind a mother to be parted with; my husband likewise continued the same as at first, and I thought myself the happiest creature alive, when an odd and surprising event put an end to all that felicity in a moment, and rendered my condition the most uncomfortable, if not the most miserable, in the world.

My mother was a mighty cheerful, good-humoured old woman – I may call her old woman, for her son was above thirty – I say she was very pleasant, good company and used to entertain me, in particular, with abundance of stories to divert me, as well of the country we were in, as of the people.

Among the rest, she often told me how the greatest part of the inhabitants of the colony came thither in very indifferent circumstances from England – that, generally speaking, they were of two sorts, either (1.) such as were brought over by masters of ships to be sold as servants – "Such we call them, my dear," says she, "but they are more properly called slaves" – or (2.) such as are transported from Newgate and other prisons after having been found guilty of felony and other crimes punishable with death.

"When they come here," says she, "we make no difference. The planters buy them, and they work together in the field till their time is out. When 'tis expired," said she, "they have encouragement given them to plant for themselves, for they have a certain number of acres of land allotted them by the country, and they go to work to clear and cure* the land, and then to plant it with tobacco and corn for their own use, and as the tradesmen and merchants will trust them with tools and clothes, and other necessaries upon the credit of their crop before it is grown, so they again plant every year a little more than the year before, and so buy whatever they want with the crop that is before them.

"Hence, child," says she, "many a Newgate bird becomes a great man, and we have," continued she, "several Justices of the Peace, officers of the train bands* and magistrates of the towns they live in that have been burnt in the hand."*

She was going on with that part of the story when her own part in it interrupted her, and with a great deal of good-humoured confidence she told me she was one of the second sort of inhabitants herself, that she came away openly, having ventured too far in a particular case, so that she was become a criminal. "And here's the mark of it, child," says she, and pulling off her glove, "Look ye here," says she, turning up the palm of her hand, and showed me a very fine white arm and hand, but branded in the inside of the hand, as in such cases it must be.

This story was very moving to me, but my mother (smiling) said, "You need not think such a thing strange, daughter, for, as I told you, some of the best men in this country are burnt in the hand, and they are not ashamed to own it. There's Major ——," says she. "He was an eminent pickpocket. There's Justice Ba——r was a shoplifter, and both of them were burnt in the hand, and I could name you several, such as they are."

We had frequent discourses of this kind, and abundance of instances she gave me of the like. After some time, as she was telling some stories of one that was transported but a few weeks ago, I began in an intimate kind of way to ask her to tell me something of her own story, which she did with the utmost plainness and sincerity – how she had fallen into very ill company in London in her young days, occasioned by her mother sending her frequently to carry victuals and other relief to a kinswoman of hers who was a prisoner in Newgate and who lay in a miserable starving condition, was afterwards condemned to be hanged, but, having got respite by pleading her belly, died afterwards in the prison.

Here my mother-in-law ran out in a long account of the wicked practices in that dreadful place, and how it ruined more young people than all the town besides. "And, child," says my mother, "perhaps you may know little of it, or it may be have heard nothing about it, but depend upon it," says she, "we all know here that there are more thieves and rogues made by that one prison of Newgate than by all the clubs and societies of villains in the nation. 'Tis that cursed place," says my mother, "that half peoples this colony."

Here she went on with her own story so long, and in so particular a manner, that I began to be very uneasy, but coming to
one particular that required telling her name, I thought I should
have sunk down in the place. She perceived I was out of order,
and asked me if I was not well, and what ailed me. I told her I
was so affected with the melancholy story she had told, and the
terrible things she had gone through, that it had overcome me,
and I begged of her to talk no more of it. "Why, my dear," says
she very kindly, "what need these things trouble you? These pas-
sages were long before your time, and they give me no trouble at
all now – nay, I look back on them with a particular satisfaction,
as they have been a means to bring me to this place." Then she
went on to tell me how she very luckily fell into a good family,
where, behaving herself well, and her mistress dying, her master
married her, by whom she had my husband and his sister, and
that by her diligence and good management after her husband's
death she had improved the plantations to such a degree as they
then were, so that most of the estate was of her getting, not her
husband's, for she had been a widow upwards of sixteen year.

I heard this part of the story with very little attention, because
I wanted much to retire and give vent to my passions, which I did
soon after, and let anyone judge what must be the anguish of my
mind when I came to reflect that this was certainly no more or less
than my own mother, and I had now had two children, and was big
with another, by my own brother, and lay with him still every night.

I was now the most unhappy of all women in the world. Oh,
had the story never been told me, all had been well – it had been
no crime to have lain with my husband, since as to his being my
relation, I had known nothing of it.

I had now such a load on my mind that it kept me perpetually
waking. To reveal it, which would have been some ease to me,
I could not find would be to any purpose, and yet to conceal it
would be next to impossible. Nay, I did not doubt but I should
talk of it in my sleep and tell my husband of it whether I would
or no. If I discovered it, the least thing I could expect was to lose

my husband, for he was too nice and too honest a man to have continued my husband after he had known I had been his sister, so that I was perplexed to the last degree.

I leave it to any man to judge what difficulties presented to my view. I was away from my native country at a distance prodigious, and the return to me unpassable. I lived very well, but in a circumstance insufferable in itself. If I had discovered myself to my mother, it might be difficult to convince her of the particulars, and I had no way to prove them. On the other hand, if she had questioned or doubted me, I had been undone, for the bare suggestion would have immediately separated me from my husband without gaining my mother or him, who would have been neither a husband or a brother – so that, between the surprise on one hand and the uncertainty on the other, I had been sure to be undone.

In the mean time, as I was but too sure of the fact, I lived therefore in open avowed incest and whoredom, and all under the appearance of an honest wife, and though I was not much touched with the crime of it, yet the action had something in it shocking to nature, and made my husband, as he thought himself, even nauseous to me.

However, upon the most sedate consideration, I resolved that it was absolutely necessary to conceal it all, and not make the least discovery of it either to mother or husband, and thus I lived with the greatest pressure imaginable for three year more, but had no more children.

During this time my mother used to be frequently telling me old stories of her former adventures which, however, were no ways pleasant to me. For by it, though she did not tell it me in plain terms, yet I could easily understand – joined with what I had heard myself of my first tutors – that in her younger days she had been both whore and thief. But I verily believe she had lived to repent sincerely of both, and that she was then a very pious, sober and religious woman.

Well, let her life have been what it would then, it was certain that my life was very uneasy to me. For I lived, as I have said, but in the worst sort of whoredom, and as I could expect no good of it, so really no good issue came of it, and all my seeming prosperity wore off and ended in misery and destruction. It was some time indeed before it came to this, for, but I know not by what ill fate guided, everything went wrong with us afterwards, and that which was worse, my husband grew strangely altered – froward,* jealous and unkind – and I was as impatient of bearing his carriage as the carriage was unreasonable and unjust. These things proceeded so far that we came at last to be in such ill terms with one another that I claimed a promise of him which he entered willingly into with me when I consented to come from England with him, viz. that if I found the country not to agree with me, or that I did not like to live there, I should come away to England again when I pleased, giving him a year's warning to settle his affairs.

I say I now claimed this promise of him, and I must confess I did it not in the most obliging terms that could be in the world neither, but I insisted that he treated me ill, that I was remote from my friends and could do myself no justice, and that he was jealous without cause, my conversation having been unblameable and he having no pretence for it, and that to remove to England would take away all occasion from him.

I insisted so peremptorily upon it that he could not avoid coming to a point, either to keep his word with me or to break it, and this notwithstanding he used all the skill he was master of and employed his mother and other agents to prevail with me to alter my resolutions. Indeed, the bottom of the thing lay at my heart, and that made all his endeavours fruitless, for my heart was alienated from him as a husband. I loathed the thoughts of bedding with him, and used a thousand pretences of illness and humour to prevent his touching me, fearing nothing more than to be with child again by him, which to be sure would have prevented, or at least delayed, my going over to England.

However, at last I put him so out of humour that he took up a rash and fatal resolution. In short, I should not go to England, and though he had promised me, yet it was an unreasonable thing for me to desire it – that it would be ruinous to his affairs, would unhinge his whole family and be next to an undoing him in the world; that therefore I ought not to desire it of him, and that no wife in the world that valued her family and her husband's prosperity would insist upon such a thing.

This plunged me again, for when I considered the thing calmly and took my husband as he really was – a diligent, careful man in the main work of laying up an estate for his children, and that he knew nothing of the dreadful circumstances that he was in – I could not but confess to myself that my proposal was very unreasonable, and what no wife that had the good of her family at heart would have desired.

But my discontents were of another nature. I looked upon him no longer as a husband, but as a near relation, the son of my own mother, and I resolved somehow or other to be clear of him, but which way I did not know, nor did it seem possible.

It is said by the ill-natured world of our sex that if we are set on a thing, it is impossible to turn us from our resolutions. In short, I never ceased poring upon the means to bring to pass my voyage, and came that length with my husband at last as to propose going without him. This provoked him to the last degree, and he called me not only an unkind wife, but an unnatural mother, and asked me how I could entertain such a thought without horror as that of leaving my two children (for one was dead) without a mother, and to be brought up by strangers, and never to see them more. It was true: had things been right I should not have done it, but now it was my real desire never to see them, or him either, any more, and as to the charge of unnatural I could easily answer it to myself, while I knew that the whole relation was unnatural in the highest degree in the world.

However, it was plain there was no bringing my husband to anything. He would neither go with me or let me go without him, and it was quite out of my power to stir without his consent, as anyone that knows the constitution of the country I was in knows very well.

We had many family quarrels about it, and they began (in time) to grow up to a dangerous height, for as I was quite estranged from my husband (as he was called) in affection, so I took no heed to my words, but sometimes gave him language that was provoking – and, in short, strove all I could to bring him to a parting with me, which was what above all things in the world I desired most.

He took my carriage very ill, and indeed he might well do so, for at last I refused to bed with him, and, carrying on the breach upon all occasions to extremity, he told me once he thought I was mad, and if I did not alter my conduct he would put me under cure – that is to say, into a madhouse. I told him he should find I was far enough from mad, and that it was not in his power, or any other villain's, to murder me. I confess at the same time I was heartily frighted at his thoughts of putting me into a madhouse, which would at once have destroyed all the possibility of breaking the truth out, whatever the occasion might be – for that then no one would have given credit to a word of it.

This therefore brought me to a resolution: whatever came of it, to lay open my whole case. But which way to do it, or to whom, was an inextricable difficulty, and took me up many months to resolve. In the mean time, another quarrel with my husband happened, which came up to such a mad extreme as almost pushed me on to tell it him all to his face, but though I kept it in so as not to come to the particulars, I spoke so much as put him into the utmost confusion, and in the end brought out the whole story.

He began with a calm expostulation upon my being so resolute to go to England. I defended it, and, one hard word bringing on another as is usual in all family strife, he told me I did not treat him as if he was my husband, or talk of my children as if I was a mother, and, in short, that I did not deserve to be used as a wife; that he had used all the fair means possible with me, that he had argued with all the kindness and calmness that a husband or a Christian ought to do, and that I made him such a vile return that I treated him rather like a dog than a man, and rather like the most contemptible stranger than a husband; that he was very loath to use violence with me, but that, in short, he saw a necessity of it now, and that for the future he should be obliged to take such measures as should reduce me to my duty.

My blood was now fired to the utmost, though I knew what he had said was very true, and nothing could appear more provoked. I told him – for his fair means and his foul, they were equally contemned* by me – that, for my going to England, I was resolved on it, come what would, and that as to treating him not like a husband and not showing myself a mother to my children, there might be something more in it than he understood at present. But, for his further consideration, I thought fit to tell him thus much: that he neither was my lawful husband nor they lawful children, and that I had reason to regard neither of them more than I did.

I confess I was moved to pity him when I spoke it, for he turned pale as death and stood mute as one thunderstruck, and once or twice I thought he would have fainted. In short, it put him in a fit something like an apoplex: he trembled, a sweat or dew ran off his face, and yet he was cold as a clod, so that I was forced to run and fetch something for him to keep life in him. When he recovered of that, he grew sick and vomited, and in a little after was put to bed, and in the next morning was, as he had been indeed all night, in a violent fever.

However, it went off again, and he recovered, though but slowly, and when he came to be a little better, he told me I had given him a mortal wound with my tongue, and he had only one thing to ask before he desired an explanation. I interrupted him, and told him I was sorry I had gone so far, since I saw what disorder it put him into, but I desired him not to talk to me of explanations, for that would but make things worse.

This heightened his impatience, and indeed perplexed him beyond all bearing, for now he began to suspect that there was some mystery yet unfolded, but could not make the least guess at the real particulars of it. All that ran in his brain was that I had another husband alive, which I could not say in fact might not be true. But I assured him, however, there was not the least of that in it – and indeed, as to my other husband, he was effectually dead in law to me, and had told me I should look on him as such, so I had not the least uneasiness on that score.

But now I found the thing too far gone to conceal it much longer, and my husband himself gave me an opportunity to ease myself of the secret, much to my satisfaction. He had laboured with me three or four weeks, but to no purpose, only to tell him whether I had spoken those words only as the effect of my passion, to put him in a passion, or whether there was anything of truth in the bottom of them. But I continued inflexible, and would explain nothing unless he would first consent to my going to England – which he would never do, he said, while he lived. On the other hand, I said it was in my power to make him willing when I pleased – nay, to make him entreat me to go – and this increased his curiosity, and made him importunate to the highest degree, but it was all to no purpose.

At length, he tells all this story to his mother, and sets her upon me to get the main secret out of me, and she used her utmost skill with me indeed. But I put her to a full stop at once by telling her that the reason and mystery of the whole matter lay in herself, and that it was my respect to her that had made me conceal it, and that in short I could go no further, and therefore conjured* her not to insist upon it.

She was struck dumb at this suggestion, and could not tell what to say or to think, but, laying aside the supposition as a policy of mine, continued her importunity on account of her son, and if possible to make up the breach between us two. As to that, I told her that it was indeed a good design in her, but that it was impossible to be done, and that if I should reveal to her the truth of what she desired, she would grant it to be impossible and cease to desire it. At last I seemed to be prevailed on by her importunity, and told her I dared trust her with a secret of the greatest importance, and she would soon see that this was so, and that I would consent to lodge it in her breast if she would engage solemnly not to acquaint her son with it without my consent.

She was long in promising this part, but rather than not come at the main secret she agreed to that too, and after a great many other preliminaries I began and told her the whole story. First I told her how much she was concerned in all the unhappy breach which had happened between her son and me, by telling me her own story and her London name, and that the surprise she saw I was in was upon that occasion. Then I told her my own story and my name, and assured her by such other tokens as she could not deny that I was no other, nor more or less, than her own child, her daughter, born of her body in Newgate – the same that had saved her from the gallows by being in her belly, and the same that she left in such and such hands when she was transported.

It is impossible to express the astonishment she was in. She was not inclined to believe the story or to remember the particulars, for she immediately foresaw the confusions that must follow in the family upon it. But everything concurred so exactly with the stories she had told me of herself – and which, if she had not told me, she would perhaps have been content to have denied – that she had stopped her own mouth, and she had nothing to do but to take me about the neck and kiss me, and cry most vehemently over me, without speaking one word for a long time together. At last she broke out: "Unhappy child!" says she. "What miserable chance could bring thee hither? And in the arms of my own son too! Dreadful girl," says she. "Why, we are all undone! Married to thy own brother! Three children, and two alive, all of the same flesh and blood! My son and my daughter lying together as husband and wife! All confusion and distraction for ever! Miserable family! What will become of us? What is to be said? What is to be done?" And thus she ran on for a great while. Nor had I any power to speak – or, if I had, did I know what to say, for every word wounded me to the soul. With this kind of amazement on our thoughts we parted for the first time, though my mother was more surprised than I was, because it was more news to her than to me. However, she promised again to me at parting that she would say nothing of it to her son till we had talked of it again.

It was not long, you may be sure, before we had a second conference upon the same subject – when, as if she had been willing to forget the story she had told me of herself or to suppose that I had forgot some of the particulars, she began to tell them with alterations and omissions. But I refreshed her memory and set her to rights in many things which I supposed she had forgot, and then came in so opportunely with the whole history that it was impossible for her to go from it, and then she fell into her rhapsodies again, and exclamations at the severity of her misfortunes. When these things were a little over with her, we fell into a close debate about what should be first done before we gave an account of the matter to my husband – but to what purpose could be all our consultations? We could neither of us see our way through it, nor see how it could be safe to open such a scene to him. It was impossible to make any judgement, or give any guess at what temper he would receive it in, or what measures he would take upon it, and if he should have so little government of himself as to make it public, we easily foresaw that it would be the ruin of the whole family, and expose my mother and me to the last degree. And if at last he should take the advantage the law would give him, he might put me away with disdain, and leave me to sue for the little portion that I had, and perhaps waste it all in the suit, and then be a beggar. The children would be ruined too, having no legal claim to any of his effects, and thus I should see him perhaps in the arms of another wife in a few months, and be myself the most miserable creature alive.

My mother was as sensible of this as I, and, upon the whole, we knew not what to do. After some time, we came to more sober resolutions, but then it was with this misfortune too: that my mother's opinion and mine were quite different from one another, and indeed inconsistent with one another. For my mother's opinion was that I should bury the whole thing entirely and continue to live with him as my husband till some other event should make the discovery of it more convenient, and that in the mean time she would endeavour to reconcile us together again, and restore our mutual comfort and family peace, that we might lie as we used to do together, and so let the whole matter remain a secret as close as death. "For, child," says she, "we are both undone if it comes out."

To encourage me to this, she promised to make me easy in my circumstances as far as she was able, and to leave me what she could at her death, secured for me separately from my husband. So that if it should come out afterwards, I should not be left destitute, but be able to stand on my own feet and procure justice from him.

This proposal did not agree at all with my judgement of the thing, though it was very fair and kind in my mother, but my thoughts ran quite another way.

As to keeping the thing in our own breasts and letting it all remain as it was, I told her it was impossible – and I asked her how she could think I could bear the thoughts of lying with my own brother. In the next place, I told her that her being alive was the only support of the discovery, and that while she owned me for her child and saw reason to be satisfied that I was so, nobody else would doubt it, but that if she should die before the discovery, I should be taken for an impudent creature that had forged such a thing to go away from my husband, or should be counted crazed and distracted. Then I told her how he had threatened already to put me into a madhouse, and what concern I had been in about it, and how that was the thing that drove me to the necessity of discovering it to her as I had done.

From all which I told her that I had on the most serious reflections I was able to make in the case come to this resolution, which I hoped she would like, as a medium between both: viz. that she should use her endeavours with her son to give me leave to go for England, as I had desired, and to furnish me with a sufficient sum of money, either in goods along with me or in bills for my support there, all along suggesting that he might one time or other think it proper to come over to me; that when I was gone she should then in cold blood, and after first obliging him in the solemnest manner possible to secrecy, discover the case to him – doing it gradually, and as her own discretion should guide her, so that he might not be surprised with it and fly out into any passions and excesses on my account, or on hers; and that she should concern herself to prevent his slighting the children or marrying again, unless he had a certain account of my being dead.

This was my scheme, and my reasons were good. I was really alienated from him in the consequence of these things – indeed, I mortally hated him as a husband, and it was impossible to remove that riveted aversion I had to him. At the same time, it being an unlawful incestuous living added to that aversion, and though I had no great concern about it in point of conscience, yet everything added to make cohabiting with him the most nauseous thing to me in the world, and I think verily it was come to such a height that I could almost as willingly have embraced a dog as have let him offer anything of that kind to me – for which reason I could not bear the thoughts of coming between the sheets with him. I cannot say that I was right in point of policy in carrying it such a length, while at the same time I did not resolve to discover the thing to him, but I am giving an account of what was, not of what ought or ought not to be.

In this directly opposite opinion to one another my mother and I continued a long time, and it was impossible to reconcile our judgements. Many disputes we had about it, but we could never either of us yield our own or bring over the other.

I insisted on my aversion to lying with my own brother, and she insisted upon its being impossible to bring him to consent to my going from him to England, and in this uncertainty we continued, not differing so as to quarrel, or anything like it, but so as not to be able to resolve what we should do to make up that terrible breach that was before us.

At last I resolved on a desperate course, and told my mother my resolution: viz. that, in short, I would tell him of it myself. My mother was frighted to the last degree at the very thoughts of it, but I bid her be easy, told her I would do it gradually and softly, and with all the art and good humour I was mistress of, and time it also as well as I could, taking him in good humour too. I told her I did not question but if I could be hypocrite enough to feign more affection to him than I really had, I should succeed in all my design, and we might part by consent, and with a good agreement, for I might love him well enough for a brother, though I could not for a husband.

All this while he lay at my mother to find out, if possible, what was the meaning of that dreadful expression of mine, as he called it, which I mentioned before – namely, that I was not his lawful wife, nor my children his legal children. My mother put him off, told him she could bring me to no explanations, but found there was something that disturbed me very much, and she hoped she should get it out of me in time, and in the mean time recommended to him earnestly to use me more tenderly and win me with his usual good carriage – told him of his terrifying and affrighting me with his threats of sending me to a madhouse and the like, and advised him not to make a woman desperate on any account whatever.

He promised her to soften his behaviour, and bid her assure me that he loved me as well as ever, and that he had no such design as that of sending me to a madhouse, whatever he might say in his passion. Also, he desired my mother to use the same persuasions to me too, that our affections might be renewed, and we might live together in a good understanding as we used to do.

I found the effects of this treaty presently. My husband's conduct was immediately altered, and he was quite another man to me. Nothing could be kinder and more obliging than he was to me upon all occasions, and I could do no less than make some return to it, which I did as well as I could. But it was but in an awkward manner at best, for nothing was more frightful to me than his caresses, and the apprehensions of being with child again by him was ready to throw me into fits, and this made me see that there was an absolute necessity of breaking the case to him without any more delay – which, however, I did with all the caution and reserve imaginable.

He had continued his altered carriage to me near a month, and we began to live a new kind of life with one another – and could

I have satisfied myself to have gone on with it, I believe it might have continued as long as we had continued alive together. One evening, as we were sitting and talking very friendly together under a little awning which served as an arbour at the entrance from our house into the garden, he was in a very pleasant, agreeable humour, and said abundance of kind things to me relating to the pleasure of our present good agreement and the disorders of our past breach, and what a satisfaction it was to him that we had room to hope we should never have any more of it.

I fetched a deep sigh, and told him there was nobody in the world could be more delighted than I was in the good agreement we had always kept up, or more afflicted with the breach of it, and should be so still, but I was sorry to tell him that there was an unhappy circumstance in our case which lay too close to my heart, and which I knew not how to break to him, that rendered my part of it very miserable, and took from me all the comfort of the rest.

He importuned me to tell him what it was. I told him I could not tell how to do it – that while it was concealed from him, I alone was unhappy. But if he knew it also, we should be both so, and that therefore to keep him in the dark about it was the kindest thing that I could do, and it was on that account alone that I kept a secret from him – the very keeping of which, I thought, would first or last be my destruction.

It is impossible to express his surprise at this relation, and the double importunity which he used with me to discover it to him. He told me I could not be called kind to him – nay, I could not be faithful to him if I concealed it from him. I told him I thought so too, and yet I could not do it. He went back to what I had said before to him, and told me he hoped it did not relate to what I had said in my passion, and that he had resolved to forget all that as the effect of a rash provoked spirit. I told him I wished I could forget it all too, but that it was not to be done: the impression was too deep, and I could not do it – it was impossible.

He then told me he was resolved not to differ with me in anything, and that therefore he would importune me no more about it, resolving to acquiesce in whatever I did or said – only begged I would then agree that, whatever it was, it should no more interrupt our quiet and our mutual kindness.

This was the most provoking thing he could have said to me, for I really wanted his further importunities, that I might be prevailed with to bring out that which indeed it was like death to me to conceal. So I answered him plainly that I could not say I was glad not to be importuned, though I could not tell how to comply. "But come, my dear," said I, "what conditions will you make with me upon the opening this affair to you?"

"Any conditions in the world," said he, "that you can in reason desire of me." "Well," said I, "come, give it me under your hand that if you do not find I am in any fault, or that I am willingly concerned in the causes of the misfortune that is to follow, you will not blame me, use me the worse, do me any injury or make me be the sufferer for that which is not my fault."

"That," says he, "is the most reasonable demand in the world – not to blame you for that which is not your fault. Give me a pen and ink," says he, so I ran in and fetched a pen, ink and paper, and he wrote the condition down in the very words I had proposed it, and signed it with his name. "Well," says he, "what is next, my dear?"

"Why," says I, "the next is that you will not blame me for not discovering the secret of it to you before I knew it."

"Very just again," says he, "with all my heart." So he wrote down that also and signed it.

"Well, my dear," says I, "then I have but one condition more to make with you, and that is that as there is nobody concerned in it but you and I, you shall not discover it to any person in the world except your own mother, and that in all the measures you shall take upon the discovery, as I am equally concerned in it with you, though as innocent as yourself, you shall do nothing in a passion, nothing to my prejudice or to your mother's prejudice, without my knowledge and consent."

This a little amazed him, and he wrote down the words distinctly, but read them over and over before he signed them, hesitating at them several times and repeating them. "My mother's prejudice! And your prejudice! What mysterious thing can this be?" However, at last he signed it.

"Well," says I, "my dear, I'll ask you no more under your hand, but as you are to bear the most unexpected and surprising thing that perhaps ever befell any family in the world, I beg you to promise me you will receive it with composure and a presence of mind suitable to a man of sense."

"I'll do my utmost," says he, "upon condition you will keep me no longer in suspense, for you terrify me with all these preliminaries."

"Well then," says I, "it is this: as I told you before in a heat that I was not your lawful wife, and that our children were not legal children, so I must let you know now, in calmness, and in kindness, but with affliction enough, that I am your own sister, and you my own brother, and that we are both the children of our mother now alive and in the house, who is convinced of the truth of it, in a manner not to be denied or contradicted."

I saw him turn pale and look wild, and I said, "Now, remember your promise, and receive it with presence of mind. For who could have said more to prepare you for it than I have done?" However, I called a servant, and got him a little glass of rum, which is the usual dram of the country, for he was just fainting away.

When he was a little recovered, I said to him, "This story, you may be sure, requires a long explanation, and therefore have patience and compose your mind to hear it out, and I'll make it as short as I can." And with this, I told him what I thought was needful of the fact, and particularly how my mother came to discover it to me, as above. "And now, my dear," says I, "you will see reason for my capitulations, and that I neither have been the cause of this matter, nor could be so, and that I could know nothing of it before now."

"I am fully satisfied of that," says he, "but 'tis a dreadful surprise to me. However, I know a remedy for it all, and a remedy that shall put an end to all your difficulties without your going to England." "That would be strange," said I, "as all the rest." "No, no," says he, "I'll make it easy. There's nobody in the way of it all but myself." He looked a little disordered when he said this, but I did not apprehend anything from it at that time, believing, as it used to be said, that they who do those things never talk of them, or that they who talk of such things never do them.

But things were not come their height with him, and I observed he became pensive and melancholy – and, in a word, as I thought, a little distempered in his head. I endeavoured to talk him into temper, and to reason him into a kind of scheme for our government in the affair, and sometimes he would be well and talk with some courage about it, but the weight of it lay too heavy upon his thoughts – and, in short, it went so far that he made two attempts upon himself, and in one of them had actually strangled himself, and, had not his mother come into the room in the very moment, he had died. But, with the help of a Negro servant, she cut him down and recovered him.

Things were now come to a lamentable height in the family. My pity for him now began to revive that affection which at first I really had for him, and I endeavoured sincerely by all the kind carriage I could to make up the breach. But, in short, it had gotten too great a head – it preyed upon his spirits, and it threw him into a long lingering consumption, though it happened not to be mortal. In this distress I did not know what to do, as his life was apparently declining, and I might perhaps have married again there, very much to my advantage. It had been certainly my business to have stayed in the country, but my mind was restless too, and uneasy. I hankered after coming to England, and nothing would satisfy me without it.

In short, by an unwearied importunity, my husband, who was apparently decaying, as I observed, was at last prevailed with, and so, my own fate pushing me on, the way was made clear for me, and, my mother concurring, I obtained a very good cargo for my coming to England.

When I parted with my brother, for such I am now to call him, we agreed that after I arrived he should pretend to have an account that I was dead in England, and so might marry again when he would. He promised, and engaged to me to correspond with me as a sister, and to assist and support me as long as I lived, and that if he died before me he would leave sufficient to his mother to take care of me still, in the name of a sister, and he was in some respect careful of me, when he heard of me. But it was so oddly managed that I felt the disappointments very sensibly afterwards, as you shall hear in its time.

I came away for England in the month of August, after I had been eight years in that country, and now a new scene of misfortunes attended me which perhaps few women have gone through the like of.

We had an indifferent good voyage, till we came just upon the coast of England, and where we arrived in two-and-thirty days, but were then ruffled with two or three storms, one of which drove us away to the coast of Ireland, and we put in at Kinsale.* We remained there about thirteen days, got some refreshment on shore and put to sea again, though we met with very bad weather again, in which the ship sprung her mainmast, as they called it, for I knew not what they meant. But we got at last into Milford Haven* in Wales, where, though it was remote from our port, yet having my foot safe upon the firm ground of my native country, the isle of Britain, I resolved to venture it no more upon the waters, which had been so terrible to me. So, getting my clothes and money on shore with my bills of loading* and other papers, I resolved to come for London and leave the ship to get to her port as she could. The port whither she was bound was to Bristol, where my brother's chief correspondent lived.

I got to London in about three weeks, where I heard a little while after that the ship was arrived in Bristol, but at the same time had the misfortune to know that by the violent weather she had been in, and the breaking of her mainmast, she had great damage on board, and that a great part of her cargo was spoilt.

I had now a new scene of life upon my hands, and a dreadful appearance it had. I was come away with a kind of final farewell. What I brought with me was indeed considerable, had it come safe, and by the help of it I might have married again tolerably well, but as it was, I was reduced to between two or three hundred pounds in the whole, and this without any hope of recruit.* I was entirely without friends – nay, even so much as without acquaintance, for I found it was absolutely necessary not to revive former acquaintances. And as for my subtle friend that set me up formerly for a fortune, she was dead, and her husband also – as I was informed upon sending a person unknown to enquire.

The looking after my cargo of goods soon after obliged me to take a journey to Bristol, and during my attendance upon that affair, I took the diversion of going to the Bath, for, as I was still far from being old, so my humour, which was always gay, continued so to an extreme. And being now, as it were, a woman of fortune, though I was a woman without a fortune, I expected something or other might happen in my way that might mend my circumstances as had been my case before.

The Bath is a place of gallantry enough – expensive and full of snares. I went thither indeed in the view of taking anything that might offer, but I must do myself that justice as to protest I knew nothing amiss; I meant nothing but in an honest way, nor had I any thoughts about me at first that looked the way which afterwards I suffered them to be guided.

Here I stayed the whole latter season, as it is called there, and contracted some unhappy acquaintance, which rather prompted the follies I fell afterwards into than fortified me against them. I lived pleasantly enough, kept good company – that is to say, gay, fine company – but had the discouragement to find this way of living sunk me exceedingly, and that as I had no settled income, so spending upon the main stock was but a certain kind of bleeding to death, and this gave me many sad reflections in the intervals of my other thoughts. However, I shook them off, and still flattered myself that something or other might offer for my advantage.

But I was in the wrong place for it. I was not now at Redriff, where if I had set myself tolerably up some honest sea captain or other might have talked with me upon the honourable terms of matrimony. But I was at the Bath, where men find a mistress sometimes, but very rarely look for a wife, and consequently all the particular acquaintances a woman can expect to make there must have some tendency that way.

I had spent the first season well enough, for though I had contracted some acquaintance with a gentleman who came to the Bath for his diversion, yet I had entered into no felonious treaty, as it might be called. I had resisted some casual offers of gallantry, and had managed that way well enough. I was not wicked enough to come into the crime for the mere vice of it, and I had no extraordinary offers made me that tempted me with the main thing which I wanted.

However, I went this length the first season, viz. I contracted an acquaintance with a woman in whose house I lodged, who, though she did not keep an ill house,* as we call it, yet had none of the best principles in herself. I had on all occasions behaved myself so well as not to get the least slur upon my reputation on any account whatever, and all the men that I had conversed with were of so good reputation that I had not given the least reflection by conversing with them. Nor did any of them seem to think there was room for a wicked correspondence, if they had any of them offered it. Yet there was one gentleman, as above, who always singled me out for the diversion of my company, as he called it – which, as he was pleased to say, was very agreeable to him – but at that time there was no more in it.

I had many melancholy hours at the Bath after all the company was gone, for though I went to Bristol sometimes for the disposing my effects and for recruits of money, yet I chose to come back to Bath for my residence, because, being on good terms with the woman in whose house I lodged in the summer, I found that during the winter I lived rather cheaper there than I could do anywhere else. Here, I say, I passed the winter as heavily as I had passed the autumn cheerfully, but having contracted a nearer intimacy with the said woman in whose house I lodged, I could not avoid communicating to her something of what lay hardest upon my mind, and particularly the narrowness of my circumstances and the loss of my fortune by the damage of my goods by sea. I told her also that I had a mother and a brother in Virginia in good circumstances, and as I had really written back to my mother in particular to represent my condition, and the great loss I had received, which indeed came to almost 500*l.*, so I did not fail to let my new friend know that I expected a supply from thence, and so indeed I did. And as the ships went from Bristol to York River in Virginia and back again generally in less time than from London, and that my brother corresponded chiefly at Bristol, I thought it was much better for me to wait here for my returns than to go to London, where also I had not the least acquaintance.

My new friend appeared sensibly affected with my condition, and indeed was so very kind as to reduce the rate of my living with her to so low a price during the winter that she convinced me she got nothing by me – and as for lodging during the winter, I paid nothing at all.

When the spring season came on, she continued to be as kind to me as she could, and I lodged with her for a time, till it was found necessary to do otherwise. She had some persons of character that frequently lodged in her house, and in particular the gentleman who, as I said, singled me out for his companion the winter before – and he came down again with another gentleman in his company and two servants, and lodged in the same house. I suspected that my landlady had invited him thither, letting him know that I was still with her, but she denied it, and protested to me that she did not, and he said the same.

In a word, this gentleman came down and continued to single me out for his peculiar confidence as well as conversation. He was a complete gentleman, that must be confessed, and his company was very agreeable to me, as mine, if I might believe him, was to him. He made no professions to me but of an extraordinary respect, and he had such an opinion of my virtue that, as he often professed, he believed if he should offer anything else, I should reject him with contempt. He soon understood from me that I was a widow, that I had arrived at Bristol from Virginia by the last ships, and that I waited at Bath till the next Virginia fleet should arrive, by which I expected considerable effects. I understood by him, and by others of him, that he had a wife, but that the lady was distempered in her head, and was under the conduct of her own relations – which he consented to, to avoid any reflections that might, as was not unusual in such cases, be cast on him for mismanaging her cure, and in the mean time he came to the Bath to divert his thoughts from the disturbance of such a melancholy circumstance as that was.

My landlady, who of her own accord encouraged the correspondence on all occasions, gave me an advantageous character of him as of a man of honour and of virtue, as well as of a great estate. And indeed I had a great deal of reason to say so of him too, for though we lodged both on a floor, and he had frequently come into my chamber, even when I was in bed, and I also into his when he was in bed, yet he never offered anything to me further than a kiss, or so much as solicited me to anything till long after, as you shall hear.

I frequently took notice to my landlady of his exceeding modesty, and she again used to tell me she believed it was so from the beginning. However, she used to tell me that she thought I ought to expect some gratification from him for my company, for indeed he did, as it were, engross me, and I was seldom from him. I told her I had not given him the least occasion to think I wanted it, or that I would accept of it from him. She told me she would take that part upon her, and she did so, and managed it so dextrously that the first time we were together alone, after she had talked with him, he began to enquire a little into my circumstances – as how I had subsisted myself since I came on shore, and whether I did not want money. I stood off very boldly: I told him that though my cargo of tobacco was damaged, yet that it was not quite lost; that the merchant I had been consigned to had so honestly managed for me that I had not wanted, and that I hoped, with frugal management, I should make it hold out till more would come, which I expected by the next fleet; that in the mean time I had retrenched my expenses, and whereas I kept a maid last season, now I lived without, and whereas I had a chamber and a dining room then on the first floor, as he knew, I now had but one room two pair of stairs, and the like. "But I live," said I, "as well satisfied now as I did then" – adding that his company had been a means to make me live much more cheerfully than otherwise I should have done, for which I was much obliged to him. And so I put off all room for any offer for the present. However, it was not long before he attacked me again, and told me he found that I was backward to trust him with the secret of my circumstances, which he was sorry for, assuring me that he enquired into it with no design to satisfy his own curiosity, but merely to assist me, if there was any occasion. But since I would not own myself to stand in need of any assistance, he had but one thing more to desire of me, and that was that I would promise him that when I was any way straitened, or like to be so, I would frankly tell him of it, and that I would make use of him with the same freedom that he made the offer, adding that I should always find I had a true friend, though perhaps I was afraid to trust him.

I omitted nothing that was fit to be said by one infinitely obliged, to let him know that I had a due sense of his kindness, and indeed from that time I did not appear so much reserved to him as I had done before, though still within the bounds of the strictest virtue on both sides. But how free soever our conversation was, I could not arrive to that sort of freedom which he desired, viz. to tell him I wanted money, though I was secretly very glad of his offer.

Some weeks passed after this, and still I never asked him for money – when my landlady, a cunning creature, who had often pressed me to it but found that I could not do it, makes a story of her own inventing, and comes in bluntly to me when we were together. "Oh, widow," says she, "I have bad news to tell you this morning." "What is that?" said I. "Are the Virginia ships taken by the French?"* – for that was my fear. "No, no," says she, "but the man you sent to Bristol yesterday for money is come back, and says he has brought none."

Now, I could by no means like her project: I thought it looked too much like prompting him, which indeed he did not want, and I saw clearly that I should lose nothing by being backward to ask, so I took her up short. "I can't imagine why he should say so to you," said I, "for I assure you he brought me all the money I sent him for, and here it is," said I (pulling out my purse with about twelve guineas in it), and added, "I intend you shall have most of it by and by."

He seemed distasted a little at her talking as she did at first, as well as I – taking it, as I fancied he would, as something forward of her – but when he saw me give such an answer, he came immediately to himself again. The next morning we talked of it again, when I found he was fully satisfied, and smiling said he hoped I would not want money and not tell him of it, and that I had promised him otherwise. I told him I had been very much dissatisfied at my landlady's talking so publicly the day before of what she had nothing to do with, but I supposed she wanted what I owed her, which was about eight guineas, which I had resolved to give her, and had accordingly given it her the same night she talked so foolishly.

He was in a mighty good humour when he heard me say I had paid her, and it went off into some other discourse at that time, but the next morning, he having heard me up about my room before him, he called to me, and I answering, he asked me to come into his chamber. He was in bed when I came in, and he made me come and sit down on his bedside, for he said he had something to say to me which was of some moment. After some very kind expressions he asked me if I would be very honest to him, and give a sincere answer to one thing he would desire of me. After some little cavil with him at the word "sincere", and asking him if I had ever given him any answers which were not sincere, I promised him I would. Why then, his request was, he said, to let him see my purse. I immediately put my hand into my pocket and, laughing at him, pulled it out, and there was in it three guineas and a half. Then he asked me if there was all the money I had. I told him no, laughing again, not by a great deal.

Well then, he said, he would have me promise to go and fetch him all the money I had, every farthing. I told him I would, and I went into my chamber and fetched him a little private drawer, where I had about six guineas more, and some silver, and threw it all down upon the bed, and told him there was all my wealth, honestly to a shilling. He looked a little at it, but did not tell it, and huddled it all into the drawer again, and then, reaching his pocket, pulled out a key, and bade me open a little walnut-tree box he had upon the table, and bring him such a drawer, which I did. In which drawer there was a great deal of money in gold – I believe near 200 guineas, but I knew not how much. He took the drawer and, taking my hand, made me put it in and take a whole handful. I was backward at that, but he held my hand hard in his hand, and put it into the drawer, and made me take out as many guineas almost as I could well take up at once.

When I had done so, he made me put them into my lap, and took my little drawer, and poured out all my own money among his, and bade me get me gone and carry it all home into my own chamber.

I relate this story the more particularly because of the good humour there was in it, and to show the temper with which we conversed. It was not long after this but he began every day to find fault with my clothes, with my laces and headdresses, and, in a word, pressed me to buy better – which by the way I was willing enough to do, though I did not seem to be so, for I loved nothing in the world better than fine clothes. I told him I must housewife the money he had lent me, or else I should not be able to pay him again. He then told me in a few words that as he had a sincere respect for me and knew my circumstances, he had not lent me that money, but given it me, and that he thought I had merited it from him by giving him my company so entirely as I had done. After this, he made me take a maid and keep house, and, his friend that came with him to Bath being gone, he obliged me to diet him* – which I did very willingly, believing, as it appeared, that I should lose nothing by it, nor did the woman of the house fail to find her account in it too.

We had lived thus near three months when, the company beginning to wear away at the Bath, he talked of going away, and fain he would have me to go to London with him. I was not very easy in that proposal, not knowing what posture I was to live in there, or how he might use me. But while this was in debate he fell very sick: he had gone out to a place in Somersetshire called Shepton where he had some business, and was there taken very ill, and so ill that he could not travel, so he sent his man back to Bath to beg me that I would hire a coach and come over to him. Before he went, he had left all his money and other things of value with me, and what to do with them I did not know, but I secured them as well as I could, and locked up the lodgings and went to him, where I found him very ill indeed. However, I persuaded him to be carried in a litter to the Bath, where there was more help and better advice to be had.

He consented, and I brought him to the Bath, which was about fifteen miles, as I remember. Here he continued very ill of a fever, and kept his bed five weeks, all which time I nursed him and tended him myself, as much and as carefully as if I had been his wife. Indeed, if I had been his wife I could not have done more. I sat up with him so much and so often that at last indeed he would not let me sit up any longer, and then I got a pallet bed into his room, and lay in it just at his bed's feet.

I was indeed sensibly affected with his condition, and with the apprehension of losing such a friend as he was and was like to be to me, and I used to sit and cry by him many hours together. However, at last he grew better, and gave hopes that he would recover, as indeed he did, though very slowly.

Were it otherwise than what I am going to say, I should not be backward to disclose it, as it is apparent I have done in other cases in this account. But I affirm that through all this conversation, abating the freedom of coming into the chamber when I or he was in bed, and abating the necessary offices of attending him night and day when he was sick, there had not passed the least immodest word or action between us. Oh, that it had been so to the last!

After some time he gathered strength, and grew well apace, and I would have removed my pallet bed, but he would not let me till he was able to venture himself without anybody to sit up with him, and then I removed to my own chamber.

He took many occasions to express his sense of my tenderness and concern for him, and when he grew quite well he made me a present of fifty guineas for my care and, as he called it, for hazarding my life to save his.

And now he made deep protestations of a sincere inviolable affection for me, but all along attested it to be with the utmost reserve for my virtue, and his own. I told him I was fully satisfied of it. He carried it that length that he protested to me that if he was naked in bed with me, he would as sacredly preserve my virtue as he would defend it if I was assaulted by a ravisher. I believed him, and told him I did so, but this did not satisfy him. He would, he said, wait for some opportunity to give me an undoubted testimony of it.

It was a great while after this that I had occasion, on my own business, to go to Bristol, upon which he hired me a coach, and would go with me, and did so. And now indeed our intimacy increased. From Bristol he carried me to Gloucester, which was merely a journey of pleasure to take the air, and here it was our hap to have no lodging in the inn but in one large chamber with two beds in it. The master of the house, going up with us to show his rooms and coming into that room, said very frankly to him, "Sir, it is none of my business to enquire whether the lady be your spouse or no, but if not, you may lie as honestly in these two beds as if you were in two chambers" – and with that he pulls a great curtain which drew quite cross the room, and effectually divided the beds. "Well," says my friend very readily, "these beds will do, and as for the rest, we are too near a kin to lie together, though we may lodge near one another" – and this put an honest face on the thing too. When we came to go to bed, he decently went out of the room till I was in bed, and then went to bed in the bed on his own side of the room, but lay there talking to me a great while.

At last, repeating his usual saying that he could lie naked in the bed with me and not offer me the least injury, he starts out of his bed. "And now, my dear," says he, "you shall see how just I will be to you, and that I can keep my word" – and away he comes to my bed.

I resisted a little, but I must confess I should not have resisted him much if he had not made those promises at all. So after a little struggle, as I said, I lay still and let him come to bed. When he was there, he took me in his arms, and so I lay all night with him, but he had no more to do with me, or offered anything to me other than embracing me, as I say, in his arms – no, not the whole night, but rose up and dressed him in the morning, and left me as innocent for him as I was the day I was born.

This was a surprising thing to me, and perhaps may be so to others who know how the laws of nature work, for he was a strong, vigorous, brisk person – nor did he act thus on a principle of religion at all, but of mere affection, insisting on it that though I was to him the most agreeable woman in the world, yet because he loved me he could not injure me.

I own it was a noble principle, but as it was what I never understood before, so it was to me perfectly amazing. We travelled the rest of the journey as we did before, and came back to the Bath, where, as he had opportunity to come to me when he would, he often repeated the moderation, and I frequently lay with him, and he with me, and although all the familiarities between man and wife were common to us, yet he never once offered to go any farther, and he valued himself much upon it. I do not say that I was so wholly pleased with it as he thought I was, for I own I was much wickeder than he, as you shall hear presently.

We lived thus near two year, only with this exception: that he went three times to London in that time, and once he continued there four months. But, to do him justice, he always supplied me with money to subsist me very handsomely.

Had we continued thus, I confess we had had much to boast of, but, as wise men say, it is ill venturing too near the brink of a command – so we found it. And here again I must do him the justice to own that the first breach was not on his part. It was one night that we were in bed together warm and merry, and having drunk, I think, a little more wine that night, both of us, than usual, though not in the least to disorder either of us, when after some other follies which I cannot name, and being clasped close in his arms, I told him (I repeat it with shame and horror of soul) that I could find in my heart to discharge him of his engagement for one night and no more.

He took me at my word immediately, and after that, there was no resisting him – neither, indeed, had I any mind to resist him any more, let what would come of it.

Thus the government of our virtue was broken, and I exchanged the place of friend for that unmusical, harsh-sounding title of whore. In the morning we were both at our penitentials: I cried very heartily; he expressed himself very sorry – but that was all either of us could do at that time, and the way being thus cleared, and the bars of virtue and conscience thus removed, we had the less difficulty afterwards to struggle with.

It was but a dull kind of conversation that we had together for all the rest of that week. I looked on him with blushes, and every now and then started that melancholy objection: "What if I should be with child now? What will become of me then?" He encouraged me by telling me that as long as I was true to him he would be so to me, and since it was gone such a length (which indeed he never intended), yet if I was with child, he would take care of that, and of me too. This hardened us both: I assured him if I was with child, I would die for want of a midwife rather than name him as the father of it, and he assured me I should never want if I should be with child. These mutual assurances hardened us in the thing, and after this we repeated the crime as often as we pleased – till at length, as I had feared, so it came to pass, and I was indeed with child.

After I was sure it was so and I had satisfied him of it too, we began to think of taking measures for the managing it, and I proposed trusting the secret to my landlady and asking her advice, which he agreed to. My landlady, a woman (as I found) used to such things, made light of it: she said she knew it would come to that at last, and made us very merry about it. As I said above, we found her an experienced old lady at such work: she undertook everything, engaged to procure a midwife and a nurse, to satisfy all enquiries and bring us off with reputation, and she did so very dextrously indeed.

When I grew near my time, she desired my gentleman to go away to London, or make as if he did so. When he was gone, she acquainted the parish officers that there was a lady ready to lie in at her house, but that she knew her husband very well, and gave them, as she pretended, an account of his name – which she called Sir Walter Cleave – telling them he was a very worthy gentleman, and that she would answer for all enquiries, and the like. This satisfied the parish officers presently, and I lay in with as much credit as I could have done if I had really been My Lady Cleave, and was assisted in my travail by three or four of the best citizens' wives of Bath who lived in the neighbourhood – which, however, made me a little the more expensive to him. I often expressed my concern to him about it, but he bid me not be concerned at it.

As he had furnished me very sufficiently with money for the extraordinary expenses of my lying-in,* I had everything very handsome about me, but did not affect to be gay or extravagant neither. Besides, knowing my own circumstances and knowing the world as I had done, and that such kind of things do not often last long, I took care to lay up as much money as I could for a wet day, as I called it – making him believe it was all spent upon the extraordinary appearance of things in my lying-in.

By this means, and including what he had given me as above, I had at the end of my lying-in about 200 guineas by me, including also what was left of my own.

I was brought to bed of a fine boy indeed, and a charming child it was, and when he heard of it he wrote me a very kind, obliging letter about it, and then told me he thought it would look better for me to come away for London as soon as I was up and well, that he had provided apartments for me at Hammersmith,* as if I came thither only from London, and that after a little while I should go back to the Bath, and he would go with me.

I liked this offer very well, and accordingly hired a coach on purpose, and taking my child and a wet nurse to tend and suckle it, and a maidservant with me, away I went for London.

He met me at Reading in his own chariot, and, taking me into that, left the servant and the child in the hired coach, and so he brought me to my new lodgings at Hammersmith – with which I had abundance of reason to be very well pleased, for they were very handsome rooms, and I was very well accommodated.

And now I was indeed in the height of what I might call my prosperity, and I wanted nothing but to be a wife – which, however, could not be in this case: there was no room for it. And therefore on all occasions I studied to save what I could, as I have said above, against a time of scarcity, knowing well enough that such things as these do not always continue – that men that keep mistresses often change them, grow weary of them or jealous of them, or something or other happens to make them withdraw their bounty, and sometimes the ladies that are thus well used are not careful by a prudent conduct to preserve the esteem of their persons, or the nice article of their fidelity, and then they are justly cast off with contempt.

But I was secured in this point, for as I had no inclination to change, so I had no manner of acquaintance in the whole house, and so no temptation to look any further. I kept no company but in the family where I lodged, and with a clergyman's lady at next door, so that when he was absent I visited nobody, nor did he ever find me out of my chamber or parlour whenever he came down. If I went anywhere to take the air, it was always with him.

The living in this manner with him, and his with me, was certainly the most undesigned thing in the world. He often protested to me that when he became first acquainted with me, and even to the very night when we first broke in upon our rules, he never had the least design of lying with me – that he always had a sincere affection for me, but not the least real inclination to do what he had done. I assured him I never suspected him – that if I had, I should not so easily have yielded to the freedoms which brought it on, but that it was all a surprise, and was owing to the accident of our having yielded too far to our mutual inclinations that night. And indeed I have often observed since, and leave it as a caution to the readers of this story, that we ought to be cautious of gratifying our inclinations in loose and lewd freedoms, lest we find our resolutions of virtue fail us in the juncture when their assistance should be most necessary.

It is true, and I have confessed it before, that from the first hour I began to converse with him, I resolved to let him lie with me, if he offered it – but it was because I wanted his help and assistance, and I knew no other way of securing him than that. But when we were that night together and, as I have said, had gone such a length, I found my weakness. The inclination was not to be resisted, but I was obliged to yield up all even before he asked it.

However, he was so just to me that he never upbraided me with that, nor did he ever express the least dislike of my conduct on any other occasion, but always protested he was as much delighted with my company as he was the first hour we came together – I mean came together as bedfellows.

It is true that he had no wife – that is to say, she was as no wife to him – and so I was in no danger that way, but the just reflections of conscience oftentimes snatch a man, especially a man of sense, from the arms of a mistress, as it did him at last, though on another occasion.

On the other hand, though I was not without secret reproaches of my own conscience for the life I led, and that even in the greatest height of the satisfaction I ever took, yet I had the terrible prospect of poverty and starving which lay on me as a frightful spectre, so that there was no looking behind me. But as poverty brought me into it, so fear of poverty kept me in it, and I frequently resolved to leave it quite off if I could but come to lay up money enough to maintain me. But these were thoughts of no weight, and whenever he came to me they vanished, for his company was so delightful that there was no being melancholy when he was there. The reflections were all the subject of those hours when I was alone.

I lived six year in this happy but unhappy condition, in which time I brought him three children, but only the first of them lived, and though I removed twice in those six years, yet I came back the sixth year to my first lodgings at Hammersmith. Here it was that I was one morning surprised with a kind but melancholy letter from my gentleman, intimating that he was very ill, and was afraid he should have another fit of sickness, but that, his wife's relations being in the house with him, it would not be practicable to have me with him – which, however, he expressed his great dissatisfaction in – and that he wished I could be allowed to tend and nurse him as I did before.

I was very much concerned at this account, and was very impatient to know how it was with him. I waited a fortnight or thereabouts, and heard nothing, which surprised me, and I began to be very uneasy indeed. I think I may say that for the next fortnight I was near to distracted. It was my particular difficulty that I did not know directly where he was, for I understood at first he was in the lodgings of his wife's mother, but, having removed myself to London, I soon found by the help of the direction I had for writing my letters to him how to enquire after him, and there I found that he was at a house in Bloomsbury – whither he had, a little before he fell sick, removed his whole family – and that his wife and wife's mother were in the same house, though the wife was not suffered to know that she was in the same house with her husband.

Here I also soon understood that he was at the last extremity, which made me almost at the last extremity too, to have a true account. One night I had the curiosity to disguise myself like a servant maid, in a round cap and straw hat, and went to the door, as sent by a lady of his neighbourhood, where he lived before, and giving master and mistress's service, I said I was sent to know how Mr —— did, and how he had rested that night. In delivering this message I got the opportunity I desired, for, speaking with one of the maids, I held a long gossip's tale with her, and had all the particulars of his illness, which I found was a pleurisy attended with a cough and a fever. She told me also who was in the house, and how his wife was – who, by her relation, they were in some hopes might recover her understanding. But as to the gentleman himself, in short she told me the doctors said there was very little hopes of him – that in the morning they thought he had been dying, and that he was but little better then, for they did not expect that he could live over the next night.

This was heavy news for me, and I began now to see an end of my prosperity, and to see also that it was very well I had played the good housewife and secured or saved something while he was alive, for that now I had no view of my own living before me.

It lay very heavy upon my mind, too, that I had a son, a fine lovely boy, above five years old, and no provision made for it, at least that I knew of. With these considerations and a sad heart, I went home that evening, and began to cast with myself how I should live, and in what manner to bestow myself for the residue of my life.

You may be sure I could not rest without enquiring again very quickly what was become of him, and, not venturing to go myself, I sent several sham messengers, till after a fortnight's waiting longer, I found that there was hopes of his life, though he was still very ill. Then I abated my sending any more to the house, and in some time after I learnt in the neighbourhood that he was about house, and then that he was abroad again.

I made no doubt then but that I should soon hear of him, and began to comfort myself with my circumstances being, as

I thought, recovered. I waited a week, and two weeks, and with much surprise and amazement I waited near two months and heard nothing but that being recovered he was gone into the country for the air, and for the better recovery after his distemper. After this it was yet two months more, and then I understood he was come to his city house again, but still I heard nothing from him.

I had written several letters for him, and directed them as usual, and found two or three of them had been called for, but not the rest. I wrote again in a more pressing manner than ever, and in one of them let him know that I must be forced to wait on him myself, representing my circumstances, the rent of lodgings to pay and the provision for the child wanting, and my own deplorable condition, destitute of subsistence after his most solemn engagement to take care of and provide for me. I took a copy of this letter, and, finding it lay at the house near a month and was not called for, I found means to have the copy of it put into his own hands at a coffee house, where I had by enquiry found he used to go.

This letter forced an answer from him, by which, though I found I was to be abandoned, yet I found he had sent a letter to me some time before, desiring me to go down to the Bath again. Its contents I shall come to presently.

It is true that sickbeds are the times when such correspondences as this are looked on with different countenance, and seen with other eyes than we saw them with, or than they appeared with before. My lover had been at the gates of death, and at the very brink of eternity, and it seems had been struck with a due remorse, and with sad reflections upon his past life of gallantry and levity. And among the rest, this criminal correspondence with me, which was neither more or less than a long-continued life of adultery, had represented itself as it really was, not as it had been formerly thought by him to be, and he looked upon it now with a just and a religious abhorrence.

I cannot but observe also, and leave it for the direction of my sex in such cases of pleasure, that whenever sincere repentance succeeds such a crime as this, there never fails to attend a hatred of the object, and the more the affection might seem to be before, the hatred will be the more in proportion. It will always be so – indeed, it can be no otherwise, for there cannot be a true and sincere abhorrence of the offence, and the love to the cause of it remain. There will with an abhorrence of the sin be found a detestation of the fellow sinner – you can expect no other.

I found it so here, though good manners and justice in this gentleman kept him from carrying it on to any extreme. But the short history of his part in this affair was thus: he perceived by my last letter, and by all the rest, which he went for after, that I was not gone to the Bath, that his first letter had not come to my hand – upon which he writes me this following:

Madam,
I am surprised that my letter dated the 8th of last month did not come to your hand. I give you my word it was delivered at your lodgings, and to the hands of your maid.

I need not acquaint you with what has been my condition for some time past, and how, having been at the edge of the grave, I am by the unexpected and undeserved mercy of Heaven restored again. In the condition I have been in, it cannot be strange to you that our unhappy correspondence has not been the least of the burdens which lay upon my conscience. I need say no more – those things that must be repented of must be also reformed.

I wish you would think of going back to the Bath. I enclose you here a bill for 50l. for clearing yourself at your lodgings and carrying you down, and hope it will be no surprise to you to add that, on this account only, and not for any offence given me on your side, I can see you no more. I will take due care of the child – leave him where he is or take him with you, as you please. I wish you the like reflections, and that they may be to your advantage. I am, etc.

I was struck with this letter as with a thousand wounds, such as I cannot describe. The reproaches of my own conscience were such as I cannot express, for I was not blind to my own crime. And I reflected that I might with less offence have continued with my brother and lived with him as a wife, since there was no crime in our marriage on that score, neither of us knowing it.

But I never once reflected that I was all this while a married woman, a wife to Mr ——, the linen draper, who, though he had left me by the necessity of his circumstances, had no power to discharge me from the marriage contract which was between us, or to give me a legal liberty to marry again – so that I had been no less than a whore and an adulteress all this while. I then reproached myself with the liberties I had taken, and how I had been a snare to this gentleman, and that indeed I was principal in the crime – that now he was mercifully snatched out of the gulf by a convincing work upon his mind, but that I was left as if I was forsaken of God's grace, and abandoned by Heaven to a continuing in my wickedness.

Under these reflections I continued very pensive and sad for near a month, and did not go down to the Bath, having no inclination to be with the woman who I was with before, lest, as I thought, she should prompt me to some wicked course of life again, as she had done – and besides, I was very loath she should know I was cast off as above.

And now I was greatly perplexed about my little boy. It was death to me to part with the child, and yet when I considered the danger of being one time or other left with him to keep without a maintenance to support him, I then resolved to leave him where he was. But then I concluded also to be near him myself too, that I might have the satisfaction of seeing him without the care of providing for him.

I sent my gentleman a short letter, therefore, that I had obeyed his orders in all things, but that of going back to the Bath, which I could not think of for many reasons; that however parting from him was a wound to me that I could never recover, yet that I was fully satisfied his reflections were just, and would be very far from desiring to obstruct his reformation or repentance.

Then I represented my own circumstances to him in the most moving terms that I was able. I told him that those unhappy distresses which first moved him to a generous and an honest friendship for me would, I hope, move him to a little concern for me now, though the criminal part of our correspondence, which I believed neither of us intended to fall into at that time, was broken off; that I desired to repent as sincerely as he had done, but entreated him to put me in some condition that I might not be exposed to the temptations which the Devil never fails to excite us to from the frightful prospect of poverty and distress. And if he had the least apprehensions of my being troublesome to him, I begged he would put me in a posture to go back to my mother in Virginia, from whence he knew I came, and that would put an end to all his fears on that account. I concluded that if he would send me 50*l.* more to facilitate my going away, I would send him back a general release, and would promise never to disturb him more with any importunities, unless it was to hear of the well-doing of the child – who, if I found my mother living and my circumstances able, I would send for to come over to me, and take him also effectually off of his hands.

This was indeed all a cheat thus far, viz. that I had no intention to go to Virginia, as the account of my former affairs there may convince anybody of. But the business was to get this last fifty pounds of him, if possible, knowing well enough it would be the last penny I was ever to expect.

However, the argument I used – namely, of giving him a general release and never troubling him any more – prevailed effectually with him, and he sent me a bill for the money by a person who brought with him a general release for me to sign, and which I frankly signed, and received the money. And thus, though full sore against my will, a final end was put to this affair.

And here I cannot but reflect upon the unhappy consequence of too great freedoms between persons stated as we were, upon the pretence of innocent intentions, love of friendship and the like. For the flesh has generally so great a share in those friendships that it is great odds but inclination prevails at last over the most solemn resolutions, and that vice breaks in at the breaches of decency, which really innocent friendship ought to preserve with the greatest strictness. But I leave the readers of these things to their own just reflections, which they will be more able to make effectual than I, who so soon forgot myself, and am therefore but a very indifferent monitor.*

I was now a single person again, as I may call myself. I was loosed from all the obligations either of wedlock or mistress-ship in the world – except my husband the linen draper, who, I having not now heard from in almost fifteen year, nobody could blame me for thinking myself entirely freed from, seeing also he had, at his going away, told me that if I did not hear frequently from him, I should conclude he was dead, and I might freely marry again to whom I pleased.

I now began to cast up my accounts. I had by many letters, and much importunity, and with the intercession of my mother too, had a second return of some goods from my brother, as I now call him, in Virginia, to make up the damage of the cargo I brought away with me, and this too was upon the condition of my sealing a general release to him and to send it him by his correspondent at Bristol – which, though I thought hard of, yet I was obliged to promise to do. However, I managed so well in this case that I got my goods away before the release was signed, and then I always found something or other to say to evade the thing, and to put off the signing it at all, till at length I pretended I must write to my brother and have his answer before I could do it.

Including this recruit, and before I got the last 50*l*., I found my strength to amount, put all together, to about 400*l*., so that with that I had above 450*l*. I had saved above 100*l*. more, but I met with a disaster with that, which was this: that a goldsmith in whose hands I had trusted it, broke, so I lost 70*l*. of my money, the man's composition not making above 30*l*. out of his 100*l*. I had a little plate, but not much, and was well enough stocked with clothes and linen.

With this stock I had the world to begin again. But you are to consider that I was not now the same woman as when I lived at Redriff, for first of all I was near twenty years older, and did not look the better for my age, nor for my rambles to Virginia and back again. And though I omitted nothing that might set me out to advantage except painting – for that I never stooped to, and had pride enough to think I did not want it – yet there would always be some difference seen between five-and-twenty and two-and-forty.

I cast about innumerable ways for my future state of life, and began to consider very seriously what I should do, but nothing offered. I took care to make the world take me for something more than I was, and had it given out that I was a fortune, and that my estate was in my own hands – the last of which was very true; the first of it was as above. I had no acquaintance, which was one of my worst misfortunes, and the consequence of that was I had no adviser, at least who could advise and assist together. And, above all, I had nobody to whom I could in confidence commit the secret of my circumstances to, and could depend upon for their secrecy and fidelity, and I found by experience that to be friendless is the worst condition, next to being in want, that a woman can be reduced to. I say a woman, because 'tis evident men can be their own advisers and their own directors, and know how to work themselves out of difficulties and into business better than women. But if a woman has no friend to communicate her affairs to, and to advise and assist her, 'tis ten to one but she is undone – nay, and the more money she has, the more danger she is in of being wronged and deceived. And this was my case in the affair of the hundred pound which I left in the hand of the goldsmith, as above, whose credit, it seems, was upon the ebb before, but I that had no knowledge of things, and nobody to consult with, knew nothing of it, and so lost my money.

In the next place, when a woman is thus left desolate and void of counsel,* she is just like a bag of money, or a jewel dropped on the highway, which is a prey to the next comer. If a man of virtue and upright principles happens to find it, he will have it cried, and the owner may come to hear of it again. But how many times shall such a thing fall into hands that will make no scruple of seizing it for their own to once that it shall come into good hands?

This was evidently my case, for I was now a loose, unguided creature, and had no help, no assistance, no guide for my conduct. I knew what I aimed at, and what I wanted, but knew nothing how to pursue the end by direct means. I wanted to be placed in a settled state of living, and had I happened to meet with a sober, good husband, I should have been as faithful and true a wife to him as virtue itself could have formed. If I had been otherwise, the vice came in always at the door of necessity, not at the door of inclination, and I understood too well, by the want of it, what the value of a settled life was to do anything to forfeit the felicity of it – nay, I should have made the better wife for all the difficulties I had passed through, by a great deal; nor did I in any of the times that I had been a wife give my husbands the least uneasiness on account of my behaviour.

But all this was nothing. I found no encouraging prospect. I waited; I lived regularly and with as much frugality as became my circumstances, but nothing offered. Nothing presented, and the main stock wasted apace. What to do I knew not. The terror of approaching poverty lay hard upon my spirits. I had some money, but where to place it I knew not, nor would the interest of it maintain me, at least not in London.

At length a new scene opened. There was in the house where I lodged a north-country woman that went for a gentlewoman, and nothing was more frequent in her discourse than her account of the cheapness of provisions and the easy way of living in her county – how plentiful and how cheap everything was, what good company they kept, and the like – till at last I told her she almost tempted me to go and live in her county, for I that was a widow, though I had sufficient to live on, yet had no way of increasing it, and that London was an expensive and extravagant place – that I found I could not live here under a hundred pound a year, unless I kept no company, no servant, made no appearance and buried myself in privacy, as if I was obliged to it by necessity.

I should have observed that she was always made to believe, as everybody else was, that I was a great fortune, or at least that I had three or four thousand pounds, if not more, and all in my own hands, and she was mighty sweet upon me when she thought me inclined in the least to go into her country. She said she had a sister lived near Liverpool – that her brother was a considerable gentleman there, and had a great estate also in Ireland, that she would go down there in about two months, and if I would give her my company thither, I should be as welcome as herself for a month or more as I pleased, till I should see how I liked the country. And if I thought fit to live there, she would undertake they would take care, though they did not entertain lodgers themselves, they would recommend me to some agreeable family, where I should be placed to my content.

If this woman had known my real circumstances, she would never have laid so many snares and taken so many weary steps to catch a poor, desolate creature that was good for little when it was caught. And indeed I, whose case was almost desperate, and thought I could not be much worse, was not very anxious about what might befall me, provided they did me no personal injury. So I suffered myself, though not without a great deal of invitation and great professions of sincere friendship and real kindness – I say I suffered myself to be prevailed upon to go with her, and accordingly I packed up my baggage and put myself in a posture for a journey, though I did not absolutely know whither I was to go.

And now I found myself in great distress. What little I had in the world was all in money, except, as before, a little plate, some linen and my clothes. As for household stuff, I had little or none, for I had lived always in lodgings. But I had not one friend in the world with whom to trust that little I had, or to direct me how to dispose of it, and this perplexed me night and day. I thought of the bank, and of the other companies in London, but I had no friend to commit the management of it to, and to keep and carry about with me bank bills, tallies, orders and such things, I looked upon it as unsafe – that if they were lost my money was lost, and then I was undone. And on the other hand I might be robbed, and perhaps murdered in a strange place for them. This perplexed me strangely, and what to do I knew not.

It came in my thoughts one morning that I would go to the bank myself, where I had often been to receive the interest of some bills I had which had interest payable on them, and where I had found the clerk to whom I applied myself very honest and just to me, and particularly so fair one time that, when I had mistold my money and taken less than my due, and was coming away, he set me to rights and gave me the rest, which he might have put into his own pocket.

I went to him and represented my case very plainly, and asked if he would trouble himself to be my adviser, who was a poor friendless widow and knew not what to do. He told me if I desired his opinion of anything within the reach of his business, he would do his endeavour that I should not be wronged, but that he would also help me to a good, sober person who was a grave man of his acquaintance, who was a clerk in such business too, though not in their house, whose judgement was good, and whose honesty I might depend upon. "For," added he, "I will answer for him, and for every step he takes. If he wrongs you, madam, of one farthing, it shall lie at my door – I will make it good. And he delights to assist people in such cases: he does it as an act of charity."

I was a little at a stand at this discourse, but after some pause I told him I had rather have depended upon him, because I had found him honest, but if that could not be, I would take his recommendation sooner than anyone else's. "I dare say, madam," says he, "that you will be as well satisfied with my friend as with me, and he is thoroughly able to assist you, which I am not." It seems he had his hands full of the business of the bank, and had engaged to meddle with no other business than that of his office, which I heard afterwards but did not understand then. He added that his friend should take nothing of me for his advice or assistance, and this indeed encouraged me very much.

He appointed the same evening after the bank was shut, and business over, for me to meet him and his friend. And, indeed, as soon as I saw his friend, and he began but to talk of the affair, I was fully satisfied that I had a very honest man to deal with. His countenance spoke it, and his character, as I heard afterwards, was everywhere so good that I had no room for any more doubts upon me.

After the first meeting, in which I only said what I had said before, we parted, and he appointed me to come the next day to him, telling me I might in the mean time satisfy myself of him by enquiry – which, however, I knew not how well to do, having no acquaintance myself.

Accordingly I met him the next day, when I entered more freely with him into my case. I told him my circumstances at large: that I was a widow come over from America, perfectly desolate and friendless; that I had a little money, and but a little, and was almost distracted for fear of losing it, having no friend in the world to trust with the management of it; that I was going into the north of England to live cheap, that my stock might not waste; that I would willingly lodge my money in the bank, but that I durst not carry the bills about me, and the like, as above – and how to correspond about it, or with who, I knew not.

He told me I might lodge the money in the bank as an account, and its being entered in the books would entitle me to the money at any time, and if I was in the north I might draw bills on the cashier and receive it when I would, but that then it would be esteemed as running cash, and the bank would give no interest for it; that I might buy stock with it, and so it would lie in store for me, but that then if I wanted to dispose of it, I must come up to town on purpose to transfer it, and even it would be with some difficulty I should receive the half-yearly dividend, unless I was here in person or had some friend I could trust with having the stock in his name to do it for me, and that would have the same difficulty in it as before. And with that he looked hard at me and smiled a little. "At last," says he, "why do you not get a head steward, madam, that may take you and your money together into keeping, and then you would have the trouble taken off of your hands?" "Ay, sir, and the money too it may be," said I, "for truly I find the hazard that way is as much as 'tis t'other way." But I remember I said secretly to myself, "I wish you would ask me the question fairly – I would consider very seriously on it before I said no."

He went on a good way with me, and I thought once or twice he was in earnest, but, to my real affliction, I found at last he had a wife. But when he owned he had a wife he shook his head, and said with some concern that indeed he had a wife and no wife. I began to think he had been in the condition of my late lover, and that his wife had been distempered or lunatic, or some such thing. However, we had not much more discourse at that time, but he told me he was in too much hurry of business then, but that if I would come home to his house after their business was over, he would by that time consider what might be done for me, to put my affairs in a posture of security. I told him I would come, and desired to know where he lived. He gave me a direction in writing, and when he gave it me he read it to me, and said, "There 'tis, madam, if you dare trust yourself with me." "Yes, sir," said I. "I believe I may venture to trust you with myself, for you have a wife, you say, and I don't want a husband. Besides, I dare trust you with my money, which is all I have in the world, and if that were gone, I may trust myself anywhere."

He said some things in jest that were very handsome and mannerly, and would have pleased me very well if they had been in earnest. But that passed over, I took the directions and appointed to attend him at his house at seven o'clock the same evening.

When I came he made several proposals for my placing my money in the bank in order to my having interest for it, but still some difficulty or other came in the way which he objected as not safe, and I found such a sincere, disinterested honesty in him that I began to muse with myself that I had certainly found the honest man I wanted, and that I could never put myself into better hands. So I told him with a great deal of frankness that I had never met with man or woman yet that I could trust, or in whom I could think myself safe, but that I saw he was so disinterestedly concerned for my safety that I said I would freely trust him with the management of that little I had, if he would accept to be steward for a poor widow that could give him no salary.

He smiled, and, standing up with great respect, saluted me. He told me he could not but take it very kindly that I had so good an opinion of him – that he would not deceive me, that he would do anything in his power to serve me and expect no salary, but that he could not by any means accept of a trust; that it might bring him to be suspected of self-interest, and that if I should die he might have disputes with my executors, which he should be very loath to encumber himself with.

I told him if those were all his objections I would soon remove them, and convince him that there was not the least room for any difficulty. For that, first, as for suspecting him, if ever I should do it, now was the time to suspect him, and not put the trust into his hands, and whenever I did suspect him, he could but throw it up then and refuse to go any farther. Then, as to executors, I assured him I had no heirs, nor any relations in England, and I would have neither heirs or executors but himself, unless I should alter my condition before I died, and then his trust and trouble should cease together – which, however, I had no prospect of yet. But I told him if I died as I was, it should be all his own, and he would deserve it by being so faithful to me as I was satisfied he would be.

He changed his countenance at this discourse, and asked me how I came to have so much goodwill for him – and, looking very much pleased, said he might very lawfully wish he was a single man for my sake. I smiled and told him that, as he was not, my offer could have no design upon him in it, and to wish as he did was not to be allowed – 'twas criminal to his wife.

He told me I was wrong. "For," says he, "madam, as I said before, I have a wife and no wife, and 'twould be no sin to me to wish her hanged, if that were all." "I know nothing of your circumstances that way, sir," said I, "but it cannot be innocent to wish your wife dead." "I tell you," says he again, "she is a wife and no wife – you don't know what I am, or what she is."

"That's true," said I, "sir, I do not know what you are, but I believe you to be an honest man, and that's the cause of all my confidence in you."

"Well, well," says he, "and so I am, I hope, too, but I am something else too, madam. For," says he, "to be plain with you, I am a cuckold, and she is a whore." He spoke it in a kind of jest, but it was with such an awkward smile that I perceived it was what stuck very close to him, and he looked dismally when he said it.

"That alters the case indeed, sir," said I, "as to that part you were speaking of. But a cuckold, you know, may be an honest man – it does not alter that case at all. Besides, I think," said I, "since your wife is so dishonest to you, you are too honest to her to own her for your wife. But that," said I, "is what I have nothing to do with."

"Nay," says he, "I do think to clear my hands of her, for to be plain with you, madam," added he, "I am no contented cuckold neither. On the other hand, I assure you it provokes me to the highest degree, but I can't help myself – she that will be a whore will be a whore."

I waived the discourse and began to talk of my business, but I found he could not have done with it, so I let him alone, and he went on to tell me all the circumstances of his case, too long to relate here – particularly that, having been out of England some time before he came to the post he was in, she had had two children in the mean time by an officer of the army, and that when he came to England and, upon her submission, took her again, and maintained her very well, yet she ran away from him with a linen draper's apprentice, robbed him of what she could come at and continued to live from him still. "So that, madam," says he, "she is a whore not by necessity, which is the common bait of your sex, but by inclination, and for the sake of the vice."

Well, I pitied him and wished him well rid of her, and still would have talked of my business, but it would not do. At last he looks steadily at me: "Look you, madam," says he, "you came to ask advice of me, and I will serve you as faithfully as if you were my own sister, but I must turn the tables, since you oblige me to do it and are so friendly to me, and I think I must ask advice of you: tell me what must a poor, abused fellow do with a whore? What can I do to do myself justice upon her?"

"Alas, sir," says I, "'tis a case too nice* for me to advise in, but it seems she has run away from you, so you are rid of her fairly. What can you desire more?" "Ay, she is gone indeed," said he, "but I am not clear of her for all that."

"That's true," says I, "she may indeed run you into debt, but the law has furnished you with methods to prevent that also – you may cry her down, as they call it."

"No, no," says he, "that is not the case neither – I have taken care of all that. 'Tis not that part that I speak of, but I would be rid of her so that I might marry again."

"Well, sir," says I, "then you must divorce her. If you can prove what you say, you may certainly get that done, and then, I suppose, you are free."

"That's very tedious and expensive," says he.

"Why," says I, "if you can get any woman you like to take your word, I suppose your wife would not dispute the liberty with you that she takes herself."

"Ay," says he, "but 'twould be hard to bring an honest woman to do that. And for the other sort," says he, "I have had enough of her to meddle with any more whores."

It occurred to me presently: "I would have taken your word with all my heart if you had but asked me the question" – but that was to myself. To him I replied, "Why, you shut the door against any honest woman accepting you, for you condemn all that should venture upon you at once, and conclude that really a woman that takes you now can't be honest."

"Why," says he, "I wish you would satisfy me that an honest woman would take me – I'd venture it." And then turns short upon me: "Will you take me, madam?"

"That's not a fair question," says I, "after what you have said. However, lest you should think I wait only for a recantation of it, I shall answer you plainly: no, not I – my business is of another kind with you, and I did not expect you would have turned my serious application to you in my own distracted case into a comedy."

"Why, madam," says he, "my case is as distracted as yours can be, and I stand in as much need of advice as you do, for I think if I have not relief somewhere, I shall be mad myself, and I know not what course to take, I protest to you."

"Why, sir," says I, "'tis easy to give advice in your case, much easier than it is in mine." "Speak then," says he, "I beg of you, for now you encourage me."

"Why," says I, "if your case is so plain as you say it is, you may be legally divorced, and then you may find honest women enough to ask the question of fairly. The sex is not so scarce that you can want a wife."

"Well then," said he, "I am in earnest. I'll take your advice, but shall I ask you one question seriously beforehand?"

"Any question," said I, "but that you did before."

"No, that answer will not do," said he, "for, in short, that is the question I shall ask."

"You may ask what questions you please, but you have my answer to that already," said I. "Besides, sir," said I, "can you think so ill of me as that I would give any answer to such a question beforehand? Can any woman alive believe you in earnest, or think you design anything but to banter her?"

"Well, well," says he, "I do not banter you – I am in earnest, consider of it."

"But, sir," says I, a little gravely, "I came to you about my own business. I beg of you, let me know what you will advise me to do."

"I will be prepared," says he, "against you come again."

"Nay," says I, "you have forbid my coming any more."

"Why so?" said he, and looked a little surprised.

"Because," said I, "you can't expect I should visit you on the account you talk of."

"Well," says he, "you shall promise me to come again, however, and I will not say any more of it till I have gotten the divorce, but I desire you will prepare to be better conditioned when that's done, for you shall be the woman, or I will not be divorced at all. Why, I owe it to your unlooked-for kindness, if it were to nothing else, but I have other reasons too."

He could not have said anything in the world that pleased me better. However, I knew that the way to secure him was to stand off while the thing was so remote, as it appeared to be, and that it was time enough to accept of it when he was able to perform it. So I said, very respectfully to him, it was time enough to consider of these things when he was in a condition to talk of them. In the mean time, I told him, I was going a great way from him, and he would find objects enough to please him better. We broke off here for the present, and he made me promise him to come again the next day for his resolutions upon my own business, which after some pressing I did – though had he seen farther into me, I wanted no pressing on that account.

I came the next evening accordingly, and brought my maid with me, to let him see that I kept a maid, but I sent her away as soon as I was gone in. He would have had me let the maid have stayed, but I would not, but ordered her aloud to come for me again about nine o'clock, but he forbid that, and told me he would see me safe home, which by the way I was not very well pleased with, supposing he might do that to know where I lived, and enquire into my character and circumstances. However, I ventured that, for all that the people there or thereabout knew of me, was to my advantage – and all the character he had of me, after he had enquired, was that I was a woman of fortune, and that I was a very modest, sober body, which, whether true or not in the main, yet you may see how necessary it is for all women who expect anything in the world to preserve the character of their virtue, even when perhaps they may have sacrificed the thing itself.

I found, and was not a little pleased with it, that he had provided a supper for me. I found also he lived very handsomely, and had a house very handsomely furnished, all which I was rejoiced at indeed, for I looked upon it as all my own.

We had now a second conference upon the subject matter of the last conference. He laid his business very home indeed – he protested his affection to me, and indeed I had no room to doubt it. He declared that it began from the first moment I talked with him, and long before I had mentioned leaving my effects with him. "'Tis no matter when it began," thought I, "if it will but hold, 'twill be well enough." He then told me how much the offer I had made of trusting him with my effects, and leaving them to him, had engaged him. "So I intended it should," thought I, "but then I thought you had been a single man too." After we had supped, I observed he pressed me very hard to drink two or three glasses of wine – which, however, I declined, but drank one glass or two. He then told me he had a proposal to make to me which I should promise him I would not take ill if I should not grant it. I told him I hoped he would make no dishonourable proposal to me, especially in his own house, and that if it was such, I desired he would not propose it, that I might not be obliged to offer any resentment to him that did not become the respect I professed for him and the trust I had placed in him in coming to his house, and begged of him he would give me leave to go away, and accordingly began to put on my gloves and prepare to be gone, though at the same time I no more intended it than he intended to let me.

Well, he importuned me not to talk of going. He assured me he had no dishonourable thing in his thoughts about me, and was very far from offering anything to me that was dishonourable, and if I thought so, he would choose to say no more of it.

That part I did not relish at all. I told him I was ready to hear anything that he had to say, depending that he would say nothing unworthy of himself or unfit for me to hear. Upon this, he told me his proposal was this: that I would marry him, though he had not yet obtained the divorce from the whore, his wife. And to satisfy me that he meant honourably, he would promise not to desire me to live with him, or go to bed to him till the divorce was obtained. My heart said yes to this offer at first word, but it was necessary to play the hypocrite a little more with him – so I seemed to decline the motion with some warmth, and besides a little condemning the thing as unfair, told him that such a proposal could be of no signification but to entangle us both in great difficulties. For if he should not at last obtain the divorce, yet we could not dissolve the marriage, neither could we proceed in it, so that if he was disappointed in the divorce, I left him to consider what a condition we should both be in.

In short, I carried on the argument against this so far that I convinced him it was not a proposal that had any sense in it. Well, then he went from it to another, and that was that I would sign and seal a contract with him, conditioning to marry him as soon as the divorce was obtained, and to be void if he could not obtain it.

I told him such a thing was more rational than the other, but as this was the first time that ever I could imagine him weak enough to be in earnest in this affair, I did not use to say yes at first asking – I would consider of it.

I played with this lover as an angler does with a trout. I found I had him fast on the hook, so I jested with his new proposal, and put him off. I told him he knew little of me, and bade him enquire about me. I let him also go home with me to my lodging, though I would not ask him to go in, for I told him it was not decent.

In short, I ventured to avoid signing a contract of marriage, and the reason why I did it was because the lady that had invited me so earnestly to go with her into Lancashire insisted so positively upon it, and promised me such great fortunes and such fine things there, that I was tempted to go and try. "Perhaps," said I, "I may mend myself very much." And then I made no scruple in my thoughts of quitting my honest citizen, who I was not so much in love with as not to leave him for a richer.

In a word, I avoided a contract, but told him I would go into the north – that he should know where to write to me by the consequence of the business I had entrusted with him, that I would give him a sufficient pledge of my respect for him, for I would leave almost all I had in the world in his hands, and I would thus far give him my word that as soon as he had sued out a divorce from his first wife, if he would send me an account of it, I would come up to London, and that then we would talk seriously of the matter.

It was a base design I went with, that I must confess, though I was invited thither with a design much worse than mine was, as the sequel will discover. Well, I went with my friend, as I called her, into Lancashire. All the way we went she caressed me with the utmost appearance of a sincere, undissembled affection – treated me, except my coach hire, all the way, and her brother brought a gentleman's coach to Warrington to receive us, and we were carried from thence to Liverpool with as much ceremony as I could desire. We were also entertained at a merchant's house in Liverpool three or four days very handsomely – I forbear to tell his name because of what followed. Then she told me she would carry me to an uncle's house of hers, where we should be nobly entertained. She did so – her uncle, as she called him, sent a coach and four horses for us, and we were carried near forty miles I know not whither.

We came, however, to a gentleman's seat, where was a numerous family,* a large park, extraordinary company indeed, and where she was called "cousin". I told her if she had resolved to bring me into such company as this she should have let me have prepared myself, and have furnished myself with better clothes. The ladies took notice of that, and told me very genteelly they did not value people in their country so much by their clothes as they did in London – that their cousin had fully informed them of my quality, and that I did not want clothes to set me off. In short, they entertained me not like what I was, but like what they thought I had been – namely, a widow lady of a great fortune.

The first discovery I made here was that the family were all Roman Catholics, and the cousin too, who I called my friend. However, I must say that nothing in the world could behave better to me, and I had all the civility shown me that I could have had if I had been of their opinion. The truth is I had not so much principle of any kind as to be nice in point of religion, and I presently learnt to speak favourably of the Romish Church – particularly, I told them I saw little but the prejudice of education in all the differences that were among Christians about religion, and if it had so happened that my father had been a Roman Catholic, I doubted not but I should have been as well pleased with their religion as my own.

This obliged them in the highest degree, and as I was besieged day and night with good company and pleasant discourse, so I had two or three old ladies that lay at me upon the subject of religion too. I was so complaisant that though I would not completely engage, yet I made no scruple to be present at their mass and to conform to all their gestures as they showed me the pattern, but I would not come too cheap – so that I only in the main encouraged them to expect that I would turn Roman Catholic if I was instructed in the Catholic doctrine, as they called it, and so the matter rested.

I stayed here about six weeks, and then my conductor led me back to a country village about six miles from Liverpool, where her brother (as she called him) came to visit me in his own chariot, and in a very good figure, with two footmen in a good livery – and the next thing was to make love to me. As it had happened to me, one would think I could not have been cheated, and indeed I thought so myself, having a safe card at home, which I resolved not to quit unless I could mend myself very much. However, in all appearance this brother was a match worth my listening to, and the least his estate was valued at was 1,000*l.* a year, but the sister said it was worth 1,500*l.* a year, and lay most of it in Ireland.

I that was a great fortune, and passed for such, was above being asked how much my estate was, and my false friend, taking it upon a foolish hearsay, had raised it from 500*l.* to 5,000*l.*, and by the time she came into the country she called it 15,000*l.* The Irishman, for such I understood him to be, was stark mad at this bait – in short, he courted me, made me presents and ran in debt like a madman for the expenses of his equipage and of his courtship. He had, to give him his due, the appearance of an extraordinary fine gentleman: he was tall, well shaped and had an extraordinary address, talked as naturally of his park and his stables, of his horses, his gamekeepers, his woods, his tenants and his servants, as if we had been in the mansion house and I had seen them all about me.

He never so much as asked me about my fortune or estate, but assured me that when we came to Dublin he would jointure me in 600*l.*-a-year good land, and that he would enter into a deed of settlement or contract here for the performance of it.

This was such language indeed as I had not been used to, and I was here beaten out of all my measures. I had a she-devil in my bosom, every hour telling me how great her brother lived. One time she would come for my orders – how I would have my coaches painted, and how lined – and another time what clothes my page should wear. In short, my eyes were dazzled. I had now lost my power of saying no, and, to cut the story short, I consented to be married. But to be the more private we were carried farther into the country, and married by a Romish clergyman, which I was assured would marry us as effectually as a Church of England parson.

I cannot say but I had some reflections in this affair upon the dishonourable forsaking my faithful citizen, who loved me sincerely and who was endeavouring to quit himself of a scandalous whore by whom he had been indeed barbarously used, and promised himself infinite happiness in his new choice – which choice was now giving up herself to another in a manner almost as scandalous as hers could be.

But the glittering show of a great estate and of fine things, which the deceived creature that was now my deceiver represented every hour to my imagination, hurried me away, and gave me no time to think of London or of anything there, much less of the obligation I had to a person of infinitely more real merit than what was now before me.

But the thing was done. I was now in the arms of my new spouse, who appeared still the same as before: great even to magnificence, and nothing less than a thousand pound a year could support the ordinary equipage he appeared in.

After we had been married about a month, he began to talk of my going to West Chester* in order to embark for Ireland. However, he did not hurry me, for we stayed near three weeks longer, and then he sent to Chester for a coach to meet us at the Black Rock,* as they call it, over against Liverpool. Thither we went in a fine boat they call a pinnace, with six oars – his servants and horses and baggage going in the ferry boat. He made his excuse to me that he had no acquaintance at Chester, but he would go before and get some handsome apartment for me at a private house. I asked him how long we should stay at Chester. He said not at all any longer than one night or two, but he would immediately hire a coach to go to Holyhead. Then I told him he should by no means give himself the trouble to get private lodgings for one night or two, for that Chester being a great place, I made no doubt but there would be very good inns and accommodation enough. So we lodged at an inn in the West Street, not far from the cathedral – I forget what sign it was at.

Here my spouse talking of my going to Ireland, asked me if I had no affairs to settle at London before we went off. I told him no, not of any great consequence, but what might be done as well by letter from Dublin. "Madam," says he very respectfully, "I suppose the greatest part of your estate, which my sister tells me is most of it in money in the Bank of England, lies secure enough, but in case it required transferring, or any way altering its property, it might be necessary to go up to London and settle those things before we went over."

I seemed to look strange at it, and told him I knew not what he meant – that I had no effects in the Bank of England that I knew of, and I hoped he could not say that I had ever told him I had. No, he said, I had not told him so, but his sister had said the greatest part of my estate lay there. "And I only mentioned it, my dear," said he, "that if there was any occasion to settle it, or order anything about it, we might not be obliged to the hazard and trouble of another voyage back again" – for he added that he did not care to venture me too much upon the sea.

I was surprised at this talk, and began to consider very seriously what the meaning of it must be – and it presently occurred to me that my friend, who called him brother, had represented me in colours which were not my due, and I thought, since it was come to that pitch, that I would know the bottom of it before I went out of England, and before I should put myself into I knew not whose hands, in a strange country.

Upon this I called his sister into my chamber the next morning, and letting her know the discourse her brother and I had been upon the evening before, I conjured her to tell me what she had said to him, and upon what foot it was that she had made this marriage. She owned that she had told him that I was a great fortune, and said that she was told so at London. "Told so!" says I warmly. "Did I ever tell you so?" No, she said, it was true I did not tell her so, but I had said several times that what I had was in my own disposal. "I did so," returned I very quickly and hastily, "but I never told you I had anything called a fortune – no, not that I had one hundred pounds, or the value of an hundred pounds in the world. And how did it consist with my being a fortune," said I, "that I should come here into the north of England with you only upon the account of living cheap?" At these words, which I spoke warm and high, my husband and her brother, as she called him, came into the room, and I desired him to come and sit down, for I had something of moment to say before them both, which it was absolutely necessary he should hear.

He looked a little disturbed at the assurance with which I seemed to speak it, and came and sat down by me, having first shut the door. Upon which I began, for I was very much provoked, and turning myself to him: "I am afraid," says I, "my dear" – for I spoke with kindness on his side – "that you have a very great abuse put upon you and an injury done you never to be repaired in your marrying me – which, however, as I have had no hand in it, I desire I may be fairly acquitted of it, and that the blame may lie where it ought to lie and nowhere else, for I wash my hands of every part of it."

"What injury can be done me, my dear," says he, "in marrying you? I hope it is to my honour and advantage every way." "I will soon explain it to you," says I, "and I fear you will have no reason to think yourself well used, but I will convince you, my dear," says I again, "that I have had no hand in it" – and there I stopped awhile.

He looked now scared and wild, and began, I believed, to suspect what followed. However, looking towards me and saying only "Go on", he sat silent, as if to hear what I had more to say – so I went on. "I asked you last night," said I, speaking to him, "if ever I made any boast to you of my estate, or ever told you I had any estate in the Bank of England or anywhere else, and you owned I had not, as is most true. And I desire you will tell me here, before your sister, if ever I gave you any reason from me to think so, or that ever we had any discourse about it." And he owned again I had not, but said I had appeared always as a woman of fortune, and he depended on it that I was so, and hoped he was not deceived. "I am not enquiring yet whether you have been deceived or not," said I. "I fear you have, and I too, but I am clearing myself from the unjust charge of being concerned in deceiving you.

"I have been now asking your sister if ever I told her of any fortune or estate I had, or gave her any particulars of it, and she owns I never did. And pray, madam," said I, turning myself to her, "be so just to me, before your brother, to charge me, if you can, if ever I pretended to you that I had an estate. And why, if I had, should I come down into this country with you on purpose to spare that little I had, and live cheap?" She could not deny one word, but said she had been told in London that I had a very great fortune, and that it lay in the Bank of England.

"And now, dear sir," said I, turning myself to my new spouse again, "be so just to me as to tell me who has abused both you and me so much as to make you believe I was a fortune, and prompt you to court me to this marriage." He could not speak a word, but pointed to her, and after some more pause flew out in the most furious passion that ever I saw a man in my life, cursing her and calling her all the whores and hard names he could think of, and that she had ruined him, declaring that she had told him I had fifteen thousand pounds, and that she was to have five hundred pounds of him for procuring this match for him. He then added, directing his speech to me, that she was none of his sister, but had been his whore for two years before, that she had had one hundred pound of him in part of this bargain, and that he was utterly undone if things were as I said. And in his raving he swore he would let her heart's blood out immediately, which frighted her, and me too – she cried, said she had been told so in the house where I lodged, but this aggravated him more than before: that she should put so far upon him and run things such a length upon no other authority than a hearsay. And then, turning to me again, said very honestly he was afraid we were both undone: "For to be plain, my dear, I have no estate," says he. "What little I had, this devil has made me run out in waiting on you and putting me into this equipage." She took the opportunity of his being earnest in talking with me, and got out of the room, and I never saw her more.

I was confounded now as much as he, and knew not what to say. I thought many ways that I had the worst of it, but his saying he was undone, and that he had no estate neither, put me into a mere distraction. "Why," says I to him, "this has been a hellish juggle, for we are married here upon the foot of a double fraud. You are undone by the disappointment, it seems, and if I had had a fortune I had been cheated too, for you say you have nothing."

"You would indeed have been cheated, my dear," says he, "but you would not have been undone, for fifteen thousand pound would have maintained us both very handsomely in this country. And I assure you," added he, "I had resolved to have dedicated every groat of it to you. I would not have wronged you of a shilling, and the rest I would have made up in my affection to you, and tenderness of you as long as I lived."

This was very honest indeed, and I really believe he spoke as he intended, and that he was a man that was as well qualified to make me happy, as to his temper and behaviour, as any man ever was. But his having no estate, and being run into debt on this ridiculous account in the country, made all the prospect dismal and dreadful, and I knew not what to say, or what to think of myself.

I told him it was very unhappy that so much love and so much good nature as I discovered in him should be thus precipitated into misery – that I saw nothing before us but ruin, for, as to me, it was my unhappiness that what little I had was not able to relieve us a week, and with that I pulled out a bank bill of 20*l*. and eleven guineas, which I told him I had saved out of my little income; and that by the account that creature had given me of the way of living in that country, I expected it would maintain me three or four year; that if it was taken from me I was left destitute, and he knew what the condition of a woman among strangers must be if she had no money in her pocket. However, I told him if he would take it, there it was.

He told me with a great concern, and I thought I saw tears stand in his eyes, that he would not touch it, that he abhorred the thoughts of stripping me and making me miserable – that, on the contrary, he had fifty guineas left, which was all he had in the world, and he pulled it out and threw it down on the table, bidding me take it, though he were to starve for want of it.

I returned, with the same concern for him, that I could not bear to hear him talk so – that on the contrary, if he could propose any probable method of living, I would do anything that became me on my part, and that I would live as close and as narrow as he could desire.

He begged of me to talk no more at that rate, for it would make him distracted. He said he was bred a gentleman, though he was reduced to a low fortune, and that there was but one way left which he could think of, and that would not do unless I could answer him one question – which, however, he said he would not press me to. I told him I would answer it honestly – whether it would be to his satisfaction or no, that I could not tell.

"Why then, my dear, tell me plainly," says he, "will the little you have keep us together in any figure, or in any station or place, or will it not?"

It was my happiness hitherto that I had not discovered myself or my circumstances at all – no, not so much as my name – and seeing there was nothing to be expected from him, however good-humoured and however honest he seemed to be, but to live on what I knew would soon be wasted, I resolved to conceal everything but the bank bill and the eleven guineas, which I had owned. And I would have been very glad to have lost that, and have been set down where he took me up. I had indeed another bank bill about me of 30*l*., which was the whole of what I brought with me, as well to subsist on in the country, as not knowing what might offer, because this creature, the go-between that had thus betrayed us both, had made me believe strange things of my marrying to my advantage in the country, and I was not willing to be without money whatever might happen. This bill I concealed, and that made me the freer of the rest, in consideration of his circumstances, for I really pitied him heartily.

But to return to his question, I told him I never willingly deceived him, and I never would. I was very sorry to tell him that the little I had would not subsist us, that it was not sufficient to subsist me alone in the south country, and that this was the reason that made me put myself into the hands of that woman who called him brother, she having assured me that I might board very handsomely at a town called Manchester, where I had not yet been, for about six pound a year. And my whole income not being above 15*l*. a year, I thought I might live easy upon it, and wait for better things.

He shook his head and remained silent, and a very melancholy evening we had. However, we supped together, and lay together that night, and when we had almost supped he looked a little better and more cheerful, and called for a bottle of wine. "Come, my dear," says he, "though the case is bad, it is to no purpose to be dejected. Come, be as easy as you can – I will endeavour to find out some way or other to live. If you can but subsist yourself, that is better than nothing. I must try the world again. A man ought to think like a man – to be discouraged is to yield to the misfortune." With this he filled a glass and drank to me, holding my hand and pressing it hard in his hand all the while the wine went down, and protesting afterwards his main concern was for me.

It was really a truly gallant spirit he was of, and it was the more grievous to me. 'Tis something of relief even to be undone by a man of honour rather than by a scoundrel. But here the greatest disappointment was on his side, for he had really spent a great deal of money, deluded by this madam the procuress, and it was very remarkable on what poor terms she proceeded. First, the baseness of the creature herself is to be observed, who for the getting one hundred pound herself could be content to let him spend three or four more, though perhaps it was all he had in the world, and more than all – when she had not the least ground, more than a little tea-table chat – to say that I had any estate, or was a fortune, or the like. It is true the design of deluding a woman of a fortune, if I had been so, was base enough – the putting the face of great things upon poor circumstances was a fraud, and bad enough. But the case a little differed too, and that in his favour, for he was not a rake that made a trade to delude women, and as some have done get six or seven fortunes after one another and then riffle and run away from them. But he was really a gentleman, unfortunate and low, but had lived well, and though if I had had a fortune I should have been enraged at the slut for betraying me, yet really for the man a fortune would not have been ill bestowed on him, for he was a lovely person indeed: of generous principles, good sense and of abundance of good humour.

We had a great deal of close conversation that night, for we neither of us slept much. He was as penitent for having put all those cheats upon me as if it had been felony, and that he was going to execution. He offered me again every shilling of the money he had about him, and said he would go into the army and seek the world for more.

I asked him why he would be so unkind to carry me into Ireland, when I might suppose he could not have subsisted me there? He took me in his arms. "My dear," said he, "depend upon it, I never designed to go to Ireland at all, much less to have carried you thither, but came hither to be out of the observation of the people, who had heard what I pretended to – and, withal, that nobody might ask me for money before I was furnished to supply them."

"But where, then," said I, "were we to have gone next?"

"Why, my dear," said he, "I'll confess the whole scheme to you as I had laid it. I purposed here to ask you something about your estate, as you see I did, and when you, as I expected you would, had entered into some account with me of the particular, I would have made an excuse to you to have put off our voyage to Ireland for some time, and to have gone first towards London.

"Then, my dear," said he, "I resolved to have confessed all the circumstances of my own affairs to you, and let you know I had indeed made use of these artifices to obtain your consent to marry me, but had now nothing to do but to ask your pardon, and to tell you how abundantly, as I have said above, I would endeavour to make you forget what was past, by the felicity of the days to come."

"Truly," said I to him, "I find you would soon have conquered me, and it is my affliction now that I am not in a condition to let you see how easily I should have been reconciled to you, and have passed by all the tricks you had put upon me in recompense of so much good humour. But, my dear," said I, "what can we do now? We are both undone, and what better are we for our being reconciled together, seeing we have nothing to live on?"

We proposed a great many things, but nothing could offer where there is nothing to begin with. He begged me at last to talk no more of it, for he said I would break his heart. So we talked of other things a little, till at last he took a husband's leave of me, and so we went to sleep.

He rose before me in the morning, and indeed, having lain awake almost all night, I was very sleepy, and lay till near eleven o'clock. In this time he took his horses and three servants, and all his linen and baggage, and away he went, leaving a short but moving letter for me on the table, as follows.

My dear,
I am a dog. I have abused you, but I have been drawn in to do it by a base creature, contrary to my principle and the general practice of my life. Forgive me, my dear! I ask you pardon with the greatest sincerity. I am the most miserable of men in having deluded you. I have been so happy to possess you, and am now so wretched as to be forced to fly from you. Forgive me, my dear – once more I say forgive me! I am not able to see you ruined by me, and myself unable to support you. Our marriage is nothing. I shall never be able to see you again. I here discharge you from it – if you can marry to your advantage do not decline it on my account. I here swear to you on my faith, and on the word of a man of honour, I will never disturb your repose if I should know of it, which, however, is not likely. On the other hand, if you should not marry, and if good fortune should befall me, it shall be all yours wherever you are.

I have put some of the stock of money I have left into your pocket. Take places for yourself and your maid in the stage-coach, and go for London. I hope it will bear your charges thither without breaking into your own. Again I sincerely ask your pardon, and will do so as often as I shall ever think of you.
Adieu, my dear, for ever,
I am yours most affectionately,
J.E.

Nothing that ever befell me in my life sank so deep into my heart as this farewell. I reproached him a thousand times in my thoughts for leaving me, for I would have gone with him through the world if I had begged my bread. I felt in my pocket, and there I found ten guineas, his gold watch and two little rings, one a small diamond ring, worth only about six pound, and the other a plain gold ring.

I sat me down and looked upon these things two hours together, and scarce spoke a word, till my maid interrupted me by telling me my dinner was ready. I ate but little, and after dinner I fell into a vehement fit of crying, every now and then calling him by his name, which was James. "Oh, Jemy!" said I. "Come back, come back! I'll give you all I have – I'll beg, I'll starve with you!" And thus I ran raving about the room several times, and then sat down between whiles, and then, walking about again, called upon him to come back, and then cried again. And thus I passed the afternoon, till about seven o'clock, when it was near dusk in the evening, being August, when to my unspeakable surprise he comes back into the inn, but without a servant, and comes directly up into my chamber.

I was in the greatest confusion imaginable, and so was he too. I could not imagine what should be the occasion of it, and began to be at odds with myself whether to be glad or sorry. But my affection biased all the rest, and it was impossible to conceal my joy, which was too great for smiles, for it burst out into tears. He was no sooner entered the room but he ran to me and took me in his arms, holding me fast and almost stopping my breath with his kisses, but spoke not a word. At length I began, "My dear," said I, "how could you go away from me?" To which he gave no answer, for it was impossible for him to speak.

When our ecstasies were a little over, he told me he was gone about fifteen mile, but it was not in his power to go any farther without coming back to see me again, and to take his leave of me once more.

I told him how I had passed my time, and how loud I had called him to come back again. He told me he heard me very plain upon

Delamere Forest, at a place about twelve miles off. I smiled. "Nay," says he, "do not think I am in jest, for if ever I heard your voice in my life, I heard you call me aloud, and sometimes I thought I saw you running after me." "Why," said I, "what did I say?" – for I had not named the words to him. "You called aloud," says he, "and said, 'Oh, Jemy! Oh, Jemy! Come back, come back.'"

I laughed at him. "My dear," says he, "do not laugh, for depend upon it, I heard your voice as plain as you hear mine now. If you please, I'll go before a magistrate and make oath of it." I then began to be amazed and surprised, and indeed frighted, and told him what I had really done, and how I had called after him, as above.

When we had amused ourselves a while about this, I said to him, "Well, you shall go away from me no more. I'll go all over the world with you, rather." He told me it would be a very difficult thing for him to leave me, but since it must be, he hoped I would make it as easy to me as I could. But as for him, it would be his destruction – that he foresaw.

However, he told me that he considered he had left me to travel to London alone, which was too long a journey, and that as he might as well go that way as any way else, he was resolved to see me safe thither, or near it, and if he did go away then without taking his leave, I should not take it ill of him, and this he made me promise.

He told me how he had dismissed his three servants, sold their horses and sent the fellows away to seek their fortunes, and all in a little time, at a town on the road, I know not where. "And," says he, "it cost me some tears, all alone by myself, to think how much happier they were than their master, for they could go to the next gentleman's house to see for a service, whereas," said he, "I knew not whither to go or what to do with myself."

I told him I was so completely miserable in parting with him that I could not be worse, and that now he was come again, I would not go from him, if he would take me with him, let him go whither he would or do what he would. And in the mean time I agreed that we would go together to London, but I could not be brought to consent he should go away at last and not take his leave of me, as he proposed to do, but told him jesting that if he did, I would call him back again as loud as I did before. Then I pulled out his watch and gave it him back, and his two rings, and his ten guineas – but he would not take them, which made me very much suspect that he resolved to go off upon the road and leave me.

The truth is, the circumstances he was in, the passionate expressions of his letter, the kind, gentlemanly treatment I had from him in all the affair, with the concern he showed for me in it, his manner of parting with that large share which he gave me of his little stock left – all these had joined to make such impressions on me that I really loved him most tenderly, and could not bear the thoughts of parting with him.

Two days after this we quitted Chester, I in the stagecoach and he on horseback. I dismissed my maid at Chester. He was very much against my being without a maid, but she being a servant hired in the country and I resolving to keep no servant at London, I told him it would have been barbarous to have taken the poor wench and have turned her away as soon as I came to town – and it would also have been a needless charge on the road, so I satisfied him, and he was easy enough on that score.

He came with me as far as Dunstable, within thirty miles of London, and then he told me fate and his own misfortunes obliged him to leave me, and that it was not convenient for him to go to London, for reasons which it was of no value to me to know, and I saw him preparing to go. The stagecoach we were in did not usually stop at Dunstable, but I desiring it but for a quarter of an hour, they were content to stand at an inn door awhile, and we went into the house.

Being in the inn, I told him I had but one favour more to ask of him, and that was that since he could not go any farther, he would give me leave to stay a week or two in the town with him, that we might in that time think of something to prevent such a ruinous thing to us both as a final separation would be, and that I had something of moment to offer to him that I had never said yet, and which perhaps he might find practicable to our mutual advantage.

This was too reasonable a proposal to be denied, so he called the landlady of the house and told her his wife was taken ill, and so ill that she could not think of going any farther in the stagecoach, which had tired her almost to death, and asked if she could not get us a lodging for two or three days in a private house where I might rest me a little, for the journey had been too much for me. The landlady, a good sort of woman, well bred and very obliging, came immediately to see me – told me she had two or three very good rooms in a part of the house quite out of the noise, and if I saw them she did not doubt but I would like them, and I should have one of her maids, that should do nothing else but be appointed to wait on me. This was so very kind that I could not but accept of it and thank her, so I went to look on the rooms, and liked them very well, and indeed they were extraordinarily furnished and very pleasant lodgings – so we paid the stagecoach, took out our baggage and resolved to stay here awhile.

Here I told him I would live with him now till all my money was spent, but would not let him spend a shilling of his own. We had some kind squabble about that, but I told him it was the last time I was like to enjoy his company, and I desired he would let me be master in that thing only, and he should govern in everything else, so he acquiesced.

Here one evening, taking a walk into the fields, I told him I would now make the proposal to him I had told him of. Accordingly, I related to him how I had lived in Virginia, that I had a mother I believed was alive there still, though my husband was dead some years. I told him that, had not my effects miscarried, which by the way I magnified pretty much, I might have been fortune good enough to him to have kept us from being parted in this manner. Then I entered into the manner of people's going over to those countries to settle, how they had a quantity of land given them by the constitution of the place – and if not, that it might be purchased at so easy a rate that it was not worth naming.

I then gave him a full and distinct account of the nature of planting, how with carrying over but two or three hundred pounds' value in English goods, with some servants and tools, a man of application would presently lay a foundation for a family, and in a very few years be certain to raise an estate.

I let him into the nature of the product of the earth, how the ground was cured and prepared, and what the usual increase of it was, and demonstrated to him that in a very few years, with such a beginning, we should be as certain of being rich as we were now certain of being poor.

He was surprised at my discourse, for we made it the whole subject of our conversation for near a week together, in which time I laid it down in black and white, as we say, that it was morally impossible, with a supposition of any reasonable good conduct, but that we must thrive there and do very well.

Then I told him what measures I would take to raise such a sum as 300*l*. or thereabouts, and I argued with him how good a method it would be to put an end to our misfortunes and restore our circumstances in the world to what we had both expected. And I added that after seven years, if we lived, we might be in a posture to leave our plantation in good hands and come over again and receive the income of it, and live here and enjoy it, and I gave him examples of some that had done so, and lived now in very good circumstances in London.

In short, I pressed him so to it that he almost agreed to it, but still something or other broke it off again, till at last he turned the tables, and he began to talk almost to the same purpose of Ireland.

He told me that a man that could confine himself to a country life, and that could but find stock to enter upon any land, should have farms there for 50*l*. a year as good as were here let for 200*l*. a year – that the produce was such, and so rich the land, that if much was not laid up we were sure to live as handsomely upon it as a gentleman of 3000*l*. a year could do in England, and that he had laid a scheme to leave me in London and go over and try, and if he found he could lay a handsome foundation of living suitable to the respect he had for me, as he doubted not he should do, he would come over and fetch me.

I was dreadfully afraid that upon such a proposal he would have taken me at my word, viz. to sell my little income, as I called it, and turn it into money, and let him carry it over into Ireland and try his experiment with it. But he was too just to desire it, or to have accepted it if I had offered it, and he anticipated me in that, for he added that he would go and try his fortune that way, and if he found he could do anything at it to live, then, by adding mine to it when I went over, we should live like ourselves, but that he would not hazard a shilling of mine till he had made the experiment with a little, and he assured me that if he found nothing to be done in Ireland, he would then come to me and join in my project for Virginia.

He was so earnest upon his project being to be tried first that I could not withstand him. However, he promised to let me hear from him in a very little time after his arriving there, to let me know whether his prospect answered his design – that if there was not a probability of success, I might take the occasion to prepare for our other voyage – and then, he assured me, he would go with me to America with all his heart.

I could bring him to nothing further than this. However, those consultations entertained us near a month, during which I enjoyed his company, which indeed was the most entertaining that ever I met with in my life before. In this time he let me into the whole story of his own life, which was indeed surprising and full of an infinite variety sufficient to fill up a much brighter history for its adventures and incidents than any I ever saw in print. But I shall have occasion to say more of him hereafter.

We parted at last, though with the utmost reluctance on my side, and indeed he took his leave very unwillingly too, but necessity obliged him, for his reasons were very good why he would not come to London, as I understood more fully some time afterwards.

I gave him a direction how to write to me, though still I reserved the grand secret, and never broke my resolution, which was not to let him ever know my true name, who I was or where to be found. He likewise let me know how to write a letter to him, so that, he said, he would be sure to receive it.

I came to London the next day after we parted, but did not go directly to my old lodgings, but for another nameless reason took a private lodging in St John Street – or, as it is vulgarly called, St Jones's, near Clerkenwell – and here, being perfectly alone, I had leisure to sit down and reflect seriously upon the last seven months' ramble I had made, for I had been abroad no less. The pleasant hours I had with my last husband I looked back on with an infinite deal of pleasure, but that pleasure was very much lessened when I found some time after that I was really with child.

This was a perplexing thing because of the difficulty which was before me where I should get leave to lie in, it being one of the nicest* things in the world, at that time of day, for a woman that was a stranger and had no friends, to be entertained in that circumstance without security – which by the way I had not, neither could I procure any.

I had taken care all this while to preserve a correspondence with my honest friend at the bank, or rather he took care to correspond with me, for he wrote to me once a week. And though I had not spent my money so fast as to want any from him, yet I often wrote also to let him know I was alive. I had left directions in Lancashire, so that I had these letters, which he sent, conveyed to me, and during my recess at St Jones's I received a very obliging letter from him, assuring me that his process for a divorce from his wife went on with success, though he met with some difficulties in it that he did not expect.

I was not displeased with the news that his process was more tedious than he expected, for though I was in no condition to have had him yet, not being so foolish to marry him when I knew myself to be with child by another man, as some I know have ventured to do, yet I was not willing to lose him – and, in a word, resolved to have him if he continued in the same mind as soon as I was up again – for I saw apparently I should hear no more from my other husband, and as he had all along pressed me to marry and had assured me he would not be at all disgusted at it, or ever offer to claim me again, so I made no scruple to resolve to do it if I could and if my other friend stood to his bargain. And I had a great deal of reason to be assured that he would stand to it by the letters he wrote to me, which were the kindest and most obliging that could be.

I now grew big, and the people where I lodged perceived it and began to take notice of it to me – and, as far as civility would allow, intimated that I must think of removing. This put me to extreme perplexity, and I grew very melancholy, for indeed I knew not what course to take. I had money, but no friends, and was like now to have a child upon my hands to keep, which was a difficulty I had never had upon me yet, as the particulars of my story hitherto make appear.

In the course of this affair I fell very ill, and my melancholy really increased my distemper. My illness proved at length to be only an ague, but my apprehensions were really that I should miscarry – I should not say apprehensions, for indeed I would have been glad to miscarry, but I could never be brought to entertain so much as a thought of endeavouring to miscarry, or of taking anything to make me miscarry. I abhorred, I say, so much as the thought of it.

However, speaking of it in the house, the gentlewoman who kept the house proposed to me to send for a midwife. I scrupled it at first, but after some time consented to it, but told her I had no particular acquaintance with any midwife, and so left it to her.

It seems the mistress of the house was not so great a stranger to such cases as mine was as I thought at first she had been, as will appear presently, and she sent for a midwife of the right sort – that is to say, the right sort for me.

The woman appeared to be an experienced woman in her business, I mean as a midwife, but she had another calling too, in which she was as expert as most women, if not more. My landlady had told her I was very melancholy, and that she believed that had done me harm, and once, before me, said to her, "Mrs B——" (meaning the midwife) "I believe this lady's trouble is of a kind that is pretty much in your way, and therefore if you can do anything for her, pray do, for she is a very civil gentlewoman" – and so she went out of the room.

I really did not understand her, but my Mother Midnight* began very seriously to explain what she meant, as soon as she was gone. "Madam," says she, "you seem not to understand what your landlady means, and when you do understand it, you need not let her know at all that you do so.

"She means that you are under some circumstances that may render your lying-in difficult to you, and that you are not willing to be exposed. I need say no more, but to tell you that if you think fit to communicate so much of your case to me, if it be so, as is necessary, for I do not desire to pry into those things, I perhaps may be in a condition to assist you, and to make you perfectly easy, and remove all your dull thoughts upon that subject."

Every word this creature said was a cordial to me, and put new life and new spirit into my very heart. My blood began to circulate immediately, and I was quite another body. I ate my victuals again, and grew better presently after it. She said a great deal more to the same purpose, and then, having pressed me to be free with her and promised in the solemnest manner to be secret, she stopped a little, as if waiting to see what impression it made on me and what I would say.

I was too sensible of the want I was in of such a woman not to accept her offer. I told her my case was partly as she guessed and partly not, for I was really married and had a husband, though he was in such circumstances, and so remote at that time, as that he could not appear publicly.

She took me short, and told me that was none of her business – all the ladies that came under her care were married women to her. "Every woman," says she, "that is with child has a father for it" – and whether that father was a husband or no husband was no business of hers. Her business was to assist me in my present circumstances whether I had a husband or no. "For, madam," says she, "to have a husband that cannot appear is to have no husband in the sense of the case, and therefore whether you are a wife or a mistress is all one to me."

I found presently that whether I was a whore or a wife, I was to pass for a whore here, so I let that go. I told her it was true as she said, but that, however, if I must tell her my case, I must tell it her as it was. So I related it to her as short as I could, and I concluded it to her thus: "I trouble you with all this, madam," said I, "not that, as you said before, it is much to the purpose in your affair, but this is to the purpose: namely, that I am not in any pain about being seen or being public or concealed, for 'tis perfectly indifferent to me – but my difficulty is that I have no acquaintance in this part of the nation."

"I understand you, madam," says she. "You have no security to bring to prevent the parish impertinences* usual in such cases, and perhaps," says she, "do not know very well how to dispose of the child when it comes." "The last," says I, "is not so much my concern as the first." "Well, madam," answers the midwife, "dare you put yourself into my hands, I live in such a place. Though I do not enquire after you, you may enquire after me: my name is B——. I live in such a street" – naming the street – "at the sign of the Cradle. My profession is a midwife, and I have many ladies that come to my house to lie in. I have given security to the parish in general terms to secure them from any charge from whatsoever shall come into the world under my roof. I have but one question to ask in the whole affair, madam," says she, "and if that be answered, you shall be entirely easy for all the rest."

I presently understood what she meant, and told her, "Madam, I believe I understand you. I thank God, though I want friends in this part of the world, I do not want money, so far as may be necessary, though I do not abound in that neither" – this I added because I would not make her expect great things. "Well, madam," says she, "that is the thing indeed without which nothing can be done in these cases. And yet," says she, "you shall see that I will not impose upon you, or offer anything that is unkind to you, and if you desire it, you shall know everything beforehand, that you may suit yourself to the occasion, and be either costly or sparing as you see fit."

I told her she seemed to be so perfectly sensible of my condition that I had nothing to ask of her but this: that, as I had told her that I had money sufficient but not a great quantity, she would order it so that I might be at as little superfluous charge as possible.

She replied that she would bring in an account of the expenses of it, in two or three shapes, and, like a bill of fare, I should choose as I pleased – and I desired her to do so.

The next day she brought it, and the copy of her three bills was as follows:

	l.	*s.*	*d.*
1. For three months' lodging in her house, including my diet at 10s. a week	06	00	0
2. For a nurse for the month, and use of childbed linen	01	10	0
3. For a minister to christen the child, and to the godfathers and clerk	01	10	0
4. For a supper at the christening if I had five friends at it	01	00	0
For her fees as a midwife, and the taking off the trouble of the parish	03	03	0
To her maidservant attending	00	10	0
	13	13	0

This was the first bill; the second was in the same terms:

	l.	*s.*	*d.*
1. For three months' lodging and diet, etc., at 20s. per week	13	00	0
2. For a nurse for the month, and the use of linen and lace	02	10	0
3. For the minister to christen the child, etc., as above	02	00	0
4. For a supper, and for sweetmeats	03	03	0
For her fees, as above	05	05	0
For a servant maid	01	00	0
	26	18	0

This was the second rate bill. The third, she said, was for a degree higher, and when the father or friends appeared:

1. For three months' lodging and diet, having two rooms and a garret for a servant	30	00	0
2. For a nurse for the month, and the finest suit of childbed linen	04	04	0
3. For the minister to christen the child, etc.	02	10	0
4. For a supper, the gentlemen to send in the wine	06	00	0
For my fees, etc.	10	10	0
The maid, besides their own maid only	00	10	0
	53	14	0

I looked upon all the three bills and smiled, and told her I did not see but that she was very reasonable in her demands, all things considered, and for that I did not doubt but her accommodations were good.

She told me I should be judge of that when I saw them. I told her I was sorry to tell her that I feared I must be her lowest-rated customer. "And perhaps, madam," said I, "you will make me the less welcome upon that account." "No, not at all," said she, "for where I have one of the third sort, I have two of the second, and four to one of the first, and I get as much by them in proportion as by any. But if you doubt my care of you, I will allow any friend you have to overlook, and see if you are well waited on or no."

Then she explained the particulars of her bill. "In the first place, madam," said she, "I would have you observe that here is three months' keeping. You are but 10s. a week – I undertake to say you will not complain of my table. I suppose," says she, "you do not live cheaper where you are now." "No, indeed," said I, "nor so cheap, for I give six shillings per week for my chamber, and find my own diet as well as I can, which costs me a great deal more."

"Then, madam," says she, "if the child should not live, or should be dead-born, as you know sometime happens, then there is the minister's article saved. And if you have no friends to come to you, you may save the expense of a supper. So that take those articles out, madam," says she, "your lying-in will not cost you above 5l. 3s., in all, more than your ordinary charge of living."

This was the most reasonable thing that I ever heard of, so I smiled and told her I would come and be her customer. But I told her also that as I had two months and more to go, I might perhaps be obliged to stay longer with her than three months, and desired to know if she would not be obliged to remove me before it was proper. No, she said, her house was large, and besides, she never put anybody to remove that had lain in till they were willing to go, and if she had more ladies offered, she was not so ill-beloved among her neighbours but she could provide accommodation for twenty, if there was occasion.

I found she was an eminent lady in her way, and, in short, I agreed to put myself into her hands, and promised her. She then talked of other things, looked about into my accommodations, where was found fault with my wanting attendance and conveniences, and that I should not be used so at her house. I told her I was shy of speaking, for the woman of the house looked stranger, or at least I thought so since I had been ill, because I was with child, and I was afraid she would put some affront or other upon me, supposing that I had been able to give but a slight account of myself.

"Oh dear," said she, "Her Ladyship is no stranger to these things. She has tried to entertain ladies in your condition several times, but could not secure the parish. And besides, she is not such a nice lady as you take her to be. However, since you are a-going you shall not meddle with her, but I'll see you are a little better looked after while you are here than I think you are, and it shall not cost you the more neither."

I did not understand her at all. However, I thanked her, and so we parted. The next morning she sent me a chicken roasted and hot, and a pint bottle of sherry, and ordered the maid to tell me that she was to wait on me every day as long as I stayed there.

This was surprisingly good and kind, and I accepted it very willingly. At night she sent to me again, to know if I wanted anything, and how I did, and to order the maid to come to her in the morning for my dinner. The maid had order to make me some chocolate in the morning before she came away, and did so, and at noon she brought me the sweetbread of a breast of veal whole, and a dish of soup for my dinner, and after this manner she nursed me up at a distance, so that I was mightily well pleased, and quickly well, for indeed my dejections before were the principal part of my illness.

I expected, as usually is the case among such people, that the servant she sent me would have been some impudent, brazen wench of Drury Lane breeding,* and I was very uneasy at having her with me upon that account. So I would not let her lie in that house the first night by any means, but had my eyes about me as narrowly as if she had been a public thief.

My gentlewoman guessed presently what was the matter, and sent her back with a short note that I might depend upon the honesty of her maid – that she would be answerable for her upon all accounts, and that she took no servants into her house without very good security for their fidelity. I was then perfectly easy, and indeed the maid's behaviour spoke for itself, for a modester, quieter, soberer girl never came into anybody's family, and I found her so afterwards.

As soon as I was well enough to go abroad, I went with the maid to see the house and to see the apartment I was to have, and everything was so handsome and so clean and well that, in short, I had nothing to say, but was wonderfully pleased and satisfied with what I had met with – which, considering the melancholy circumstances I was in, was far beyond what I looked for.

It might be expected that I should give some account of the nature of the wicked practice of this woman in whose hands I was now fallen, but it would be but too much encouragement to the vice to let the world see what easy measures were here taken to rid the women's unwelcome burden of a child clandestinely gotten. This grave matron had several sorts of practice, and this was one particular: that if a child was born, though not in her house (for she had the occasion to be called to many private labours), she had people at hand who for a piece of money would take the child off their hands, and off from the hands of the parish too – and those children, as she said, were honestly provided for and taken care of. What should become of them all, considering so many as by her account she was concerned with, I cannot conceive.

I had many times discourses upon that subject with her, but she was full of this argument: that she saved the life of many an innocent lamb, as she called them, which would otherwise perhaps have been murdered, and of many a woman who, made desperate by the misfortune, would otherwise be tempted to destroy their children and bring themselves to the gallows. I granted her that this was true, and a very commendable thing, provided the poor children fell into good hands afterwards and were not abused, starved and neglected by the nurses that bred them up. She answered that she always took care of that, and had no nurses in her business but what were very good, honest people, and such as might be depended upon.

I could say nothing to the contrary, and so was obliged to say, "Madam, I do not question you do your part honestly, but what those people do afterwards is the main question" – and she stopped my mouth again with saying that she took the utmost care about it.

The only thing I found in all her conversation on these subjects that gave me any distaste was that one time, in discoursing about my being so far gone with child and the time I expected to come, she said something that looked as if she could help me off with my burden sooner, if I was willing – or, in English, that she could give me something to make me miscarry, if I had a desire to put an end to my troubles that way. But I soon let her see that I abhorred the thoughts of it, and, to do her justice, she put it off so cleverly that I could not say she really intended it or whether she only mentioned the practice as a horrible thing, for she couched her words so well, and took my meaning so quickly, that she gave her negative before I could explain myself.

To bring this part into as narrow a compass as possible, I quitted my lodging at St Jones's and went to my new governess, for so they called her in the house, and there I was indeed treated with so much courtesy, so carefully looked to, so handsomely provided, and everything so well, that I was surprised at it, and could not at first see what advantage my governess made of it. But I found afterwards that she professed to make no profit of the lodgers' diet, nor indeed could she get much by it, but that her profit lay in the other articles of her management, and she made enough that way, I assure you, for 'tis scarce credible what practice she had, as well abroad as at home, and yet all upon the private account – or, in plain English, the whoring account.

While I was in her house, which was near four months, she had no less than twelve ladies of pleasure brought to bed within doors, and I think she had two-and-thirty, or thereabouts, under her conduct without doors, whereof one, as nice as she was with me, was lodged with my old landlady at St Jones's.

This was a strange testimony of the growing vice of the age, and such a one that, as bad as I had been myself, it shocked my very senses. I began to nauseate the place I was in and, above all, the wicked practice, and yet I must say that I never saw, or do I believe there was to be seen, the least indecency in the house the whole time I was there.

Not a man was ever seen to come upstairs, except to visit the lying-in ladies within their month,* nor then without the old lady with them, who made it a piece of the honour of her management that no man should touch a woman – no, not his own wife – within the month. Nor would she permit any man to lie in the house upon any pretence whatever – no, not though she was sure it was with his own wife – and her general saying for it was that she cared not how many children was born in her house, but she would have none got there if she could help it.

It might perhaps be carried further than was needful, but it was an error of the right hand,* if it was an error, for by this she kept up the reputation, such as it was, of her business, and obtained this character: that though she did take care of the women when they were debauched, yet she was not instrumental to their being debauched at all – and yet it was a wicked trade she drove too.

While I was here, and before I was brought to bed, I received a letter from my trustee at the bank full of kind, obliging things, and earnestly pressing me to return to London. It was near a fortnight old when it came to me, because it had been first sent into Lancashire and then returned to me. He concludes with telling me that he had obtained a decree, I think he called it, against his wife, and that he would be ready to make good his engagement to me if I would accept of him, adding a great many protestations of kindness and affection, such as he would have been far from offering if he had known the circumstances I had been in, and which as it was I had been very far from deserving.

I returned an answer to this letter, and dated it at Liverpool, but sent it by a messenger, alleging that it came in cover to a friend in town. I gave him joy of his deliverance, but raised some scruples at the lawfulness of his marrying again, and told him I supposed he would consider very seriously upon that point before he resolved on it, the consequence being too great for a man of his judgement to venture rashly upon a thing of that nature – so concluded, wishing him very well in whatever he resolved, without letting him into anything of my own mind or giving any answer to his proposal of my coming to London to him, but mentioned at a distance my intention to return the latter end of the year, this being dated in April.

I was brought to bed about the middle of May, and had another brave boy, and myself in as good condition as usual on such occasions. My governess did her part as a midwife with the greatest art and dexterity imaginable, and far beyond all that ever I had had any experience of before.

Her care of me in my travail, and after in my lying-in, was such that if she had been my own mother it could not have been better. Let none be encouraged in their loose practices from this dextrous lady's management, for she is gone to her place, and I dare say has left nothing behind her that can or will come up to it.

I think I had been brought to bed about twenty-two days when I received another letter from my friend at the bank, with the surprising news that he had obtained a final sentence of divorce against his wife, and had served her with it on such a day, and that he had such an answer to give to all my scruples about his marrying again as I could not expect, and as he had no desire of – for that his wife, who had been under some remorse before for her usage of him, as soon as she had the account that he had gained his point, had very unhappily destroyed herself that same evening.

He expressed himself very handsomely as to his being concerned at her disaster, but cleared himself of having any hand in it, and that he had only done himself justice in a case in which he was notoriously injured and abused. However, he said that he was extremely afflicted at it, and had no view of any satisfaction left in this world, but only in the hope that I would come and relieve him by my company. And then he pressed me violently indeed to give him some hopes that I would at least come up to town and let him see me, when he would further enter into discourse about it.

I was exceedingly surprised at the news, and began now seriously to reflect on my present circumstances, and the inexpressible misfortune it was to me to have a child upon my hands – and what to do in it I knew not. At last I opened my case at a distance to my governess. I appeared melancholy and uneasy for several days, and she lay at me continually to know what troubled me. I could not for my life tell her that I had an offer of marriage, after I had so often told her that I had a husband, so that I really knew not what to say to her. I owned I had something which very much troubled me, but at the same time told her I could not speak of it to anyone alive.

She continued importuning me several days, but it was impossible, I told her, for me to commit the secret to anybody. This, instead of being an answer to her, increased her importunities. She urged her having been trusted with the greatest secrets of this nature – that it was her business to conceal everything, and that to discover things of that nature would be her ruin. She asked me if ever I had found her tattling of other people's affairs, and how could I suspect her.1 She told me to unfold myself to her was telling it to nobody – that she was silent as death, that it must be a very strange case indeed that she could not help me out of, but to conceal it was to deprive myself of all possible help, or means of help, and to deprive her of the opportunity of serving me. In short, she had such a bewitching eloquence, and so great a power of persuasion, that there was no concealing anything from her.

So I resolved to unbosom myself to her. I told her the history of my Lancashire marriage, and how both of us had been disappointed; how we came together, and how we parted; how he absolutely discharged me, as far as lay in him, and gave me free liberty to marry again, protesting that if he knew it he would never claim me, or disturb or expose me; that I thought I was free, but was dreadfully afraid to venture for fear of the consequences that might follow in case of a discovery.

Then I told her what a good offer I had, showed her my friend's two last letters, inviting me to come to London, and let her see with what affection and earnestness they were written, but blotted out the name, and also the story about the disaster of his wife, only that she was dead.

She fell a-laughing at my scruples about marrying, and told me the other was no marriage, but a cheat on both sides, and that as we were parted by mutual consent, the nature of the contract was destroyed, and the obligation was mutually discharged. She had arguments for this at the tip of her tongue, and, in short, reasoned me out of my reason – not but that it was too by the help of my own inclination.

But then came the great and main difficulty, and that was the child. This she told me in so many words must be removed, and that so as that it should never be possible for anyone to discover it. I knew there was no marrying without entirely concealing that I had had a child, for he would soon have discovered by the age of it that it was born – nay, and gotten too since my parley with him, and that would have destroyed all the affair.

But it touched my heart so forcibly to think of parting entirely with the child – and, for ought I knew, of having it murdered or starved by neglect and ill-usage (which was much the same) – that I could not think of it without horror. I wish all those women who consent to the disposing their children out of the way, as it is called for decency sake, would consider that 'tis only a contrived method for murder – that is to say, a killing their children with safety.

It is manifest to all that understand anything of children that we are born into the world helpless and incapable, either to supply our own wants or so much as make them known, and that without help we must perish, and this help requires not only an assisting hand, whether of the mother or somebody else, but there are two things necessary in that assisting hand: that is, care and skill, without both which half the children that are born would die – nay, though they were not to be denied food. And one half more of those that remained would be cripples or fools, lose their limbs and perhaps their sense. I question not but that these are partly the reasons why affection was placed by nature in the hearts of mothers to their children, without which they would never be able to give themselves up, as 'tis necessary they should, to the care and waking pains needful to the support of their children.

Since this care is needful to the life of children, to neglect them is to murder them. Again, to give them up to be managed by those people who have none of that needful affection placed by nature in them is to neglect them in the highest degree – nay, in some it goes further, and is a neglect in order to their being lost, so that 'tis even an intentional murder, whether the child lives or dies.

All those things represented themselves to my view, and that in the blackest and most frightful form, and as I was very free with my governess, who I had now learnt to call "Mother", I represented to her all the dark thoughts which I had upon me about it, and told her what distress I was in. She seemed graver by much at this part than at the other, but as she was hardened in these things beyond all possibility of being touched with the religious part, and the scruples about the murder, so she was equally impenetrable in that part which related to affection. She asked me if she had not been careful and tender of me in my lying-in, as if I had been her own child. I told her I owned she had. "Well, my dear," says she, "and when you are gone, what are you to me? And what would it be to me if you were to be hanged? Do you think there are not women who, as it is their trade and they get their bread by it, value themselves upon their being as careful of children as their own mothers can be, and understand it rather better? Yes, yes, child," says she, "fear it not. How were we nursed ourselves? Are you sure you was nursed up by your own mother? And yet you look fat and fair, child," says the old beldam, and with that she stroked me over the face. "Never be concerned, child," says she, going on in her drolling way. "I have no murderers about me. I employ the best and the honestest nurses that can be had, and have as few children miscarry under their hands as there would if they were all nursed by mothers. We want neither care nor skill."

She touched me to the quick when she asked if I was sure that I was nursed by my own mother. On the contrary, I was sure I was not, and I trembled and looked pale at the very expression. "Sure," said I to myself, "this creature cannot be a witch, or have any conversation with a spirit that can inform her what was done with me before I was able to know it myself." And I looked at her as if I had been frighted, but, reflecting that it could not be possible for her to know anything about me, that disorder went off, and I began to be easy, but it was not presently.

She perceived the disorder I was in, but did not know the meaning of it, so she ran on in her wild talk upon the weakness of my supposing that children were murdered because they were not all nursed by the mother, and to persuade me that the children she disposed of were as well used as if the mothers had the nursing of them themselves.

"It may be true, Mother," says I, "for ought I know, but my doubts are very strongly grounded, indeed." "Come then," says she, "let's hear some of them." "Why, first," says I, "you give a piece of money to these people to take the child off the parent's hands, and to take care of it as long as it lives. Now, we know, Mother," said I, "that those are poor people, and their gain consists in being quit of the charge as soon as they can. How can I doubt but that, as it is best for them to have the child die, they are not over-solicitous about its life?"

"This is all vapours and fancy," says the old woman. "I tell you their credit depends upon the child's life, and they are as careful as any mother of you all."

"Oh, Mother," says I, "if I was but sure my little baby would be carefully looked to, and have justice done it, I should be happy indeed. But it is impossible I can be satisfied in that point unless I saw it, and to see it would be ruin and destruction to me, as now my case stands – so what to do I know not."

"A fine story!" says the governess. "You would see the child and you would not see the child; you would be concealed and discovered both together – these are things impossible, my dear, so you must e'n do as other conscientious mothers have done before you, and be contented with things as they must be, though they are not as you wish them to be."

I understood what she meant by "conscientious mothers" – she would have said "conscientious whores", but she was not willing to disoblige me, for really in this case I was not a whore, because legally married, the force of my former marriage excepted.

However, let me be what I would, I was not come up to that pitch of hardness common to the profession – I mean to be unnatural, and regardless of the safety of my child – and I preserved this honest affection so long that I was upon the point of giving up my friend at the bank, who lay so hard at me to come to him and marry him that, in short, there was hardly any room to deny him.

At last my old governess came to me with her usual assurance. "Come, my dear," says she. "I have found out a way how you shall be at a certainty that your child shall be used well, and yet the people that take care of it shall never know you, or who the mother of the child is."

"Oh, Mother," says I, "if you can do so, you will engage me to you for ever." "Well," says she, "are you willing to be at some small annual expense, more than what we usually give to the people we contract with?" "Ay," says I, "with all my heart, provided I may be concealed." "As to that," says the governess, "you shall be secure, for the nurse shall never so much as dare to enquire about you, and you shall once or twice a year go with me and see your child, and see how 'tis used, and be satisfied that it is in good hands, nobody knowing who you are."

"Why," said I, "do you think, Mother, that when I come to see my child I shall be able to conceal my being the mother of it? Do you think that possible?"

"Well, well," says my governess, "if you discover it, the nurse shall be never the wiser, for she shall be forbid to ask any questions about you, or to take any notice. If she offers it, she shall lose the money which you are to be supposed to give her, and the child be taken from her too."

I was very well pleased with this, so the next week a country woman was brought from Hertford, or thereabouts, who was to take the child off our hands entirely, for 10*l*. in money. But if I would allow 5*l*. a year more to her, she would be obliged to bring the child to my governess's house as often as we desired, or we should come down and look at it, and see how well she used it.

The woman was a very wholesome-looked, likely woman, a cottager's wife, but she had very good clothes and linen, and everything well about her, and with a heavy heart and many a tear I let her have my child. I had been down at Hertford and looked at her and at her dwelling, which I liked well enough, and I promised her great things if she would be kind to the child, so she knew at first word that I was the child's mother. But she seemed to be so much out of the way, and to have no room to enquire after me, that I thought I was safe enough, so in short I consented to let her have the child, and I gave her ten pound – that is to say, I gave it to my governess, who gave it the poor woman before my face, she agreeing never to return the child back to me or to claim anything more for its keeping or bringing up, only that I promised, if she took a great deal of care of it, I would give her something more as often as I came to see it. So that I was not bound to pay the 5*l*., only that I promised my governess I would do it. And thus my great care was over, after a manner which, though it did not at all satisfy my mind, yet was the most convenient for me, as my affairs then stood, of any that could be thought of at that time.

I then began to write to my friend at the bank in a more kindly style, and particularly about the beginning of July I sent him a letter, that I purposed to be in town some time in August. He returned me an answer in the most passionate terms imaginable, and desired me to let him have timely notice, and he would come and meet me two days' journey. This puzzled me scurvily, and I did not know what answer to make to it. Once I was resolved to take the stagecoach to West Chester on purpose only, to have the satisfaction of coming back, that he might see me really come in the same coach. For I had a jealous thought, though I had no ground for it at all, lest he should think I was not really in the country – and it was no ill-grounded thought, as you shall hear presently.

I endeavoured to reason myself out of it, but it was in vain: the impression lay so strong on my mind that it was not to be resisted. At last it came as an addition to my new design of going in the country that it would be an excellent blind to my old governess, and would cover entirely all my other affairs, for she did not know in the least whether my new lover lived in London or in Lancashire – and when I told her my resolution, she was fully persuaded it was in Lancashire.

Having taken my measures for this journey, I let her know it, and sent the maid that tended me from the beginning to take a place for me in the coach. She would have had me let the maid have waited on me down to the last stage and come up again in the wagon, but I convinced her it would not be convenient. When I went away, she told me, she would enter into no measures for correspondence, for she saw evidently that my affection to my child would cause me to write to her, and to visit her too when I came to town again. I assured her it would, and so took my leave, well satisfied to have been freed from such a house, however good my accommodations there had been, as I have related above.

I took the place in the coach not to its full extent, but to a place called Stone in Cheshire,* I think it is, where I not only had no manner of business, but not so much as the least acquaintance with any person in the town or near it. But I knew that with money in the pocket one is at home anywhere, so I lodged there two or three days, till, watching my opportunity, I found room in another stagecoach, and took passage back again for London, sending a letter to my gentleman that I should be such a certain day at Stony Stratford,* where the coachman told me he was to lodge.

It happened to be a chance coach that I had taken up – which, having been hired on purpose to carry some gentlemen to West Chester who were going for Ireland, was now returning, and did not tie itself up to exact times or places as the stages did, so that having been obliged to lie still a Sunday,* he had time to get himself ready to come out, which otherwise he could not have done.

However, his warning was so short that he could not reach to Stony Stratford time enough to be with me at night, but he met me at a place called Brickhill* the next morning, as we were just coming into the town.

I confess I was very glad to see him, for I had thought myself a little disappointed overnight, seeing I had gone so far to contrive my coming on purpose. He pleased me doubly too by the figure he came in, for he brought a very handsome (gentleman's) coach and four horses with a servant to attend him.

He took me out of the stagecoach immediately, which stopped at an inn in Brickhill, and, putting in to the same inn, he set up his own coach and bespoke his dinner. I asked him what he meant by that, for I was for going forward with the journey. He said no, I had need of a little rest upon the road, and that was a very good sort of a house, though it was but a little town. So we would go no farther that night, whatever came of it.

I did not press him much, for since he had come so far to meet me, and put himself to so much expense, it was but reasonable I should oblige him a little too, so I was easy as to that point.

After dinner we walked to see the town, to see the church and to view the fields and the country, as is usual for strangers to do, and our landlord was our guide in going to see the church. I observed my gentleman enquired pretty much about the parson, and I took the hint immediately that he certainly would propose to be married, and though it was a sudden thought, it followed presently that in short I would not refuse him, for to be plain with my circumstances, I was in no condition now to say no – I had no reason now to run any more such hazards.

But while these thoughts ran round in my head, which was the work but of a few moments, I observed my landlord took him aside and whispered to him, though not very softly neither, for so much I overheard: "Sir, if you shall have occasion…" The rest I could not hear, but it seems it was to this purpose: "Sir, if you shall have occasion for a minister, I have a friend a little way off that will serve you, and be as private as you please." My gentleman answered loud enough for me to hear: "Very well, I believe I shall."

I was no sooner come back to the inn but he fell upon me with irresistible words – that since he had had the good fortune to meet me, and everything concurred, it would be hastening his felicity if I would put an end to the matter just there. "What do you mean?" says I, colouring a little. "What, in an inn, and upon the road! Bless us all," said I, as if I had been surprised. "How can you talk so?" "Oh, I can talk so very well," says he. "I came a-purpose to talk so, and I'll show you that I did" – and with that he pulls out a great bundle of papers. "You fright me," said I. "What are all these?" "Don't be frighted, my dear," said he, and kissed me. This was the first time that he had been so free to call me "my dear". Then he repeated it: "Don't be frighted – you shall see what it is all." Then he laid them all abroad. There was first the deed or sentence of divorce from his wife, and the full evidence of her playing the whore. Then there was the certificates of the minister and churchwardens of the parish where she lived, proving that she was buried, and intimating the manner of her death; the copy of the coroner's warrant for a jury to sit upon her, and the verdict of the jury, who brought it in non compos mentis. All this was indeed to the purpose, and to give me satisfaction – though, by the way, I was not so scrupulous, had he known all, but that I might have taken him without it. However, I looked them all over as well as I could, and told him that this was all very clear indeed, but that he need not have given himself the trouble to have brought them out with him, for it was time enough. Well, he said, it might be time enough for me, but no time but the present time was time enough for him.

There were other papers rolled up, and I asked him what they were. "Why, ay," says he, "that's the question I wanted to have you ask me." So he unrolls them, and takes out a little shagreen* case, and gives me out of it a very fine diamond ring. I could not refuse it if I had a mind to do so, for he put it upon my finger.

So I made him a curtsy and accepted it. Then he takes out another ring. "And this," says he, "is for another occasion" – so he puts that in his pocket. "Well, but let me see it, though," says I, and smiled. "I guess what it is – I think you are mad." "I should have been mad if I had done less," says he, and still he did not show it me, and I had a great mind to see it. So I says, "Well, but let me see it." "Hold," says he, "first look here." Then he took up the roll again and read it, and behold! it was a licence for us to be married. "Why," says I, "are you distracted? Why, you were fully satisfied that I would comply and yield at first word, or resolved to take no denial." "The last is certainly the case," said he. "But you may be mistaken," said I. "No, no," says he, "how can you think so? I must not be denied – I can't be denied" – and with that he fell to kissing me so violently I could not get rid of him.

There was a bed in the room, and we were walking to and again, eager in the discourse. At last he takes me by surprise in his arms, and threw me on the bed and himself with me, and, holding me fast in his arms, but without the least offer of any indecency, courted me to consent with such repeated entreaties and arguments, protesting his affection and vowing he would not let me go till I had promised him, that at last I said, "Why, you resolve not to be denied indeed, I think." "No, no," says he, "I must not be denied, I won't be denied, I can't be denied." "Well, well," said I, and giving him a slight kiss, "then you shan't be denied," said I. "Let me get up."

He was so transported with my consent, and the kind manner of it, that I began to think once he took it for a marriage and would not stay for the form, but I wronged him, for he gave over kissing me, took me by the hand, pulled me up again, and then, giving me two or three kisses again, thanked me for my kind yielding to him, and was so overcome with the satisfaction and joy of it that I saw tears stand in his eyes.

I turned from him, for it filled my eyes with tears too, and I asked him leave to retire a little to my chamber. If ever I had a grain of true repentance for a vicious and abominable life for twenty-four years past, it was then. Oh, what a felicity is it to mankind, said I to myself, that they cannot see into the hearts of one another! How happy had it been for me if I had been wife to a man of so much honesty and so much affection from the beginning!

Then it occurred to me: "What an abominable creature am I! And how is this innocent gentleman going to be abused by me! How little does he think that, having divorced a whore, he is throwing himself into the arms of another! That he is going to marry one that has lain with two brothers, and has had three children by her own brother! One that was born in Newgate, whose mother was a whore, and is now a transported thief! One that has lain with thirteen men, and has had a child since he saw me! Poor gentleman!" said I. "What is he going to do?" After this reproaching myself was over, it followed thus: "Well, if I must be his wife, if it please God to give me grace, I'll be a true wife to him, and love him suitably to the strange excess of his passion for me. I will make him amends, if possible, by what he shall see, for the cheats and abuses I put upon him, which he does not see."

He was impatient for my coming out of my chamber, but finding me long, he went downstairs and talked with my landlord about the parson.

My landlord – an officious, though well-meaning fellow – had sent away for the neighbouring clergyman, and when my gentleman began to speak of it to him and talk of sending for him, "Sir," says he to him, "my friend is in the house." So without any more words he brought them together. When he came to the minister, he asked him if he would venture to marry a couple of strangers that were both willing. The parson said that Mr —— had said something to him of it, that he hoped it was no clandestine business, that he seemed to be a grave gentleman, and he supposed madam was not a girl, so that the consent of friends should be wanted. "To put you out of doubt of that," says my gentleman, "read this paper" – and out he pulls the licence. "I am satisfied," says the minister. "Where is the lady?" "You shall see her presently," says my gentleman.

When he had said thus, he comes upstairs, and I was by that time come out of my room, so he tells me the minister was below, and that he had talked with him, and that upon showing him the licence he was free to marry us with all his heart. "But he asks to see you" – so he asked if I would let him come up.

"'Tis time enough," said I, "in the morning, is it not?" "Why," said he, "my dear, he seemed to scruple whether it was not some young girl stolen from her parents, and I assured him we were both of age to command our own consent, and that made him ask to see you." "Well," said I, "do as you please." So up they brings the parson, and a merry good sort of gentleman he was. He had been told, it seems, that we had met there by accident, that I came in the Chester coach and my gentleman in his own coach to meet me, that we were to have met last night at Stony Stratford, but that he could not reach so far. "Well, sir," says the parson, "every ill turn has some good in it. The disappointment, sir," says he to my gentleman, "was yours, and the good turn is mine, for if you had met at Stony Stratford I had not had the honour to marry you. Landlord, have you a Common Prayer Book?"

I started as if I had been frighted. "Lord, sir," says I, "what do you mean? What, to marry in an inn, and at night too?" "Madam," says the minister, "if you will have it be in the church you shall, but I assure you your marriage will be as firm here as in the church. We are not tied by the canons to marry nowhere but in the church, and if you will have it in the church it will be as public as a country fair. And as for the time of day, it does not at all weigh in this case. Our princes are married in their chambers, and at eight or ten o'clock at night."

I was a great while before I could be persuaded, and pretended not to be willing at all to be married but in the church. But it was all grimace,* so I seemed at last to be prevailed on, and my landlord, and his wife and daughter, were called up. My landlord was father and clerk and all together, and we were married, and very merry we were – though I confess the self-reproaches which I had upon me before lay close to me, and extorted every now and then a deep sigh from me, which my bridegroom took notice of and endeavoured to encourage me, thinking, poor man, that I had some little hesitations at the step I had taken so hastily.

We enjoyed ourselves that evening completely, and yet all was kept so private in the inn that not a servant in the house knew of it, for my landlady and her daughter waited on me, and would not let any of the maids come upstairs except while we were at supper. My landlady's daughter I called my bridesmaid, and, sending for a shopkeeper the next morning, I gave the young woman a good suit of knots,* as good as the town would afford – and, finding it was a lacemaking town, I gave her mother a piece of bone lace* for a head.

One reason that my landlord was so close was that he was unwilling the minister of the parish should hear of it, but for all that somebody heard of it, so as that we had the bells set a-ringing the next morning early, and the music, such as the town would afford, under our window. But my landlord brazened it out – that we were married before we came thither, only that, being his former guests, we would have our wedding supper at his house.

We could not find in our hearts to stir the next day, for, in short, having been disturbed by the bells in the morning and having perhaps not slept overmuch before, we were so sleepy afterwards that we lay in bed till almost twelve o'clock.

I begged my landlady that we might not have any more music in the town, nor ringing of bells, and she managed it so well that we were very quiet – but an odd passage interrupted all my mirth for a good while. The great room of the house looked into the street, and, my new spouse being below stairs, I had walked to the end of the room, and it being a pleasant warm day, I had opened the window, and was standing at it for some air when I saw three gentlemen come by on horseback and go into an inn just against us.

It was not to be concealed, nor was it so doubtful as to leave me any room to question it, but the second of the three was my Lancashire husband. I was frighted to death – I never was in such a consternation in my life. I thought I should have sunk into the ground; my blood run chill in my veins, and I trembled as if I had been in a cold fit of an ague. I say, there was no room to question the truth of it: I knew his clothes, I knew his horse, and I knew his face.

The first sensible reflection I made was that my husband was not by to see my disorder – and *that* I was very glad of. The gentlemen had not been long in the house but they came to the window of their room, as is usual – but my window was shut, you may be sure. However, I could not keep from peeping at them, and there I saw him again, heard him call out to one of the servants of the house for something he wanted, and received all the terrifying confirmations of its being the same person that were possible to be had.

My next concern was to know, if possible, what was his business there, but that was impossible. Sometimes my imagination formed an idea of one frightful thing, sometimes of another; sometimes I thought he had discovered me, and was come to upbraid me with ingratitude and breach of honour, and every moment I fancied he was coming up the stairs to insult me, and innumerable fancies came into my head of what was never in his head, nor ever could be, unless the Devil had revealed it to him.

I remained in this fright near two hours, and scarce ever kept my eye from the window or door of the inn where they were. At last, hearing a great clutter in the passage of their inn, I run to the window and, to my great satisfaction, see them all three go out again and travel on westward. Had they gone towards London, I should have been still in a fright, lest I should meet him on the road again, and that he should know me – but he went the contrary way, and so I was eased of that disorder.

We resolved to be going the next day, but about six o'clock at night we were alarmed with a great uproar in the street, and people riding as if they had been out of their wits, and what was it but a hue and cry after three highwaymen that had robbed two coaches and some other travellers near Dunstable Hill – and notice had, it seems, been given that they had been seen at Brickhill at such a house, meaning the house where those gentlemen had been.

The house was immediately beset and searched, but there were witnesses enough that the gentlemen had been gone above three hours. The crowd having gathered about, we had the news presently, and I was heartily concerned now another way. I presently told the people of the house that I durst to say those were not the persons, for that I knew one of the gentlemen to be a very honest person, and of a good estate in Lancashire.

The constable, who came with the hue and cry, was immediately informed of this, and came over to me to be satisfied from my own mouth, and I assured him that I saw the three gentlemen as I was at the window – that I saw them afterwards at the windows of the room they dined in, that I saw them afterwards take horse, and I could assure him I knew one of them to be such a man, that he was a gentleman of a very good estate and an undoubted character in Lancashire, from whence I was just now upon my journey.

The assurance with which I delivered this gave the mob gentry a check, and gave the constable such satisfaction that he immediately sounded a retreat, told his people these were not the men, but that he had an account they were very honest gentlemen, and so they went all back again. What the truth of the matter was I knew not, but certain it was that the coaches were robbed at Dunstable Hill, and 560*l*. in money taken, besides some of the lace merchants that always travel that way had been visited too. As to the three gentlemen, that remains to be explained hereafter.

Well, this alarm stopped us another day, though my spouse was for travelling and told me that it was always safest travelling after a robbery, for that the thieves were sure to be gone far enough off when they had alarmed the country. But I was afraid and uneasy, and indeed principally lest my old acquaintance should be upon the road still, and should chance to see me.

I never lived four pleasanter days together in my life. I was a mere bride all this while, and my new spouse strove to make me entirely easy in everything. Oh, could this state of life have continued! How had all my past troubles been forgot, and my future sorrows been avoided! But I had a past life of a most wretched kind to account for, some of it in this world as well as in another.

We came away the fifth day, and my landlord, because he saw me uneasy, mounted himself, his son and three honest country fellows with good firearms, and, without telling us of it, followed the coach, and would see us safe into Dunstable. We could do no less than treat them very handsomely at Dunstable, which cost my spouse about ten or twelve shillings, and something he gave the men for their time too, but my landlord would take nothing for himself.

This was the most happy contrivance for me that could have fallen out, for had I come to London unmarried, I must either have come to him for the first night's entertainment or have discovered to him that I had not one acquaintance in the whole city of London that could receive a poor bride for the first night's lodging with her spouse. But now, being an old married woman, I made no scruple of going directly home with him, and there I took possession at once of a house well furnished and a husband in very good circumstances, so that I had a prospect of a very happy life, if I knew how to manage it. And I had leisure to consider of the real value of the life I was likely to live – how different it was to be from the loose, ungoverned part I had acted before, and how much happier a life of virtue and sobriety is than that which we call a life of pleasure.

Oh, had this particular scene of life lasted, or had I learnt from that time I enjoyed it to have tasted the true sweetness of it, and had I not fallen into that poverty which is the sure bane of virtue, how happy had I been, not only here, but perhaps for ever! For while I lived thus, I was really a penitent for all my life past – I looked back on it with abhorrence, and might truly be said to hate myself for it. I often reflected how my lover at the Bath, struck by the hand of God, repented and abandoned me, and refused to see me any more, though he loved me to an extreme. But I, prompted by that worst of devils, poverty, returned to the vile practice, and made the advantage of what they call a handsome face be the relief to my necessities, and beauty be a pimp to vice.

Now I seemed landed in a safe harbour after the stormy voyage of life past was at an end, and I began to be thankful for my deliverance. I sat many an hour by myself, and wept over the remembrance of past follies and the dreadful extravagances of a wicked life, and sometimes I flattered myself that I had sincerely repented.

But there are temptations which it is not in the power of human nature to resist, and few know what would be their case if driven to the same exigences. As covetousness is the root of all evil, so poverty is, I believe, the worst of all snares – but I waive that discourse till I come to the experiment.*

I lived with this husband in the utmost tranquillity. He was a quiet, sensible, sober man – virtuous, modest, sincere, and in his business diligent and just. His business was in a narrow compass, and his income sufficient to a plentiful way of living in the ordinary way – I do not say to keep an equipage and make a figure, as the world calls it. Nor did I expect it or desire it, for as I abhorred the levity and extravagance of my former life, so I chose now to live retired, frugal and within ourselves. I kept no company, made no visits, minded my family and obliged my husband – and this kind of life became a pleasure to me.

We lived in an uninterrupted course of ease and content for five years, when a sudden blow from an almost invisible hand blasted all my happiness and turned me out into the world in a condition the reverse of all that had been before it.

My husband having trusted one of his fellow clerks with a sum of money too much for our fortunes to bear the loss of, the clerk failed, and the loss fell very heavy on my husband – yet it was not so great neither but that if he had had spirit and courage to have looked his misfortunes in the face, his credit was so good that, as I told him, he would easily recover it, for to sink under trouble is to double the weight, and he that will die in it shall die in it.

It was in vain to speak comfortably to him – the wound had sunk too deep. It was a stab that touched the vitals. He grew melancholy and disconsolate, and from thence lethargic, and died. I foresaw the blow, and was extremely oppressed in my mind, for I saw evidently that if he died I was undone.

I had had two children by him and no more – for, to tell the truth, it began to be time for me to leave bearing children, for I was now eight-and-forty, and I suppose if he had lived I should have had no more.

I was now left in a dismal and disconsolate case indeed, and in several things worse than ever. First, it was past the flourishing time with me when I might expect to be courted for a mistress. That agreeable part had declined some time, and the ruins only appeared of what had been. And that which was worse than all was this: that I was the most dejected, disconsolate creature alive – I that had encouraged my husband, and endeavoured to support his spirits under his trouble, could not support my own. I wanted that spirit in trouble which I told him was so necessary to him for bearing the burden.

But my case was indeed deplorable, for I was left perfectly friendless and helpless, and the loss my husband had sustained had reduced his circumstances so low that though indeed I was not in debt, yet I could easily foresee that what was left would not support me long – that while it wasted daily for subsistence, I had no way to increase it one shilling, so that it would be soon all spent, and then I saw nothing before me but the utmost distress, and this represented itself so lively to my thoughts that it seemed as if it was come before it was really very near. Also, my very apprehensions doubled the misery, for I fancied every sixpence that I paid but for a loaf of bread was the last that I had in the world, and that tomorrow I was to fast and be starved to death.

In this distress I had no assistant, no friend to comfort or advise me. I sat and cried and tormented myself night and day, wringing my hands and sometimes raving like a distracted woman, and indeed I have often wondered it had not affected my reason, for I had the vapours to such a degree that my understanding was sometimes quite lost in fancies and imaginations.

I lived two years in this dismal condition, wasting that little I had, weeping continually over my dismal circumstances, and as it were only bleeding to death, without the least hope or prospect of help from God or man. And now I had cried so long, and so often, that tears were, as I might say, exhausted, and I began to be desperate, for I grew poor apace.

For a little relief I had put off my house and took lodgings, and as I was reducing my living so I sold off most of my goods, which put a little money in my pocket, and I lived near a year upon that, spending very sparingly and eking things out to the utmost. But still, when I looked before me, my very heart would sink within me at the inevitable approach of misery and want. Oh, let none read this part without seriously reflecting on the circumstances of a desolate state, and how they would grapple with mere want of friends and want of bread! It will certainly make them think not of sparing what they have only, but of looking up to heaven for support, and of the wise man's prayer: "Give me not poverty lest I steal."*

Let 'em remember that a time of distress is a time of dreadful temptation, and all the strength to resist is taken away. Poverty presses, the soul is made desperate by distress, and what can be done? It was one evening, when being brought, as I may say, to the last gasp, I think I may truly say I was distracted and raving, when prompted by I know not what spirit and, as it were, doing I did not know what or why, I dressed me, for I had still pretty good clothes, and went out. I am very sure I had no manner of design in my head when I went out – I neither knew or considered where to go, or on what business – but, as the Devil carried me out and laid his bait for me, so he brought me to be sure to the place, for I knew not whither I was going or what I did.

Wandering thus about I knew not whither, I passed by an apothecary's shop in Leadenhall Street, where I saw lie on a stool just before the counter a little bundle wrapped in a white cloth. Beyond it stood a maidservant with her back to it, looking up towards the top of the shop, where the apothecary's apprentice, as I suppose, was standing up on the counter, with his back also to the door, and a candle in his hand, looking and reaching up to the upper shelf for something he wanted, so that both were engaged mighty earnestly, and nobody else in the shop.

This was the bait, and the Devil, who I said laid the snare, as readily prompted me as if he had spoke, for I remember, and shall never forget it, 'twas like a voice spoken to me over my shoulder, "Take the bundle. Be quick – do it this moment." It was no sooner said but I stepped into the shop, and, with my back to the wench, as if I had stood up for a cart that was going by, I put my hand behind me and took the bundle, and went off with it, the maid or the fellow not perceiving me, or anyone else.

It is impossible to express the horror of my soul all the while I did it. When I went away I had no heart to run, or scarce to mend my pace. I crossed the street, indeed, and went down the first turning I came to, and I think it was a street that went through into Fenchurch Street. From thence I crossed and turned through so many ways and turnings that I could never tell which way it was, nor where I went, for I felt not the ground I stepped on, and the farther I was out of danger the faster I went, till, tired and out of breath, I was forced to sit down on a little bench at a door, and then I began to recover, and found I was got into Thames Street near Billingsgate. I rested me a little and went on. My blood was all in a fire; my heart beat as if I was in a sudden fright – in short, I was under such a surprise that I still knew not whither I was a-going, or what to do.

After I had tired myself thus with walking a long way about, and so eagerly, I began to consider and make home to my lodging, where I came about nine o'clock at night.

What the bundle was made up for, or on what occasion laid where I found it, I knew not. But when I came to open it I found there was a suit of childbed linen in it, very good and almost new, the lace very fine. There was a silver porringer of a pint, a small silver mug and six spoons, with some other linen, a good smock and three silk handkerchiefs, and in the mug, wrapped up in a paper, eighteen shillings and sixpence in money.

All the while I was opening these things I was under such dreadful impressions of fear, and in such terror of mind, though I was perfectly safe, that I cannot express the manner of it. I sat me down and cried most vehemently. "Lord," said I, "what am I now? A thief! Why, I shall be taken next time and be carried to Newgate and be tried for my life!" And with that I cried again a long time, and I am sure, as poor as I was, if I had durst for fear, I would certainly have carried the things back again – but that went off after a while. Well, I went to bed for that night, but slept little – the horror of the fact was upon my mind, and I knew not what I said or did all night, and all the next day. Then I was impatient to hear some news of the loss, and would fain know how it was, whether they were a poor body's goods or a rich. "Perhaps," said I, "it may be some poor widow like me, that had packed up these goods to go and sell them for a little bread for herself and a poor child, and are now starving and breaking their hearts for want of that little they would have fetched" – and this thought tormented me worse than all the rest for three or four days' time.

But my own distresses silenced all these reflections, and the prospect of my own starving, which grew every day more frightful to me, hardened my heart by degrees. It was then particularly heavy upon my mind that I had been reformed, and had, as I hoped, repented of all my past wickednesses – that I had lived a sober, grave, retired life for several years. But now I should be driven by the dreadful necessity of my circumstances to the gates of destruction, soul and body, and two or three times I fell upon my knees, praying to God, as well as I could, for deliverance. But I cannot but say my prayers had no hope in them. I knew not what to do. It was all fear without and dark within, and I reflected on my past life as not sincerely repented of – that Heaven was now beginning to punish me on this side the grave, and would make me as miserable as I had been wicked.

Had I gone on here I had perhaps been a true penitent, but I had an evil counsellor within, and he was continually prompting me to relieve myself by the worst means. So, one evening, he tempted me again by the same wicked impulse that had said "Take that bundle", to go out again and seek for what might happen.

I went out now by daylight, and wandered about I knew not whither, and in search of I knew not what, when the Devil put a snare in my way of a dreadful nature indeed, and such a one as I have never had before or since. Going through Aldersgate Street, there was a pretty little child had been at a dancing school and was going home all alone, and my prompter, like a true devil, set me upon this innocent creature. I talked to it, and it prattled to me again, and I took it by the hand and led it along till I came to a paved alley that goes into Bartholomew Close, and I led it in there. The child said that was not its way home. I said, "Yes, my dear, it is. I'll show you the way home." The child had a little necklace on of gold beads, and I had my eye upon that, and in the dark of the alley I stooped, pretending to mend the child's clog that was loose, and took off her necklace, and the child never felt it, and so led the child on again. Here, I say, the Devil put me upon killing the child in the dark alley, that it might not cry, but the very thought frighted me so that I was ready to drop down, but I turned the child about and bade it go back again, for that was not its way home. The child said so she would, and I went through into Bartholomew Close, and then turned round to another passage that goes into Long Lane, so away into Charterhouse Yard and out into St John Street, then crossing into Smithfield, went down Chick Lane and into Field Lane to Holborn Bridge,* when mixing with the crowd of people usually passing there, it was not possible to have been found out. And thus I enterprised my second sally into the world.

The thoughts of this booty put out all the thoughts of the first, and the reflections I had made wore quickly off. Poverty, as I have said, hardened my heart, and my own necessities made me regardless of anything. The last affair left no great concern upon me, for as I did the poor child no harm, I only said to myself I had given the parents a just reproof for their negligence in leaving the poor little lamb to come home by itself, and it would teach them to take more care of it another time.

This string of beads was worth about twelve or fourteen pounds. I suppose it might have been formerly the mother's, for it was too big for the child's wear, but that, perhaps, the vanity of the mother to have her child look fine at the dancing school had made her let the child wear it, and no doubt the child had a maid sent to take care of it – but she, like a careless jade, was taken up perhaps with some fellow that had met her by the way, and so the poor baby wandered till it fell into my hands.

However, I did the child no harm. I did not so much as fright it, for I had a great many tender thoughts about me yet, and did nothing but what, as I may say, mere necessity drove me to.

I had a great many adventures after this, but I was young in the business, and did not know how to manage otherwise than as the Devil put things into my head – and indeed he was seldom backward to me. One adventure I had which was very lucky to me: I was going through Lombard Street in the dusk of the evening, just by the end of Three King Court, when on a sudden comes a fellow running by me as swift as lightning and throws a bundle that was in his hand just behind me, as I stood up against the corner of the house at the turning into the alley. Just as he threw it in, he said, "God bless you, mistress, let it lie there a little" – and away he runs, swift as the wind. After him comes two more, and immediately a young fellow without his hat crying "Stop thief!" – and after him two or three more. They pursued the two last fellows so close that they were forced to drop what they had got, and one of them was taken into the bargain. The other got off free.

I stood stock-still all this while, till they came back, dragging the poor fellow they had taken and lugging the things they had found, extremely well satisfied that they had recovered the booty and taken the thief. And thus they passed by me, for I looked only like one who stood up while the crowd was gone.

Once or twice I asked what was the matter, but the people neglected answering me, and I was not very importunate. But after the crowd was wholly passed, I took my opportunity to turn about and take up what was behind me and walk away. This indeed I did with less disturbance than I had done formerly, for these things I did not steal, but they were stolen to my hand. I got safe to my lodgings with this cargo, which was a piece of fine black lustring* silk and a piece of velvet. The latter was but part of a piece of about eleven yards; the former was a whole piece of near fifty yards. It seems it was a mercer's shop that they had rifled – I say rifled because the goods were so considerable that they had lost, for the goods that they recovered were pretty many, and I believe came to about six or seven several pieces of silk. How they came to get so many I could not tell, but as I had only robbed the thief, I made no scruple at taking these goods, and being very glad of them too.

I had pretty good luck thus far, and I made several adventures more, though with but small purchase, yet with good success, but I went in daily dread that some mischief would befall me, and that I should certainly come to be hanged at last. The impression this made on me was too strong to be slighted, and it kept me from making attempts that for ought I know might have been very safely performed. But one thing I cannot omit, which was a bait to me many a day. I walked frequently out into the villages round the town to see if nothing would fall in my way there, and, going by a house near Stepney,* I saw on the window board two rings, one a small diamond ring and the other a plain gold ring, to be sure laid there by some thoughtless lady that had more money than forecast,* perhaps only till she washed her hands.

I walked several times by the window to observe if I could see whether there was anybody in the room or no, and I could see nobody, but still I was not sure. It came presently into my thoughts to rap at the glass as if I wanted to speak with somebody, and if anybody was there they would be sure to come to the window, and then I would tell them to remove those rings, for that I had seen two suspicious fellows take notice of them. This was a ready thought. I rapped once or twice and nobody came – when, seeing the coast clear, I thrust hard against the square of glass and broke it with very little noise, and took out the two rings, and walked away with them very safe. The diamond ring was worth about 3*l.* and the other about 9*s.*

I was now at a loss for a market for my goods, and especially for my two pieces of silk. I was very loath to dispose of them for a trifle, as the poor, unhappy thieves in general do – who, after they have ventured their lives for perhaps a thing of value, are fain to sell it for a song when they have done. But I was resolved I would not do thus whatever shift I made, unless I was driven to the last extremity. However, I did not well know what course to take. At last I resolved to go to my old governess and acquaint myself with her again. I had punctually supplied the 5*l.* a year to her for my little boy as long as I was able, but at last was obliged to put a stop to it. However, I had written a letter to her, wherein I had told her that my circumstances were reduced very low, that I had lost my husband, and that I was not able to do it any longer, and so begged that the poor child might not suffer too much for its mother's misfortunes.

I now made her a visit, and I found that she drove something of the old trade still, but that she was not in such flourishing circumstances as before, for she had been sued by a certain gentleman who had had his daughter stolen from him, and who, it seems, she had helped to convey away, and it was very narrowly that she escaped the gallows. The expense also had ravaged her, and she was become very poor – her house was but meanly furnished, and she was not in such repute for her practice as before. However, she stood upon her legs, as they say, and, as she was a stirring, bustling woman, and had some stock left, she was turned pawn-broker, and lived pretty well.

She received me very civilly, and with her usual obliging manner told me she would not have the less respect for me for my being reduced – that she had taken care my boy was very well looked after, though I could not pay for him, and that the woman that had him was easy, so that I needed not to trouble myself about him till I might be better able to do it effectually.

I told her I had not much money left, but that I had some things that were money's worth, if she could tell me how I might turn them into money. She asked me what it was I had. I pulled out the string of gold beads, and told her it was one of my husband's presents to me. Then I showed her the two parcels of silk, which I told her I had from Ireland and brought up to town with me, and the little diamond ring. As to the small parcel of plate and spoons, I had found means to dispose of them myself before. And as for the childbed linen I had, she offered me to take it herself, believing it to have been my own. She told me that she was turned pawnbroker, and that she would sell those things for me as pawned to her. And so she sent presently for proper agents that bought them, being in her hands, without any scruple, and gave good prices too.

I now began to think this necessary* woman might help me a little, in my low condition, to some business – for I would gladly have turned my hand to any honest employment if I could have got it. But here she was deficient: honest business did not come within her reach. If I had been younger, perhaps she might have helped me to a spark,* but my thoughts were off of that kind of livelihood, as being quite out of the way after fifty, which was my case, and so I told her.

She invited me at last to come and be at her house till I could find something to do, and it should cost me very little, and this I gladly accepted of. And now, living a little easier, I entered into some measures to have my little son by my last husband taken off, and this she made easy too, reserving a payment only of 5*l.* a year, if I could pay it. This was such a help to me that for a good while I left off the wicked trade that I had so newly taken up, and gladly I would have got my bread by the help of my needle if I could have got work, but that was very hard to do for one that had no manner of acquaintance in the world.

However, at last I got some quilting work for ladies' beds, petticoats and the like, and this I liked very well and worked very hard, and with this I began to live – but the diligent devil, who resolved I should continue in his service, continually prompted me to go out and take a walk – that is to say, to see if anything would offer in the old way.

One evening I blindly obeyed his summons and fetched a long circuit through the streets, but met with no purchase and came home very weary, and empty. But not content with that, I went out the next evening too, when, going by an alehouse, I saw the door of a little room open, next the very street, and on the table a silver tankard, things much in use in public houses at that time. It seems some company had been drinking there, and the careless boys had forgot to take it away.

I went into the box frankly, and, setting the silver tankard on the corner of the bench, I sat down before it and knocked with my foot. A boy came presently, and I bade him fetch me a pint of warm ale, for it was cold weather. The boy ran, and I heard him go down the cellar to draw the ale. While the boy was gone, another boy came into the room, and cried, "D'ye call?" I spoke with a melancholy air, and said, "No child, the boy is gone for a pint of ale for me."

While I sat here, I heard the woman in the bar say, "Are they all gone in the five?" – which was the box I sat in – and the boy said yes. "Who fetched the tankard away?" says the woman. "I did," says another boy. "That's it" – pointing, it seems, to another tankard, which he had fetched from another box by mistake. Or else it must be that the rogue forgot that he had not brought it in, which certainly he had not.

I heard all this, much to my satisfaction, for I found plainly that the tankard was not missed, and yet they concluded it was fetched away. So I drank my ale, called to pay, and, as I went away, I said, "Take care of your plate, child" – meaning a silver pint mug which he brought me drink in. The boy said, "Yes, madam, very welcome" – and away I came.

I came home to my governess, and now I thought it was a time to try her, that if I might be put to the necessity of being exposed, she might offer me some assistance. When I had been at home some time and had an opportunity of talking to her, I told her I had a secret of the greatest consequence in the world to commit to her if she had respect enough for me to keep it a secret. She told me she had kept one of my secrets faithfully – why should I doubt her keeping another? I told her the strangest thing in the world had befallen me, and that it had made a thief of me, even without any design – and so told her the whole story of the tankard. "And have you brought it away with you, my dear?" says she. "To be sure I have," says I, and showed it her. "But what shall I do now," says I. "Must not I carry it again?"

"Carry it again!" says she. "Ay, if you are minded to be sent to Newgate for stealing it." "Why," says I, "they can't be so base to stop me when I carry it to them again?" "You don't know those sort of people, child," says she. "They'll not only carry you to Newgate, but hang you too without any regard to the honesty of returning it, or bring in an account of all the other tankards they have lost for you to pay for." "What must I do then?" says I. "Nay," says she, "as you have played the cunning part and stole it, you must e'n keep it – there's no going back now. Besides, child," says she, "don't you want it more than they do? I wish you could light of such a bargain once a week."

This gave me a new notion of my governess, and that since she was turned pawnbroker, she had a sort of people about her that were none of the honest ones that I had met with there before.

I had not been long there but I discovered it more plainly than before, for every now and then I saw hilts of swords, spoons, forks, tankards, and all such kind of ware brought in – not to be pawned, but to be sold downright. And she bought everything that came without asking any questions, but had very good bargains, as I found by her discourse.

I found also that, in the following this trade, she always melted down the plate she bought, that it might not be challenged, and she came to me and told me one morning that she was going to melt, and, if I would, she would put my tankard in, that it might not be seen by anybody. I told her with all my heart, so she weighed it and allowed me the full value in silver again. But I found she did not do the same to the rest of her customers.

Some time after this, as I was at work, and very melancholy, she begins to ask me what the matter was, as she was used to do. I told her my heart was heavy: I had little work and nothing to live on, and knew not what course to take. She laughed and told me I must go out again and try my fortune – it might be that I might meet with another piece of plate. "Oh, Mother!" says I. "That is a trade I have no skill in, and if I should be taken I am undone at once." Says she, "I could help you to a schoolmistress that shall make you as dextrous as herself." I trembled at that proposal, for hitherto I had had no confederates, nor any acquaintance among that tribe. But she conquered all my modesty and all my fears, and in a little time, by the help of this confederate, I grew as impudent a thief and as dextrous as ever Moll Cutpurse* was – though, if fame does not belie her, not half so handsome.

The comrade she helped me to dealt in three sorts of craft, viz. shoplifting, stealing of shop books and pocketbooks, and taking off gold watches from the ladies' sides, and this last she did so dextrously that no woman ever arrived to the perfection of that art so as to do it like her. I liked the first and the last of these things very well, and I attended her sometime in the practice, just as a deputy attends a midwife without any pay.

At length she put me to practice. She had shown me her art, and I had several times unhooked a watch from her own side with great dexterity. At last she showed me a prize, and this was a young lady big with child who had a charming watch. The thing was to be done as she came out of church. She goes on one side of the lady and pretends, just as she came to the steps, to fall, and fell against the lady with so much violence as put her into a great fright, and both cried out terribly. In the very moment that she jostled the lady, I had hold of the watch, and, holding it the right way, the start she gave drew the hook out, and she never felt it. I made off immediately, and left my schoolmistress to come out of her pretended fright gradually, and the lady too, and presently the watch was missed. "Ay," says my comrade, "then it was those rogues that thrust me down, I warrant ye. I wonder the gentlewoman did not miss her watch before, then we might have taken them."

She humoured the thing so well that nobody suspected her, and I was got home a full hour before her. This was my first adventure in company. The watch was indeed a very fine one, and had a great many trinkets about it, and my governess allowed us 20*l.* for it, of which I had half, and thus I was entered a complete thief, hardened to a pitch above all the reflections of conscience or modesty, and to a degree which I must acknowledge I never thought possible in me.

Thus the Devil, who began, by the help of an irresistible poverty, to push me into this wickedness, brought me onto a height beyond the common rate, even when my necessities were not so great or the prospect of my misery so terrifying. For I had now got into a little vein of work, and as I was not at a loss to handle my needle, it was very probable, as acquaintance came in, I might have got my bread honestly enough.

I must say that if such a prospect of work had presented itself at first, when I began to feel the approach of my miserable circumstances – I say, had such a prospect of getting my bread by working presented itself then, I had never fallen into this wicked trade or into such a wicked gang as I was now embarked with. But practice had hardened me, and I grew audacious to the last degree, and the more so because I had carried it on so long and had never been taken. For, in a word, my new partner in wickedness and I went on together so long without being ever detected that we not only grew bold, but we grew rich, and we had at one time one-and-twenty gold watches in our hands.

I remember that one day, being a little more serious than ordinary, and finding I had so good a stock beforehand as I had, for

I had near 200*l.* in money for my share, it came strongly into my mind – no doubt from some kind spirit, if such there be – that as at first poverty excited me and my distresses drove me to these dreadful shifts, so seeing those distresses were now relieved, and I could also get something towards a maintenance by working, and had so good a bank to support me, why should I not now leave off, as they say, while I was well? That I could not expect to go always free, and if I was once surprised and miscarried, I was undone.

This was doubtless the happy minute when, if I had hearkened to the blessed hint from whatsoever hand it came, I had still a cast for an easy life. But my fate was otherwise determined – the busy devil that so industriously drew me in had too fast hold of me to let me go back. But as poverty brought me into the mire, so avarice kept me in, till there was no going back. As to the arguments which my reason dictated for persuading me to lay down, avarice stepped in and said, "Go on, go on. You have had very good luck – go on till you have gotten four or five hundred pound, and then you shall leave off, and then you may live easy without working at all."

Thus I, that was once in the Devil's clutches, was held fast there as with a charm, and had no power to go without the circle, till I was engulfed in labyrinths of trouble too great to get out at all.

However, these thoughts left some impression upon me, and made me act with some more caution than before, and more than my directors used for themselves. My comrade, as I called her – but rather she should have been called my teacher – with another of her scholars, was the first in the misfortune, for, happening to be upon the hunt for purchase, they made an attempt upon a linen draper in Cheapside, but were snapped by a hawk-eyed journeyman,* and seized with two pieces of cambric, which were taken also upon them.

This was enough to lodge them both in Newgate, where they had the misfortune to have some of their former sins brought to remembrance. Two other indictments being brought against them, and the facts being proved upon them, they were both condemned to die. They both pleaded their bellies, and were both voted quick with child, though my tutress was no more with child than I was.

I went frequently to see them and condole with them, expecting that it would be my turn next, but the place gave me so much horror, reflecting that it was the place of my unhappy birth and of my mother's misfortunes, that I could not bear it, so I was forced to leave off going to see them.

And oh, could I have but taken warning by their disasters I had been happy still! For I was yet free and had nothing brought against me, but it could not be – my measure was not yet filled up.

My comrade, having the brand of an old offender, was executed.* The young offender was spared, having obtained a reprieve, but lay starving a long while in prison, till at last she got her name into what they call a circuit pardon,* and so came off.

This terrible example of my comrade frighted me heartily, and for a good while I made no excursions. But one night, in the neighbourhood of my governess's house, they cried fire. My governess looked out, for we were all up, and cried immediately that such a gentlewoman's house was all of a light fire atop, and so indeed it was. Here she gives me a jog. "Now, child," says she, "there is a rare opportunity, the fire being so near, that you may go to it before the street is blocked up with the crowd." She presently gave me my cue. "Go, child," says she, "to the house, and run in and tell the lady, or anybody you see, that you come to help them, and that you came from such a gentlewoman" (that is, one of her acquaintance farther up the street). She gave me the like cue to the next house, naming another name that was also an acquaintance of the gentlewoman of the house.

Away I went, and, coming to the house, I found them all in confusion, you may be sure. I ran in, and, finding one of the maids: "Lord! Sweetheart," said I, "how came this dismal accident? Where is your mistress? And how does she do? Is she safe? And where are the children? I come from Madam —— to help you." Away runs the maid. "Madam, madam," says she, screaming as loud as she could yell, "here is a gentlewoman come from Madam —— to help us." The poor woman, half out of her wits, with a bundle under her arm and two little children, comes towards me. "Lord, madam," says I, "let me carry the poor children to madam – she desires you to send them. She'll take care of the poor lambs." And immediately I takes one of them out of her hand, and she lifts the other up into my arms. "Ay, do, for God's sake," says she, "carry them to her. Oh, thank her for her kindness." "Have you anything else to secure, madam?" says I. "She will take care of it." "Oh dear! Ay," says she. "God bless her, and thank her – take this bundle of plate and carry it to her too. Oh, she is a good woman. Oh, Lord, we are utterly ruined, utterly undone" – and away she runs from me out of her wits, and the maids after her, and away comes I with the two children and the bundle.

I was no sooner got into the street but I saw another woman come to me. "Oh," says she, "mistress" – in a piteous tone – "you will let fall the child. Come, this is a sad time – let me help you" – and immediately lays hold of my bundle to carry it for me. "No," says I, "if you will help me, take the child by the hand, and lead it for me but to the upper end of the street. I'll go with you and satisfy you for your pains."

She could not avoid going, after what I said, but the creature, in short, was one of the same business with me, and wanted nothing but the bundle. However, she went with me to the door, for she could not help it. When we were come there, I whispered her: "Go, child," said I, "I understand your trade – you may meet with purchase enough."

She understood me and walked off. I thundered at the door with the children, and as the people were raised before by the noise of the fire, I was soon let in, and I said, "Is madam awake? Pray tell her Mrs —— desires the favour of her to take the two children in. Poor lady, she will be undone – their house is all of a flame." They took the children in very civilly, pitied the family in distress, and away came I with my bundle. One of the maids asked me if I was not to leave the bundle too. I said, "No, sweetheart, 'tis to go to another place. It does not belong to them."

I was a great way out of the hurry now, and so I went on, clear of anybody's enquiry, and brought the bundle of plate, which was very considerable, straight home, and gave it to my old governess. She told me she would not look into it, but bade me go out again to look for more.

She gave me the like cue to the gentlewoman of the next house to that which was on fire, and I did my endeavour to go, but by this time the alarm of fire was so great, and so many engines playing, and the street so thronged with people, that I could not get near the house, whatever I could do. So I came back again to my governess's and, taking the bundle up into my chamber, I began to examine it. It is with horror that I tell what a treasure I found there – 'tis enough to say that besides most of the family plate, which was considerable, I found a gold chain, an old-fashioned thing, the locket of which was broken, so that I suppose it had not been used some years, but the gold was not the worse for that. Also a little box of burying rings,* the lady's wedding ring and some broken bits of old lockets of gold, a gold watch and a purse with about 24*l.* value in old pieces of gold coin, and several other things of value.

This was the greatest and the worst prize that ever I was concerned in, for indeed, though, as I have said above, I was hardened now beyond the power of all reflection in other cases, yet it really touched me to the very soul, when I looked into this treasure, to think of the poor, disconsolate gentlewoman who had lost so much by the fire besides, and who would think to be sure that she had saved her plate and best things – how she would be surprised and afflicted when she should find that she had been deceived, and should find that the person that took her children and her goods had not come, as was pretended, from the gentlewoman in the next street, but that the children had been put upon her without her own knowledge.

I say I confess the inhumanity of this action moved me very much and made me relent exceedingly, and tears stood in my eyes upon that subject, but with all my sense of its being cruel and inhuman, I could never find in my heart to make any restitution. The reflection wore off, and I began quickly to forget the circumstances that attended the taking them.

Nor was this all, for though by this job I was become considerably richer than before, yet the resolution I had formerly taken of leaving off this horrid trade when I had gotten a little more did not return, but I must still get further, and more. And the avarice joined so with the success that I had no more thoughts of coming to a timely alteration of life, though without it I could expect no safety, no tranquillity in the possession of what I had so wickedly gained – but a little more, and a little more, was the case still.

At length, yielding to the importunities of my crime, I cast off all remorse and repentance, and all the reflections on that head turned to no more than this: that I might perhaps come to have one booty more that might complete my desires. But though I certainly had that one booty, yet every hit looked towards another, and was so encouraging to me to go on with the trade that I had no gust to the thought of laying it down.

In this condition, hardened by success and resolving to go on, I fell into the snare in which I was appointed to meet with my last reward for this kind of life – but even this was not yet, for I met with several successful adventures more in this way of being undone.

I remained still with my governess, who was for a while really concerned for the misfortune of my comrade that had been hanged, and who it seems knew enough of my governess to have sent her the same way, and which made her very uneasy – indeed, she was in a very great fright.

It is true that when she was gone, and had not opened her mouth to tell what she knew, my governess was easy as to that point, and perhaps glad she was hanged, for it was in her power to have obtained a pardon at the expense of her friends. But, on the other hand, the loss of her, and the sense of her kindness in not making her market of what she knew, moved my governess to mourn very sincerely for her. I comforted her as well as I could, and she in return hardened me to merit more completely the same fate.

However, as I have said, it made me the more wary, and particularly I was very shy of shoplifting, especially among the mercers and drapers, who are a set of fellows that have their eyes very much about them. I made a venture or two among the lace folks and the milliners, and particularly at one shop, where I got notice of two young women who were newly set up, and had not been bred to the trade. There, I think I carried off a piece of bone lace worth six or seven pound, and a paper of thread – but this was but once. It was a trick that would not serve again.

It was always reckoned a safe job when we heard of a new shop, and especially when the people were such as were not bred to shops. Such may depend upon it that they will be visited once or twice at their beginning, and they must be very sharp indeed if they can prevent it.

I made another adventure or two, but they were but trifles too, though sufficient to live on. After this, nothing considerable offering for a good while, I began to think that I must give over the trade in earnest. But my governess, who was not willing to lose me and expected great things of me, brought me one day into company with a young woman and a fellow that went for her husband, though as it appeared afterwards she was not his wife, but they were partners, it seems, in the trade they carried on – and partners in something else too. In short, they robbed together, lay together, were taken together and, at last, were hanged together.

I came into a kind of league with these two, by the help of my governess, and they carried me out into three or four adventures, where I rather saw them commit some coarse and unhandy robberies in which nothing but a great stock of impudence on their side and gross negligence on the people's side who were robbed could have made them successful. So I resolved from that time forward to be very cautious how I adventured upon anything with them, and indeed when two or three unlucky projects were proposed by them, I declined the offer, and persuaded them against it. One time, they particularly proposed robbing a watchmaker of three gold watches which they had eyed in the daytime, and found the place where he laid them. One of them had so many keys of all kinds that he made no question to open the place where the watchmaker had laid them, and so we made a kind of an appointment. But when I came to look narrowly into the thing, I found they proposed breaking open the house – and this, as a thing out of my way, I would not embark in, so they went without me. They did get into the house by main force, and broke up the locked place where the watches were, but found but one of the gold watches, and a silver one, which they took, and got out of the house again very clear. But the family, being alarmed, cried out thieves, and the man was pursued and taken. The young woman had got off too, but unhappily was stopped at a distance, and the watches found upon her. And thus I had a second escape, for they were convicted, and both hanged, being old offenders, though but young people – as I said before, that they robbed together and lay together, so now they hanged together, and there ended my new partnership.

I began now to be very wary, having so narrowly escaped a scouring and having such an example before me. But I had a new tempter, who prompted me every day – I mean my governess. And now a prize presented – which, as it came by her management, so she expected a good share of the booty. There was a good quantity of Flanders lace lodged in a private house, where she had gotten intelligence of it, and Flanders lace, being then prohibited,* it was a good booty to any custom-house officer that could come at it. I had a full account from my governess, as well of the quantity as of the very place where it was concealed, and I went to a custom-house officer and told him I had such a discovery to make to him of such a quantity of lace, if he would assure me that I should have my due share of the reward. This was so just an offer that nothing could be fairer, so he agreed and, taking a constable, and me with him, we beset the house. As I told him I could go directly to the place, he left it to me, and the hole being very dark, I squeezed myself into it with a candle in my hand, and so reached the pieces out to him, taking care as I gave him some, so to secure as much about myself as I could conveniently dispose of. There was near

300*l.* worth of lace in the whole, and I secured about 50*l.* worth of it to myself. The people of the house were not owners of the lace, but a merchant who had entrusted them with it, so that they were not so surprised as I thought they would be.

I left the officer overjoyed with his prize, and fully satisfied with what he had got, and appointed to meet him at a house of his own directing, where I came after I had disposed of the cargo I had about me, of which he had not the least suspicion. When I came to him, he began to capitulate with me, believing I did not understand the right I had to a share in the prize, and would fain have put me off with twenty pound, but I let him know that I was not so ignorant as he supposed I was – and yet I was glad too that he offered to bring me to a certainty. I asked 100*l.*, and he rose up to 30*l.* I fell to 80*l.*, and he rose again to 40*l.* In a word, he offered 50*l.*, and I consented, only demanding a piece of lace, which I thought came to about eight or nine pound, as if it had been for my own wear, and he agreed to it, so I got 50*l.* in money paid me that same night, and made an end of the bargain. Nor did he ever know who I was or where to enquire for me – so that if it had been discovered that part of the goods were embezzled, he could have made no challenge upon me for it.

I very punctually* divided this spoil with my governess, and I passed with her from this time for a very dextrous manager in the nicest cases. I found that this last was the best and easiest sort of work that was in my way, and I made it my business to enquire out prohibited goods, and, after buying some, usually betrayed them. But none of these discoveries amounted to anything considerable – not like that I related just now. But I was willing to act safe, and was still cautious of running the great risks which I found others did, and in which they miscarried every day.

The next thing of moment was an attempt at a gentlewoman's gold watch. It happened in a crowd, at a meeting house, where I was in very great danger of being taken. I had full hold of her watch, but, giving a great jostle, as if somebody had thrust me against her, and in the juncture giving the watch a fair pull,

I found it would not come, so I let it go that moment, and cried out, as if I had been killed, that somebody had trod upon my foot, and that there was certainly pickpockets there, for somebody or other had given a pull at my watch – for you are to observe that on these adventures we always went very well dressed, and I had very good clothes on, and a gold watch by my side, as like a lady as other folks.

I had no sooner said so but the other gentlewoman cried out a pickpocket too, for somebody, she said, had tried to pull her watch away.

When I touched her watch, I was close to her, but when I cried out, I stopped as it were short, and, the crowd bearing her forward a little, she made a noise too, but it was at some distance from me, so that she did not in the least suspect me. But when she cried out a pickpocket, somebody cried, "Ay, and here has been another – this gentlewoman has been attempted too."

At that very instant, a little farther in the crowd, and very luckily too, they cried out a pickpocket again, and really seized a young fellow in the very fact. This, though unhappy for the wretch, was very opportunely for my case, though I had carried it off handsomely enough before. But now it was out of doubt, and all the loose part of the crowd ran that way, and the poor boy was delivered up to the rage of the street, which is a cruelty I need not describe, and which, however, they are always glad of, rather than to be sent to Newgate, where they lie often a long time, till they are almost perished, and sometimes they are hanged, and the best they can look for, if they are convicted, is to be transported.

This was a narrow escape to me, and I was so frighted that I ventured no more at gold watches a great while. There was indeed a great many concurring circumstances in this adventure which assisted to my escape, but the chief was that the woman whose watch I had pulled at was a fool – that is to say, she was ignorant of the nature of the attempt, which one would have thought she should not have been, seeing she was wise enough to fasten her watch so that it could not be slipped up. But she was in such a fright that she had no thought about her, for she, when she felt the pull, screamed out and pushed herself forward, and put all the people about her into disorder, but said not a word of her watch or of a pickpocket for at least two minutes' time, which was time enough for me, and to spare. For as I had cried out behind her, as I have said, and bore myself back in the crowd as she bore forward, there were several people – at least seven or eight, the throng being still moving on – that were got between me and her in that time, and then I crying out a pickpocket rather sooner than she, or at least as soon, she might as well be the person suspected as I, and the people were confused in their enquiry. Whereas had she, with a presence of mind needful on such an occasion, as soon as she felt the pull, not screamed out as she did, but turned immediately round and seized the next body that was behind her, she had infallibly taken me.

This is a direction not of the kindest sort to the fraternity, but 'tis certainly a key to the clue of a pickpocket's motions, and whoever can follow it will as certainly catch the thief as he will be sure to miss if he does not.

I had another adventure which puts this matter out of doubt, and which may be an instruction for posterity in the case of a pickpocket. My good old governess, to give a short touch at her history, though she had left off the trade, was, as I may say, born a pickpocket, and as I understood afterwards had run through all the several degrees of that art, and yet had never been taken but once, when she was so grossly detected that she was convicted and ordered to be transported. But, being a woman of a rare tongue, and withal having money in her pocket, she found means, the ship putting into Ireland for provisions, to get on shore there, where she lived and practised her old trade for some years – when, falling into another sort of bad company, she turned midwife and procuress, and played a hundred pranks there, which she gave me a little history of in confidence between us as we grew more intimate. And it was to this wicked creature that I owed all the art and dexterity I arrived to, in which there were few that ever went beyond me, or that practised so long without any misfortune.

It was after those adventures in Ireland, and when she was pretty well known in that country, that she left Dublin and came over to England – where, the time of her transportation being not expired, she left her former trade for fear of falling into bad hands again, for then she was sure to have gone to wreck. Here she set up the same trade she had followed in Ireland, in which she soon, by her admirable management and a good tongue, arrived to the height which I have already described, and indeed began to be rich, though her trade fell off again afterwards, as I have hinted before.

I mention thus much of the history of this woman here, the better to account for the concern she had in the wicked life I was now leading, into all the particulars of which she led me, as it were, by the hand, and gave me such directions, and I so well followed them, that I grew the greatest artist of my time, and worked myself out of every danger with such dexterity that when several more of my comrades ran themselves into Newgate presently, and by that time they had been half a year at the trade, I had now practised upwards of five year, and the people at Newgate did not so much as know me. They had heard much of me, indeed, and often expected me there, but I always got off, though many times in the extremest danger.

One of the greatest dangers I was now in was that I was too well known among the trade, and some of them whose hatred was owing rather to envy than any injury I had done them began to be angry that I should always escape when they were always catched and hurried to Newgate. These were they that gave me the name of Moll Flanders. For it was no more of affinity with my real name, or with any of the names I had ever gone by, than black is of kin to white, except that once, as before, I called myself Mrs Flanders when I sheltered myself in the Mint – but that these rogues never knew, nor could I ever learn how they came to give me the name, or what the occasion of it was.

I was soon informed that some of these who were gotten fast into Newgate had vowed to impeach me, and as I knew that two or three of them were but too able to do it, I was under a great concern about it, and kept within doors for a good while. But my governess – who I always made partner in my success, and who now played a sure game with me, for that she had a share of the gain and no share in the hazard – I say, my governess was something impatient of my leading such a useless, unprofitable life, as she called it, and she laid a new contrivance for my going abroad, and this was to dress me up in men's clothes, and so put me into a new kind of practice.

I was tall and personable, but a little too smooth-faced for a man. However, as I seldom went abroad but in the night, it did well enough, but it was a long time before I could behave in my new clothes – I mean as to my craft. It was impossible to be so nimble, so ready, so dextrous at these things in a dress so contrary to nature, and as I did everything clumsily, so I had neither the success or the easiness of escape that I had before, and I resolved to leave it off, but that resolution was confirmed soon after by the following accident.

As my governess had disguised me like a man, so she joined me with a man, a young fellow that was nimble enough at his business, and for about three weeks we did very well together. Our principal trade was watching shopkeepers' compters* and slipping off any kind of goods we could see carelessly laid anywhere, and we made several very good bargains, as we called them, at this work. And as we kept always together, so we grew very intimate, yet he never knew that I was not a man – nay, though I several times went home with him to his lodgings, according as our business directed, and four or five times lay with him all night. But our design lay another way, and it was absolutely necessary to me to conceal my sex from him, as appeared afterwards. The circumstances of our living, coming in late, and having such and such business to do as required that nobody should be trusted with coming into our lodgings, were such as made it impossible to me to refuse lying with him, unless I would have owned my sex, and as it was I effectually concealed myself.

But his ill and my good fortune soon put an end to this life, which I must own I was sick of too, on several other accounts. We had made several prizes in this new way of business, but the last would have been extraordinary. There was a shop in a certain street which had a warehouse behind it that looked into another street, the house making the corner of the turning.

Through the window of the warehouse we saw, lying on the counter, or show board which was just before it, five pieces of silks, besides other stuffs, and though it was almost dark, yet the people, being busy in the fore shop with customers, had not had time to shut up those windows, or else had forgot it.

This the young fellow was so overjoyed with that he could not restrain himself. It lay all within his reach, he said, and he swore violently to me that he would have it if he broke down the house for it. I dissuaded him a little, but saw there was no remedy, so he ran rashly upon it, slipped out a square out of the sash window dextrously enough and without noise, and got out four pieces of the silks, and came with them towards me, but was immediately pursued with a terrible clutter and noise. We were standing together indeed, but I had not taken any of the goods out of his hand, when I said to him hastily, "You are undone – fly, for God's sake!" He ran like lightning, and I too, but the pursuit was hotter after him, because he had the goods, than after me. He dropped two of the pieces, which stopped them a little, but the crowd increased and pursued us both. They took him soon after with the other two pieces upon him, and then the rest followed me. I ran for it and got into my governess's house, whither some quick-eyed people followed me so warmly as to fix me there. They did not immediately knock at the door, by which I got time to throw off my disguise and dress me in my own clothes. Besides, when they came there, my governess, who had her tale ready, kept her door shut, and called out to them and told them there was no man came in there. The people affirmed there did a man come in there, and swore they would break open the door.

My governess, not at all surprised, spoke calmly to them, told them they should very freely come and search her house if they would bring a constable, and let in none but such as the constable would admit, for it was unreasonable to let in a whole crowd. This they could not refuse, though they were a crowd, so a constable was fetched immediately, and she very freely opened the door. The constable kept the door, and the men he appointed searched the house, my governess going with them from room to room. When she came to my room she called to me, and said aloud: "Cousin, pray open the door. Here's some gentlemen that must come and look into your room."

I had a little girl with me, which was my governess's grandchild, as she called her, and I bade her open the door, and there sat I at work with a great litter of things about me, as if I had been at work all day, being myself quite undressed,* with only night clothes on my head and a loose morning gown wrapped about me. My governess made a kind of excuse for their disturbing me, telling me partly the occasion of it, and that she had no remedy but to open the doors to them and let them satisfy themselves, for all she could say to them would not satisfy them. I sat still, and bid them search the room if they pleased, for if there was anybody in the house, I was sure they was not in my room, and as for the rest of the house, I had nothing to say to that – I did not understand what they looked for.

Everything looked so innocent and so honest about me that they treated me civiller than I expected, but it was not till they had searched the room to a nicety, even under the bed, in the bed and everywhere else where it was possible anything could be hid. When they had done this and could find nothing, they asked my pardon for troubling me and went down.

When they had thus searched the house from bottom to top, and then from top to bottom, and could find nothing, they appeased the mob pretty well, but they carried my governess before the justice. Two men swore that they saw the man who they pursued go into her house. My governess rattled and made a great noise that her house should be insulted, and that she should be used thus for nothing; that if a man did come in, he might go out again presently, for ought she knew, for she was ready to make oath that no man had been within her doors all that day as she knew of, and that was very true indeed; that it might be indeed that as she was above stairs any fellow in a fright might find the door open and run in for shelter when he was pursued, but that she knew nothing of it – and if it had been so, he certainly went out again, perhaps at the other door, for she had another door into an alley, and so had made his escape and cheated them all.

This was indeed probable enough, and the justice satisfied himself with giving her an oath that she had not received or admitted any man into her house to conceal him, or protect or hide him from justice. This oath she might justly take, and did so, and so she was dismissed.

It is easy to judge what a fright I was in upon this occasion, and it was impossible for my governess ever to bring me to dress in that disguise again – for, as I told her, I should certainly betray myself.

My poor partner in this mischief was now in a bad case, for he was carried away before My Lord Mayor, and by His Worship committed to Newgate, and the people that took him were so willing, as well as able, to prosecute him that they offered themselves to enter into recognizances* to appear at the sessions and pursue the charge against him.

However, he got his indictment deferred, upon promise to discover his accomplices, and particularly the man that was concerned with him in this robbery, and he failed not to do his endeavour, for he gave in my name, who he called Gabriel Spencer, which was the name I went by to him, and here appeared the wisdom of my concealing my name and sex from him – which, if he had ever known, I had been undone.

He did all he could to discover this Gabriel Spencer. He described me; he discovered the place where he said I lodged, and, in a word, all the particulars that he could of my dwelling. But having concealed the main circumstances of my sex from him, I had a vast advantage, and he never could hear of me. He brought two or three families into trouble by his endeavouring to find me out, but they knew nothing of me, any more than that he had a fellow with him that they had seen but knew nothing of. And as for my governess, though she was the means of his coming to me, yet it was done at second hand, and he knew nothing of her.

This turned to his disadvantage, for, having promised discoveries but not being able to make it good, it was looked upon as a trifling with the justice of the City, and he was the more fiercely pursued by the shopkeepers who took him.

I was, however, terribly uneasy all this while, and that I might be quite out of the way, I went away from my governess's for a while. But not knowing whither to wander, I took a maidservant with me, and took the stagecoach to Dunstable to my old landlord and landlady, where I had lived so handsomely with my Lancashire husband. Here I told her a formal* story: that I expected my husband every day from Ireland, and that I had sent a letter to him that I would meet him at Dunstable at her house, and that he would certainly land, if the wind was fair, in a few days, so that I was come to spend a few days with them till he should come, for he would either come post or in the West Chester coach, I knew not which – but whichsoever it was, he would be sure to come to that house to meet me.

My landlady was mighty glad to see me, and my landlord made such a stir with me that if I had been a princess I could not have been better used, and here I might have been welcome a month or two if I had thought fit.

But my business was of another nature. I was very uneasy (though so well disguised that it was scarce possible to detect me) lest this fellow should somehow or other find me out, and though he could not charge me with this robbery, having persuaded him not to venture, and having also done nothing in it myself but run away, yet he might have charged me with other things, and have bought his own life at the expense of mine.

This filled me with horrible apprehensions. I had no recourse, no friend, no confidant but my old governess, and I knew no remedy but to put my life in her hands, and so I did, for I let her know where to send to me, and had several letters from her while I stayed here. Some of them almost scared me out of my wits, but at last she sent me the joyful news that he was hanged, which was the best news to me that I had heard a great while.

I had stayed here five weeks, and lived very comfortably indeed (the secret anxiety of my mind excepted), but when I received this letter I looked pleasantly again, and told my landlady that I had received a letter from my spouse in Ireland, that I had the good news of his being very well, but had the bad news that his business would not permit him to come away so soon as he expected, and so I was like to go back again without him.

My landlady complimented me upon the good news, however, that I had heard he was well. "For I have observed, madam," says she, "you han't been so pleasant as you used to be. You have been over head and ears in care for him, I dare say," says the good woman. "'Tis easy to be seen there's an alteration in you for the better," says she. "Well, I am sorry the esquire can't come yet," says my landlord. "I should have been heartily glad to have seen him, but I hope, when you have certain news of his coming, you'll take a step hither again, madam," says he. "You shall be very welcome whenever you please to come."

With all these fine compliments we parted, and I came merry enough to London, and found my governess as well pleased as I was. And now she told me she would never recommend any partner to me again, for she always found, she said, that I had the best luck when I ventured by myself. And so indeed I had, for I was seldom in any danger when I was by myself – or, if I was, I got out of it with more dexterity than when I was entangled with the dull measures of other people, who had perhaps less forecast and were more rash and impatient than I. For though I had as much courage to venture as any of them, yet I used more caution before I undertook a thing, and had more presence of mind when I was to bring myself off.

I have often wondered even at my own hardiness another way: that when all my companions were surprised and fell so suddenly into the hand of justice, and that I so narrowly escaped, yet I could not all that while enter into one serious resolution to leave off this trade – and especially considering that I was now very far from being poor, that the temptation of necessity, which is generally the introduction of all such wickedness, was now removed. For I had near 500*l.* by me in ready money, on which I might have lived very well if I had thought fit to have retired. But, I say, I had not so much as the least inclination to leave off – no, not so much as I had before when I had but 200*l.* beforehand, and when I had no such frightful examples before my eyes as these were. From hence 'tis evident to me that when once we are hardened in crime, no fear can affect us, no example give us any warning.

I had indeed one comrade whose fate went very near me for a good while, though I wore it off too in time. That case was indeed very unhappy. I had made a prize of a piece of very good damask in a mercer's shop, and went clear off myself, but had conveyed the piece to this companion of mine when we went out of the shop, and she went one way and I went another. We had not been long out of the shop but the mercer missed his piece of stuff, and sent his messengers, one one way and one another, and they presently seized her that had the piece with the damask upon her. As for me, I had very luckily stepped into a house where there was a lace chamber, up one pair of stairs, and had the satisfaction, or the terror indeed, of looking out of the window upon the noise they made and seeing the poor creature dragged away in triumph to the justice, who immediately committed her to Newgate.

I was careful to attempt nothing in the lace chamber, but tumbled their goods pretty much to spend time, then bought a few yards of edging and paid for it, and came away very sad-hearted indeed for the poor woman, who was in tribulation for what I only had stolen.

Here again my old caution stood me in good stead – namely, that though I often robbed with these people, yet I never let them know who I was or where I lodged. Nor could they ever find out my lodging, though they often endeavoured to watch me to it. They all knew me by the name of Moll Flanders, though even some of them rather believed I was she than knew me to be so. My name was public among them indeed, but how to find me out they knew not, nor so much as how to guess at my quarters, whether they were at the east end of the town or the west, and this wariness was my safety upon all these occasions.

I kept close a great while upon the occasion of this woman's disaster. I knew that if I should do anything that should miscarry, and should be carried to prison, she would be there, and ready to witness against me, and perhaps save her life at my expense. I considered that I began to be very well known by name at the Old Bailey, though they did not know my face, and that if I should fall into their hands, I should be treated as an old offender. And for this reason I was resolved to see what this poor creature's fate should be before I stirred abroad, though several times in her distress I conveyed money to her for her relief.

At length she came to her trial. She pleaded she did not steal the things, but that one Mrs Flanders, as she heard her called (for she did not know her), gave the bundle to her after they came out of the shop, and bade her carry it home to her lodging. They asked her where this Mrs Flanders was, but she could not produce her, neither could she give the least account of me. And the mercer's men swearing positively that she was in the shop when the goods were stolen, that they immediately missed them and pursued her, and found them upon her – thereupon the jury brought her in guilty. But the court – considering that she really was not the person that stole the goods, an inferior assistant, and that it was very possible she could not find out this Mrs Flanders, meaning me, though it would save her life, which indeed was true – I say, considering all this, they allowed her to be transported, which was the utmost favour she could obtain, only that the court told her that if she could in the mean time produce the said Mrs Flanders, they would intercede for her pardon – that is to say, if she could find me out, and hang me, she should not be transported. This I took care to make impossible to her, and so she was shipped off in pursuance of her sentence a little while after.

I must repeat it again: that the fate of this poor woman troubled me exceedingly, and I began to be very pensive, knowing that I was really the instrument of her disaster. But the preservation of my own life, which was so evidently in danger, took off all my tenderness, and, seeing she was not put to death, I was very easy at her transportation, because she was then out of the way of doing me any mischief, whatever should happen.

The disaster of this woman was some months before that of the last recited story, and was indeed partly the occasion of my governess proposing to dress me up in men's clothes, that I might go about unobserved, as indeed I did. But I was soon tired of that disguise, as I have said, for indeed it exposed me to too many difficulties.

I was now easy as to all fear of witnesses against me, for all those that had either been concerned with me or that knew me by the name of Moll Flanders were either hanged or transported, and if I should have had the misfortune to be taken, I might call myself anything else as well as Moll Flanders, and no old sins could be placed to my account. So I began to run a-tick* again, with the more freedom, and several successful adventures I made, though not such as I had made before.

We had at that time another fire happened not a great way off from the place where my governess lived, and I made an attempt there, as before, but as I was not soon enough before the crowd of people came in, and could not get to the house I aimed at, instead of a prize I got a mischief which had almost put a period to my life and all my wicked doings together. For the fire being very furious, and the people in a great fright in removing their goods and throwing them out of window, a wench from out of a window threw a feather bed just upon me. It is true, the bed being soft it broke no bones, but as the weight was great, and made greater by the fall, it beat me down and laid me dead for a while. Nor did the people concern themselves much to deliver me from it, or to recover me at all, but I lay like one dead and neglected a good while, till somebody going to remove the bed out of the way helped me up. It was indeed a wonder the people in the house had not thrown other goods out after it, and which might have fallen upon it, and then I had been inevitably killed, but I was reserved for further afflictions.

This accident, however, spoilt my market for that time, and I came home to my governess very much hurt and bruised, and frighted to the last degree, and it was a good while before she could set me upon my feet again.

It was now a merry time of the year, and Bartholomew Fair* was begun. I had never made any walks that way, nor was the common part of the fair of much advantage to me, but I took a turn this year into the cloisters, and, among the rest, I fell into one of the raffling shops.* It was a thing of no great consequence to me, nor did I expect to make much of it, but there came a gentleman extremely well dressed, and very rich, and as 'tis frequent to talk to everybody in those shops, he singled me out, and was very particular with me. First he told me he would put in for me to raffle, and did so, and some small matter coming to his lot, he presented it to me – I think it was a feather muff. Then he continued to keep talking to me with a more than common appearance of respect, but still very civil and much like a gentleman.

He held me in talk so long, till at last he drew me out of the raffling place to the shop door, and then to take a walk in the cloister, still talking of a thousand things cursorily without anything to the purpose. At last, he told me that without compliment he was charmed with my company, and asked me if I durst trust myself in a coach with him. He told me he was a man of honour, and would not offer anything to me unbecoming him as such. I seemed to decline it awhile, but suffered myself to be importuned a little, and then yielded.

I was at a loss in my thoughts to conclude at first what this gentleman designed, but I found afterwards he had had some drink in his head, and that he was not very unwilling to have some more. He carried me in the coach to the Spring Garden at Knightsbridge,* where we walked in the gardens, and he treated me very handsomely, but I found he drank very freely. He pressed me also to drink, but I declined it.

Hitherto he kept his word with me, and offered me nothing amiss. We came away in the coach again, and he brought me into the streets, and by this time it was near ten o'clock at night, and he stopped the coach at a house where it seems he was acquainted, and where they made no scruple to show us upstairs into a room with a bed in it. At first I seemed to be unwilling to go up, but after a few words I yielded to that too, being indeed willing to see the end of it, and in hopes to make something of it at last. As for the bed, etc., I was not much concerned about that part.

Here he began to be a little freer with me than he had promised, and I by little and little yielded to everything, so that, in a word, he did what he pleased with me. I need say no more. All this while he drank freely too, and about one in the morning we went into the coach again. The air and the shaking of the coach made the drink he had get more up in his head than it was before, and he grew uneasy in the coach, and was for acting over again what he had been doing before. But as I thought my game now secure, I resisted him, and brought him to be a little still, which had not lasted five minutes but he fell fast asleep.

I took this opportunity to search him to a nicety. I took a gold watch, with a silk purse of gold, his fine, full-bottom periwig and silver-fringed gloves, his sword and fine snuffbox, and, gently opening the coach door, stood ready to jump out while the coach was going on. But the coach stopping in the narrow street beyond Temple Bar* to let another coach pass, I got softly out, fastened the door again, and gave my gentleman and the coach the slip both together, and never heard more of them.

This was an adventure indeed unlooked for, and perfectly unde-signed by me, though I was not so past the merry part of life as to forget how to behave when a fop so blinded by his appetite should not know an old woman from a young. I did not, indeed, look so old as I was by ten or twelve year, yet I was not a young wench of seventeen, and it was easy enough to be distinguished. There is nothing so absurd, so surfeiting, so ridiculous as a man heated by wine in his head and a wicked gust in his inclination together. He is in the possession of two devils at once, and can no more govern himself by his reason than a mill can grind without water. His vice tramples upon all that was in him that had any good in it, if any such thing there was – nay, his very sense is blinded by its own rage, and he acts absurdities even in his view: such as drinking more when he is drunk already, picking up a common woman without regard to what she is or who she is, whether sound or rotten, clean or unclean, whether ugly or handsome, whether old or young, and so blinded as not really to distinguish. Such a man is worse than lunatic – prompted by his vicious corrupted head he no more knows what he is doing than this wretch of mine knew when I picked his pocket of his watch and his purse of gold.

These are the men of whom Solomon says, "They go like an ox to the slaughter, till a dart strikes through their liver"* – an admirable description, by the way, of the foul disease,* which is a poisonous, deadly contagion mingling with the blood, whose centre or fountain is in the liver. From whence, by the swift circu-lation of the whole mass, that dreadful, nauseous plague strikes immediately through his liver, and his spirits are infected, his vitals stabbed through as with a dart.

It is true this poor, unguarded wretch was in no danger from me, though I was greatly apprehensive at first of what danger I might be in from him, but he was really to be pitied in one respect: that he seemed to be a good sort of a man in himself, a gentleman that had no harm in his design, a man of sense and of a fine behav-iour – a comely, handsome person, a sober solid countenance, a charming beautiful face and everything that could be agreeable

– only had unhappily had some drink the night before, had not been in bed, as he told me when we were together, was hot, and his blood fired with wine, and in that condition his reason, as it were asleep, had given him up.

As for me, my business was his money and what I could make of him, and after that, if I could have found out any way to have done it, I would have sent him safe home to his house, and to his family, for 'twas ten to one but he had an honest, virtuous wife and innocent children that were anxious for his safety, and would have been glad to have gotten him home and have taken care of him till he was restored to himself. And then with what shame and regret would he look back upon himself? How would he reproach himself with associating himself with a whore picked up in the worst of all holes, the cloister, among the dirt and filth of all the town? How would he be trembling for fear he had got the pox, for fear a dart had struck through his liver, and hate himself every time he looked back upon the madness and brutality of his debauch? How would he, if he had any principles of honour, as I verily believe he had – I say, how would he abhor the thought of giving any ill distemper, if he had it, as for ought he knew he might, to his modest and virtuous wife, and thereby sowing the contagion in the lifeblood of his posterity?

Would such gentlemen but consider the contemptible thoughts which the very women they are concerned with in such cases as these have of them, it would be a surfeit to them. As I said above, they value not the pleasure; they are raised by no inclination to the man; the passive jade thinks of no pleasure but the money, and when he is, as it were, drunk in the ecstasies of his wicked pleasure, her hands are in his pockets searching for what she can find there, and of which he can no more be sensible in the moment of his folly than he can forethink of it when he goes about it.

I knew a woman that was so dextrous with a fellow, who indeed deserved no better usage, that while he was busy with her another way, conveyed his purse with twenty guineas in it out of his fob pocket, where he had put it for fear of her, and put another purse with gilded counters* in it into the room of it. After he had done, he says to her, "Now, han't you picked my pocket?" She jested with him, and told him she supposed he had not much to lose. He put his hand to his fob, and with his fingers felt that his purse was there, which fully satisfied him, and so she brought off his money. And this was a trade with her: she kept a sham gold watch – that is, a watch of silver gilt and a purse of counters in her pocket to be ready on all such occasions, and I doubt not practised it with success.

I came home with this last booty to my governess, and really when I told her the story, it so affected her that she was hardly able to forbear tears to think how such a gentleman ran a daily risk of being undone every time a glass of wine got into his head.

But as to the purchase I got, and how entirely I stripped him, she told me it pleased her wonderfully. "Nay, child," says she, "the usage may, for ought I know, do more to reform him than all the sermons that ever he will hear in his life." And if the remainder of the story be true, so it did.

I found the next day she was wonderful inquisitive about this gentleman. The description I had given her of him, his dress, his person, his face, everything concurred to make her think of a gentleman whose character she knew, and family too. She mused a while, and I going still on with the particulars, she starts up – says she, "I'll lay a hundred pound I know the gentleman."

"I am sorry you do," says I, "for I would not have him exposed on any account in the world. He has had injury enough already by me, and I would not be instrumental to do him any more." "No, no," says she, "I will do him no injury, I assure you, but you may let me satisfy my curiosity a little, for if it is he, I warrant you I find it out." I was a little startled at that, and told her with an apparent concern in my face that by the same rule he might find me out, and then I was undone. She returned warmly, "Why, do you think I will betray you, child? No, no," says she, "not for all he is worth in the world. I have kept your counsel in worse things than these – sure you may trust me in this." So I said no more at that time.

She laid her scheme another way, and without acquainting me of it, but she was resolved to find it out, if possible. So she goes to a certain friend of hers who was acquainted in the family that she guessed at, and told her friend she had some extraordinary business with such a gentleman (who, by the way, was no less than a baronet, and of a very good family), and that she knew not how to come at him without somebody to introduce her. Her friend promised her very readily to do it, and accordingly goes to the house to see if the gentleman was in town.

The next day she comes to my governess and tells her that Sir —— was at home, but that he had met with a disaster and was very ill, and there was no speaking with him. "What disaster?" says my governess hastily, as if she was surprised at it. "Why," says her friend, "he had been at Hampstead to visit a gentleman of his acquaintance, and as he came back again he was set upon and robbed, and having got a little drink too, as they suppose, the rogues abused him, and he is very ill." "Robbed!" says my governess. "And what did they take from him?" "Why," says her friend, "they took his gold watch, and his gold snuffbox, his fine periwig, and what money he had in his pocket, which was considerable, to be sure, for Sir —— never goes without a purse of guineas about him."

"Pshaw!" says my old governess jeering. "I warrant you he has got drunk now and got a whore, and she has picked his pocket, and so he comes home to his wife and tells her he has been robbed. That's an old sham – a thousand such tricks are put upon the poor women every day."

"Fie!" says her friend. "I find you don't know Sir ——. Why, he is as civil a gentleman – there is not a finer man, nor a soberer, graver, modester person in the whole city. He abhors such things – there's nobody that knows him will think such a thing of him." "Well, well," says my governess, "that's none of my business. If it was, I warrant I should find there was something of that kind in it. Your modest men in common opinion are sometimes no better than other people, only they keep a better character – or, if you please, are the better hypocrites."

"No, no," says her friend, "I can assure you, Sir —— is no hypocrite. He is really an honest, sober gentleman, and he has certainly been robbed." "Nay," says my governess, "it may be he has – it is no business of mine, I tell you. I only want to speak with him. My business is of another nature." "But," says her friend, "let your business be of what nature it will, you cannot see him yet, for he is not fit to be seen, for he is very ill, and bruised very much." "Ay," says my governess. "Nay, then he has fallen into bad hands to be sure." And then she asked gravely, "Pray, where is he bruised?" "Why, in his head," says her friend, "and one of his hands, and his face, for they used him barbarously." "Poor gentleman," says my governess. "I must wait, then, till he recovers" – and adds, "I hope it will not be long, for I want very much to speak with him."

Away she comes to me and tells me this story. "I have found out your fine gentleman, and a fine gentleman he was," says she, "but mercy on him, he is in a sad pickle now. I wonder what the Devil you have done to him. Why, you have almost killed him." I looked at her with disorder enough. "I killed him!" says I. "You must mistake the person. I am sure I did nothing to him – he was very well when I left him," said I, "only drunk and fast asleep." "I know nothing of that," says she, "but he is in a sad pickle now." And so she told me all that her friend had said to her. "Well, then," says I, "he fell into bad hands after I left him, for I am sure I left him safe enough."

About ten days after, or a little more, my governess goes again to her friend to introduce her to this gentleman. She had enquired other ways in the mean time, and found that he was about again, if not abroad again, so she got leave to speak with him.

She was a woman of an admirable address, and wanted nobody to introduce her. She told her tale much better than I shall be able to tell it for her, for she was a mistress of her tongue, as I have said already. She told him that she came, though a stranger, with a single design of doing him a service, and he should find she had no other end in it – that as she came purely on so friendly an account, she begged a promise from him that if he did not accept what she should officiously* propose, he would not take ill that she meddled with what was not her business. She assured him that as what she had to say was a secret that belonged to him only, so, whether he accepted her offer or not, it should remain a secret to all the world, unless he exposed it himself. Nor should his refusing her service in it make her so little show her respect as to do him the least injury, so that he should be entirely at liberty to act as he thought fit.

He looked very shy at first, and said he knew nothing that related to him that required much secrecy; that he had never done any man any wrong, and cared not what anybody might say of him; that it was no part of his character to be unjust to anybody, nor could he imagine in what any man could render him any service; but that if it was so disinterested a service as she said, he could not take it ill from anyone that they should endeavour to serve him – and so, as it were, left her at liberty either to tell him or not to tell him, as she thought fit.

She found him so perfectly indifferent that she was almost afraid to enter into the point with him. But, however, after some other circumlocutions, she told him that by a strange and unaccountable accident she came to have a particular knowledge of the late unhappy adventure he had fallen into, and that in such a manner that there was nobody in the world but herself and him that were acquainted with it – no, not the very person that was with him.

He looked a little angrily at first. "What adventure?" said he. "Why, sir," said she, "of your being robbed coming from Knightsbr... – Hampstead, sir, I should say," says she. "Be not surprised, sir," says she, "that I am able to tell you every step you took that day from the cloister in Smithfield to the Spring Garden at Knightsbridge, and thence to the —— in the Strand, and how you were left asleep in the coach afterwards. I say, let not this surprise you, for, sir, I do not come to make a booty of you. I ask nothing of you, and I assure you the woman that was with you knows nothing who you are, and never shall. And yet perhaps I may serve you further still, for I did not come barely to let you know that I was informed of these things, as if I wanted a bribe to conceal them – assure yourself, sir," said she, "that whatever you think fit to do or say to me, it shall be all a secret as it is, as much as if I were in my grave."

He was astonished at her discourse, and said gravely to her, "Madam, you are a stranger to me, but it is very unfortunate that you should be let into the secret of the worst action of my life, and a thing that I am so justly ashamed of that the only satisfaction of it to me was that I thought it was known only to God and my own conscience." "Pray, sir," says she, "do not reckon the discovery of it to me to be any part of your misfortune. It was a thing, I believe, you were surprised into, and perhaps the woman used some art to prompt you to it. However, you will never find any just cause," said she, "to repent that I came to hear of it. Nor can your own mouth be more silent in it than I have been, and ever shall be."

"Well," says he, "but let me do some justice to the woman too. Whoever she is, I do assure you she prompted me to nothing – she rather declined me. It was my own folly and madness that brought me into it all – ay, and brought her into it too. I must give her her due so far. As to what she took from me, I could expect no less from her in the condition I was in, and to this hour I know not whether she robbed me or the coachman. If she did it, I forgive her, and I think all gentlemen that do so should be used in the same manner. But I am more concerned for some other things than I am for all that she took from me."

My governess now began to come into the whole matter, and he opened himself freely to her. First, she said to him, in answer to what he had said about me, "I am glad, sir, you are so just to the person that you were with. I assure you she is a gentlewoman, and no woman of the town, and however you prevailed with her so far as you did, I am sure 'tis not her practice. You ran a great venture indeed, sir, but if that be any part of your care, I am persuaded you may be perfectly easy, for I dare assure you no man has touched her, before you, since her husband, and he has been dead now almost eight year."

It appeared that this was his grievance, and that he was in a very great fright about it. However, when my governess said this to him, he appeared very well pleased, and said, "Well, madam, to be plain with you, if I was satisfied of that, I should not so much value what I lost. For as to that, the temptation was great, and perhaps she was poor and wanted it." "If she had not been poor, Sir ——," says my governess, "I assure you she would never have yielded to you, and as her poverty first prevailed with her to let you do as you did, so the same poverty prevailed with her to pay herself at last, when she saw you was in such a condition that if she had not done it, perhaps the next coachman or chairman* might have done it."

"Well," says he, "much good may it do her. I say again, all the gentlemen that do so ought to be used in the same manner, and then they would be cautious of themselves. I have no more concern about it, but on the score which you hinted at before, madam." Here he entered into some freedoms with her on the subject of what passed between us, which are not so proper for a woman to write, and the great terror that was upon his mind with relation to his wife, for fear he should have received any injury from me and should communicate it further; and asked her at last if she could not procure him an opportunity to speak with me. My governess gave him further assurances of my being a woman clear from any such thing, and that he was as entirely safe in that respect as he was with his own lady. But as for seeing me, she said it might be of dangerous consequence – but, however, that she would talk with me, and let him know my answer, using at the same time some arguments to persuade him not to desire it, and that it could be of no service to him, seeing she hoped he had no desire to renew a correspondence with me, and that on my account it was a kind of putting my life in his hands.

He told her he had a great desire to see me – that he would give her any assurances that were in his power not to take any advantages of me, and that in the first place he would give me a general release from all demands of any kind. She insisted how it might tend to a further divulging the secret, and might in the end be injurious to him, entreating him not to press for it, so at length he desisted.

They had some discourse upon the subject of the things he had lost, and he seemed to be very desirous of his gold watch, and told her if she could procure that for him, he would willingly give as much for it as it was worth. She told him she would endeavour to procure it for him and leave the valuing it to himself.

Accordingly, the next day she carried the watch, and he gave her thirty guineas for it, which was more than I should have been able to make of it, though it seems it cost much more. He spoke something of his periwig, which it seems cost him threescore guineas, and his snuffbox, and in a few days more she carried them too, which obliged him very much, and he gave her thirty more. The next day I sent him his fine sword and cane gratis, and demanded nothing of him, but I had no mind to see him, unless it had been so that he might be satisfied I knew who he was, which he was not willing to.

Then he entered into a long talk with her of the manner how she came to know all this matter. She formed a long tale of that part: how she had it from one that I had told the whole story to, and that was to help me dispose of the goods, and this confidant brought the things to her, she being by profession a pawnbroker; and she, hearing of His Worship's disaster, guessed at the thing in general; that having gotten the things into her hands, she had resolved to come and try as she had done. She then gave him repeated assurances that it should never go out of her mouth, and though she knew the woman very well, yet she had not let her know, meaning me, anything of it – that is to say, who the person was, which by the way was false, but, however, it was not to his damage, for I never opened my mouth of it to anybody.

I had a great many thoughts in my head about my seeing him again, and was often sorry that I had refused it. I was persuaded that if I had seen him and let him know that I knew him, I should have made some advantage of him, and perhaps have had some maintenance from him, and though it was a life wicked enough, yet it was not so full of danger as this I was engaged in. However, those thoughts wore off, and I declined seeing him again, for that time, but my governess saw him often, and he was very kind to her, giving her something almost every time he saw her. One time in particular she found him very merry, and as she thought he had some wine in his head, and he pressed her again very earnestly to let him see that woman that, as he said, had bewitched him so that night, my governess, who was from the beginning for my seeing him, told him he was so desirous of it that she could almost yield to it, if she could prevail upon me – adding that if he would please to come to her house in the evening she would endeavour it, upon his repeated assurances of forgetting what was past.

Accordingly, she came to me and told me all the discourse. In short, she soon biased me to consent in a case which I had some regret in my mind for declining before. So I prepared to see him. I dressed me to all the advantage possible, I assure you, and for the first time used a little art – I say for the first time, for I had never yielded to the baseness of paint before, having always had vanity enough to believe I had no need of it.

At the hour appointed he came, and as she observed before, so it was plain still that he had been drinking, though very far from what we call being in drink. He appeared exceeding pleased to see me, and entered into a long discourse with me upon the old affair. I begged his pardon very often for my share of it, protested I had not any such design when first I met him – that I had not gone out with him but that I took him for a very civil gentleman, and that he made me so many promises of offering no uncivility to me.

He alleged the wine he drank, and that he scarce knew what he did, and that if it had not been so I should never have let him take the freedom with me that he had done. He protested to me that he never touched any woman but me since he was married to his wife, and it was a surprise upon him, complimented me upon being so particularly agreeable to him, and the like, and talked so much of that kind till I found he had talked himself almost into a temper to do the same thing over again. But I took him up short: I protested I had never suffered any man to touch me since my husband died, which was near eight year. He said he believed it to be so truly, and added that madam had intimated as much to him, and that it was his opinion of that part which made him desire to see me again, and that since he had once broke in upon his virtue with me and found no ill consequences, he could be safe in venturing there again. And so in short it went on to what I expected, and to what will not bear relating.

My old governess had foreseen it, as well as I, and therefore led him into a room which had not a bed in it, and yet had a chamber within it which had a bed, whither we withdrew for the rest of the night. And, in short, after some time being together, he went to bed and lay there all night. I withdrew, but came again undressed in the morning before it was day, and lay with him the rest of the time.

Thus, you see, having committed a crime once is a sad handle to the committing of it again, whereas all the regret and reflections wear off when the temptation renews itself. Had I not yielded to see him again, the corrupt desire in him had worn off, and 'tis very probable he had never fallen into it with anybody else, as I really believe he had not done before.

When he went away, I told him I hoped he was satisfied he had not been robbed again. He told me he was satisfied in that point, and could trust me again, and, putting his hand in his pocket, gave me five guineas, which was the first money I had gained that way for many years.

I had several visits of the like kind from him, but he never came into a settled way of maintenance, which was what I would have been best pleased with. Once, indeed, he asked me how I did to live. I answered him pretty quick that I assured him I had never taken that course that I took with him, but that indeed I worked at my needle, and could just maintain myself – that sometimes it was as much as I was able to do, and I shifted hard enough.

He seemed to reflect upon himself that he should be the first person to lead me into that which he assured me he never intended to do himself, and it touched him a little, he said, that he should be the cause of his own sin, and mine too. He would often make just reflections also upon the crime itself, and upon the particular circumstances of it, with respect to himself: how wine introduced the inclinations, how the Devil led him to the place and found out an object to tempt him, and he made the moral always himself.

When these thoughts were upon him he would go away, and perhaps not come again in a month's time or longer, but then as the serious part wore off, the lewd part would wear in, and then he came prepared for the wicked part. Thus we lived for some time. Though he did not keep, as they call it, yet he never failed doing things that were handsome and sufficient to maintain me without working, and, which was better, without following my old trade.

But this affair had its end too, for after about a year I found that he did not come so often as usual, and at last he left it off altogether without any dislike or bidding adieu. And so there was an end of that short scene of life, which added no great store to me, only to make more work for repentance.

However, during this interval, I confined myself pretty much at home. At least, being thus provided for, I made no adventures – no, not for a quarter of a year after he left me. But then, finding the fund fail and being loath to spend upon the main stock, I began to think of my old trade, and to look abroad into the street again, and my first step was lucky enough.

I had dressed myself up in a very mean habit, for as I had several shapes to appear in I was now in an ordinary stuff gown, a blue apron and a straw hat, and I placed myself at the door of the Three Cups Inn in St John Street. There were several carriers used the inn, and the stagecoaches for Barnet, for Totteridge and other towns that way stood always in the street in the evening, when they prepared to set out, so that I was ready for anything that offered for either one or other. The meaning was this: people come frequently with bundles and small parcels to those inns, and call for such carriers or coaches as they want to carry them into the country, and there generally attends women, porters' wives or daughters, ready to take in such things for their respective people that employ them.

It happened very oddly that I was standing at the inn gate, and a woman that had stood there before, and which was the porter's wife belonging to the Barnet stagecoach, having observed me, asked if I waited for any of the coaches. I told her yes, I waited for my mistress, that was coming to go to Barnet. She asked me who was my mistress, and I told her any madam's name that came next me. But as it seemed, I happened upon a name, a family of which name lived at Hadley, just beyond Barnet.

I said no more to her, or she to me, a good while, but by and by, somebody calling her at a door a little way off, she desired me that if anybody called for the Barnet coach, I would step and call her at the house, which it seems was an alehouse. I said yes very readily, and away she went.

She was no sooner gone but comes a wench and a child, puffing and sweating, and asks for the Barnet coach. I answered presently, "Here." "Do you belong to the Barnet coach?" says she. "Yes, sweetheart," said I. "What do ye want?" "I want room for two passengers," says she. "Where are they, sweetheart?" said I. "Here's this girl – pray let her go into the coach," says she, "and I'll go and fetch my mistress." "Make haste then, sweetheart," says I, "for we may be full, else." The maid had a great bundle under arm, so she put the child into the coach, and I said, "You had best put your bundle into the coach too." "No," says she, "I am afraid somebody should slip it away from the child." "Give it me, then," said I, "and I'll take care of it." "Do then," says she, "and be sure you take care of it." "I'll answer for it," said I, "if it were for twenty-pound value." "There, take it then," says she, and away she goes.

As soon as I had got the bundle and the maid was out of sight, I goes on towards the alehouse where the porter's wife was, so that if I had met her, I had then only been going to give her the bundle and to call her to her business, as if I was going away and could stay no longer. But as I did not meet her I walked away, and, turning into Charterhouse Lane, made off through Charterhouse Yard, into Long Lane, then crossed into Bartholomew Close, so into Little Britain and through the Bluecoat Hospital* into Newgate Street.

To prevent my being known, I pulled off my blue apron and wrapped the bundle in it, which before was made up in a piece of painted calico, and very remarkable. I also wrapped up my straw hat in it, and so put the bundle upon my head – and it was very well that I did thus, for, coming through the Bluecoat Hospital, who should I meet but the wench that had given me the bundle to hold. It seems she was going with her mistress, who she had been gone to fetch to the Barnet coaches.

I saw she was in haste, and I had no business to stop her. So away she went, and I brought my bundle safe home to my governess. There was no money, nor plate or jewels in the bundle, but a very good suit of Indian damask, a gown and petticoat, a laced head and ruffles of very good Flanders lace, and some linen and other things, such as I knew very well the value of.

This was not indeed my own invention, but was given me by one that had practised it with success, and my governess liked it extremely. And, indeed, I tried it again several times, though never twice near the same place, for the next time I tried it in Whitechapel just by the corner of Petticoat Lane, where the coaches stand that go out to Stratford and Bow and that side of the country, and another time at the Flying Horse, without Bishopsgate, where the Cheston* coaches then lay, and I had always the good luck to come off with some booty.

Another time I placed myself at a warehouse by the waterside, where the coasting vessels from the north come, such as from Newcastle upon Tyne, Sunderland and other places. Here, the warehouse being shut, comes a young fellow with a letter, and he wanted a box and a hamper that was come from Newcastle upon Tyne. I asked him if he had the marks of it, so he shows me the letter, by virtue of which he was to ask for it, and which gave an account of the contents, the box being full of linen, and the hamper full of glassware. I read the letter and took care to see the name and the marks, the name of the person that sent the goods, the name of the person that they were sent to – then I bade the messenger come in the morning, for that the warehouse keeper would not be there any more that night.

Away went I, and, getting materials in a public house, I wrote a letter from Mr John Richardson of Newcastle to his dear cousin Jemey Cole in London, with an account that he had sent by such a vessel (for I remembered all the particulars to a tittle)* so many pieces of huckaback linen,* so many ells* of Dutch holland and the like, in a box, and a hamper of flint glasses from Mr Henzell's glasshouse,* and that the box was marked "I.C. No. 1" and the hamper was directed by a label on the cording.

About an hour after, I came to the warehouse, found the warehouse keeper and had the goods delivered me without any scruple – the value of the linen being about twenty-two pound.

I could fill up this whole discourse with the variety of such adventures which daily invention directed to, and which I managed with the utmost dexterity, and always with success.

At length – as when does the pitcher come safe home that goes so very often to the well? – I fell into some small broils, which though they could not affect me fatally, yet made me known, which was the worst thing next to being found guilty that could befall me.

I had taken up the disguise of a widow's dress. It was without any real design in view, but only waiting for anything that might offer, as I often did. It happened that while I was going along the street in Covent Garden, there was a great cry of "Stop thief, stop thief!" Some artists had, it seems, put a trick upon a shopkeeper, and, being pursued, some of them fled one way and some another. And one of them was, they said, dressed up in widow's weeds, upon which the mob gathered about me, and some said I was the person, others said no. Immediately came the mercer's journeyman, and he swore aloud I was the person, and so seized on me. However, when I was brought back by the mob to the mercer's shop, the master of the house said freely that I was not the woman that was in his shop, and would have let me go immediately, but another fellow said gravely, "Pray stay till Mr ———" (meaning the journeyman) "comes back, for he knows her." So they kept me by force near half an hour. They had called a constable, and he stood in the shop as my jailer, and in talking with the constable I enquired where he lived and what trade he was. The man not apprehending in the least what happened afterwards, readily told me his name and trade, and where he lived, and told me as a jest that I might be sure to hear of his name when I came to the Old Bailey.

Some of the servants likewise used me saucily, and had much ado to keep their hands off of me. The master, indeed, was civiller to me than they, but he would not yet let me go, though he owned he could not say I was in his shop before.

I began to be a little surly with him, and told him I hoped he would not take it ill if I made myself amends upon him in a more legal way another time, and desired I might send for friends to see me have right done me. No, he said, he could give no such liberty – I might ask it when I came before the Justice of Peace, and, seeing I threatened him, he would take care of me in the mean time, and would lodge me safe in Newgate. I told him it was his time now, but it would be mine by and by, and governed my passion as well as I was able. However, I spoke to the constable to call me a porter, which he did, and then I called for pen, ink and paper, but they would let me have none. I asked the porter his name, and where he lived, and the poor man told it me very willingly. I bade him observe and remember how I was treated there – that he saw I was detained there by force. I told him I should want his evidence in another place, and it should not be the worse for him to speak. The porter said he would serve me with all his heart. "But, madam," says he, "let me hear them refuse to let you go, then I may be able to speak the plainer."

With that I spoke aloud to the master of the shop, and said, "Sir, you know in your own conscience that I am not the person you look for, and that I was not in your shop before. Therefore, I demand that you detain me here no longer, or tell me the reason of your stopping me." The fellow grew surlier upon this than before, and said he would do neither till he thought fit. "Very well," said I to the constable and to the porter. "You will be pleased to remember this, gentlemen, another time." The porter said, "Yes, madam," and the constable began not to like it, and would have persuaded the mercer to dismiss him and let me go, since, as he said, he owned I was not the person. "Good sir," says the mercer to him tauntingly, "are you a Justice of Peace, or a constable? I charged you with her – pray do you do your duty." The constable told him, a little moved, but very handsomely, "I know my duty, and what I am, sir – I doubt you hardly know what you are doing." They had some other hard words, and in the mean time the journeymen, impudent and unmanly to the last degree, used me barbarously, and one of them, the same that first seized upon me, pretended he would search me, and began to lay hands on me. I spit in his face, called out to the constable and bade him take notice of my usage. "And pray, Mr Constable," said I, "ask that villain's name" – pointing to the man. The constable reproved him decently, told him that he did not know what he did, for he knew that his master acknowledged I was not the person that was in his shop. "And," says the constable, "I am afraid your master is bringing himself and me too into trouble, if this gentlewoman comes to prove who she is and where she was, and it appears that she is not the woman you pretend to." "Damn her," says the fellow again, with an impudent, hardened face. "She is the lady, you may depend upon it. I'll swear she is the same body that was in the shop, and that I gave the pieces of satin that is lost into her own hand. You shall hear more of it when Mr William and Anthony" – those were other journeymen – "come back. They will know her again as well as I."

Just as the insolent rogue was talking thus to the constable, comes back Mr William and Mr Anthony, as he called them, and a great rabble with them, bringing along with them the true widow that I was pretended to be. And they came sweating and blowing into the shop, and with a great deal of triumph dragging the poor creature in a most butcherly manner up towards their master, who was in the back shop, and cried out aloud, "Here's the widow, sir – we have catched her at last." "What do ye mean by that?" says the master. "Why, we have her already – there she sits," says he, "and Mr —— says he can swear this is she." The other man, who they called Mr Anthony, replied, "Mr —— may say what he will and swear what he will, but this is the woman, and there's the remnant of satin she stole – I took it out of her clothes with my own hand."

I sat still now, and began to take a better heart, but smiled and said nothing. The master looked pale. The constable turned about and looked at me. "Let 'em alone, Mr Constable," said I. "Let 'em go on." The case was plain and could not be denied, so the constable was charged with the right thief, and the mercer told me very civilly he was sorry for the mistake, and hoped I would not take it ill – that they had so many things of this nature put upon them every day that they could not be blamed for being very sharp in doing themselves justice. "Not take it ill, sir!" said I. "How can I take it well? If you had dismissed me when your insolent fellow seized on me in the street and brought me to you, and when you yourself acknowledged I was not the person, I would have put it by and not taken it ill, because of the many ill things I believe you have put upon you daily. But your treatment of me since has been insufferable, and especially that of your servant – I must and will have reparation for that."

Then he began to parley with me – said he would make me any reasonable satisfaction, and would fain have had me told him what it was I expected. I told him I should not be my own judge – the law should decide it for me – and as I was to be carried before a magistrate, I should let him hear there what I had to say. He told me there was no occasion to go before the justice now – I was at liberty to go where I pleased; and so, calling to the constable, told him he might let me go, for I was discharged. The constable said calmly to him, "Sir, you asked me just now if I knew whether I was a constable or a justice, and bade me do my duty, and charged me with this gentlewoman as a prisoner. Now, sir, I find you do not understand what is my duty, for you would make me a justice indeed, but I must tell you it is not in my power. I may keep a prisoner when I am charged with him, but 'tis the law and the magistrate alone that can discharge that prisoner. Therefore 'tis a mistake, sir – I must carry her before a justice now whether you think well of it or not." The mercer was very high with the constable at first, but the constable happening to be not a hired officer, but a good substantial kind of man – I think he was a corn chandler – and a man of good sense, stood to his business, would not discharge me without going to a Justice of the Peace – and I insisted upon it too. When the mercer saw that, "Well," says he to the constable, "you may carry her where you please. I have nothing to say to her." "But, sir," says the constable, "you will go with us, I hope, for 'tis you that charged me with her." "No, not I," says the mercer. "I tell you I have nothing to say to her." "But pray, sir, do," says the constable. "I desire it of you for your own sake, for the justice can do nothing without you." "Prithee, fellow," says the mercer, "go about your business. I tell you I have nothing to say to the gentlewoman. I charge you in the King's name to dismiss her." "Sir," says the constable, "I find you don't know what it is to be a constable. I beg of you don't oblige me to be rude to you." "I think I need not – you are rude enough already," says the mercer. "No, sir," says the constable, "I am not rude. You have broken the peace in bringing an honest woman out of the street when she was about her lawful occasion,* confining her in your shop and ill-using her here by your servants. And now can you say I am rude to you? I think I am civil to you in not commanding or charging you in the King's name to go with me, and charging every man I see that passes your door to aid and assist me in carrying you by force. This you cannot but know I have power to do, and yet I forbear it, and once more entreat you to go with me." Well, he would not for all this, and gave the constable ill language. However, the constable kept his temper, and would not be provoked, and then I put in and said, "Come, Mr Constable, let him alone. I shall find ways enough to fetch him before a magistrate, I don't fear that. But there's the fellow," says I. "He was the man that seized on me as I was innocently going along the street, and you are a witness of his violence with me since. Give me leave to charge you with him, and carry him before the justice." "Yes, madam," says the constable, and, turning to the fellow, "Come, young gentleman," says he to the journeyman, "you must go along with us. I hope you are not above the constable's power, though your master is."

The fellow looked like a condemned thief and hung back, then looked at his master, as if he could help him. And he, like a fool, encouraged the fellow to be rude, and he truly resisted the constable, and pushed him back with a good force when he went to lay hold on him, at which the constable knocked him down and called out for help, and immediately the shop was filled with people, and the constable seized the master and man, and all his servants.

The first ill consequence of this fray was that the woman they had taken, who was really the thief, made off and got clear away in the crowd, and two others that they had stopped also – whether they were really guilty or not, that I can say nothing to.

By this time, some of his neighbours, having come in and, upon enquiry, seeing how things went, had endeavoured to bring the hot-brained mercer to his senses, and he began to be convinced that he was in the wrong. And so at length we went all very quietly before the justice, with a mob of about five hundred people at our heels, and all the way I went I could hear the people ask what was the matter, and others reply and say a mercer had stopped a gentlewoman instead of a thief, and had afterwards taken the thief, and now the gentlewoman had taken the mercer and was carrying him before the justice. This pleased the people strangely, and made the crowd increase, and they cried out as they went, "Which is the rogue? Which is the mercer?" – and especially the women. Then, when they saw him, they cried out, "That's he, that's he!" – and every now and then came a good dab of dirt at him. And thus we marched a good while, till the mercer thought fit to desire the constable to call a coach to protect himself from the rabble, so we rode the rest of the way, the constable and I, and the mercer and his man.

When we came to the justice, which was an ancient gentleman in Bloomsbury, the constable giving first a summary account of the matter, the justice bade me speak and tell what I had to say. And first he asked my name, which I was very loath to give, but there was no remedy, so I told him my name was Mary Flanders, that I was a widow – my husband, being a sea captain, died on a voyage to Virginia. And some other circumstances I told which he could never contradict, and that I lodged at present in town with such a person, naming my governess, but that I was preparing to go over to America, where my husband's effects lay, and that I was going that day to buy some clothes to put myself into second mourning,* but had not yet been in any shop, when that fellow, pointing to the mercer's journeyman, came rushing upon me with such fury as very much frighted me, and carried me back to his master's shop, where, though his master acknowledged I was not the person, yet he would not dismiss me, but charged a constable with me.

Then I proceeded to tell how the journeyman treated me, how they would not suffer me to send for any of my friends, how afterwards they found the real thief and took the very goods they had lost upon her, and all the particulars as before.

Then the constable related his case: his dialogue with the mercer about discharging me, and at last his servants refusing to go with him when I had charged him with him, and his master encouraging him to do so, and at last his striking the constable, and the like, all as I have told it already.

The justice then heard the mercer and his man. The mercer, indeed, made a long harangue of the great loss they have daily by lifters and thieves – that it was easy for them to mistake, and that when he found it, he would have dismissed me, etc., as above. As to the journeyman, he had very little to say, but that he pretended other of the servants told him that I was really the person.

Upon the whole, the justice first of all told me very courteously I was discharged – that he was very sorry that the mercer's man should in his eager pursuit have so little discretion as to take up an innocent person for a guilty person; that if he had not been so unjust as to detain me afterwards, he believed I would have forgiven the first affront; that, however, it was not in his power to award me any reparation for anything, other than by openly reproving them, which he should do. But he supposed I would apply to such methods as the law directed. In the mean time he would bind him over.

But as to the breach of the peace committed by the journeyman, he told me he should give me some satisfaction for that, for he should commit him to Newgate for assaulting the constable, and for assaulting of me also.

Accordingly, he sent the fellow to Newgate for that assault, and his master gave bail, and so we came away. But I had the satisfaction of seeing the mob wait upon them both as they came out, hallooing and throwing stones and dirt at the coaches they rode in, and so I came home to my governess.

After this hustle, coming home and telling my governess the story, she falls a-laughing at me. "Why are you merry?" says I. "The story has not so much laughing room in it as you imagine. I am sure I have had a great deal of hurry and fright too, with a pack of ugly rogues." "Laugh!" says my governess. "I laugh, child, to see what a lucky creature you are. Why, this job will be the best bargain to you that ever you made in your life, if you manage it well. I warrant you," says she, "you shall make the mercer pay you 500*l.* for damages, besides what you shall get of the journeyman."

I had other thoughts of the matter than she had, and especially because I had given in my name to the Justice of Peace, and I knew that my name was so well known among the people at Hicks Hall,* the Old Bailey and such places that if this cause came to be tried openly and my name came to be enquired into, no court would give much damages for the reputation of a person of such a character. However, I was obliged to begin a prosecution in form, and accordingly my governess found me out a very creditable sort of a man to manage it, being an attorney of very good business and of good reputation – and she was certainly in the right of this, for had she employed a pettifogging hedge solicitor, or a man not known and not in good reputation, I should have brought it to but little.

I met this attorney and gave him all the particulars at large, as they are recited above, and he assured me it was a case, as he said, that would very well support itself, and that he did not question but that a jury would give very considerable damages on such an occasion. So, taking his full instructions, he began the prosecution, and the mercer, being arrested, gave bail. A few days after his giving bail, he comes with his attorney to my attorney, to let him know that he desired to accommodate the matter – that it was all carried on in the heat of an unhappy passion; that his client, meaning me, had a sharp, provoking tongue; that I used them ill, gibing at them and jeering them even while they believed me to be the very person, and that I had provoked them, and the like.

My attorney managed as well on my side: made them believe I was a widow of fortune, that I was able to do myself justice, and had great friends to stand by me, too, who had all made me promise to sue to the utmost, and that if it cost me a thousand pound, I would be sure to have satisfaction, for that the affronts I had received were insufferable.

However, they brought my attorney to this: that he promised he would not blow the coals; that if I inclined to an accommodation, he would not hinder me, and that he would rather persuade me to peace than to war, for which they told him he should be no loser. All which he told me very honestly, and told me that if they offered him any bribe, I should certainly know it. But upon the whole he told me very honestly that if I would take his opinion, he would advise me to make it up with them, for that as they were in a great fright and were desirous above all things to make it up, and knew that, let it be what it would, they would be allotted to bear all the costs of the suit, he believed they would give me freely more than any jury or court of justice would give upon a trial. I asked him what he thought they would be brought to. He told me he could not tell as to that, but he would tell me more when I saw him again.

Some time after this, they came again to know if he had talked with me. He told them he had, that he found me not so averse to an accommodation as some of my friends were, who resented the disgrace offered me, and set me on – that they blowed the coals in secret, prompting me to revenge, or to do myself justice, as they called it, so that he could not tell what to say to it. He told them he would do his endeavour to persuade me, but he ought to be able to tell me what proposal they made. They pretended they could not make any proposal, because it might be made use of against them, and he told them that by the same rule he could not make any offers, for that might be pleaded in abatement of what damages a jury might be inclined to give. However, after some discourse and mutual promises that no advantage should be taken on either side by what was transacted then, or at any other of those meetings, they came to a kind of a treaty, but so remote, and so wide from one another, that nothing could be expected from it – for my attorney demanded 500*l*. and charges, and they offered 50*l*. without charges. So they broke off, and the mercer proposed to have a meeting with me myself, and my attorney agreed to that very readily.

My attorney gave me notice to come to this meeting in good clothes, and with some state, that the mercer might see I was something more than I seemed to be that time they had me. Accordingly, I came in a new suit of second mourning, according to what I had said at the justice's. I set myself out too, as well as a widow's dress in second mourning would admit. My governess also furnished me with a good pearl necklace, that shut in behind with a locket of diamonds, which she had in pawn. And I had a very good gold watch by my side, so that, in a word, I made a very good figure, and as I stayed till I was sure they were come, I came in a coach to the door with my maid with me.

When I came into the room, the mercer was surprised. He stood up and made his bow, which I took a little notice of, and but a little, and went and sat down where my own attorney had pointed to me to sit, for it was his house. After a little while, the mercer said he did not know me again, and began to make some compliments his way. I told him I believed he did not know me at first, and that if he had, I believed he would not have treated me as he did.

He told me he was very sorry for what had happened, and that it was to testify the willingness he had to make all possible reparation that he had appointed this meeting; that he hoped I would not carry things to extremity, which might be not only too great a loss to him, but might be the ruin of his business and shop, in which case I might have the satisfaction of repaying an injury with an injury ten times greater – but that I would then get nothing, whereas he was willing to do me any justice that was in his power, without putting himself or me to the trouble or charge of a suit at law.

I told him I was glad to hear him talk so much more like a man of sense than he did before; that it was true: acknowledgement in most cases of affronts was counted reparation sufficient, but this had gone too far to be made up so; that I was not revengeful – nor did I seek his ruin or any man's else, but that all my friends were unanimous not to let me so far neglect my character as to adjust a thing of this kind without a sufficient reparation of honour; that to be taken up for a thief was such an indignity as could not be put up; that my character was above being treated so by any that knew me – but because, in my condition of a widow, I had been for some time careless of myself and negligent of myself, I might be taken for such a creature, but that for the particular usage I had from him afterwards. And then I repeated all as before – it was so provoking I had scarce patience to repeat it.

Well, he acknowledged all, and was mighty humble indeed. He made proposals very handsome: he came up to a hundred pounds, and to pay all the law charges, and added that he would make me a present of a very good suit of clothes. I came down to three hundred pounds, and I demanded that I should publish an advertisement of the particulars in the common newspapers.

This was a clause he never could comply with. However, at last he came up, by good management of my attorney, to 150*l.* and a suit of black silk clothes, and there I agreed and, as it were at my attorney's request, complied with it, he paying my attorney's bill and charges, and gave us a good supper into the bargain.

When I came to receive the money, I brought my governess with me, dressed like an old duchess, and a gentleman very well dressed, who we pretended courted me, but I called him "cousin", and the lawyer was only to hint privately to him that this gentleman courted the widow.

He treated us handsomely indeed, and paid the money cheerfully enough, so that it cost him 200*l.* in all, or rather more. At our last meeting, when all was agreed, the case of the journeyman came up, and the mercer begged very hard for him, told me he was a man that had kept a shop of his own and been in good business, had a wife and several children, and was very poor; that he had nothing to make satisfaction with, but he should come to beg my pardon on his knees, if I desired it as openly as I pleased. I had no spleen at the saucy rogue, nor were his submissions anything to me, since there was nothing to be got by him, so I thought it was as good to throw that in generously as not. So I told him I did not desire the ruin of any man, and therefore at his request I would forgive the wretch – it was below me to seek any revenge.

When we were at supper, he brought the poor fellow in to make acknowledgement, which he would have done with as much mean humility as his offence was with insulting haughtiness and pride, in which he was an instance of a complete baseness of spirit – imperious, cruel and relentless when uppermost and in prosperity, abject and low-spirited when down in affliction. However, I abated his cringes, told him I forgave him and desired he might withdraw, as if I did not care for the sight of him, though I had forgiven him.

I was now in good circumstances indeed, if I could have known my time for leaving off, and my governess often said I was the richest of the trade in England, and so I believe I was, for I had 700*l.* by me in money, besides clothes, rings, some plate and two gold watches – and all of them stolen, for I had innumerable jobs, besides these I have mentioned. Oh, had I even now had the grace of repentance, I had still leisure to have looked back upon my follies and have made some reparation! But the satisfaction I was to make for the public mischiefs I had done was yet left behind, and I could not forbear going abroad again, as I called it now, any more than I could when my extremity really drove me out for bread.

It was not long after the affair with the mercer was made up that I went out in an equipage quite different from any I had ever appeared in before. I dressed myself like a beggarwoman, in the coarsest and most despicable rags I could get, and I walked about peering and peeping into every door and window I came near – and, indeed, I was in such a plight now that I knew as ill how to behave in as ever I did in any. I naturally abhorred dirt and rags – I had been bred up tight and cleanly, and could be no other, whatever condition I was in, so that this was the most uneasy disguise to me that ever I put on. I said presently to myself that this would not do, for this was a dress that everybody was shy and afraid of, and I thought everybody looked at me as if they were afraid I should come near them, lest I should take something from them, or afraid to come near me lest they should get something from me. I wandered about all the evening the first time I went out, and made nothing of it, but came home again wet, draggled and tired. However, I went out again the next night, and then I met with a little adventure, which had like to have cost me dear. As I was standing near a tavern door, there comes a gentleman on horseback and lights at the door, and, wanting to go into the tavern, he calls one of the drawers* to hold his horse. He stayed pretty long in the tavern, and the drawer heard his master call, and thought he would be angry with him. Seeing me stand by him, when he called to me, "Here, woman," says he, "hold this horse awhile, till I go in. If the gentleman comes, he'll give you something." "Yes," says I, and takes the horse, and walks off with him very soberly, and carried him to my governess.

This had been a booty to those that had understood it, but never was poor thief more at a loss to know what to do with anything that was stolen, for when I came home, my governess was quite confounded, and what to do with the creature we neither of us knew. To send him to a stable was doing nothing, for it was certain that public notice would be given in the *Gazette*,* and the horse described, so that we durst not go to fetch it again.

All the remedy we had for this unlucky adventure was to go and set up the horse at an inn, and send a note by a porter to the tavern that the gentleman's horse that was lost such a time was left at such an inn, and that he might be had there; that the poor woman that held him, having led him about the street, not being able to lead him back again, had left him there. We might have waited till the owner had published and offered a reward, but we did not care to venture the receiving the reward.

So this was a robbery and no robbery, for little was lost by it and nothing was got by it, and I was quite sick of going out in a beggar's dress – it did not answer at all, and besides, I thought it was ominous and threatening.

While I was in this disguise, I fell in with a parcel of folks of a worse kind than any I ever sorted with, and I saw a little into their ways too. These were coiners of money, and they made some very good offers to me as to profit, but the part they would have had me have embarked in was the most dangerous part – I mean that of the very working the dye, as they call it, which, had I been taken, had been certain death, and that at a stake – I say, to be burnt to death at a stake. So that though I was to appearance but a beggar and they promised mountains of gold and silver to me to engage, yet it would not do. It is true, if I had been really a beggar or had been desperate as when I began, I might perhaps have closed with it, for what care they to die that can't tell how to live? But at present this was not my condition – at least, I was for no such terrible risks as those. Besides, the very thoughts of being burnt at a stake struck terror into my very soul, chilled my blood and gave me the vapours to such a degree as I could not think of it without trembling.

This put an end to my disguise, too, for as I did not like the proposal, so I did not tell them so, but seemed to relish it, and promised to meet again. But I durst see them no more, for if I had seen them and not complied, though I had declined it with the greatest assurances of secrecy in the world, they would have gone near to have murdered me, to make sure work and make themselves easy, as they call it. What kind of easiness that is, they may best judge that understand how easy men are that can murder people to prevent danger.

This and horse-stealing were things quite out of my way, and I might easily resolve I would have no more to say to them. My business seemed to lie another way, and though it had hazard enough in it too, yet it was more suitable to me, and what had more of art in it, more room to escape and more chances for a-coming off if a surprise should happen.

I had several proposals made also to me about that time to come into a gang of housebreakers, but that was a thing I had no mind to venture at neither, any more than I had at the coining trade. I offered to go along with two men and a woman that made it their business to get into houses by stratagem, and with them I was willing enough to venture, but there was three of them already, and they did not care to part, nor I to have too many in a gang, so I did not close with them, but declined them, and they paid dear for their next attempt.

But at length I met with a woman that had often told me what adventures she had made, and with success, at the waterside, and I closed with her, and we drove on our business pretty well. One day we came among some Dutch people at St Katherine's,* where we went on pretence to buy goods that were privately got on shore. I was two or three times in a house where we saw a good quantity of prohibited goods, and my companion once brought away three pieces of Dutch black silk that turned to good account, and I had my share of it. But in all the journeys I made by myself, I could not get an opportunity to do anything, so I laid it aside, for I had been so often that they began to suspect something, and were so shy that I saw nothing was to be done.

This baulked me a little, and I resolved to push at something or other, for I was not used to come back so often without purchase. So, the next day I dressed myself up fine and took a walk to the other end of the town. I passed through the Exchange in the Strand,* but had no notion of finding anything to do there, when on a sudden I saw a great clutter in the place, and all the people, shopkeepers as well as others, standing up and staring, and what should it be but some great duchess come into the Exchange, and they said the Queen was coming. I set myself close up to a shop side with my back to the compter, as if to let the crowd pass by, when, keeping my eye upon a parcel of lace which the shopkeeper was showing to some ladies that stood by me, the shopkeeper and her maid were so taken up with looking to see who was a-coming and what shop they would go to, that I found means to slip a paper of lace into my pocket and come clear off with it, so the lady milliner paid dear enough for her gaping after the Queen.

I went off from the shop as if driven along by the throng, and, mingling myself with the crowd, went out at the other door of the Exchange, and so got away before they missed their lace. And because I would not be followed, I called a coach and shut myself up in it. I had scarce shut the coach doors up but I saw the milliner's maid and five or six more come running out into the street and crying out as if they were frighted. They did not cry "Stop thief!", because nobody ran away, but I could hear the word "robbed" and "lace" two or three times, and saw the wench wringing her hands, and run staring, to and again, like one scared. The coachman that had taken me up was getting up into the box, but was not quite up, so that the horses had not begun to move, so that I was terrible uneasy, and I took the packet of lace and laid it ready to have dropped it out at the flap of the coach, which opens before just behind the coachman. But to my great satisfaction, in less than a minute the coach began to move – that is to say, as soon as the coachman had got up and spoken to his horses. So he drove away without any interruption, and I brought off my purchase, which was worth near twenty pound.

The next day I dressed me up again, but in quite different clothes, and walked the same way again, but nothing offered till I came into St James's Park, where I saw abundance of fine ladies in the park, walking in the Mall,* and among the rest there was a little miss, a young lady of about twelve or thirteen years old, and she had a sister, as I suppose it was, with her, that might be about nine year old. I observed the biggest had a fine gold watch on and a good necklace of pearl, and they had a footman in livery with them, but as it is not usual for the footmen to go behind the ladies in the Mall, so I observed the footman stopped at their going into the Mall, and the biggest of the sisters spoke to him, which I perceived was to bid him be just there when they came back.

When I heard her dismiss the footman, I stepped up to him and asked him what little lady that was, and held a little chat with him about what a pretty child it was with her, and how genteel and well carriaged the lady, the eldest, would be – how womanish and how grave. And the fool of a fellow told me presently who she was, that she was Sir Thomas ——'s eldest daughter of Essex, and that she was a great fortune – that her mother was not come to town yet, but she was with Sir William ——'s lady of Suffolk, at her lodgings in Suffolk Street, and a great deal more: that they had a maid and a woman to wait on them, besides Sir Thomas's coach, the coachman and himself, and that young lady was governess to the whole family as well here as at home too – and, in short, told me abundance of things enough for my business.

I was very well dressed, and had my gold watch, as well as she. So I left the footman, and I puts myself in a rank with* this young lady, having stayed till she had taken one double turn in the Mall, and was going forward again. By and by, I saluted her by her name, with the title of Lady Betty. I asked her when she heard from her father, when My Lady her mother would be in town and how she did.

I talked so familiarly to her of her whole family that she could not suspect but that I knew them all intimately. I asked her why she would come abroad without Mrs Chime with her (that was the name of her woman) to take care of Mrs Judith – that was her sister. Then I entered into a long chat with her about her sister, what a fine little lady she was, and asked her if she had learnt French and a thousand such little things to entertain her, when on a sudden we see the guards come, and the crowd run to see the King* go by to the Parliament house.

The ladies ran all to the side of the Mall, and I helped My Lady to stand upon the edge of the boards on the side of the Mall, that she might be high enough to see, and took the little one and lifted her quite up – during which I took care to convey the gold watch so clean away from the Lady Betty that she never felt it, nor missed it, till all the crowd was gone and she was gotten into the middle of the Mall among the other ladies.

I took my leave of her in the very crowd, and said to her, as if in haste, "Dear Lady Betty, take care of your little sister" – and so the crowd did, as it were, thrust me away from her, and that I was obliged unwillingly to take my leave.

The hurry in such cases is immediately over, and the place clear as soon as the King is gone by, but as there is always a great running and clutter just as the King passes, so having dropped the two little ladies and done my business with them without any miscarriage, I kept hurrying on among the crowd, as if I ran to see the King, and so I got before the crowd and kept so till I came to the end of the Mall, when, the King going on toward the Horse Guards,* I went forward to the passage which went then through against the lower end of the Haymarket, and there I bestowed a coach upon myself and made off, and I confess I have not yet been so good as my word, viz. to go and visit My Lady Betty.

I was once of the mind to venture staying with Lady Betty till she missed the watch, and so have made a great outcry about it with her, and have got her into her coach, and put myself in the coach with her, and have gone home with her – for she appeared so fond of me, and so perfectly deceived by my so readily talking to her of all her relations and family, that I thought it was very easy to push the thing further, and to have got at least the necklace of pearl. But when I considered that, though the child would not perhaps have suspected me, other people might, and that if I was searched I should be discovered, I thought it was best to go off with what I had got and be satisfied.

I came accidentally afterwards to hear that when the young lady missed her watch, she made a great outcry in the park, and sent her footman up and down to see if he could find me out, she having described me so perfectly that he knew presently that it was the same person that had stood and talked so long with him and asked him so many questions about them. But I was gone far enough out of their reach before she could come at her footman to tell him the story.

I made another adventure after this, of a nature different from all I had been concerned in yet, and this was at a gaming house near Covent Garden.

I saw several people go in and out, and I stood in the passage a good while with another woman with me, and, seeing a gentleman go up that seemed to be of more than ordinary fashion, I said to him, "Sir, pray, don't they give women leave to go up?" "Yes, madam," says he, "and to play, too, if they please." "I mean so, sir," said I, and with that he said he would introduce me if I had a mind, so I followed him to the door, and he looking in: "There, madam," says he, "are the gamesters, if you have a mind to venture." I looked in and said to my comrade, aloud, "Here's nothing but men – I won't venture among them" – at which one of the gentlemen cried out, "You need not be afraid, madam – here's none but fair gamesters. You are very welcome to come and set* what you please." So I went a little nearer and looked on, and some of them brought me a chair, and I sat down and saw the box and dice go round a pace.* Then I said to my comrade, "The gentlemen play too high for us – come, let us go."

The people were all very civil, and one gentleman in particular encouraged me, and said, "Come, madam, if you please to venture – if you dare trust me, I'll answer for it you shall have nothing put upon you here." "No, sir," said I, smiling. "I hope the gentlemen would not cheat a woman." But still I declined venturing, though I pulled out a purse with money in it, that they might see I did not want money.

After I had sat awhile, one gentleman said to me, jeering, "Come, madam, I see you are afraid to venture for yourself. I always had good luck with the ladies – you shall set for me, if you won't set for yourself." I told him, "Sir, I should be very loath to lose your money" – though I added, "I am pretty lucky too, but the gentlemen play so high that I dare not indeed venture my own."

"Well, well," says he, "there's ten guineas, madam – set them for me." So I took his money and set, himself looking on. I ran out nine of the guineas by one and two at a time, and then, the box coming to the next man to me, my gentleman gave me ten guineas more, and made me set five of them at once, and the gentleman who had the box threw out, so there was five guineas of his money again. He was encouraged at this, and made me take the box, which was a bold venture. However, I held the box so long that I had gained him his whole money, and had a good handful of guineas in my lap – and, which was the better luck, when I threw out, I threw but at one or two of those that had set me, and so went off easy.

When I was come this length, I offered the gentleman all the gold, for it was his own, and so would have had him play for himself, pretending I did not understand the game well enough. He laughed, and said if I had but good luck, it was no matter whether I understood the game or no, but I should not leave off. However, he took out the fifteen guineas that he had put in at first and bade me play with the rest. I would have told them to see how much I had got, but he said, "No, no, don't tell them – I believe you are very honest, and 'tis bad luck to tell them" – so I played on.

I understood the game well enough, though I pretended I did not, and played cautiously. It was to keep a good stock in my lap, out of which I every now and then conveyed some into my pocket, but in such a manner and at such convenient times as I was sure he could not see it.

I played a great while, and had very good luck for him, but the last time I held the box, they set me high, and I threw boldly at all. I held the box till I gained near fourscore guineas, but lost above half of it back at the last throw, so I got up, for I was afraid I should lose it all back again, and said to him, "Pray come, sir, now, and take it and play for yourself – I think I have done pretty well for you." He would have had me play on, but it grew late, and I desired to be excused. When I gave it up to him, I told him I hoped he would give me leave to tell it now, that I might see what I had gained and how lucky I had been for him. When I told them, there was threescore and three guineas. "Ay," says I, "if it had not been for that unlucky throw I had got you a hundred guineas." So I gave him all the money, but he would not take it till I had put my hand into it and taken some for myself, and bid me please myself. I refused it, and was positive I would not take it myself – if he had a mind to anything of that kind, it should be all his own doings.

The rest of the gentlemen, seeing us striving, cried "Give it her all", but I absolutely refused that. Then one of them said, "Damn ye, Jack, half it with her – don't you know you should be always upon even terms with the ladies?" So, in short, he divided it with me, and I brought away thirty guineas, besides about forty-three which I had stole privately, which I was sorry for afterwards, because he was so generous.

Thus I brought home seventy-three guineas, and let my old governess see what good luck I had at play. However, it was her advice that I should not venture again, and I took her counsel, for I never went there any more. For I knew as well as she, if the itch of play came in, I might soon lose that, and all the rest of what I had got.

Fortune had smiled upon me to that degree, and I had thriven so much, and my governess too, for she always had a share with me, that really the old gentlewoman began to talk of leaving off while we were well and being satisfied with what we had got. But I know not what fate guided me – I was as backward to it now as she was when I proposed it to her before, and so in an ill hour we gave over the thoughts of it for the present, and, in a word, I grew more hardened and audacious than ever, and the success I had made my name as famous as any thief of my sort ever had been at Newgate and in the Old Bailey.

I had sometimes taken the liberty to play the same game over again, which is not according to practice – which, however, succeeded not amiss. But generally I took up new figures, and contrived to appear in new shapes every time I went abroad.

It was now a rumbling time of the year, and the gentlemen being most of them gone out of town, Tunbridge and Epsom* and such places were full of people, but the city was thin, and I thought our trade felt it a little, as well as others, so that at the latter end of the year I joined myself with a gang, who usually go every year to Stourbridge Fair, and from thence to Bury Fair, in Suffolk.* We promised ourselves great things here, but when I came to see how things were, I was weary of it presently, for except mere picking of pockets, there was little worth meddling with. Neither, if a booty had been made, was it so easy carrying it off, nor was there such a variety of occasion for business in our way as in London. All that I made of the whole journey was a gold watch at Bury Fair and a small parcel of linen at Cambridge, which gave me an occasion to take leave of the place. It was an old bite,* and I thought might do with a country shopkeeper, though in London it would not.

I bought at a linen draper's shop – not in the fair, but in the town of Cambridge – as much fine holland and other things as came to about seven pound. When I had done, I bade them be sent to such an inn, where I had purposely taken up my being the same morning, as if I was to lodge there that night.

I ordered the draper to send them home to me, about such an hour, to the inn where I lay, and I would pay him his money. At the time appointed the draper sends the goods, and I placed one of our gang at the chamber door, and when the innkeeper's maid brought the messenger to the door – who was a young fellow, an apprentice, almost a man – she tells him her mistress was asleep, but if he would leave the things and call in about an hour, I should be awake, and he might have the money. He left the parcel very readily, and goes his way, and in about half an hour my maid and I walked off, and that very evening I hired a horse and a man to ride before me, and went to Newmarket, and from thence got my passage in a coach that was not quite full to St Edmund's Bury, where, as I told you, I could make but little of my trade – only at a little country opera house made a shift to carry off a gold watch from a lady's side, who was not only intolerably merry, but as I thought a little fuddled, which made my work much easier.

I made off with this little booty to Ipswich, and from thence to Harwich,* where I went into an inn, as if I had newly arrived from Holland, not doubting but I should make some purchase among the foreigners that came on shore there. But I found them generally empty of things of value, except what was in their portmanteaus and Dutch hampers, which were generally guarded by footmen. However, I fairly got one of their portmanteaus one evening out of the chamber where the gentleman lay, the footman being fast asleep on the bed, and I suppose very drunk.

The room in which I lodged lay next to the Dutchman's, and, having dragged the heavy thing with much ado out of the chamber into mine, I went out into the street to see if I could find any possibility of carrying it off. I walked about a great while, but could see no probability either of getting out the thing or of conveying away the goods that was in it if I had opened it, the town being so small, and I a perfect stranger in it. So I was returning with a resolution to carry it back again and leave it where I found it. Just in that very moment I heard a man make a noise to some people to make haste, for the boat was going to put off, and the tide would be spent. I called to the fellow: "What boat is it, friend," says I, "that you belong to?" "The Ipswich wherry, madam," says he. "When do you go off?" says I. "This moment, madam," says he. "Do you want to go thither?" "Yes," said I, "if you can stay till I fetch my things." "Where are your things, madam?" says he. "At such an inn," said I. "Well, I'll go with you, madam," says he, very civilly, "and bring them for you." "Come away, then," says I, and takes him with me.

The people of the inn were in great hurry, the packet boat from Holland being just come in, and two coaches just come also with passengers from London for another packet boat that was going off for Holland – which coaches were to go back next day with the passengers that were just landed. In this hurry it was not much minded that I came to the bar and paid my reckoning, telling my landlady I had gotten my passage by sea in a wherry.

These wherries are large vessels, with good accommodation for carrying passengers from Harwich to London, and though they are called wherries, which is a word used in the Thames for a small boat rowed with one or two men, yet these are vessels able to carry twenty passengers, and ten or fifteen ton of goods, and fitted to bear the sea. All this I had found out by enquiring the night before into the several ways of going to London.

My landlady was very courteous, took my money for my reckoning, but was called away, all the house being in a hurry. So I left her, took the fellow up to my chamber, gave him the trunk, or portmanteau, for it was like a trunk, and wrapped it about with an old apron, and he went directly to his boat with it, and I after him, nobody asking us the least question about it. As for the drunken Dutch footman, he was still asleep, and his master with other foreign gentlemen at supper, and very merry below. So I went clean off with it to Ipswich, and, going in the night, the people of the house knew nothing but that I was gone to London by the Harwich wherry, as I had told my landlady.

I was plagued at Ipswich with the custom-house officers, who stopped my trunk, as I called it, and would open and search it.

I was willing, I told them: they should search it, but my husband had the key, and he was not yet come from Harwich. This I said: that if upon searching it they should find all the things be such as properly belonged to a man rather than a woman, it should not seem strange to them. However, they being positive to open the trunk, I consented to have it be broken open – that is to say, to have the lock taken off, which was not difficult.

They found nothing for their turn, for the trunk had been searched before, but they discovered several things very much to my satisfaction, as particularly a parcel of money in French pistoles, and some Dutch ducatoons, or rix-dollars,* and the rest was chiefly two periwigs, wearing linen and razors, wash balls,* perfumes and other useful things necessary for a gentleman, which all passed for my husband's, and so I was quit of them.

It was now very early in the morning, and not light, and I knew not well what course to take, for I made no doubt but I should be pursued in the morning, and perhaps be taken with the things about me, so I resolved upon taking new measures. I went publicly to an inn in the town with my trunk, as I called it, and having taken the substance out, I did not think the lumber of it worth my concern. However, I gave it the landlady of the house with a charge to take great care of it and lay it up safe till I should come again, and away I walked into the street.

When I was got into the town a great way from the inn, I met with an ancient woman who had just opened her door, and I fell into chat with her, and asked her a great many wild questions of things all remote to my purpose and design, but in my discourse I found by her how the town was situated – that I was in a street which went out towards Hadley, but that such a street went towards the water-side, such a street went into the heart of the town and at last such a street went towards Colchester, and so the London road lay there.

I had soon my ends of this old woman, for I only wanted to know which was London road, and away I walked as fast as I could – not that I intended to go on foot either to London or to Colchester, but I wanted to get quietly away from Ipswich.

I walked about two or three mile, and then I met a plain countryman, who was busy about some husbandry work, I did not know what, and I asked him a great many questions first, not much to the purpose, but at last told him I was going for London, and the coach was full, and I could not get a passage, and asked him if he could not tell me where to hire a horse that would carry double, and an honest man to ride before me to Colchester, so that I might get a place there in the coaches. The honest clown* looked earnestly at me and said nothing for above half a minute, when, scratching his poll,* "A horse, say you, and to Colchester to carry double. Why, yes, mistress, alack-a-day, you may have horses enough for money." "Well, friend," says I, "that I take for granted – I don't expect it without money." "Why, but mistress," says he, "how much are you willing to give?" "Nay," says I again, "friend, I don't know what your rates are in the country here, for I am a stranger, but if you can get one for me, get it as cheap as you can, and I'll give you somewhat for your pains."

"Why, that's honestly said too," says the countryman. "Not so honest, neither," said I to myself, "if thou knewest all." "Why, mistress," says he, "I have a horse that will carry double, and I don't much care if I go myself with you" – and the like. "Will you?" says I. "Well, I believe you are an honest man. If you will, I shall be glad of it. I'll pay you in reason." "Why, look ye, mistress," says he, "I won't be out of reason with you, then. If I carry you to Colchester, it will be worth five shillings for myself and my horse, for I shall hardly come back tonight."

In short, I hired the honest man and his horse, but when we came to a town upon the road – I do not remember the name of it, but it stands upon a river – I pretended myself very ill, and I could go no farther that night, but, if he would stay there with me, because I was a stranger, I would pay him for himself and his horse with all my heart.

This I did because I knew the Dutch gentlemen and their servants would be upon the road that day, either in the stagecoaches or riding post, and I did not know but the drunken fellow, or somebody else that might have seen me at Harwich, might see me again, and so I thought that in one day's stop they would be all gone by.

We lay all that night there, and the next morning it was not very early when I set out, so that it was near ten o'clock by that time I got to Colchester. It was no little pleasure that I saw the town where I had so many pleasant days, and I made many enquiries after the good old friends I had once had there, but could make little out – they were all dead or removed. The young ladies had been all married or gone to London; the old gentleman and the old lady that had been my early benefactress all dead; and, which troubled me most, the young gentleman my first lover, and afterwards my brother-in-law, was dead – but two sons, men grown, were left of him, but they too were transplanted to London.

I dismissed my old man here, and stayed incognito for three or four days in Colchester, and then took a passage in a wagon, because I would not venture being seen in the Harwich coaches. But I needed not have used so much caution, for there was nobody in Harwich but the woman of the house could have known me, nor was it rational to think that she, considering the hurry she was in and that she never saw me but once, and that by candlelight, should have ever discovered me.

I was now returned to London, and though by the accident of the last adventure I got something considerable, yet I was not fond of any more country rambles, nor should I have ventured abroad again if I had carried the trade on to the end of my days. I gave my governess a history of my travels – she liked the Harwich journey well enough, and in discoursing of these things between ourselves she observed that a thief being a creature that watches the advantages of other people's mistakes, 'tis impossible but that to one that is vigilant and industrious many opportunities must happen, and therefore she thought that one so exquisitely keen in the trade as I was would scarce fail of something extraordinary wherever I went.

On the other hand, every branch of my story, if duly considered, may be useful to honest people and afford a due caution to people of some sort or other to guard against the like surprises, and to have their eyes about them when they have to do with strangers of any kind, for 'tis very seldom that some snare or other is not in their way. The moral indeed of all my history is left to be gathered by the senses and judgement of the reader – I am not qualified to preach to them. Let the experience of one creature completely wicked and completely miserable be a storehouse of useful warning to those that read.

I am drawing now towards a new variety of the scenes of life. Upon my return, being hardened by a long race of crime, and success unparalleled, at least in the reach of my own knowledge, I had, as I have said, no thoughts of laying down a trade which, if I was to judge by the example of others, must however end at last in misery and sorrow.

It was on the Christmas Day following, in the evening, that, to finish a long train of wickedness, I went abroad to see what might offer in my way, when going by a working silversmith's in Foster Lane, I saw a tempting bait indeed, and not to be resisted by one of my occupation, for the shop had nobody in it, as I could see, and a great deal of loose plate lay in the window and at the seat of the man who usually, as I suppose, worked at one side of the shop.

I went boldly in, and was just going to lay my hand upon a piece of plate – and might have done it and carried it clear off, for any care that the men who belonged to the shop had taken of it – but an officious fellow in a house, not a shop, on the other side of the way, seeing me go in and observing that there was nobody in the shop, comes running over the street and into the shop, and without asking me what I was or who, seizes upon me and cries out for the people of the house.

I had not, as I said above, touched anything in the shop, and seeing a glimpse of somebody running over to the shop, I had so much presence of mind as to knock very hard with my foot on the floor of the house, and was just calling out too when the fellow laid hands on me.

However, as I had always most courage when I was in most danger, so when the fellow laid hands on me I stood very high upon it that I came in to buy half a dozen of silver spoons, and to my good fortune it was a silversmith's that sold plate, as well as worked plate, for other shops. The fellow laughed at that part, and put such a value upon the service that he had done his neighbour that he would have it be that I came not to buy but to steal, and, raising a great crowd, I said to the master of the shop, who by this time was fetched home from some neighbouring place, that it was in vain to make noise and enter into talk there of the case. The fellow had insisted that I came to steal, and he must prove it, and I desired we might go before a magistrate without any more words, for I began to see I should be too hard for the man that had seized me.

The master and mistress of the shop were really not so violent as the man from t'other side of the way, and the man said, "Mistress, you might come into the shop with a good design, for ought I know, but it seemed a dangerous thing for you to come into such a shop as mine is when you see nobody there, and I cannot do so little justice to my neighbour, who was so kind to me, as not to acknowledge he had reason on his side – though, upon the whole, I do not find you attempted to take anything, and I really know not what to do in it." I pressed him to go before a magistrate with me, and if anything could be proved on me that was like a design of robbery, I should willingly submit, but if not I expected reparation.

Just while we were in this debate and a crowd of people gathered about the door, came by Sir T.B., an alderman of the City and Justice of the Peace, and the goldsmith, hearing of it, goes out, and entreated His Worship to come in and decide the case.

Give the goldsmith his due, he told his story with a great deal of justice and moderation, and the fellow that had come over and seized upon me told his with as much heat and foolish passion, which did me good still, rather than harm. It came then to my turn to speak, and I told His Worship that I was a stranger in London, being newly come out of the north, that I lodged in such a place, that I was passing this street and went into the goldsmith's shop to buy half a dozen of spoons. By great good luck I had an old silver spoon in my pocket, which I pulled out, and told him I had carried that spoon to match it with half a dozen of new ones, that it might match some I had in the country; that, seeing nobody in the shop, I knocked with my foot very hard to make the people hear, and had also called aloud with my voice – 'tis true there was loose plate in the shop, but that nobody could say I had touched any of it or gone near it; that a fellow came running into the shop out of the street and laid hands on me in a furious manner, in the very moments while I was calling for the people of the house; that if he had really had a mind to have done his neighbour any service, he should have stood at a distance, and silently watched to see whether I had touched anything or no, and then have clapped in upon me,* and taken me in the fact.*

"That is very true," says Mr Alderman, and, turning to the fellow that stopped me, he asked him if it was true that I knocked with my foot. He said yes, I had knocked, but that might be because of his coming. "Nay," says the alderman, taking him short, "now you contradict yourself, for just now you said she was in the shop with her back to you, and did not see you till you came upon her." Now, it was true that my back was partly to the street, but yet, as my business was of a kind that required me to have my eyes every way, so I really had a glance of him running over, as I said before, though he did not perceive it.

After a full hearing, the alderman gave it as his opinion that his neighbour was under a mistake, and that I was innocent, and the goldsmith acquiesced in it too, and his wife, and so I was dismissed. But as I was going to depart, Mr Alderman said, "But hold, madam – if you were designing to buy spoons, I hope you will not let my friend here lose his customer by the mistake." I readily answered, "No, sir – I'll buy the spoons still if he can match my odd spoon, which I brought for a pattern" – and the goldsmith showed me some of the very same fashion. So he weighed the spoons, and they came to five-and-thirty shillings, so I pulls out my purse to pay him, in which I had near twenty guineas, for I never went without such a sum about me, whatever might happen, and I found it of use at other times as well as now.

When Mr Alderman saw my money, he said, "Well, madam, now I am satisfied you were wronged, and it was for this reason that I moved you should buy the spoons, and stayed till you had bought them, for if you had not had money to pay for them, I should have suspected that you did not come into the shop with an intent to buy, for indeed the sort of people who come upon those designs that you have been charged with are seldom troubled with much gold in their pockets, as I see you are."

I smiled, and told His Worship that then I owed something of his favour to my money, but I hoped he saw reason also in the justice he had done me before. He said yes, he had, but this had confirmed his opinion, and he was fully satisfied now of my having been injured. So I came off with flying colours, though from an affair in which I was at the very brink of destruction.

It was but three days after this that, not at all made cautious by my former danger as I used to be, and still pursuing the art which I had so long been employed in, I ventured into a house where I saw the doors open, and furnished myself – as I thought verily without being perceived – with two pieces of flowered silks, such as they call brocaded silk, very rich. It was not a mercer's shop, nor a warehouse of a mercer, but looked like a private dwelling house, and was it seems inhabited by a man that sold goods for the weavers to the mercers, like a broker or factor.

That I may make short of this black part of this story, I was attacked by two wenches that came open-mouthed at me just as I was going out at the door, and one of them pulled me back into the room, while the other shut the door upon me. I would have given them good words, but there was no room for it – two fiery dragons could not have been more furious than they were. They tore my clothes, bullied and roared as if they would have murdered me. The mistress of the house came next, and then the master, and all outrageous, for a while especially.

I gave the master very good words, told him the door was open, and things were a temptation to me, that I was poor and distressed, and poverty was what many could not resist, and begged him with tears to have pity on me. The mistress of the house was moved with compassion, and inclined to have let me go, and had almost persuaded her husband to it also, but the saucy wenches were run even before they were sent and had fetched a constable, and then the master said he could not go back: I must go before a justice, and answered his wife that he might come into trouble himself if he should let me go.

The sight of the constable indeed struck me with terror, and I thought I should have sunk into the ground. I fell into faintings, and indeed the people themselves thought I would have died – when the woman argued again for me, and entreated her husband, seeing they had lost nothing to let me go. I offered him to pay for the two pieces, whatever the value was, though I had not got them, and argued that as he had his goods and had really lost nothing, it would be cruel to pursue me to death and have my blood for the bare attempt of taking them. I put the constable in mind that I had broke no doors, nor carried anything away, and when I came to the justice and pleaded there that I had neither broken anything to get in nor carried anything out, the justice was inclined to have released me, but the first saucy jade that stopped me affirming that I was going out with the goods but that she stopped me and pulled me back as I was upon the threshold, the justice upon that point committed me, and I was carried to Newgate – that horrid place! My very blood chills at the mention of its name – the place where so many of my comrades had been locked up, and from whence they went to the fatal tree.* The place where my mother suffered so deeply, where I was brought into the world, and from whence I expected no redemption but by an infamous death! To conclude, the place that had so long expected me, and which with so much art and success I had so long avoided!

I was now fixed indeed. 'Tis impossible to describe the terror of my mind when I was first brought in, and when I looked round upon all the horrors of that dismal place. I looked on myself as lost, and that I had nothing to think of but of going out of the world – and that with the utmost infamy. The hellish noise, the roaring, swearing and clamour, the stench and nastiness, and all the dreadful crowd of afflicting things that I saw there, joined together to make the place seem an emblem of hell itself, and a kind of an entrance into it.

Now I reproached myself with the many hints I had had, as I have mentioned above, from my own reason, from the sense of my good circumstances, and of the many dangers I had escaped, to leave off while I was well, and how I had withstood them all, and hardened my thoughts against all fear. It seemed to me that I was hurried on by an inevitable and unseen fate to this day of misery, and that now I was to expiate all my offences at the gallows – that I was now to give satisfaction to justice with my blood, and that I was come to the last hour of my life, and of my wickedness together. These things poured themselves in upon my thoughts in a confused manner, and left me overwhelmed with melancholy and despair.

Then I repented heartily of all my life past, but that repentance yielded me no satisfaction, no peace – no, not in the least – because, as I said to myself, it was repenting after the power of further sinning was taken away. I seemed not to mourn that I had committed such crimes, and for the fact as it was an offence against God and my neighbour, but I mourned that I was to be punished for it. I was a penitent, as I thought, not that I had sinned, but that I was to suffer – and this took away all the comfort, and even the hope of my repentance in my own thoughts.

I got no sleep for several nights or days after I came into that wretched place, and glad I would have been for some time to have died there, though I did not consider dying as it ought to be considered neither. Indeed, nothing could be filled with more horror to my imagination than the very place, nothing was more odious to me than the company that was there. Oh, if I had but been sent to any place in the world, and not to Newgate, I should have thought myself happy!

In the next place, how did the hardened wretches that were there before me triumph over me! What? Mrs Flanders come to Newgate at last? What? Mrs Mary, Mrs Molly, and after that plain Moll Flanders? They thought the Devil had helped me, they said, that I had reigned so long. They expected me there many years ago – and was I come at last? Then they flouted me with my dejections, welcomed me to the place, wished me joy, bid me have a good heart, not to be cast down: things might not be so bad as I feared, and the like. Then called for brandy, and drank to me, but put it all up to my score,* for they told me I was but just come to the college,* as they called it, and sure I had money in my pocket, though they had none.

I asked one of this crew how long she had been there. She said four months. I asked her how the place looked to her when she first came into it. Just as it did now to me, says she: dreadful and frightful – that she thought she was in hell. "And I believe so still," adds she, "but it is natural to me now – I don't disturb myself about it." "I suppose," says I, "you are in no danger of what is to follow." "Nay," says she, "for you are mistaken there, I assure you, for I am under sentence, only I pleaded my belly, but I am no more with child than the judge that tried me, and I expect to be called down next sessions." This "calling down" is calling down to their former judgement, when a woman has been respited for her belly but proves not to be with child, or if she has been with child and has been brought to bed. "Well," says I, "and are you thus easy?" "Ay," says she, "I can't help myself – what signifies being sad? If I am hanged, there's an end of me," says she, and away she turns dancing, and sings as she goes the following piece of Newgate wit:

If I swing by the string,
I shall hear the bell* ring
And then there's an end of poor Jenny.

I mention this because it would be worth the observation of any prisoner who shall hereafter fall into the same misfortune and come to that dreadful place of Newgate how time, necessity and conversing with the wretches that are there familiarizes the place to them – how at last they become reconciled to that which at first was the greatest dread upon their spirits in the world, and are as impudently cheerful and merry in their misery as they were when out of it.

I cannot say, as some do, this devil is not so black as he is painted, for indeed no colours can represent the place to the life, nor any soul conceive aright of it but those who have been sufferers there. But how hell should become by degrees so natural, and not only tolerable, but even agreeable, is a thing unintelligible but by those who have experienced it, as I have.

The same night that I was sent to Newgate, I sent the news of it to my old governess, who was surprised at it, you may be sure, and spent the night almost as ill out of Newgate as I did in it.

The next morning she came to see me. She did what she could to comfort me, but she saw that was to no purpose. However, as she said, to sink under the weight was but to increase the weight – she immediately applied herself to all the proper methods to prevent the effects of it which we feared, and first she found out the two fiery jades that had surprised me. She tampered with them, persuaded them, offered them money and, in a word, tried all imaginable ways to prevent a prosecution. She offered one of the wenches 100*l.* to go away from her mistress and not to appear against me, but she was so resolute that though she was but a serv-ant maid, at 3*l.* a year wages or thereabouts, she refused it, and would have refused it, as my governess said she believed, if she had offered her 500*l.* Then she attacked the other maid – she was not so hard-hearted in appearance as the other, and sometimes seemed inclined to be merciful, but the first wench kept her up, and changed her mind, and would not so much as let my govern-ess talk with her, but threatened to have her up for tampering with the evidence.

Then she applied to the master – that is to say, the man whose goods had been stolen – and particularly to his wife, who, as I told you, was inclined at first to have some compassion for me. She found the woman the same still, but the man alleged he was bound by the justice that committed me to prosecute, and that he should forfeit his recognizance.

My governess offered to find friends that should get his recognizances off of the file, as they call it, and that he should not suffer, but it was not possible to convince him that could be done, or that he could be safe any way in the world but by appearing against me. So I was to have three witnesses of fact against me: the master and his two maids – that is to say, I was as certain to be cast for my life as I was certain that I was alive, and I had nothing to do but to think of dying and prepare for it. I had but a sad foundation to build upon, as I said before, for all my repentance appeared to me to be only the effect of my fear of death, not a sincere regret for the wicked life that I had lived and which had brought this misery upon me, or for the offending my Creator, who was now suddenly to be my judge.

I lived many days here under the utmost horror of soul. I had death, as it were, in view, and thought of nothing night and day but of gibbets and halters, evil spirits and devils. It is not to be expressed by words how I was harassed, between the dreadful apprehensions of death and the terror of my conscience reproaching me with my past horrible life.

The ordinary* of Newgate came to me and talked a little in his way, but all his divinity ran upon confessing my crime, as he called it (though he knew not what I was in for), making a full discovery and the like, without which he told me God would never forgive me, and he said so little to the purpose that I had no manner of consolation from him. And then to observe the poor creature preaching confession and repentance to me in the morning, and find him drunk with brandy and spirits by noon – this had something in it so shocking that I began to nauseate the man more than his work, and his work too by degrees, for the sake of the man, so that I desired him to trouble me no more.

I know not how it was, but by the indefatigable application of my diligent governess I had no bill preferred against me the first sessions, I mean to the grand jury at Guildhall,* so I had another month, or five weeks, before me, and without doubt this ought to have been accepted by me as so much time given me for reflection upon what was past, and preparation for what was to come – or, in a word, I ought to have esteemed it as a space given me for repentance, and have employed it as such. But it was not in me – I was sorry (as before) for being in Newgate, but had very few signs of repentance about me.

On the contrary, like the waters in the cavities and hollows of mountains, which putrefy and turn into stone whatever they are suffered to drop upon, so the continual conversing with such a crew of hellhounds as I was had the same common operation upon me as upon other people – I degenerated into stone. I turned first stupid and senseless, then brutish and thoughtless, and at last raving mad as any of them were – and, in short, I became as naturally pleased and easy with the place as if indeed I had been born there.

It is scarce possible to imagine that our natures should be capable of so much degeneracy as to make that pleasant and agreeable that in itself is the most complete misery. Here was a circumstance that I think it is scarce possible to mention a worse – I was as exquisitely miserable as, speaking of common cases, it was possible for anyone to be that had life and health, and money to help them, as I had.

I had a weight of guilt upon me enough to sink any creature who had the least power of reflection left and had any sense upon them of the happiness of this life, or the misery of another. Then I had at first remorse indeed, but no repentance – I had now neither remorse or repentance. I had a crime charged on me, the punishment of which was death by our law, the proof so evident that there was no room for me so much as to plead not guilty. I had the name of old offender, so that I had nothing to expect but death in a few weeks' time. Neither had I myself any thoughts of escaping, and yet a certain strange lethargy of soul possessed me. I had no trouble, no apprehensions, no sorrow about me – the first surprise was gone. I was, I may well say, I know not how. My senses, my reason – nay, my conscience were all asleep. My course of life for forty years had been a horrid complication of wickedness, whoredom, adultery, incest, lying, theft and, in a word, everything but murder – and treason had been my practice from the age of eighteen, or thereabouts, to threescore. And now I was engulfed in the misery of punishment, and had an infamous death just at the door, and yet I had no sense of my condition, no thought of heaven or hell, at least that went any further than a bare flying touch, like the stitch or pain that gives a hint and goes off. I neither had a heart to ask God's mercy or indeed to think of it, and in this I think I have given a brief description of the completest misery on earth.

All my terrifying thoughts were past. The horrors of the place were become familiar, and I felt no more uneasiness at the noise and clamour of the prison than they did who made that noise. In a word, I was become a mere Newgate bird, as wicked and as outrageous as any of them. Nay, I scarce retained the habit and custom of good breeding and manners which all along till now run through my conversation. So thorough a degeneracy had possessed me that I was no more the same thing that I had been than if I had never been otherwise than what I was now.

In the middle of this hardened part of my life, I had another sudden surprise, which called me back a little to that thing called sorrow, which indeed I began to be past the sense of, before they told me one night that there was brought into the prison late the night before three highwaymen who had committed a robbery somewhere on the road to Windsor – Hounslow Heath, I think it was – and were pursued to Uxbridge by the country, and were taken there after a gallant resistance, in which I know not how many of the country people were wounded, and some killed.

It is not to be wondered that we prisoners were all desirous enough to see these brave, topping* gentlemen that were talked up to be such as their fellows had not been known, and especially because it was said they would in the morning be removed into the press yard, having given money to the headmaster of the prison to be allowed the liberty of that better part of the prison.* So we that were women placed ourselves in the way that we would be sure to see them – but nothing could express the amazement and surprise I was in when the very first man that came out I knew to be my Lancashire husband, the same with whom I lived so well at Dunstable, and the same who I afterwards saw at Brickhill, when I was married to my last husband, as has been related.

I was struck dumb at the sight, and knew neither what to say or what to do. He did not know me, and that was all the present relief I had. I quitted my company, and retired as much as that dreadful place suffers anybody to retire, and I cried vehemently for a great while. "Dreadful creature that I am," said I, "how many poor people have I made miserable? How many desperate wretches have I sent to the Devil?" This gentleman's misfortunes I placed all to my own account. He had told me at Chester he was ruined by that match, and that his fortunes were made desperate on my account – for that, thinking I had been a fortune, he was run into debt more than he was able to pay, and that he knew not what course to take; that he would go into the army and carry a musket, or buy a horse and take a tour, as he called it. And though I never told him that I was a fortune, and so did not actually deceive him myself, yet I did encourage the having it thought that I was so, and by that means I was the occasion originally of his mischief.

The surprise of this thing only struck deeper into my thoughts, and gave me stronger reflections than all that had befallen me before. I grieved day and night for him, and the more for that they told me he was the captain of the gang, and that he had committed so many robberies that Hind, or Whitney, or the Golden Farmer* were fools to him – that he would surely be hanged if there were no more men left in the country he was born in, and that there would abundance of people come in against him.

I was overwhelmed with grief for him. My own case gave me no disturbance compared to this, and I loaded myself with reproaches on his account. I bewailed his misfortunes and the ruin he was now come to, at such a rate that I relished nothing now as I did before, and the first reflections I made upon the horrid, detestable life I had lived began to return upon me, and as these things returned, my abhorrence of the place I was in, and of the way of living in it, returned also. In a word, I was perfectly changed, and become another body.

While I was under these influences of sorrow for him, came notice to me that, the next sessions approaching, there would be a bill preferred to the grand jury against me, and that I should be certainly tried for my life at the Old Bailey. My temper was touched before; the hardened wretched boldness of spirit which I had acquired in the prison abated, and conscious guilt began to flow in upon my mind. In short, I began to think, and to think is one real advance from hell to heaven. All that hellish, hardened state and temper of soul which I have said so much of before is but a deprivation of thought: he that is restored to his power of thinking is restored to himself.

As soon as I began, I say, to think, the first thing that occurred to me broke out thus: "Lord! What will become of me? I shall certainly die! I shall be cast, to be sure, and there is nothing beyond that but death! I have no friends – what shall I do? I shall be certainly cast. Lord, have mercy upon me – what will become of me?" This was a sad thought, you will say, to be the first after so long time that had started into my soul of that kind, and yet even this was nothing but fright at what was to come. There was not a word of sincere repentance in it all. However, I was indeed dreadfully dejected, and disconsolate to the last degree, and as I had no friend in the world to communicate my distressed thoughts to, it lay so heavy upon me that it threw me into fits and swoonings several times a day. I sent for my old governess, and she, give her her due, acted the part of a true friend – she left me no stone unturned to prevent the grand jury finding the bill. She went to several of the jurymen, talked with them and endeavoured to possess them with favourable dispositions, on account that nothing was taken away and no house broken, etc. But all would not do – they were overruled by the rest. The two wenches swore home to the fact, and the jury found the bill against me for robbery and housebreaking – that is, for felony and burglary.

I sank down when they brought me news of it, and after I came to myself again, I thought I should have died with the weight of it. My governess acted a true mother to me: she pitied me, she cried with me, and for me, but she could not help me, and to add to the terror of it, 'twas the discourse all over the house that I should die for it. I could hear them talk it among themselves very often, and see them shake their heads, and say they were sorry for it and the like, as is usual in the place. But still nobody came to tell me their thoughts, till at last one of the keepers came to me privately, and said with a sigh, "Well, Mrs Flanders, you will be tried a Friday" (this was but a Wednesday). "What do you intend to do?" I turned as white as a clout,* and said, "God knows what I shall do. For my part I know not what to do." "Why," says he, "I won't flatter you – I would have you prepare for death, for I doubt you will be cast – and as, they say, you are an old offender, I doubt you will find but little mercy. They say," added he, "your case is very plain, and that the witnesses swear so home against you, there will be no standing it."

This was a stab into the very vitals of one under such a burden as I was oppressed with before, and I could not speak to him a word good or bad for a great while, but at last I burst out into tears, and said to him, "Lord! Mr ——, what must I do?" "Do?" says he. "Send for the ordinary, send for a minister, and talk with him – for indeed, Mrs Flanders, unless you have very good friends, you are no woman for this world."

This was plain dealing indeed, but it was very harsh to me – at least I thought it so. He left me in the greatest confusion imaginable, and all that night I lay awake, and now I began to say my prayers, which I had scarce done before since my last husband's death, or from a little while after. And truly I may well call it "saying my prayers", for I was in such a confusion and had such horror upon my mind that, though I cried and repeated several times the ordinary expression of "Lord have mercy upon me", I never brought myself to any sense of my being a miserable sinner, as indeed I was, and of confessing my sins to God, and begging pardon for the sake of Jesus Christ. I was overwhelmed with the sense of my condition, being tried for my life, and being sure to be condemned, and then I was as sure to be executed, and on this account I cried out all night, "Lord! What will become of me? Lord! What shall I do? Lord! I shall be hanged – Lord, have mercy upon me" – and the like.

My poor afflicted governess was now as much concerned as I, and a great deal more truly penitent, though she had no prospect of being brought to trial and sentence, not but that she deserved it as much as I, and so she said herself, but she had not done anything herself for many years other than receiving what I and others stole and encouraging us to steal it. But she cried and took on like a distracted body, wringing her hands and crying out that she was undone, that she believed there was a curse from Heaven upon her, that she should be damned, that she had been the destruction of all her friends, that she had brought such a one and such a one, and such one to the gallows – and there she reckoned up ten or eleven people, some of which I have given an account of, that came to untimely ends – and that now she was the occasion of my ruin, for she had persuaded me to go on when I would have left off. I interrupted her there. "No, Mother, no," said I. "Don't speak of that, for you would have had me left off when I got the mercer's money again, and when I came home from Harwich, and I would not hearken to you. Therefore, you have not been to blame – it is I only have ruined myself. I have brought myself to this misery" – and thus we spent many hours together.

Well, there was no remedy. The prosecution went on, and on the Thursday I was carried down to the sessions house, where I was arraigned, as they called it, and the next day I was appointed to be tried. At the arraignment I pleaded not guilty, and well I might, for I was indicted for felony and burglary – that is, for feloniously stealing two pieces of brocaded silk, value 46*l*., the goods of Anthony Johnson, and for breaking open his doors, whereas I knew very well they could not pretend to prove I had broken up the doors, or so much as lifted up a latch.

On the Friday I was brought to my trial. I had exhausted my spirits with crying for two or three days before, so that I slept better the Thursday night than I expected, and had more courage for my trial than indeed I thought possible for me to have.

When the trial began and the indictment was read, I would have spoke, but they told me the witnesses must be heard first, and then I should have time to be heard. The witnesses were the two wenches, a couple of hard-mouthed jades indeed, for though the thing was truth in the main, yet they aggravated it to the utmost extremity, and swore I had the goods wholly in my possession – that I had hid them among my clothes, that I was going off with them, that I had one foot over the threshold when they discovered themselves, and then I put t'other over, so that I was quite out of the house in the street with the goods before they took hold of me, and then they seized me and brought me back again, and they took the goods upon me. The fact in general was all true, but I believe, and insisted upon it, that they stopped me before I had set my foot clear of the threshold of the house. But that did not argue much, for certain it was that I had taken the goods, and that I was bringing them away, if I had not been taken.

But I pleaded that I had stole nothing, they had lost nothing, that the door was open, and I went in seeing the goods lie there and with design to buy. If, seeing nobody in the house, I had taken any of them up in my hand, it could not be concluded that I intended to steal them, for that I never carried them farther than the door to look on them with the better light.

The court would not allow that by any means, and made a kind of a jest of my intending to buy the goods, that being no shop for the selling of anything. And as to carrying them to the door to look at them, the maids made their impudent mocks upon that, and spent their wit upon it very much – told the court I had looked at them sufficiently, and approved them very well, for I had packed them up under my clothes and was a-going with them.

In short, I was found guilty of felony, but acquitted of the burglary, which was but small comfort to me, the first bringing me to a sentence of death, and the last would have done no more. The next day, I was carried down to receive the dreadful sentence, and when they came to ask me what I had to say why sentence should not pass, I stood mute awhile, but somebody that stood behind me prompted me aloud to speak to the judges, for that they could represent things favourably for me. This encouraged me to speak, and I told them I had nothing to say to stop the sentence, but that I had much to say to bespeak the mercy of the court: that I hoped they would allow something in such a case for the circumstances of it, that I had broken no doors, had carried nothing off, that nobody had lost anything, that the person whose goods they were was pleased to say he desired mercy might be shown, which indeed he very honestly did, that at the worst it was the first offence, and that I had never been before any court of justice before – and, in a word, I spoke with more courage than I thought I could have done, and in such a moving tone, and though with tears, yet not so many tears as to obstruct my speech, that I could see it moved others to tears that heard me.

The judges sat grave and mute, gave me an easy hearing and time to say all that I would, but saying neither yes or no to it, pronounced the sentence of death upon me – a sentence that was to me like death itself, which after it was read confounded me. I had no more spirit left in me. I had no tongue to speak or eyes to look up either to God or man.

My poor governess was utterly disconsolate, and she that was my comforter before wanted comfort now herself, and sometimes mourning, sometimes raging, was as much out of herself (as to all outward appearance) as any madwoman in Bedlam. Nor was she only disconsolate as to me, but she was struck with horror at the sense of her own wicked life, and began to look back upon it with a taste quite different from mine – for she was penitent to the highest degree for her sins, as well as sorrowful for the misfortune. She sent for a minister too – a serious, pious, good man – and applied herself with such earnestness by his assistance to the work of a sincere repentance that I believe, and so did the minister too, that she was a true penitent, and, which is still more, she was not only so for the occasion and at that juncture, but she continued so, as I was informed, to the day of her death.

It is rather to be thought of than expressed what was now my condition. I had nothing before me but present death, and as I had no friends to assist me or to stir for me, I expected nothing but to find my name in the dead warrant, which was to come down for the execution the Friday afterwards, of five more and myself.

In the mean time, my poor distressed governess sent me a minister, who at her request first, and at my own afterwards, came to visit me. He exhorted me seriously to repent of all my sins, and to dally no longer with my soul – not flattering myself with hopes of life, which, he said, he was informed there was no room to expect, but unfeignedly to look up to God with my whole soul, and to cry for pardon in the name of Jesus Christ. He backed his discourses with proper quotations of Scripture encouraging the greatest sinner to repent and turn from their evil way, and when he had done, he knelt down and prayed with me.

It was now that for the first time I felt any real signs of repentance. I now began to look back upon my past life with abhorrence, and, having a kind of view into the other side of time, the things of life, as I believe they do with everybody at such a time, began to look with a different aspect and quite another shape than they did before – the greatest and best things, the views of felicity, the joy, the griefs of life were quite other things, and I had nothing in my thoughts but what was so infinitely superior to what I had known in life that it appeared to me to be the greatest stupidity in nature to lay any weight upon anything, though the most valuable in this world.

The word "eternity" represented itself with all its incomprehensible additions, and I had such extended notions of it that I know not how to express them. Among the rest, how vile, how gross, how absurd did every pleasant thing look – I mean, that we had counted pleasant before, especially when I reflected that these sordid trifles were the things for which we forfeited eternal felicity.

With these reflections came in, of mere course, severe reproaches of my own mind for my wretched behaviour in my past life: that I had forfeited all hope of any happiness in the eternity that I was just going to enter into, and, on the contrary, was entitled to all that was miserable or had been conceived of misery – and all this with the frightful addition of its being also eternal.

I am not capable of reading lectures of instruction to anybody, but I relate this in the very manner in which things then appeared to me as far as I am able, but infinitely short of the lively impressions which they made on my soul at that time. Indeed, those impressions are not to be explained by words – or, if they are, I am not mistress of words enough to express them. It must be the work of every sober reader to make just reflections on them as their own circumstances may direct, and, without question, this is what everyone at some time or other may feel something of – I mean a clearer sight into things to come than they had here, and a dark view of their own concern in them.

But I go back to my own case. The minister pressed me to tell him, as far as I thought convenient, in what state I found myself as to the sight I had of things beyond life. He told me he did not come as ordinary of the place, whose business it is to extort confessions from prisoners, for private ends or for the further detecting of other offenders – that his business was to move me to such freedom of discourse as might serve to disburden my own mind and furnish him to administer comfort to me as far as was in his power – and assured me that whatever I said to him should remain with him, and be as much a secret as if it was known only to God and myself, and that he desired to know nothing of me, but, as above, to qualify him to apply proper advice and assistance to me, and to pray to God for me.

This honest, friendly way of treating me unlocked all the sluices of my passions. He broke into my very soul by it, and I unravelled all the wickedness of my life to him. In a word, I gave him an abridgement of this whole history – I gave him the picture of my conduct for fifty years in miniature.

I hid nothing from him, and he in return exhorted me to a sincere repentance, explained to me what he meant by repentance, and then drew out such a scheme of infinite mercy, proclaimed from Heaven to sinners of the greatest magnitude, that he left me nothing to say that looked like despair or doubting of being accepted, and in this condition he left me the first night.

He visited me again the next morning, and went on with his method of explaining the terms of divine mercy, which according to him consisted of nothing more, or more difficult, than that of being sincerely desirous of it, and willing to accept it – only a sincere regret for, and hatred of, those things I had done, which rendered me so just an object of divine vengeance. I am not able to repeat the excellent discourses of this extraordinary man. 'Tis all that I am able to do to say that he revived my heart, and brought me into such a condition that I never knew anything of in my life before. I was covered with shame and tears for things past, and yet had at the same time a secret, surprising joy at the prospect of being a true penitent and obtaining the comfort of a penitent – I mean the hope of being forgiven. And so swift did thoughts circulate, and so high did the impressions they had made upon me run, that I thought I could freely have gone out that minute to execution without any uneasiness at all, casting my soul entirely into the arms of infinite mercy as a penitent.

The good gentleman was so moved also in my behalf, with a view of the influence which he saw these things had on me, that he blessed God he had come to visit me, and resolved not to leave me till the last moment – that is, not to leave visiting me.

It was no less than twelve days after our receiving sentence before any were ordered for execution, and then upon a Wednesday the dead warrant, as they call it, came down, and I found my name was among them. A terrible blow this was to my new resolutions – indeed, my heart sunk within me, and I swooned away twice, one after another, but spoke not a word. The good minister was sorely afflicted for me, and did what he could to comfort me with the same arguments and the same moving eloquence that he did before, and left me not that evening so long as the prison keepers would suffer him to stay in the prison, unless he would be locked up with me all night, which he was not willing to be.

I wondered much that I did not see him all the next day, it being but the day before the time appointed for execution, and I was greatly discouraged and dejected in my mind, and indeed almost sank for want of that comfort which he had so often, and with such success, yielded me on his former visits. I waited with great impatience, and under the greatest oppressions of spirits imaginable, till about four o'clock he came to my apartment – for I had obtained the favour by the help of money, nothing being to be done in that place without it, not to be kept in the condemned hole, as they call it, among the rest of the prisoners who were to die, but to have a little dirty chamber to myself.

My heart leapt within me for joy when I heard his voice at the door even before I saw him, but let anyone judge what kind of motion I found in my soul when, after having made a short excuse for his not coming, he showed me that his time had been employed on my account – that he had obtained a favourable report from the recorder* to the secretary of state in my particular case, and, in short, that he had brought me a reprieve.

He used all the caution that he was able in letting me know a thing which it would have been a double cruelty to have concealed, and yet it was too much for me, for as grief had overset me before, so did joy overset now, and I fell into a much more dangerous swooning than I did at first, and it was not without a great difficulty that I was recovered at all.

The good man, having made a very Christian exhortation to me not to let the joy of my reprieve put the remembrance of my past sorrow out of my mind, and having told me that he must leave me to go and enter the reprieve in the books and show it to the sheriffs, stood up just before his going away, and in a very earnest manner prayed to God for me that my repentance might be made unfeigned and sincere, and that my coming back, as it were, into life again might not be a returning to the follies of life which I had made such solemn resolutions to forsake, and to repent of them. I joined heartily in the petition, and must needs say, I had deeper impressions upon my mind all that night of the mercy of God in sparing my life, and a greater detestation of my past sins, from a sense of the goodness which I had tasted in this case, than I had in all my sorrow before.

This may be thought inconsistent in itself, and wide from the business of this book – particularly, I reflect that many of those who may be pleased and diverted with the relation of the wild and wicked part of my story may not relish this, which is really the best part of my life, the most advantageous to myself, and the most instructive to others. Such, however, will I hope allow me the liberty to make my story complete. It would be a severe satire on such to say they do not relish the repentance as much as they do the crime, and that they had rather the history were a complete tragedy, as it was very likely to have been.

But I go on with my relation. The next morning there was a sad scene indeed in the prison. The first thing I was saluted with in the morning was the tolling of the great bell at St Sepulchre's, as they call it, which ushered in the day. As soon as it began to toll, a dismal groaning and crying was heard from the condemned hole, where there lay six poor souls who were to be executed that day, some for one crime, some for another, and two of them for murder.

This was followed by a confused clamour in the house among the several sorts of prisoners, expressing their awkward sorrows for the poor creatures that were to die, but in a manner extremely differing one from another: some cried for them; some huzzaed and wished them a good journey; some damned and cursed those that had brought them to it – that is, meaning the evidence or prosecutors; many pitying them; and some few, but very few, praying for them.

There was hardly room for so much composure of mind as was required for me to bless the merciful Providence that had, as it were, snatched me out of the jaws of this destruction. I remained, as it were, dumb and silent, overcome with the sense of it and not able to express what I had in my heart, for the passions on such occasions as these are certainly so agitated as not to be able presently to regulate their own motions.

All the while the poor, condemned creatures were preparing to their death, and the ordinary, as they call him, was busy with them, disposing them to submit to their sentence. I say, all this while I was seized with a fit of trembling, as much as I could have been if I had been in the same condition as, to be sure, the day before I expected to be. I was so violently agitated by this surprising fit that I shook as if it had been in the cold fit of an ague, so that I could not speak or look but like one distracted. As soon as they were all put into the carts and gone – which, however, I had not courage enough to see – I say, as soon as they were gone, I fell into a fit of crying involuntarily, and without design, but as a mere distemper, and yet so violent, and it held me so long, that I knew not what course to take, nor could I stop or put a check to it – no, not with all the strength and courage I had.

This fit of crying held me near two hours and, as I believe, held me till they were all out of the world, and then a most humble, penitent, serious kind of joy succeeded – a real transport it was, or passion of joy and thankfulness, but still unable to give vent to it by words, and in this I continued most part of the day.

In the evening the good minister visited me again, and then fell to his usual good discourses. He congratulated my having a space yet allowed me for repentance, whereas the state of those six poor creatures was determined, and they were now past the offers of salvation. He earnestly pressed me to retain the same sentiments of the things of life that I had when I had a view of eternity, and, at the end of all, told me I should not conclude that all was over – that a reprieve was not a pardon, that he could not yet answer for the effects of it. However, I had this mercy: that I had more time given me, and that it was my business to improve that time.

This discourse, though very seasonable, left a kind of sadness on my heart, as if I might expect the affair would have a tragical issue still – which, however, he had no certainty of, and I did not indeed at that time question him about it, he having said that he would do his utmost to bring it to a good end, and that he hoped he might, but he would not have me secure – and the consequence proved that he had reason for what he said.

It was about a fortnight after this that I had some just apprehensions that I should be included in the next dead warrant at the ensuing sessions, and it was not without great difficulty, and at last an humble petition for transportation, that I avoided it, so ill was I beholding to fame, and so prevailing was the fatal report of being an old offender – though in that they did not do me strict justice, for I was not in the sense of the law an old offender, whatever I was in the eye of the judge, for I had never been before them in a judicial way before, so the judges could not charge me with being an old offender, but the recorder was pleased to represent my case as he thought fit.

I had now a certainty of life indeed, but with the hard conditions of being ordered for transportation, which indeed was a hard condition in itself, but not when comparatively considered, and therefore I shall make no comments upon the sentence, nor upon the choice I was put to. We shall all choose anything rather than death, especially when 'tis attended with an uncomfortable prospect beyond it, which was my case.

The good minister, whose interest, though a stranger to me, had obtained me the reprieve, mourned sincerely for this part. He was in hopes, he said, that I should have ended my days under the influence of good instruction, that I might not have forgot my former distresses, and that I should not have been turned loose again among such a wretched crew as they generally are who are thus sent abroad – where, as he said, I must have more than ordinary secret assistance from the grace of God if I did not turn as wicked again as ever.

I have not for a good while mentioned my governess, who had, during most if not all of this part, been dangerously sick, and being in as near a view of death, by her disease, as I was by my sentence, was a very great penitent. I say, I have not mentioned her – nor, indeed, did I see her in all this time – but being now recovering and just able to come abroad, she came to see me.

I told her my condition, and what a different flux and reflux of fears and hopes I had been agitated with. I told her what I had escaped, and upon what terms, and she was present when the minister expressed his fears of my relapsing into wickedness upon my falling into the wretched companies that are generally transported. Indeed, I had a melancholy reflection upon it in my own mind, for I knew what a dreadful gang was always sent away together, and I said to my governess that the good minister's fears were not without cause. "Well, well," says she, "but I hope you will not be tempted with such a horrid example as that" – and as soon as the minister was gone, she told me she would not have me discouraged, for perhaps ways and means might be found out to dispose of me in a particular way, by myself, of which she would talk further to me afterwards.

I looked earnestly at her, and I thought she looked more cheerful than she usually had done, and I entertained immediately a thousand notions of being delivered, but could not for my life imagine the methods, or think of one that was in the least feasible. But I was too much concerned in it to let her go from me without explaining herself – which, though she was very loath to do, yet my importunity prevailed, and while I was still pressing, she answered me in few words, thus: "Why, you have money, have you not? Did you ever know one in your life that was transported and had a hundred pound in his pocket, I'll warrant you, child?" says she.

I understood her presently, but told her I would leave all that to her, but I saw no room to hope for anything but a strict execution of the order, and as it was a severity that was esteemed a mercy, there was no doubt but it would be strictly observed. She said no more but this: "We will try what can be done" – and so we parted for that night.

I lay in the prison near fifteen weeks after this order for transportation was signed. What the reason of it was, I know not, but at the end of this time I was put on board of a ship in the Thames, and with me a gang of thirteen, as hardened vile creatures as ever Newgate produced in my time, and it would really well take up a history longer than mine to describe the degrees of impudence and audacious villainy that those thirteen were arrived to, and the manner of their behaviour in the voyage, of which I have a very diverting account by me, which the captain of the ship who carried them over gave me the minutes of, and which he caused his mate to write down at large.

It may perhaps be thought trifling to enter here into a relation of all the little incidents which attended me in this interval of my circumstances – I mean between the final order for my transportation and the time of my going on board the ship, and I am too near the end of my story to allow room for it – but something relating to me and my Lancashire husband I must not omit.

He had, as I have observed already, been carried from the master's side* of the ordinary prison into the press yard, with three of his comrades, for they found another to add to them after some time. Here, for what reason I knew not, they were kept in custody without being brought to trial almost three months. It seems they found means to bribe or buy off some of those who were expected to come in against them, and they wanted evidence some time to convict them. After some puzzle on this account, at first they made a shift to get proof enough against two of them, to carry them off, but the other two, of which my Lancashire husband was one, lay still in suspense. They had, I think, one positive evidence against each of them, but the law strictly obliging them to have two witnesses, they could make nothing of it. Yet it seems they were resolved not to part with the men neither, not doubting but a further evidence would at last come in – and, in order to this, I think publication was made that, such prisoners being taken, anyone that had been robbed by them might come to the prison and see them.

I took this opportunity to satisfy my curiosity, pretending that I had been robbed in the Dunstable coach, and that I would go to see the two highwaymen, but when I came into the press yard, I so disguised myself, and muffled my face up so, that he could see little of me, and consequently knew nothing of who I was, and when I came back, I said publicly that I knew them very well.

Immediately it was rumoured all over the prison that Moll Flanders would turn evidence against one of the highwaymen, and that I was to come off by it from the sentence of transportation.

They heard of it, and immediately my husband desired to see this Mrs Flanders that knew him so well and was to be an evidence against him, and, accordingly, I had leave given to go to him. I dressed myself up as well as the best clothes that I suffered myself ever to appear in there would allow me, and went to the press yard, but had for some time a hood over my face. He said little to me at first, but asked me if I knew him. I told him, "Yes, very well" – but as I concealed my face, so I counterfeited my voice, that he had not the least guess at who I was. He asked me where I had seen him. I told him between Dunstable and Brickhill, but, turning to the keeper that stood by, I asked if I might not be admitted to talk with him alone. He said, "Yes, yes" – as much as I pleased, and so very civilly withdrew.

As soon as he was gone and I had shut the door, I threw off my hood and, bursting out into tears, "My dear," says I, "do you not know me?" He turned pale and stood speechless, like one thunderstruck, and, not able to conquer the surprise, said no more but this: "Let me sit down" – and, sitting down by a table, he laid his elbow upon the table and, leaning his head on his hand, fixed his eyes on the ground as one stupid. I cried so vehemently, on the other hand, that it was a good while ere I could speak any more, but after I had given some vent to my passion by tears, I repeated the same words: "My dear, do you not know me?" At which he answered, "Yes" – and said no more a good while.

After some time continuing in the surprise, as above, he cast up his eyes towards me and said, "How could you be so cruel?" I did not readily understand what he meant, and I answered, "How can you call me cruel? What have I been cruel to you in?" "To come to me," says he, "in such a place as this. Is it not to insult me? I have not robbed you, at least not on the highway."

I perceived by this that he knew nothing of the miserable circumstances I was in, and thought that having got some intelligence of his being there, I had come to upbraid him with his leaving me. But I had too much to say to him to be affronted, and told him in few words that I was far from coming to insult him, but at best I came to condole mutually – that he would be easily satisfied that I had no such view when I should tell him that my condition was worse than his, and that many ways. He looked a little concerned at the general expression of my condition being worse than his, but, with a kind of a smile, looked a little wildly, and said, "How can that be? When you see me fettered, and in Newgate, and two of my companions executed already – can you say your condition is worse than mine?"

"Come, my dear," says I, "we have a long piece of work to do, if I should be to relate, or you to hear, my unfortunate history. But if you are disposed to hear it, you will soon conclude with me that my condition is worse than yours." "How is that possible," says he again, "when I expect to be cast for my life the very next sessions?" "Yes," says I, "'tis very possible: when I shall tell you that I have been cast for my life three sessions ago and am under sentence of death, is not my case worse than yours?"

Then, indeed, he stood silent again, like one struck dumb, and after a little while he starts up: "Unhappy couple!" says he. "How can this be possible?" I took him by the hand. "Come, my dear," said I, "sit down, and let us compare our sorrows. I am a prisoner in this very house, and in a much worse circumstance than you, and you will be satisfied I do not come to insult you when I tell you the particulars." And with this we sat down together, and I told him so much of my story as I thought was convenient, bringing it at last to my being reduced to great poverty, and representing myself as fallen into some company that led me to relieve my distresses by a way that I had been utterly unacquainted with and that, they making an attempt at a tradesman's house, I was seized upon for having been but just at the door, the maidservant pulling me in; that I neither had broke any lock or taken anything away, and that notwithstanding that I was brought in guilty and sentenced to die, but that the judges, having been made sensible of the hardship of my circumstances, had obtained leave to remit the sentence upon my consenting to be transported.

I told him I fared the worse for being taken in the prison for one Moll Flanders, who was a famous, successful thief that all of them had heard of, but none of them had ever seen – but that, as he knew well, was none of my name. But I placed all to the account of my ill fortune, and that under this name I was dealt with as an old offender, though this was the first thing they had ever known of me. I gave him a long particular of things that had befallen me since I saw him, but I told him I had seen him since he might think I had, and then gave him an account how I had seen him at Brickhill, how furiously he was pursued, and how by giving an account that I knew him and that he was a very honest gentleman, one Mr ——, the hue and cry was stopped, and the high constable went back again.

He listened most attentively to all my story, and smiled at most of the particulars, being all of them petty matters, and infinitely below what he had been at the head of. But when I came to the story of Little Brickhill, he was surprised. "And was it you, my dear," said he, "that gave the check to the mob that was at our heels there, at Brickhill?" "Yes," said I, "it was I indeed" – and then I told him the particulars which I had observed of him there. "Why, then," said he, "it was you that saved my life at that time, and I am glad I owe my life to you, for I will pay the debt to you now, and I'll deliver you from the present condition you are in, or I will die in the attempt."

I told him by no means – it was a risk too great, not worth his running the hazard of, and for a life not worth his saving. 'Twas no matter for that, he said – it was a life worth all the world to him, a life that had given him a new life. "For," says he, "I was never in real danger of being taken but that time, till the last minute when I was taken." Indeed, he told me his danger then lay in his believing he had not been pursued that way, for they had gone off from Hockley quite another way, and had come over the enclosed country* into Brickhill, not by the road, and were sure they had not been seen by anybody.

Here he gave a long history of his life – which indeed would make a very strange history, and be infinitely diverting. He told me he took to the road about twelve year before he married me – that the woman which called him brother was not really his sister, or any kin to him, but one that belonged to their gang, and who, keeping correspondence with them, lived always in town, having good store of acquaintance; that she gave them a perfect intelligence of persons going out of town, and that they had made several good booties by her correspondence; that she thought she had fixed a fortune for him when she brought me to him, but happened to be disappointed, which he really could not blame her for; that, if it had been his good luck that I had had the estate, which she was informed I had, he had resolved to leave off the road and live a retired, sober life, but never to appear in public till some general pardon had been passed, or till he could, for money, have got his name into some particular pardon, that so he might have been perfectly easy – but that, as it had proved otherwise, he was obliged to put off his equipage and take up the old trade again.

He gave me a long account of some of his adventures, and particularly one, when he robbed the West Chester coaches, near Lichfield, when he got a very great booty – and after that, how he robbed five graziers in the west, going to Burford Fair in

Wiltshire* to buy sheep. He told me he got so much money on those two occasions that, if he had known where to have found me, he would certainly have embraced my proposal of going with me to Virginia, or to have settled in a plantation on some other parts of the English colonies in America.

He told me he wrote two or three letters to me, directed according to my order, but heard nothing from me. This I indeed knew to be true – but the letters coming to my hand in the time of my latter husband, I could do nothing in it, and therefore chose to give no answer, that so he might rather believe they had miscarried.

Being thus disappointed, he said, he carried on the old trade ever since, though when he had gotten so much money, he said, he did not run such desperate risks as he did before. Then he gave me some account of several hard and desperate encounters which he had with gentlemen on the road, who parted too hardly with their money, and showed me some wounds he had received. And he had one or two very terrible wounds indeed, as particularly one by a pistol bullet which broke his arm, and another with a sword, which ran him quite through the body, but that missing his vitals he was cured again, one of his comrades having kept with him so faithfully and so friendly as that he assisted him in riding near eighty miles before his arm was set, and then got a surgeon in a considerable city, remote from that place where it was done, pretending they were gentlemen travelling towards Carlisle, and that they had been attacked on the road by highwaymen, and that one of them had shot him into the arm and broke the bone.

This, he said, his friend managed so well that they were not suspected at all, but lay still till he was perfectly cured. He gave me so many distinct accounts of his adventures that it is with great reluctance that I decline the relating them – but I consider that this is my own story, not his.

I then enquired into the circumstances of his present case at that time, and what it was he expected when he came to be tried. He told me that they had no evidence against him, or but very little – for that, of three robberies, which they were all charged with, it was his good fortune that he was but in one of them, and that there was but one witness to be had for that fact, which was not sufficient, but that it was expected some others would come in against him. That he thought, indeed, when he first saw me, that I had been one that came of that errand, but that if nobody came in against him, he hoped he should be cleared. That he had had some intimation that if he would submit to transport himself, he might be admitted to it without a trial, but that he could not think of it with any temper, and thought he could much easier submit to be hanged.

I blamed him for that, and told him I blamed him on two accounts. First, because if he was transported, there might be an hundred ways for him – that was a gentleman and a bold, enterprising man – to find his way back again, and perhaps some ways and means to come back before he went. He smiled at that part, and said he should like the last the best of the two, for he had a kind of horror upon his mind at his being sent over to the plantations as Romans sent condemned slaves to work in the mines; that he thought the passage into another state, let it be what it would, much more tolerable at the gallows, and that this was the general notion of all the gentlemen who were driven by the exigence of their fortunes to take the road; that at the place of execution there was at least an end of all the miseries of the present state, and as for what was to follow, a man was, in his opinion, as likely to repent sincerely in the last fortnight of his life under the pressures and agonies of a jail and the condemned hole as he would ever be in the woods and wildernesses of America; that servitude and hard labour were things gentlemen could never stoop to; that it was but the way to force them to be their own executioners afterwards, which was much worse, and that therefore he could not have any patience when he did but think of being transported.

I used the utmost of my endeavour to persuade him, and joined that known woman's rhetoric to it – I mean that of tears. I told him the infamy of a public execution was certainly a greater pressure upon the spirits of a gentleman than any of the mortifications that he could meet with abroad could be – that he had at least in the other a chance for his life, whereas here he had none at all; that it was the easiest thing in the world for him to manage the captain of the ship, who were generally speaking men of good humour and some gallantry – and a small matter of conduct, especially if there was any money to be had, would make way for him to buy himself off when he came to Virginia.

He looked wishfully at me, and I thought I guessed at what he meant – that is to say, that he had no money – but I was mistaken. His meaning was another way. "You hinted just now, my dear," said he, "that there might be a way of coming back before I went, by which I understood you that it might be possible to buy it off here. I had rather give 200*l.* to prevent going than 100*l.* to be set at liberty when I came there." "That is, my dear," said I, "because you do not know the place so well as I do." "That may be," said he, "and yet I believe, as well as you know it, you would do the same, unless it is because, as you told me, you have a mother there."

I told him, as to my mother, it was next to impossible, but that she must be dead many years before. And as for any other relations that I might have there, I knew them not now; that since the misfortunes I had been under had reduced me to the condition I had been in for some years, I had not kept up any correspondence with them, and that he would easily believe I should find but a cold reception from them, if I should be put to make my first visit in the condition of a transported felon; that, therefore, if I went thither, I resolved not to see them, but that I had many views in going there, if it should be my fate, which took off all the uneasy part of it – and if he found himself obliged to go also, I should easily instruct him how to manage himself so as never to go a servant at all, especially since I found he was not destitute of money, which was the only friend in such a condition.

He smiled, and said he did not tell me he had money. I took him up short, and told him I hoped he did not understand by my speaking that I should expect any supply from him if he had money – that, on the other hand, though I had not a great deal, yet I did not want, and while I had any I would rather add to him than weaken him in that article, seeing, whatever he had, I knew in the case of transportation he would have occasion of it all.

He expressed himself in a most tender manner upon that head. He told me what money he had was not a great deal, but that he would never hide any of it from me if I wanted it, and that he assured me he did not speak with any such apprehensions, that he was only intent upon what I had hinted to him before he went, that here he knew what to do with himself, but there he should be the most ignorant, helpless wretch alive.

I told him he frighted and terrified himself with that which had no terror in it – that if he had money, as I was glad to hear he had, he might not only avoid the servitude, supposed to be the consequence of transportation, but begin the world upon a new foundation, and that such a one as he could not fail of success in, with but the common application usual in such cases; that he could not but call to mind that it was what I had recommended to him many years before, and had proposed it for our mutual subsistence and restoring our fortunes in the world, and I would tell him now that to convince him both of the certainty of it and of my being fully acquainted with the method, and also fully satisfied in the probability of success, he should first see me deliver myself from the necessity of going over at all, and then that I would go with him freely, and of my own choice, and perhaps carry enough with me to satisfy him that I did not offer it for want of being able to live without assistance from him, but that I thought our mutual misfortunes had been such as were sufficient to reconcile us both to quitting this part of the world and living where nobody could upbraid us with what was past or we be in any dread of a prison, and without the agonies of a condemned hole to drive us to it – where we should look back on all our past disasters with infinite satisfaction, when we should consider that our enemies should entirely forget us, and that we should live as new people in a new world, nobody having anything to say to us, or we to them.

I pressed this home to him with so many arguments, and answered all his own passionate objections so effectually, that he embraced me and told me I treated him with such a sincerity and affection as overcame him – that he would take my advice and would strive to submit to his fate, in hope of having the comfort of my assistance, and of so faithful a counsellor, and such a companion in his misery. But still he put me in mind of what I had mentioned before – namely, that there might be some way to get off before he went, and that it might be possible to avoid going at all, which he said would be much better. I told him he should see, and be fully satisfied that I would do my utmost in that part too, and if it did not succeed, yet that I would make good the rest.

We parted after this long conference with such testimonies of kindness and affection as I thought were equal, if not superior, to that at our parting at Dunstable. And now I saw more plainly than before the reason why he declined coming at that time any farther with me toward London than Dunstable, and why, when we parted there, he told me it was not convenient for him to come part of the way to London to bring me going, as he would otherwise have done. I have observed that the account of his life would have made a much more pleasing history than this of mine, and indeed nothing in it was more strange than this part, viz. that he had carried on that desperate trade full five-and-twenty year and had never been taken; the success he had met with had been so very uncommon, and such that sometimes he had lived handsomely and retired in one place for a year or two at a time, keeping himself and a manservant to wait on him, and has often sat in the coffee houses, and heard the very people who he had robbed give accounts of their being robbed, and of the places and circumstances, so that he could easily remember that it was the same.

In this manner it seems he lived near Liverpool at the time he unluckily married me for a fortune. Had I been the fortune he expected, I verily believe, as he said, that he would have taken up and lived honestly all his days.

He had with the rest of his misfortunes the good luck not to be actually upon the spot when the robbery was done which he was committed for, and so none of the persons robbed could swear to him, or had anything to charge upon him. But, it seems, as he was taken with the gang, one hard-mouthed countryman swore home to him, and they were like to have others come in according to the publication they had made, so that they expected more evidence against him, and for that reason he was kept in hold.

However, the offer which was made to him of admitting him to transportation was made, as I understood, upon the intercession of some great person who pressed him hard to accept of it before a trial – and, indeed, as he knew there were several that might come in against him, I thought his friend was in the right, and I lay at him night and day to delay it no longer.

At last, with much difficulty he gave his consent, and as he was not therefore admitted to transportation in court, and on his petition, as I was, so he found himself under a difficulty to avoid embarking himself as I had said he might have done – his great friend, who was his intercessor for the favour of that grant, having given security for him that he should transport himself, and not return within the term.

This hardship broke all my measures, for the steps I took afterwards for my own deliverance were hereby rendered wholly ineffectual, unless I would abandon him and leave him to go to America by himself – than which he protested he would much rather venture, although he were certain to go directly to the gallows.

I must now return to my own case. The time of my being transported according to my sentence was near at hand. My governess, who continued my fast friend, had tried to obtain a pardon, but it could not be done unless with an expense too heavy for my purse, considering that to be left naked and empty, unless I had resolved to return to my old trade again, had been worse than my transportation, because there I knew I could live – here I could not. The good minister stood very hard on another account to prevent my being transported also, but he was answered that, indeed, my life had been given me at his first solicitations, and therefore he ought to ask no more. He was sensibly grieved at my going, because, as he said, he feared I should lose the good impressions which a prospect of death had at first made on me, and which were since increased by his instructions, and the pious gentleman was exceedingly concerned about me on that account.

On the other hand, I really was not so solicitous about it as I was before, but I industriously concealed my reasons for it from the minister, and to the last he did not know but that I went with the utmost reluctance and affliction.

It was in the month of February that I was, with thirteen other convicts, as they called us, delivered to a merchant that traded to Virginia, on board a ship, riding,* as they called it, in Deptford Reach. The officer of the prison delivered us on board, and the master of the vessel gave a discharge for us.

We were for that night clapped under hatches, and kept so close that I thought I should have been suffocated for want of air, and the next morning the ship weighed and fell down the river* to a place they call Bugby's Hole,* which was done, as they told us, by the agreement of the merchant, that all opportunity of escape should be taken from us. However, when the ship came thither and cast anchor, we were allowed more liberty, and particularly were permitted to come upon the deck, but not upon the quarterdeck, that being kept particularly for the captain and for passengers.

When, by the noise of the men over my head and the motion of the ship, I perceived that they were under sail, I was at first greatly surprised, fearing we should go away directly, and that our friends would not be admitted to see us any more, but I was easy soon after when I found they had come to an anchor again, and soon after that we had notice given by some of the men where we were that the next morning we should have the liberty to come upon deck, and to have our friends come and see us, if we had any.

All that night I lay upon the hard boards of the deck, as the other prisoners did, but we had afterwards the liberty of little cabins for such of us as had any bedding to lay in them, and room to stow any box or trunk for clothes, and linen if we had it (which might well be put in), for some of them had neither shirt or shift, or a rag of linen or woollen, but what was on their backs, or a farthing of money to help themselves – and yet I did not find but they fared well enough in the ship, especially the women, who got money of the seamen for washing their clothes sufficient to purchase any common things that they wanted.

When the next morning we had the liberty to come upon the deck, I asked one of the officers of the ship whether I might not have the liberty to send a letter on shore to let my friends know where the ship lay, and to get some necessary things sent to me. This was, it seems, the boatswain – a very civil, courteous sort of man – who told me I should have that or any other liberty that I desired, that he could allow me with safety. I told him I desired no other, and he answered that the ship's boat would go up to London the next tide, and he would order my letter to be carried.

Accordingly, when the boat went off, the boatswain came to me and told me the boat was going off – that he went in it himself, and if my letter was ready, he would take care of it. I had prepared myself, you may be sure, pen, ink and paper beforehand, and I had gotten a letter ready directed to my governess, and enclosed another for my fellow prisoner – which, however, I did not let her know was my husband, not to the last. In that to my governess, I let her know where the ship lay, and pressed her earnestly to send me what things I knew she had got ready for me for my voyage.

When I gave the boatswain the letter, I gave him a shilling with it, which I told him was for the charge of a messenger or porter, which I entreated him to send with the letter as soon as he came on shore – that, if possible, I might have an answer brought back by the same hand, that I might know what was become of my things. "For, sir," says I, "if the ship should go away before I have them on board, I am undone."

I took care when I gave him the shilling to let him see that I had a little better furniture* about me than the ordinary prisoners, for he saw that I had a purse, and in it a pretty deal of money, and I found that the very sight of it immediately furnished me with very different treatment from what I should otherwise have met with in the ship – for though he was very courteous indeed before, in a kind of natural compassion to me, as a woman in distress, yet he was more than ordinarily so afterwards, and procured me to be better treated in the ship than, I say, I might otherwise have been, as shall appear in its place.

He very honestly had my letter delivered to my governess's own hands, and brought me back an answer from her in writing – and when he gave me the answer, gave me the shilling again. "There," says he, "there's your shilling again, too, for I delivered the letter myself." I could not tell what to say, I was so surprised at the thing, but after some pause, I said, "Sir, you are too kind. It had been but reasonable that you had paid yourself coach hire, then."

"No, no," says he, "I am overpaid. What is the gentlewoman? Your sister?"

"No, sir," said I, "she is no relation to me, but she is a dear friend, and all the friends I have in the world." "Well," says he, "there are few such friends in the world. Why, she cries after you like a child." "Ay," says I again, "she would give a hundred pound, I believe, to deliver me from this dreadful condition I am in."

"Would she so?" says he. "For half the money I believe I could put you in a way how to deliver yourself." But this he spoke softly, that nobody could hear.

"Alas, sir!" said I. "But then that must be such a deliverance as, if I should be taken again, would cost me my life." "Nay," said he. "If you were once out of the ship, you must look to yourself afterwards, that I can say nothing to." So we dropped the discourse for that time.

In the mean time, my governess, faithful to the last moment, conveyed my letter to the prison, to my husband, and got an answer to it, and the next day came down herself to the ship, bringing me in the first place a sea bed, as they call it, and all its furniture, such as was convenient, but not to let the people think it was extraordinary. She brought with her a sea chest – that is, a chest such as are made for seamen – with all the conveniences in it, and filled with everything almost that I could want. And in one of the corners of the chest, where there was a private drawer, was my bank of money – that is to say, so much of it as I had resolved to carry with me, for I ordered a part of my stock to be left behind me, to be sent afterwards in such goods as I should want when I came to settle, for money in that country is not of much use where all things are bought for tobacco: much more is it a great loss to carry it from hence.

But my case was particular. It was by no means proper to me to go thither without money or goods, and for a poor convict that was to be sold as soon as I came on shore, to carry with me a cargo of goods would be to have notice taken of it, and perhaps to have them seized by the public. So I took part of my stock with me thus, and left the other part with my governess.

My governess brought me a great many other things, but it was not proper for me to look too well provided in the ship, at least till I knew what kind of a captain we should have. When she came into the ship, I thought she would have died indeed. Her heart sank at the sight of me and at the thoughts of parting with me in that condition, and she cried so intolerably I could not for a long time have any talk with her.

I took that time to read my fellow prisoner's letter – which, however, greatly perplexed me. He told me he was determined to go, but found it would be impossible for him to be discharged time enough for going in the same ship, and, which was more than all, he began to question whether they would give him leave to go in what ship he pleased, though he did voluntarily transport himself, but that they would see him put on board such a ship as they should direct, and that he would be charged upon the captain as other convict prisoners were. So that he began to be in despair of seeing me till he came to Virginia, which made him almost desperate, seeing that, on the other hand, if I should not be there, if any accident of the sea or of mortality should take me away, he should be the most undone creature there in the world.

This was very perplexing, and I knew not what course to take. I told my governess the story of the boatswain, and she was mighty eager with me to treat with him. But I had no mind to it till I heard whether my husband, or fellow prisoner, so she called him, could be at liberty to go with me or no. At last I was forced to let her into the whole matter, except only that of his being my husband. I told her I had made a positive bargain or agreement with him to go, if he could get the liberty of going in the same ship, and that I found he had money.

Then I read a long lecture to her of what I proposed to do when we came there – how we could plant, settle and, in short, grow rich without any more adventures – and, as a great secret, I told her that we were to marry as soon as he came on board.

She soon agreed cheerfully to my going, when she heard this, and she made it her business from that time to get him out of the prison in time, so that he might go in the same ship with me – which at last was brought to pass, though with great difficulty, and not without all the forms of a transported prisoner convict, which he really was not yet, for he had not been tried, and which was a great mortification to him. As our fate was now determined, and we were both on board, actually bound to Virginia, in the despicable quality of transported convicts destined to be sold for slaves, I for five year and he under bonds and security not to return to England any more as long as he lived, he was very much dejected and cast down. The mortification of being brought on board as he was, like a prisoner, piqued him very much, since it was first told him he should transport himself, and so that he might go as a gentleman at liberty. It is true he was not ordered to be sold when he came there, as we were, and for that reason he was obliged to pay for his passage to the captain, which we were not. As to the rest, he was as much at a loss as a child what to do with himself, or with what he had, but by directions.

Our first business was to compare our stock. He was very honest to me, and told me his stock was pretty good when he came into the prison, but the living there, as he did, in a figure like a gentleman – and, which was ten times as much, the making of friends, and soliciting his case – had been very expensive, and, in a word, all his stock that he had left was an hundred and eight pounds, which he had about him all in gold.

I gave him an account of my stock as faithfully – that is to say, of what I had taken to carry with me, for I was resolved, whatever should happen, to keep what I had left with my governess, in reserve, that, in case I should die, what I had with me was enough to give him, and that which was left in my governess's hands would be her own, which she had well deserved of me indeed.

My stock which I had with me was two hundred and forty-six pounds, some odd shillings, so that we had three hundred and fifty-four pound between us, but a worse-gotten estate was scarce ever put together to begin the world with.

Our greatest misfortune as to our stock was that it was all in money, which everyone knows is an unprofitable cargo to be carried to the plantations. I believe his was really all he had left in the world, as he told me it was, but I, who had between seven and eight hundred pounds in bank when this disaster befell me, and who had one of the faithfullest friends in the world to manage it for me, considering she was a woman of no manner of religious principles, had still three hundred pounds left in her hand, which I reserved, as above, besides some very valuable things, as particularly two gold watches, some small pieces of plate and some rings – all stolen goods. The plate, rings and watches were put up in my chest with the money, and with this fortune, and in the sixty-first year of my age, I launched out into a new world, as I may call it, in the condition (as to what appeared) only of a poor naked convict, ordered to be transported in respite from the gallows. My clothes were poor and mean, but not ragged or dirty, and none knew in the whole ship that I had anything of value about me.

However, as I had a great many very good clothes, and linen in abundance, which I had ordered to be packed up in two great boxes, I had them shipped on board – not as my goods, but as consigned to my real name in Virginia, and had the bills of loading signed by a captain in my pocket – and in these boxes was my plate and watches, and everything of value except my money, which I kept by itself in a private drawer in my chest, which could not be found, or opened if found, without splitting the chest to pieces.

In this condition I lay for three weeks in the ship, not knowing whether I should have my husband with me or no, and therefore not resolving how or in what manner to receive the honest boat-swain's proposal – which, indeed, he thought a little strange at first.

At the end of this time, behold, my husband came on board. He looked with a dejected, angry countenance – his great heart was swelled with rage and disdain to be dragged along with three keepers of Newgate and put on board like a convict, when he had not so much as been brought to a trial. He made loud complaints of it by his friends, for it seems he had some interest, but his friends got some check in their application, and were told he had had favour enough, and that they had received such an account of him since the last grant of his transportation that he ought to think himself very well treated that he was not prosecuted anew. This answer quieted him at once, for he knew too much what might have happened and what he had room to expect, and now he saw the goodness of the advice to him, which prevailed with him to accept of the offer of a voluntary transportation. And after his chagrin at these hellhounds, as he called them, was a little over, he looked a little composed, began to be cheerful, and, as I was telling him how glad I was to have him once more out of their hands, took me in his arms and acknowledged with great tender-ness that I had given him the best advice possible. "My dear," says he, "thou hast twice saved my life. From henceforward it shall be all employed for you, and I'll always take your advice."

The ship began now to fill. Several passengers came on board who were embarked on no criminal account, and these had accommodations assigned them in the great cabin, and other parts of the ship, whereas we as convicts were thrust down below, I know not where. But when my husband came on board, I spoke to the boatswain who had so early given me hints of his friendship in carrying my letter. I told him he had befriended me in many things, and I had not made any suitable return to him, and with that I put a guinea into his hands. I told him that my husband was now come on board – that though we were both under the present misfortunes, yet we had been persons of a differing character from the wretched crew that we came with, and desired to know of him whether the captain might not be moved to admit us to some conveniences in the ship, for which we would make him what satisfaction he pleased, and that we would gratify him for his pains in procuring this for us. He took the guinea, as I could see, with great satisfaction, and assured me of his assistance.

Then he told us he did not doubt but that the captain, who was one of the best-humoured gentlemen in the world, would be easily brought to accommodate us as well as we could desire, and to make me easy told me he would go up the next tide on purpose to speak to the captain about it. The next morning, happening to sleep a little longer than ordinary, when I got up and began to look abroad, I saw the boatswain among the men in his ordinary business. I was a little melancholy at seeing him there, and, going forwards to speak to him, he saw me and came towards me, but, not giving him time to speak first, I said, smiling, "I doubt, sir, you have forgot us, for I see you are very busy." He returned presently, "Come along with me, and you shall see." So he took me into the great cabin, and there sat a good sort of a gentlemanly man for a seaman, writing and with a great many papers before him.

"Here," says the boatswain to him that was a-writing, "is the gentlewoman that the captain spoke to you of." And turning to me, he said, "I have been so far from forgetting your business that I have been up at the captain's house, and have represented faithfully to the captain what you said relating to your being furnished with better conveniences for yourself and your husband, and the captain has sent this gentleman, who is mate of the ship, down with me on purpose to show you everything, and to accommodate you fully to your content, and bid me assure you that you shall not be treated like what you were at first expected to be, but with the same respect as other passengers are treated."

The mate then spoke to me, and, not giving me time to thank the boatswain for his kindness, confirmed what the boatswain had said, and added that it was the captain's delight to show himself kind and charitable, especially to those that were under any misfortunes, and with that he showed me several cabins built up – some in the great cabin and some partitioned off out of the steerage, but opening into the great cabin on purpose for the accommodation of passengers – and gave me leave to choose where I would. However, I chose a cabin which opened into the steerage, in which was very good conveniences to set our chest and boxes, and a table to eat on.

The mate then told me that the boatswain had given so good a character of me and of my husband, as to our civil behaviour, that he had orders to tell me we should eat with him, if we thought fit, during the whole voyage, on the common terms of passengers; that we might lay in some fresh provisions, if we pleased – or, if not, he should lay in his usual store, and we should have share with him. This was very reviving news to me after so many hardships and afflictions as I had gone through of late. I thanked him, and told him the captain should make his own terms with us, and asked him leave to go and tell my husband of it, who was not very well, and was not yet out of his cabin. Accordingly, I went, and my husband, whose spirits were still so much sunk with the indignity (as he understood it) offered him that he was scarce yet himself, was so revived with the account I gave him of the reception we were like to have in the ship that he was quite another man, and new vigour and courage appeared in his very countenance. So true is it that the greatest of spirits, when overwhelmed by their afflictions, are subject to the greatest dejections and are the most apt to despair and give themselves up.

After some little pause to recover himself, my husband came up with me and gave the mate thanks for the kindness which he had expressed to us, and sent suitable acknowledgement by him to the captain, offering to pay him by advance whatever he demanded for our passage and for the conveniences he had helped us to. The mate told him that the captain would be on board in the afternoon, and that he would leave all that till he came. Accordingly, in the afternoon the captain came, and we found him the same courteous obliging man that the boatswain had represented him to be, and he was so well pleased with my husband's conversation that, in short, he would not let us keep the cabin we had chosen, but gave us one that, as I said before, opened into the great cabin.

Nor were his conditions exorbitant, or the man craving and eager to make a prey of us, but for fifteen guineas we had our whole passage and provisions, and cabin, ate at the captain's table and were very handsomely entertained.

The captain lay himself in the other part of the great cabin, having let his roundhouse, as they call it, to a rich planter who went over with his wife and three children, who ate by themselves. He had some other ordinary passengers, who quartered in the steerage, and as for our old fraternity, they were kept under the hatches while the ship lay there, and came very little on the deck.

I could not refrain acquainting my governess with what had happened. It was but just that she, who was so really concerned for me, should have part in my good fortune – besides, I wanted her assistance to supply me with several necessaries which before I was shy of letting anybody see me have, that it might not be public. But now I had a cabin and room to set things in, I ordered abundance of good things for our comfort in the voyage, as brandy, sugar, lemons, etc., to make punch and treat our benefactor, the captain, and abundance of things for eating and drinking in the voyage – also a larger bed, and bedding proportioned to it. So that, in a word, we resolved to want for nothing in the voyage.

All this while I had provided nothing for our assistance when we should come to the place and begin to call ourselves planters, and I was far from being ignorant of what was needful on that occasion – particularly, all sorts of tools for the planter's work and for building, and all kinds of furniture for our dwelling, which, if to be bought in the country, must necessarily cost double the price.

So I discoursed that point with my governess, and she went and waited upon the captain and told him that she hoped ways might be found out for her two unfortunate cousins, as she called us, to obtain our freedom when we came into the country, and so entered into a discourse with him about the means and terms also, of which I shall say more in its place. And after thus sounding the captain, she let him know, though we were unhappy in the circumstance that occasioned our going, yet that we were not unfurnished to set ourselves to work in the country, and were resolved to settle and live there as planters, if we might be put in a way how to do it. The captain readily offered his assistance, told her the method of entering upon such business, and how easy – nay, how certain – it was for industrious people to recover their fortunes in such a manner. "Madam," says he, "'tis no reproach to any man in that country to have been sent over in worse circumstances than I perceive your cousins are in, provided they do but apply with diligence and good judgement to the business of that place when they come there."

She then enquired of him what things it was necessary we should carry over with us, and he, like a very honest as well as knowing man, told her thus: "Madam, your cousins in the first place must procure somebody to buy them as servants, in conformity to the conditions of their transportation, and then, in the name of that person, they may go about what they will. They may either purchase some plantations already begun, or they may purchase land of the government of the country, and begin where they please, and both will be done reasonably." She bespoke his favour in the first article, which he promised to her to take upon himself, and indeed faithful performed it. And as to the rest, he promised to recommend us to such as should give us the best advice, and not to impose upon us, which was as much as could be desired.

She then asked him if it would not be necessary to furnish us with a stock of tools and materials for the business of planting, and he said, "Yes, by all means" – and then she begged his assistance in it. She told him she would furnish us with everything that was convenient, whatever it cost her. He accordingly gave her a long particular of things necessary for a planter, which by his account came to about fourscore or an hundred pounds. And, in short, she went about as dextrously to buy them as if she had been an old Virginia merchant – only that she bought by my direction above twice as much of everything as he had given her a list of.

These she put on board in her own name, took his bills of loading for them, and endorsed those bills of loading to my husband, ensuring the cargo afterwards in her own name, by our order – so that we were provided for all events and for all disasters.

I should have told you that my husband gave her all his whole stock of 108*l.* – which, as I have said, he had about him in gold – to lay out thus, and I gave her a good sum besides, so that I did not break into the stock which I had left in her hands at all, but after we had sorted out our whole cargo, we had yet near 200*l.* in money, which was more than enough for our purpose.

In this condition, very cheerful, and indeed joyful, at being so happily accommodated as we were, we set sail from Bugby's Hole to Gravesend,* where the ship lay about ten days more, and where the captain came on board for good and all. Here the captain offered us a civility which, indeed, we had no reason to expect. Namely, to let us go on shore and refresh ourselves, upon giving our words in a solemn manner that we would not go from him, and that we would return peaceably on board again. This was such an evidence of his confidence in us that it overcome my husband, who, in a mere principle of gratitude, told him as he could not be in any capacity to make a suitable return for such a favour, so he could not think of accepting of it. Nor could he be easy that the captain should run such a risk. After some mutual civilities, I gave my husband a purse, in which was eighty guineas, and he puts it into the captain's hand. "There, captain," says he, "there's part of a pledge for our fidelity. If we deal dishonestly with you on any account, 'tis your own" – and on this we went on shore.

Indeed, the captain had assurance enough of our resolutions to go, for that, having made such provision to settle there, it did not seem rational that we would choose to remain here at the expense and peril of life – for such it must have been if we had been taken again. In a word, we went all on shore with the captain and supped together in Gravesend, where we were very merry, stayed all night, lay at the house where we supped and came all very honestly on board again with him in the morning. Here we bought ten dozen bottles of good beer, some wine, some fowls and such things as we thought might be acceptable on board.

My governess was with us all this while, and went with us round into the Downs,* as did also the captain's wife, with whom she went back. I was never so sorrowful at parting with my own mother as I was at parting with her, and I never saw her more. We had a fair easterly wind sprung up the third day after we came to the Downs, and we sailed from thence the 10th of April. Nor did we touch any more at any place till, being driven on the coast of Ireland by a very hard gale of wind, the ship came to an anchor in a little bay near the mouth of a river whose name I remember not, but they said the river came down from Limerick, and that it was the largest river in Ireland.*

Here being detained by bad weather for some time, the captain, who continued the same kind, good-humoured man as at first, took us two on shore with him again. He did it now in kindness to my husband, indeed, who bore the sea very ill and was very sick, especially when it blew so hard. Here we bought in, again, store of fresh provisions, especially beef, pork, mutton and fowls, and the captain stayed to pickle up five or six barrels of beef to lengthen out the ship's store. We were here not above five days, when, the weather turning mild, and a fair wind, we set sail again, and in two-and-forty days came safe to the coast of Virginia.

When we drew near to the shore, the captain called me to him and told me that he found by my discourse I had some relations in the place, and that I had been there before, and so he supposed I understood the custom in their disposing the convict prisoners when they arrived. I told him I did not, and that, as to what relations I had in the place, he might be sure I would make myself known to none of them while I was in the circumstances of a prisoner, and that, as to the rest, we left ourselves entirely to him to assist us, as he was pleased to promise us he would do. He told me I must get somebody in the place to come and buy us as servants, and who must answer for us to the governor of the country if he demanded us. I told him we should do as he should direct, so he brought a planter to treat with him, as it were, for the purchase of these two servants, my husband and me, and there we were formally sold to him, and went ashore with him. The captain went with us and carried us to a certain house, whether it was to be called a tavern or not I know not, but we had a bowl of punch there made of rum, etc., and were very merry. After some time, the planter gave us a certificate of discharge and an acknowledgement of having served him faithfully, and we were free from him the next morning to go whither we would.

For this piece of service the captain demanded of us six thousandweight* of tobacco, which he said he was accountable for to his freighter, and which we immediately bought for him, and made him a present of twenty guineas besides, with which he was abundantly satisfied.

It is not proper to enter here into the particulars of what part of the colony of Virginia we settled in, for divers reasons. It may suffice to mention that we went into the great river of Potomac, the ship being bound thither, and there we intended to have settled at first, though afterwards we altered our minds.

The first thing I did of moment after having gotten all our goods on shore and placed them in a storehouse, or warehouse, which with a lodging we hired at the small place or village where we landed – I say, the first thing was to enquire after my mother and after my brother (that fatal person who I married as a husband, as I have related at large). A little enquiry furnished me with information that Mrs —— (that is, my mother) was dead, that my brother (or husband) was alive, which I confess I was not very glad to hear – but, which was worse, I found he was removed from the plantation where he lived formerly, and where I lived with him, and lived with one of his sons in a plantation just by the place where we landed and where we had hired a warehouse.

I was a little surprised at first, but as I ventured to satisfy myself that he could not know me, I was not only perfectly easy, but had a great mind to see him, if it was possible to do so without his seeing me. In order to that, I found out by enquiry the plantation where he lived, and, with a woman of that place, who I got to help me, like what we call a charwoman, I rambled about towards the place, as if I had only a mind to see the country and look about me. At last I came so near that I saw the dwelling house. I asked the woman whose plantation that was – she said it belonged to such a man, and, looking out a little to our right hands, "There," says she, "is the gentleman that owns the plantation, and his father with him." "What are their Christian names?" said I. "I know not," said she, "what the old gentleman's name is, but his son's name is Humphry, and, I believe," says she, "the father's is so too." You may guess, if you can, what a confused mixture of joy and fright possessed my thoughts upon this occasion, for I immediately knew that this was nobody else but my own son by that father she showed me, who was my own brother. I had no mask, but I ruffled my hoods so about my face that I depended upon it that after above twenty years' absence, and withal not expecting anything of me in that part of the world, he would not be able to know anything of me. But I need not have used all that caution, for the old gentleman was grown dim-sighted by some distemper which had fallen upon his eyes, and could but just see well enough to walk about and not run against a tree or into a ditch. The woman that was with me had told me that by a mere accident, knowing nothing of what importance it was to me. As they drew near to us, I said, "Does he know you, Mrs Owen?" – so they called the woman. "Yes," said she, "if he hears me speak, he will know me. But he can't see well enough to know me, or anybody else" – and so she told me the story of his sight, as I have related. This made me secure, and so I threw open my hoods again, and let them pass by me. It was a wretched thing for a mother thus to see her own son – a handsome, comely young gentleman in flourishing circumstances – and durst not make herself known to him, and durst not take any notice of him. Let any mother of children that reads this consider it, and but think with what anguish of mind I restrained myself, what yearnings of soul I had in me to embrace him and weep over him, and how I thought all my entrails turned within me, that my very bowels moved, and I knew not what to do, as I now know not how to express those agonies. When he went from me, I stood gazing and trembling, and looking after him as long as I could see him. Then, sitting down on the grass, just at a place I had marked, I made as if I lay down to rest me, but turned from her and, lying on my face, wept and kissed the ground that he had set his foot on.

I could not conceal my disorder so much from the woman but that she perceived it, and thought I was not well, which I was obliged to pretend was true. Upon which, she pressed me to rise, the ground being damp and dangerous, which I did accordingly, and walked away.

As I was going back again, and still talking of this gentleman and his son, a new occasion of melancholy offered itself thus: the woman began, as if she would tell me a story to divert me, "There goes," says she, "a very odd tale among the neighbours where this gentleman formerly lived." "What was that?" said I. "Why," says she, "that old gentleman, going to England when he was a young man, fell in love with a young lady there, one of the finest women that ever was seen, and married her, and brought her over hither to his mother, who was then living. He lived here several years with her," continued she, "and had several children by her, of which the young gentleman that was with him now was one, but after some time, the old gentlewoman his mother talking to her of something relating to herself, when she was in England,

and of her circumstances in England, which were bad enough, the daughter-in-law began to be very much surprised and uneasy, and, in short, examining further into things, it appeared past all contradiction that she (the old gentlewoman) was her own mother, and that, consequently, that son was his wife's own brother, which struck the whole family with horror, and put them into such confusion that it had almost ruined them all. The young woman would not live with him. The son, her brother and husband, for a time went distracted, and, at last, the young woman went away for England, and has never been heard of since."

It is easy to believe that I was strangely affected with this story, but 'tis impossible to describe the nature of my disturbance. I seemed astonished at the story, and asked her a thousand questions about the particulars, which I found she was thoroughly acquainted with. At last I began to enquire into the circumstances of the family, how the old gentlewoman – I mean my mother – died, and how she left what she had – for my mother had promised me very solemnly that when she died she would do something for me, and leave it so as that, if I was living, I should one way or other come at it, without its being in the power of her son, my brother and husband, to prevent it. She told me she did not know exactly how it was ordered, but she had been told that my mother had left a sum of money, and had tied her plantation for the payment of it, to be made good to the daughter, if ever she could be heard of, either in England or elsewhere, and that the trust was left with this son, who was the person that we saw with his father.

This was news too good for me to make light of, and you may be sure filled my heart with a thousand thoughts what course I should take, how and when, and in what manner I should make myself known, or whether I should ever make myself known or no.

Here was a perplexity that I had not indeed skill to manage myself in. Neither knew I what course to take. It lay heavy upon my mind night and day. I could neither sleep or converse, so that my husband perceived it and wondered what ailed me, strove to divert me, but it was all to no purpose. He pressed me to tell him what it was troubled me, but I put it off, till at last, importuning me continually, I was forced to form a story which yet had a plain truth to lay it upon too. I told him I was troubled because I found we must shift our quarters and alter our scheme of settling, for that I found I should be known if I stayed in that part of the country, for that, my mother being dead, several of my relations were come into that part where we then was, and that I must either discover myself to them, which in our present circumstances was not proper on many accounts, or remove – and which to do I knew not, and that this it was that made me so melancholy and so thoughtful.

He joined with me in this – that it was by no means proper for me to make myself known to anybody in the circumstances in which we then were – and therefore he told me he would be willing to remove to any other part of the country, or even to any other country if I thought fit. But now I had another difficulty, which was that if I removed to any other colony, I put myself out of the way of ever making a due search after those effects which my mother had left. Again, I could never so much as think of breaking the secret of my former marriage to my new husband – it was not a story, as I thought, that would bear telling, nor could I tell what might be the consequences of it, and it was impossible to search into the bottom of the thing without making it public all over the country, as well who I was as what I now was also.

In this perplexity I continued a great while, and this made my spouse very uneasy, for he found me perplexed, and yet thought I was not open with him, and did not let him into every part of my grievance. And he would often say he wondered what he had done that I would not trust him with whatever it was, especially if it was grievous and afflicting. The truth is he ought to have been trusted with everything, for no man in the world could deserve better of a wife, but this was a thing I knew not how to open to him, and yet, having nobody to disclose any part of it to, the burden was too heavy for my mind. For let them say what they please of our sex not being able to keep a secret – my life is a plain conviction to me of the contrary. But be it our sex or the man's sex, a secret of moment should always have a confidant, a bosom friend, to whom we may communicate the joy of it or the grief of it, be it which it will, or it will be a double weight upon the spirits, and perhaps become even insupportable in itself. And this I appeal to all human testimony for the truth of.

And this is the cause why many times men, as well as women, and men of the greatest and best qualities other ways, yet have found themselves weak in this part, and have not been able to bear the weight of a secret joy or of a secret sorrow, but have been obliged to disclose it, even for the mere giving vent to themselves and to unbend the mind, oppressed with the load and weights which attended it. Nor was this any token of folly or thoughtlessness at all, but a natural consequence of the thing, and such people, had they struggled longer with the oppression, would certainly have told it in their sleep and disclosed the secret, let it have been of what fatal nature soever, without regard to the person to whom it might be exposed. This necessity of nature is a thing which works sometimes with such vehemence in the minds of those who are guilty of any atrocious villainy, such as secret murder in particular, that they have been obliged to discover it, though the consequence would necessarily be their own destruction. Now, though, it may be true that the divine justice ought to have the glory of all those discoveries and confessions, yet 'tis as certain that Providence, which ordinarily works by the hands of nature, makes use here of the same natural causes to produce those extraordinary effects.

I could give several remarkable instances of this in my long conversation with crime and with criminals. I knew one fellow that, while I was a prisoner in Newgate, was one of those they called then "night-flyers" – I know not what other word they may have understood it by since, but he was one who by connivance was admitted to go abroad every evening, when he played his pranks, and furnished those honest people they call thief-catchers with business to find out next day, and restore for a reward what they had stolen the evening before. This fellow was as sure to tell in his sleep all that he had done, and every step he had taken, what he had stole and where, as sure as if he had engaged to tell it waking, and that there was no harm or danger in it. And therefore he was obliged, after he had been out, to lock himself up or be locked up by some of the keepers that had him in fee,* that nobody should hear him. But on the other hand, if he had told all the particulars and given a full account of his rambles and success to any comrade, any brother thief, or to his employers, as I may justly call them, then all was well with him, and he slept as quietly as other people.

As the publishing this account of my life is for the sake of the just moral of every part of it and for instruction, caution, warning and improvement to every reader, so this will not pass, I hope, for an unnecessary digression concerning some people being obliged to disclose the greatest secrets either of their own or other people's affairs.

Under the certain oppression of this weight upon my mind, I laboured in the case I have been naming, and the only relief I found for it was to let my husband into so much of it as I thought would convince him of the necessity there was for us to think of settling in some other part of the world, and the next consideration before us was which part of the English settlements we should go to. My husband was a perfect stranger to the country, and had not yet so much as a geographical knowledge of the situation of the several places – and I, that till I wrote this did not know what the word "geographical" signified, had only a general knowledge from long conversation with people that came from or went to several places. But this I knew: that Maryland, Pennsylvania, East and West Jersey, New York and New England lay all north of Virginia, and that they were consequently all colder climates – to which, for that very reason, I had an aversion, for that, as I naturally loved warm weather, so, now I grew into years, I had a stronger inclination to shun a cold climate. I therefore considered of going to Carolina, which is the only southern colony of the English on the continent of America, and hither I proposed to go – and the rather because I might with great ease come from thence at any time, when it might be proper to enquire after my mother's effects, and to make myself known enough to demand them.

With this resolution, I proposed to my husband our going away from where we was and carrying all our effects with us to Carolina, where we resolved to settle, for my husband readily agreed to the first part, viz. that it was not at all proper to stay where we was, since I had assured him we should be known there, and the rest I effectually concealed from him.

But now I found a new difficulty upon me. The main affair grew heavy upon my mind still, and I could not think of going out of the country without somehow or other making enquiry into the grand affair of what my mother had done for me. Nor could I with any patience bear the thought of going away and not make myself known to my old husband (brother) or to my child, his son – only I would fain have had this done without my new husband having any knowledge of it, or they having any knowledge of him, or that I had such a thing as a husband.

I cast about innumerable ways in my thoughts how this might be done. I would gladly have sent my husband away to Carolina, with all our goods, and have come after myself, but this was impracticable – he would never stir without me, being himself perfectly unacquainted with the country and with the methods of settling there or anywhere else. Then I thought we would both go first with part of our goods, and that when we were settled I should come back to Virginia and fetch the remainder – but even then I knew he would never part with me, and be left there to go on alone. The case was plain: he was bred a gentleman, and by consequence was not only unacquainted but indolent, and, when we did settle, would much rather go out into the woods with his gun, which they call there "hunting", and which is the ordinary work of the Indians, and which they do as servants – I say, he would much rather do that than attend the natural business of his plantation.

These were, therefore, difficulties unsurmountable, and such as I knew not what to do in. I had such strong impressions on my mind about discovering myself to my brother, formerly my husband, that I could not withstand them – and the rather, because it ran constantly in my thoughts, that if I did not do it while he lived, I might in vain endeavour to convince my son afterwards that I was really the same person, and that I was his mother, and so might both lose the assistance and comfort of the relation and the benefit of whatever it was my mother had left me. And yet, on the other hand, I could never think it proper to discover myself to them in the circumstances I was in, as well relating to the having a husband with me as to my being brought over by a legal transportation as a criminal. On both which accounts it was absolutely necessary to me to remove from the place where I was – and come again to him, as from another place – and in another figure.

Upon those considerations, I went on with telling my husband the absolute necessity there was of our not settling in Potomac River, at least that we should be presently made public there, whereas if we went to any other place in the world we should come in with as much reputation as any family that came to plant – that, as it was always agreeable to the inhabitants to have families come among them to plant who brought substance with them, either to purchase plantations or begin new ones, so we should be sure of a kind, agreeable reception, and that without any possibility of a discovery of our circumstances.

I told him in general, too, that as I had several relations in the place where we was, and that I durst not now let myself be known to them, because they would soon come into a knowledge of the occasion and reason of my coming over, which would be to expose myself to the last degree, so I had reason to believe that my mother who died here had left me something, and perhaps considerable, which it might be very well worth my while to enquire after – but that this too could not be done without exposing us publicly, unless we went from hence and then, wherever we settled, I might come as it were to visit and to see my brother and nephews, make myself known to them, claim and enquire after what was my due, be received with respect, and at the same time have justice done me with cheerfulness and goodwill. Whereas if I did it now, I could expect nothing but with trouble, such as exacting it by force, receiving it with curses and reluctance, and with all kinds of affronts which he would not perhaps bear to see; that in case of being obliged to legal proofs of being really her daughter, I might be at loss, be obliged to have recourse to England, and it may be to fail at last, and so lose it, whatever it might be. With these arguments, and having thus acquainted my husband with the whole secret so far as was needful to him, we resolved to go and seek a settlement in some other colony – and, at first thoughts, Carolina was the place we pitched upon.

In order to this we began to make enquiry for vessels going to Carolina, and in a very little while got information that on the other side the bay, as they call it – namely, in Maryland – there was a ship which came from Carolina, loaden with rice and other goods, and was going back again thither, and from thence to Jamaica with provisions. On this news we hired a sloop to take in our goods, and taking, as it were, a final farewell of Potomac River, we went with all our cargo over to Maryland.

This was a long and unpleasant voyage, and my spouse said it was worse to him than all the voyage from England, because the weather was but indifferent, the water rough and the vessel small and inconvenient. In the next place we were full a hundred miles up Potomac River, in a part which they call Westmoreland County, and as that river is by far the greatest in Virginia, and, I have heard say, it is the greatest river in the world that falls into another river, and not directly into the sea, so we had base weather in it, and were frequently in great danger. For though they call it but a river 'tis frequently so broad that when we were in the middle we could not see land on either side for many leagues together. Then we had the great river or bay of Chesapeake to cross, which is where the River Potomac falls into it, near thirty miles broad, and we entered more great, vast waters, whose names I know not, so that our voyage was full two hundred mile, in a poor, sorry sloop with all our treasure, and if any accident had happened to us we might at last have been very miserable. Supposing we had lost our goods and saved our lives only, and had then been left naked and destitute, and in a wild strange place, not having one friend or acquaintance in all that part of the world? The very thoughts of it gives me some horror, even since the danger is past.

Well, we came to the place in five days' sailing – I think they call it Philip's Point. And behold, when we came thither, the ship bound to Carolina was loaded and gone away but three days before. This was a disappointment, but, however, I that was to be discouraged with nothing told my husband that since we could not get passage to Carolina, and that the country we was in was very fertile and good, we would if he liked of it see if we could find out anything for our turn where we was, and that if he liked things we would settle here.

We immediately went on shore, but found no conveniences just at that place, either for our being on shore or preserving our goods on shore, but was directed by a very honest Quaker who we found there to go to a place about sixty miles east – that is to say, nearer the mouth of the bay where he said he lived, and where we should be accommodated, either to plant or to wait for any other place to plant in that might be more convenient, and he invited us with so much kindness and simple honesty that we agreed to go, and the Quaker himself went with us.

Here we bought us two servants, viz. an English woman servant just come on shore from a ship of Liverpool, and a Negro man-servant – things absolutely necessary for all people that pretended to settle in that country. This honest Quaker was very helpful to us, and when we came to the place that he proposed to us, found us out a convenient storehouse for our goods, and lodging for ourselves and our servants. And about two months or thereabout afterwards, by his direction we took up a large piece of land from the governor of that country in order to form our plantation, and so we laid the thoughts of going to Carolina wholly aside, having been very well received here, and accommodated with a convenient lodging till we could prepare things and have land enough cured, and timber and materials provided for building us a house – all which we managed by the direction of the Quaker. So that in one year's time, we had near fifty acres of land cleared, part of it enclosed and some of it planted with tobacco, though not much. Besides, we had garden ground, and corn sufficient to help supply our servants with roots and herbs and bread.

And now I persuaded my husband to let me go over the bay again and enquire after my friends. He was the willinger to consent to it now because he had business upon his hands sufficient to employ him, besides his gun to divert him, which they call "hunting" there, and which he greatly delighted in. And, indeed, we used to look at one another sometimes with a great deal of pleasure, reflecting how much better that was, not than Newgate only, but than the most prosperous of our circumstances in the wicked trade that we had been both carrying on.

Our affair was in a very good posture. We purchased of the proprietors of the colony as much land for thirty-five pound, paid in ready money, as would make a sufficient plantation to employ between fifty and sixty servants, and which, being well improved, would be sufficient to us as long as we could either of us live – and as for children, I was past the prospect of anything of that kind.

But our good fortune did not end here. I went, as I have said, over the bay to the place where my brother, once a husband, lived – but I did not go to the same village where I was before, but went up another great river, on the east side of the River Potomac, called Rappahannock River, and by this means came on the back of his plantation, which was large, and by the help of a navigable creek, or little river, that ran into the Rappahannock, I came very near it.

I was now fully resolved to go up point-blank to my brother (husband) and to tell him who I was. But not knowing what temper I might find him in – or how much out of temper, rather, I might make him by such a rash visit – I resolved to write a letter to him first to let him know who I was, and that I was come not to give him any trouble upon the old relation, which I hoped was entirely forgot, but that I applied to him as a sister to a brother, desiring his assistance in the case of that provision which our mother at her decease had left for my support, and which I did not doubt but he would do me justice in, especially considering that I was come thus far to look after it.

I said some very tender kind things in the letter about his son, which I told him he knew to be my own child, and that as I was guilty of nothing in marrying him any more than he was in marrying me, neither of us having then known our being at all related to one another, so I hoped he would allow me the most passionate desire of once seeing my one and only child, and of showing something of the infirmities of a mother in preserving a violent affection for him, who had never been able to retain any thought of me one way or other.

I did believe that, having received this letter, he would immediately give it to his son to read – I having understood, his eyes being so dim, that he could not see to read it. But it fell out better than so, for, as his sight was dim, so he had allowed his son to open all letters that came to his hand for him, and the old gentleman being from home or out of the way when my messenger came, my letter came directly to my son's hand, and he opened and read it.

He called the messenger in, after some little stay, and asked him where the person was who gave him the letter. The messenger told him the place, which was about seven miles off, so he bid him stay and, ordering a horse to be got ready, and two servants, away he came to me with the messenger. Let anyone judge the consternation I was in when my messenger came back and told me the old gentleman was not at home, but his son was come along with him, and was just coming up to me. I was perfectly confounded, for I knew not whether it was peace or war – nor could I tell how to behave. However, I had but a very few moments to think, for my son was at the heels of the messenger, and, coming up into my lodgings, asked the fellow at the door something. I suppose it was – for I did not hear it so as to understand it – which was the gentlewoman that sent him, for the messenger said, "There she is sir," at which he comes directly up to me, kisses me, took me in his arms and embraced me with so much passion that he could not speak, but I could feel his breast heave and throb like a child that cries, but sobs and cannot cry it out.

I can neither express or describe the joy that touched my very soul when I found – for it was easy to discover that part – that he came not as a stranger, but as a son to a mother, and indeed as a son who had never before known what a mother of his own was. In short, we cried over one another a considerable while, when at last he broke out first: "My dear mother," says he, "are you still alive? I never expected to have seen your face." As for me, I could say nothing a great while.

After we had both recovered ourselves a little and were able to talk, he told me how things stood. As to what I had written to his father, he told me he had not showed my letter to his father, or told him anything about it – that what his grandmother left me was in his hands, and that he would do me justice to my full satisfaction; that as to his father, he was old and infirm both in body and mind – that he was very fretful and passionate, almost blind, and capable of nothing, and he questioned whether he would know how to act in an affair which was of so nice a nature as this, and that therefore he had come himself, as well to satisfy himself in seeing me, which he could not restrain himself from, as also to put it into my power to make a judgement, after I had seen how things were, whether I would discover myself to his father or no.

This was really so prudently and wisely managed that I found my son was a man of sense, and needed no direction from me. I told him I did not wonder that his father was as he had described him, for that his head was a little touched before I went away, and principally his disturbance was because I could not be persuaded to conceal our relation and to live with him as my husband after I knew that he was my brother; that as he knew better than I what his father's present condition was, I should readily join with him in such measures as he would direct; that I was indifferent as to seeing his father, since I had seen him first, and he could not have told me better news than to tell me that what his grandmother had left me was entrusted in his hands – who, I doubted not now he knew who I was, would, as he said, do me justice. I enquired then how long my mother had been dead, and where she died, and told so many particulars of the family that I left him no room to doubt the truth of my being really and truly his mother.

My son then enquired where I was, and how I had disposed myself. I told him I was on the Maryland side of the bay, at the plantation of a particular friend, who came from England in the same ship with me – that as for that side of the bay where he was, I had no habitation. He told me I should go home with him and live with him, if I pleased, as long as I lived – that, as to his father, he knew nobody, and would never so much as guess at me. I considered of that a little, and told him that though it was really no little concern to me to live at a distance from him, yet I could not say it would be the most comfortable thing in the world to me to live in the house with him, and to have that unhappy object always before me which had been such a blow to my peace before; that though I should be glad to have his company (my son), or to be as near him as possible while I stayed, yet I could not think of being in the house where I should be also under constant restraint, for fear of betraying myself in my discourse, nor should I be able to refrain some expressions, in my conversing with him as my son, that might discover the whole affair, which would by no means be convenient.

He acknowledged that I was right in all this. "But then, dear mother," says he, "you shall be as near me as you can." So he took me with him on horseback to a plantation next to his own, and where I was as well entertained as I could have been in his own. Having left me there, he went away home, telling me we would talk of the main business the next day, and having first called me his aunt and given a charge to the people, who it seems were his tenants, to treat me with all possible respect. About two hours after he was gone, he sent me a maidservant and a Negro boy to wait on me, and provisions ready dressed for my supper, and thus I was as if I had been in a new world, and began secretly now to wish that I had not brought my Lancashire husband from England at all.

However, that wish was not hearty neither, for I loved my Lancashire husband entirely, as indeed I had ever done from the beginning, and he merited from me as much as it was possible for a man to do – but that by the way.

The next morning my son came to visit me again almost as soon as I was up. After a little discourse, he first of all pulled out a deerskin bag and gave it me, with five-and-fifty Spanish pistoles in it, and told me that was to supply my expenses from England, for though it was not his business to enquire, yet he ought to think I did not bring a great deal of money out with me, it not being usual to bring much money into that country. Then he pulled out his grandmother's will, and read it over to me, whereby it appeared that she had left a small plantation, as he called it, on York River – that is, where my mother lived – to me, with the stock of servants and cattle upon it, and given it in trust to this son of mine for my use, whenever he should hear of my being alive, and to my heirs, if I had any children, and, in default of heirs, to whomsoever I should by will dispose of it – but gave the income of it, till I should be heard of or found, to my said son, and if I should not be living, then it was to him and his heirs.

This plantation, though remote from him, he said he did not let out, but managed it by a head clerk (steward), as he did another that was his father's that lay hard by it, and went over himself three or four times a year to look after it. I asked him what he thought the plantation might be worth. He said if I would let it out, he would give me about sixty pounds a year for it, but if I would live on it, then it would be worth much more, and he believed would bring me in about 150l. a year. But seeing I was likely either to settle on the other side the bay, or might perhaps have a mind to go back to England again, if I would let him be my steward he would manage it for me, as he had done for himself, and that he believed he should be able to send me as much tobacco to England from it as would yield me about 100l. a year, sometimes more.

This was all strange news to me, and things I had not been used to, and really my heart began to look up more seriously than I think it ever did before, and to look with great thankfulness to the hand of Providence, which had done such wonders for me, who had been myself the greatest wonder of wickedness, perhaps, that had been suffered to live in the world. And I must again observe that not on this occasion only, but even on all other occasions of thankfulness, my past wicked and abominable life never looked so monstrous to me, and I never so completely abhorred it and reproached myself with it, as when I had a sense upon me of Providence doing good to me, while I had been making those vile returns on my part.

But I leave the reader to improve these thoughts, as no doubt they will see cause, and I go on to the fact. My son's tender carriage and kind offers fetched tears from me, almost all the while he talked with me. Indeed, I could scarce discourse with him but in the intervals of my passion. However, at length I began, and, expressing myself with wonder at my being so happy to have the trust of what I had left put into the hands of my own child, I told him that, as to the inheritance of it, I had no child but him in the world, and was now past having any if I should marry, and therefore would desire him to get a writing drawn, which I was ready to execute, by which I would after me give it wholly to him and to his heirs. And in the mean time, smiling, I asked him what made him continue a bachelor so long. His answer was kind and ready, that Virginia did not yield any great plenty of wives, and that since I talked of going back to England, I should send him a wife from London.

This was the substance of our first day's conversation, the pleasantest day that ever passed over my head in my life, and which gave me the truest satisfaction. He came every day after this, and spent great part of his time with me, and carried me about to several of his friends' houses, where I was entertained with great respect. Also I dined several times at his own house, when he took care always to see his half-dead father so out of the way that I never saw him, or he me. I made him one present, and it was all I had of value, and that was one of the gold watches, of which I mentioned above that I had two in my chest, and this I happened to have with me, and I gave it him at his third visit. I told him I had nothing of any value to bestow but that, and I desired he would now and then kiss it for my sake. I did not, indeed, tell him that I had stole it from a gentlewoman's side at a meeting house in London – that's by the way.

He stood a little while hesitating, as if doubtful whether to take it or no, but I pressed it on him and made him accept it, and it was not much less worth than his leather pouch full of Spanish gold – no, though it were to be reckoned as if at London, whereas it was worth twice as much there, where I gave it him. At length he took it, kissed it, told me the watch should be a debt upon him that he would be paying as long as I lived.

A few days after he brought the writings of gift, and the scrivener with them, and I signed them very freely and delivered them to him with a hundred kisses – for sure nothing ever passed between a mother and a tender, dutiful child with more affection. The next day he brings me an obligation under his hand and seal, whereby he engaged himself to manage and improve the plantation for my account, and with his utmost skill, and to remit the produce to my order wherever I should be, and withal to be obliged himself to make up the produce a hundred pound a year to me. When he had done so, he told me that as I came to demand it before the crop was off, I had a right to the produce of the current year, and so he paid me an hundred pound in Spanish pieces of eight, and desired me to give him a receipt for it as in full for that year, ending at Christmas following, this being about the latter end of August.

I stayed here above five weeks, and indeed had much ado to get away then. Nay, he would have come over the bay with me, but I would by no means allow him to it. However, he would send me over in a sloop of his own, which was built like a yacht, and served him as well for pleasure as business. This I accepted of, and so after the utmost expressions both of duty and affection, he let me come away, and I arrived safe in two days at my friend's the Quaker's.

I brought over with me, for the use of our plantation, three horses with harness and saddles, some hogs, two cows and a thousand other things, the gift of the kindest and tenderest child that ever woman had. I related to my husband all the particulars of this voyage, except that I called my son my cousin, and first I told him that I had lost my watch, which he seemed to take as a misfortune. But then I told him how kind my cousin had been – that my mother had left me such a plantation, and that he had preserved it for me, in hopes some time or other he should hear from me. Then I told him that I had left it to his management, that he would render me a faithful account of its produce, and then I pulled him out the hundred pound in silver, as the first year's produce. And then, pulling out the deerskin purse with the pistoles: "And here, my dear," says I, "is the gold watch." My husband – so is Heaven's goodness sure to work the same effects in all sensible minds where mercies touch the heart – lifted up both his hands, and, with an ecstasy of joy, "What is God a-doing," says he, "for such an ungrateful dog as I am?" Then I let him know what I had brought over in the sloop besides all this – I mean the horses, hogs and cows, and other stores for our plantation. All which added to his surprise and filled his heart with thankfulness – and from this time forward I believe he was as sincere a penitent, and as thoroughly a reformed man, as ever God's goodness brought back from a profligate, a highwayman and a robber. I could fill a larger history than this with the evidences of this truth, and but that I doubt that part of the story will not be equally diverting as the wicked part, I have had thoughts of making a volume of it by itself.

As for myself, as this is to be my own story, not my husband's, I return to that part which relates to myself. We went on with our plantation, and managed it with the help and direction of such friends as we got there by our obliging behaviour, and especially the honest Quaker, who proved a faithful, generous and steady friend to us. And we had very good success, for, having a flourishing stock to begin with, as I have said, and this being now increased by the addition of a hundred and fifty pound sterling in money, we enlarged our number of servants, built us a very good house and cured every year a great deal of land. The second year I wrote to my old governess, giving her part with us of the joy of our success, and ordered her how to lay out the money I had left with her, which was 250*l*., as above, and to send it to us in goods, which she performed with her usual kindness and fidelity, and all this arrived safe to us.

Here we had a supply of all sorts of clothes, as well for my husband as for myself, and I took especial care to buy for him all those things that I knew he delighted to have – as two good long wigs, two silver-hilted swords, three or four fine fowling pieces, a fine saddle with holsters and pistols very handsome, with a scarlet cloak – and, in a word, everything I could think of to oblige him, and to make him appear, as he really was, a very fine gentleman. I ordered a good quantity of such household stuff as we yet wanted, with linen of all sorts for us both. As for myself, I wanted very little of clothes or linen, being very well furnished before. The rest of my cargo consisted in ironwork of all sorts, harness for horses, tools, clothes for servants, and woollen cloth, stuffs, serges, stockings, shoes, hats and the like, such as servants wear, and whole pieces also to make up for servants, all by direction of the Quaker. And all this cargo arrived safe and in good condition, with three women servants, lusty wenches, which my old governess had picked up for me, suitable enough to the place and to the work we had for them to do – one of which happened to come double, having been got with child by one of the seamen in the ship, as she owned afterwards, before the ship got so far as Gravesend. So she brought us a stout boy about seven months after her landing.

My husband, you may suppose, was a little surprised at the arriving of all this cargo from England, and, talking with me after he saw the account of the particular, "My dear," says he, "what is the meaning of all this? I fear you will run us too deep in debt. When shall we be able to make return for it all?" I smiled, and told him that it was all paid for, and then I told him that not knowing what might befall us in the voyage, and considering what our circumstances might expose us to, I had not taken my whole stock with me; that I had reserved so much in my friend's hands – which, now we were come over safe and was settled in a way to live, I had sent for, as he might see.

He was amazed, and stood awhile telling upon his fingers, but said nothing. At last, he began thus: "Hold, let's see," says he, telling upon his fingers still, and first on his thumb. "There's 246*l.* in money at first, then two gold watches, diamond rings and plate," says he, upon the forefinger. Then, upon the next finger: "Here's a plantation on York River, a 100*l.* a year, then 150*l.* in money, then a sloop load of horses, cows, hogs and stores" – and so on to the thumb again. "And now," says he, "a cargo cost 250*l.* in England, and worth here twice the money." "Well," says I, "what do you make of all that?" "Make of it?" says he. "Why, who says I was deceived when I married a wife in Lancashire? I think I have married a fortune, and a very good fortune too," says he.

In a word, we were now in very considerable circumstances, and every year increasing, for our new plantation grew upon our hands insensibly, and in eight year which we lived upon it, we brought it to such a pitch that the produce was at least 300*l.* sterling a year – I mean, worth so much in England.

After I had been a year at home again, I went over the bay to see my son, and to receive another year's income of my plantation, and I was surprised to hear, just at my landing there, that my old husband was dead, and had not been buried above a fortnight. This, I confess, was not disagreeable news, because now I could appear as I was, in a married condition. So I told my son before I came from him that I believed I should marry a gentleman who had a plantation near mine, and though I was legally free to marry, as to any obligation that was on me before, yet that I was shy of it, lest the blot should some time or other be revived, and it might make a husband uneasy. My son, the same kind, dutiful and obliging creature as ever, treated me now at his own house, paid me my hundred pound and sent me home again loaded with presents.

Some time after this, I let my son know I was married, and invited him over to see us, and my husband wrote a very obliging letter to him also, inviting him to come and see him, and he came accordingly some months after, and happened to be there just when my cargo from England came in, which I let him believe belonged all to my husband's estate, not to me.

It must be observed that when the old wretch, my brother (husband), was dead, I then freely gave my husband an account of all that affair, and of this cousin, as I had called him before, being my own son by that mistaken unhappy match. He was perfectly easy in the account, and told me he should have been as easy if the old man, as we called him, had been alive. "For," said he, "it was no fault of yours, nor of his. It was a mistake impossible to be prevented." He only reproached him with desiring me to conceal it and to live with him as a wife after I knew that he was my brother – that, he said, was a vile part. Thus all these little difficulties were made easy, and we lived together with the greatest kindness and comfort imaginable. We are now grown old – I am come back to England, being almost seventy years of age, my husband sixty-eight, having performed much more than the limited terms of my transportation. And now, notwithstanding all the fatigues and all the miseries we have both gone through, we are both in good heart and health. My husband remained there some time after me to settle our affairs, and at first I had intended to go back to him, but at his desire I altered that resolution, and he is come over to England also, where we resolve to spend the remainder of our years in sincere penitence for the wicked lives we have lived.

WRITTEN IN THE YEAR 1683

FINIS

Note on the Text

The text in the present volume is based on the first edition of *Moll Flanders* (1721, but released in January 1722), incorporating a few amendments from "The Third Edition Corrected" of the book, also published in 1722. The punctuation has been regularized, and the spelling has been standardized and modernized throughout.

Notes

p. 3, *Newgate*: A notorious prison in the City of London.

p. 4, *gust*: Taste.

p. 5, *garbled*: Cleansed.

p. 7, *midwife-keeper*: The keeper of a brothel.

p. 7, *coming out by themselves*: In fact, Defoe never produced these supplementary narratives.

p. 11, *Old Bailey*: The most important criminal court in London, located next to Newgate Prison.

p. 11, *the galleys*: Oar-propelled vessels to which French criminals were sometimes sentenced until the eighteenth century.

p. 12, *holland*: A kind of linen fabric originally from the Netherlands.

p. 12, *Cheapside*: The site of a major market in the City of London.

p. 12, *pleaded her belly*: A pregnant woman who was sentenced to death would have her execution postponed until after her baby was born.

p. 12, *I had no parish*: Prisoners were excluded from the basic level of relief provided by the parish to the poor.

p. 12, *Gypsies, or Egyptians*: Gypsies were popularly thought to have originated in Egypt.

p. 15, *4d.*: In Defoe's day and up to decimalization in 1971, the British pound (*l.* – from Latin *libra*, meaning "pound") consisted of twenty shillings (*s.*), each of which consisted in turn of twelve pence (*d.* – from Latin *denarius*, meaning "penny"), making a total of 240 pence in the pound.

p. 15, *plain work*: Simple (as opposed to ornamental) needlework.

p. 17, *laced heads*: Caps made from lace, worn by women.

p. 18, *found myself clothes*: That is, she paid for her clothes out of her own earnings.

p. 19, *mere*: True, real.

p. 19, *turn them*: A worn-out garment could be altered so that the inner side became the outer as a means of prolonging its lifespan.

p. 23, *well carriaged*: Well mannered, well behaved.

p. 28, *cast*: Reckon, calculate.

p. 28, *capitulation*: Stipulation.

p. 30, *turnover*: A linen band worn around the neck.

p. 30, *neck*: A neckcloth.

p. 31, *no dress*: That is, no formal clothing.

p. 31, *Mile End*: A village north of Colchester.

p. 31, *earnest*: Advance payment.

p. 32, *put me to my shifts*: Brought me to an extremity.

p. 38, *I told him he knew very well… as if the ceremony had passed*: Before the Marriage Act of 1753, the first statutory legislation in England requiring a formal ceremony of marriage, it was popularly believed that all that was required for a marriage to be valid was a simple exchange of consent. (In fact, a marriage had to be celebrated by a clergyman even before the 1753 Act.)

p. 40, *jogging*: Shaking.

p. 44, *expected my life*: Expected her to survive.

p. 45, *possessions*: Fixations, obsessions.

p. 46, *rallied*: Teased.

p. 47, *tittle*: Tiny amount.

p. 47, *by the ears*: In conflict with one another, fighting.

p. 54, *in form*: Formally.

p. 54, *a settlement… jointure*: A settlement was a legal arrangement guaranteeing certain money or property for an intended wife. The jointure was the money settled on a wife for the period of her widowhood.

p. 54, *Answer, and answer not, says Solomon*: "Answer not a fool according to his folly, lest thou also be like unto him. Answer a fool according to his folly, lest he be wise in his own conceit" (Proverbs 26:4–5).

p. 56, *the main chance*: The chief issue.

p. 59, *like a bear to the stake*: A reference to the blood sport of bear-baiting, in which a bear was tied to a stake and set upon by dogs.

p. 60, *conversation*: Sexual intercourse.

p. 62, *the mark of his hat upon his periwig*: A gentleman would carry (rather than wear) his hat.

p. 62, *trepanned*: Caught in a trap; deceived.

p. 63, *coach and six*: A coach pulled by six horses – a symbol of extravagance.

p. 63, *the Mint, but got into a sponging house*: The Mint was a district of Southwark, south London, that offered protection against prosecution for debtors due to its historical status as a "liberty", an area of local administration with a degree of independence from neighbouring jurisdictions. A sponging house was a place of preliminary imprisonment for debtors.

p. 66, *the Bull*: An inn in Southwark.

p. 66, *like My Lord Rochester's mistress… without the joy*: In the poem 'Phyllis, Be Gentler, I Advise' by the English courtier and poet John Wilmot, Earl of Rochester (1647–80), the speaker urges Phyllis not to be coy, lest she "Die with the scandal of a whore / And never know the joy" (ll. 15–16).

p. 66, *put a rape upon*: Committed an act of violence against.

p. 68, *lie on hand*: Remain unsold.

p. 71, *Ratcliff*: A hamlet on the north bank of the Thames, east of the City of London.

p. 72, *Redriff*: Another name for Rotherhithe, an area on the south bank of the Thames populated by seamen.

p. 72, *huffed*: Bullied.

p. 73, *A woman's ne'er... her undoer, man*: From Rochester's 'A Letter from Artemisia in the Town to Chloe in the Country', ll. 185–86.

p. 75, *nice*: Fastidious, scrupulous.

p. 76, *as a horse rushes into the battle*: See Jeremiah 8:6.

p. 82, *be transported*: To emigrate.

p. 85, *composition*: A sum paid in lieu of a larger debt.

p. 87, *cure*: Prepare for plantation.

p. 87, *train bands*: Companies of citizen soldiers; local militias.

p. 87, *burnt in the hand*: Criminals convicted of a capital offence could escape execution if they were able to read, which was established by making them read from the Bible (an extension of the medieval principle of clerical immunity from trial or punishment in the secular courts; hence "benefit of clergy"). Those who avoided the death penalty in this manner were branded.

p. 91, *froward*: Difficult, contrary.

p. 94, *contemned*: Treated with contempt.

p. 95, *conjured*: Appealed to.

p. 105, *Kinsale*: A small port in County Cork on the east coast of Ireland.

p. 105, *Milford Haven*: A port in Pembrokeshire, south-west Wales.

p. 105, *bills of loading*: A bill of loading (or lading) is a document provided by a master of a ship acknowledging receipt of cargo.

p. 106, *recruit*: Fresh or additional supply; replenishment.

p. 107, *ill house*: A brothel.

p. 111, *Are the Virginia ships taken by the French?*: England and France fought several wars during the seventeenth century (when the novel is set).

p. 113, *diet him*: Provide him with food.

p. 117, *lying-in*: Confinement before and after childbirth.

p. 118, *Hammersmith*: Now a district in west London, then a village outside the metropolis.

p. 126, *monitor*: Guide.

p. 128, *void of counsel*: See Deuteronomy 32:28.

p. 135, *nice*: Difficult.

p. 140, *a numerous family*: The term "family" here includes the household staff.

p. 143, *West Chester*: The city of Chester.

p. 143, *Black Rock*: An area at the mouth of Liverpool Bay, on the southern side of the River Mersey, opposite Liverpool itself.

p. 158, *one of the nicest*: one of the most difficult.

p. 160, *Mother Midnight*: A slang term for a midwife (also a bawd).

p. 161, *parish impertinences*: As the parish was responsible for illegitimate children born within its limits, its officers were likely to make invasive enquiries.

p. 165, *wench of Drury Lane breeding*: A prostitute. Drury Lane was the centre of prostitution in seventeenth-century London.

p. 168, *within their month*: The period of lying-in typically lasted for a month after birth.

p. 168, *error of the right hand*: An error that has good intentions behind it.

p. 176, *Stone in Cheshire*: A town roughly forty miles south-east of Chester.

p. 176, *Stony Stratford*: A town roughly one hundred miles south-east of Stone.

p. 177, *having been obliged to lie still a Sunday*: Inessential travel was forbidden on Sundays by the Sunday Observance Act 1677.

p. 177, *Brickhill*: Little Brickhill in Buckinghamshire, ten miles south-east of Stony Stratford.

p. 178, *shagreen*: Untanned, rough-surfaced leather.

p. 181, *grimace*: Affectation, sham.

p. 182, *suit of knots*: A set of bows of ribbon worn on a woman's gown as an accessory.

p. 182, *bone lace*: Lace made using fine threads wound on bobbins made of bone.

p. 186, *the experiment*: The proof.

p. 188, *wise man's prayer... lest I steal*: See Proverbs 30:8–9. The "wise man" is Solomon, king of ancient Israel, famous for his great wisdom, to whom much of the book of Proverbs is attributed.

p. 191, *Holborn Bridge*: A bridge that spanned the Fleet ditch at Holborn Street, and was a major thoroughfare.

p. 193, *lustring*: A glossy silk fabric.

p. 193, *Stepney*: A village east of the City of London, now part of the East End of the metropolis.

p. 193, *forecast*: Foresight.

p. 195, *necessary*: Of a person (especially a servant): rendering necessary, useful or personal services.

p. 195, *spark*: A young, foppish man.

p. 198, *Moll Cutpurse*: Sobriquet of the real-life Mary Frith (*c.*1584–1659), notorious London pickpocket and fence.

p. 200, *journeyman*: A trained worker (as opposed to an apprentice) who works for a master rather than himself.

p. 201, *having the brand... was executed*: One could only escape execution by claiming benefit of clergy once (see third note to p. 87).

p. 201, *circuit pardon*: Convicts who could not afford an individual pardon were sometimes included in a document called a "circuit pardon", which listed as many as two dozen or more offenders from the same jail.

p. 203, *burying rings*: Mourning rings.

p. 206, *Flanders lace, being then prohibited*: A means of protecting the domestic lacemaking industry.

p. 207, *punctually*: Scrupulously.

p. 211, *compters*: Counters.

p. 213, *undressed*: Not dressed in formal clothing.

p. 214, *recognizances*: A recognizance is a bond by which a person agrees before a court to observe some condition, such as to appear when summoned.

p. 215, *formal*: Elaborately constructed.

p. 219, *run a-tick*: To "run on tick" meant to purchase on credit – Moll compares herself to one with no outstanding debts.

p. 220, *Bartholomew Fair*: A street fair that began each year on 24th August (St Bartholomew's Day) in West Smithfield in the City of London.

p. 220, *raffling shops*: Shops that sold tickets for raffles and lotteries that were also held on the premises.

p. 221, *Spring Garden at Knightsbridge*: One of London's pleasure gardens – recreational spaces for music, dancing, eating and drinking, hosting firework displays, theatrical performances, masquerades and so on – which, despite their exclusivity (an entrance fee was charged), often had a somewhat dubious reputation.

p. 221, *Temple Bar*: Ceremonial entrance on the western boundary of the City of London, dividing it from the City of Westminster.

p. 222, *They go… through their liver*: See Proverbs 7:22–23.

p. 222, *foul disease*: Syphilis.

p. 224, *gilded counters*: In other words, fake gold coins.

p. 227, *officiously*: With eagerness to serve; courteously.

p. 229, *chairman*: One of two porters who carried a sedan chair (an enclosed box for transporting a single person, carried on poles).

p. 235, *Bluecoat Hospital*: A name for Christ's Hospital, a charity school established in 1552. Such establishments were known as "Bluecoat" schools because of the colour of the gowns worn by the pupils.

p. 235, *Cheston*: A name for the town of Cheshunt in Hertfordshire, twelve miles north of central London.

p. 236, *to a tittle*: To the tiniest detail; to a tee.

p. 236, *huckaback linen*: A robust linen fabric with a rough surface, used for towelling.

p. 236, *ells*: A measure of length used for textiles, typically about forty-five inches.

p. 236, *Mr Henzell's glasshouse*: The de Hennezels were Huguenots who came to England from France in the sixteenth century and established themselves as glassmakers, first in London and then in Newcastle upon Tyne.

p. 240, *about her lawful occasion*: About her lawful business.

p. 242, *second mourning*: The second stage of formal mourning, following strict mourning, requiring black clothes lightened by decoration of white or grey.

p. 243, *Hicks Hall*: A courthouse on St John Street in Clerkenwell.

p. 248, *drawers*: Barmen, tapsters.

p. 249, *the Gazette*: The *London Gazette*, the official journal of record of the British government, first published in 1666.

p. 250, *St Katherine's*: St Katharine Docks, on the north bank of the Thames in the East End of the capital, was one of the principal docks for the port of London.

p. 251, *Exchange in the Strand*: Exeter Exchange on the Strand, which opened in 1680, was an early version of a "shopping mall".

p. 252, *the Mall*: A fashionable promenade running alongside St James's Park.

p. 252, *I puts myself in a rank with*: I walk alongside.

p. 253, *the King*: Given that Moll claims her account was written in 1683, the king here would be Charles II (1630–85), who reigned from the Restoration in 1660 until his death in 1685.

p. 253, *Horse Guards*: The barracks of the Household Cavalry, responsible for guarding the monarch, located at the eastern end of the Mall.

p. 254, *set*: Put down a stake.

p. 255, *the box and dice go round a pace*: The gamesters are playing hazard, a gambling game dating from medieval times in which players bet on the outcome of the rolling of two dice.

p. 257, *Tunbridge and Epsom*: Fashionable spa towns.

p. 257, *Stourbridge Fair... Bury Fair, in Suffolk*: Stourbridge Fair was held annually in September on Stourbridge Common in Cambridge. The fair in Bury St Edmunds in Suffolk took place in December.

p. 257, *bite*: Swindle, deception.

p. 258, *Harwich*: An east-coast seaport in Essex. Moll has travelled north-east of London to Cambridge, then east to Bury St Edmunds, then south-east to Ipswich and Harwich.

p. 260, *French pistoles... rix-dollars*: Respectively, gold coins issued in France after 1640 (otherwise known as louis d'or); silver coins issued in the Netherlands in the seventeenth century; and silver coins used across Europe for trade from the late sixteenth century.

p. 260, *wash balls*: Balls of soap.

p. 261, *clown*: Peasant.

p. 261, *poll*: Head.

p. 265, *clapped in upon me*: Moved suddenly and decisively towards me.

p. 265, *taken me in the fact*: Caught me red-handed.

p. 267, *from whence they went to the fatal tree*: Convicted criminals were taken from Newgate to the village of Tyburn, where now Marble Arch stands in west London, to be hanged.

p. 269, *put it all up to my score*: By convention, new inmates were expected to buy drink for other prisoners.

p. 269, *the college*: Newgate was known as "Whittington's College", after former Lord Mayor of London Sir Richard Whittington (d. 1423). The notion of prisons as "universities of crime" survives to the present day.

p. 269, *the bell*: The bell at St Sepulchre's, which tolls upon execution day (DEFOE'S NOTE). As its name suggests, the church of St Sepulchre-without-Newgate was adjacent to the prison.

p. 271, *ordinary*: Chaplain.

p. 272, *Guildhall*: The ceremonial and administrative centre of the City of London, where many trials were held.

p. 273, *topping*: Distinguished, eminent.

p. 274, *press yard... prison*: A yard at Newgate from where condemned prisoners started for the place of execution – also apparently containing a higher class of accommodation. In medieval times the torture of *peine forte et dure* – in which prisoners' bodies were "pressed" by heavy objects – was carried out here, hence the name.

p. 274, *Hind, or Whitney, or the Golden Farmer*: Real-life highwaymen James Hind (executed in 1652), James Whitney (executed in 1693) and William Davies (executed in 1690), who combined his clandestine criminal career with his role as a farmer (hence his nickname).

p. 276, *as white as a clout*: An archaic expression meaning "as white as a sheet".

p. 283, *recorder*: A magistrate or judge with criminal and civil jurisdiction within a city.

p. 288, *master's side*: A ward of Newgate for wealthier prisoners. Those who could afford to pay for their own food and accommodation. It was luxurious compared to the "common side", but squalid compared to the press yard (see first note to p. 274).

p. 292, *enclosed country*: Formerly common land that has been taken into private ownership for cultivation and fenced in.

p. 293, *Burford Fair in Wiltshire*: A cattle market in Oxfordshire (not Wiltshire).

p. 299, *riding*: Lying at anchor.

p. 299, *fell down the river*: Sailed downriver.

p. 299, *Bugby's Hole*: An embarkation point on the Thames between Woolwich and Greenwich. (A "hole" was an anchorage.) It was also a place where pirates were hanged in chains.

p. 301, *furniture*: Personal belongings.

p. 310, *Gravesend*: On the south bank of the Thames Estuary in Kent.

p. 311, *the Downs*: A roadstead (a sheltered stretch of sea) off the east Kent coast.

p. 311, *the largest river in Ireland*: The River Shannon.

p. 312, *thousandweight*: A weight of a thousand pounds.

p. 318, *had him in fee*: Owned him absolutely.

ALMA CLASSICS

ALMA CLASSICS aims to publish mainstream and lesser-known European classics in an innovative and striking way, while employing the highest editorial and production standards. By way of a unique approach the range offers much more, both visually and textually, than readers have come to expect from contemporary classics publishing.

LATEST TITLES PUBLISHED BY ALMA CLASSICS

www.almaclassics.com

EVERGREENS SERIES

Greatly produced classics, affordably priced

Alma Classics is committed to making available the widest range of literature from around the globe. All the titles are provided with an extensive critical apparatus and extra reading material, including a section of photographs and notes. The texts are based on the most authoritative edition (or collated from the most authoritative editions or manuscripts) and edited using a fresh, intelligent editorial approach. With an emphasis on the production, editorial and typographical values of a book, Alma Classics aspires to revitalize the whole experience of reading the classics.

∽◦∾

Erasmus	*Praise of Folly*
F. Scott Fitzgerald	*The Great Gatsby*
Gustave Flaubert	*Madame Bovary*
Ford Madox Ford	*The Good Soldier*
J.W. von Goethe	*The Sorrows of Young Werther*
Nikolai Gogol	*Petersburg Tales*
Thomas Hardy	*Tess of the d'Urbervilles*
Nathaniel Hawthorne	*The Scarlet Letter*
Henry James	*The Portrait of a Lady*
Franz Kafka	*The Metamorphosis and Other Stories*
D.H. Lawrence	*Lady Chatterley's Lover*
Mikhail Lermontov	*A Hero of Our Time*
Niccolò Machiavelli	*The Prince*
Edgar Allan Poe	*Tales of Horror*
Alexander Pushkin	*Eugene Onegin*
William Shakespeare	*Sonnets*
Mary Shelley	*Frankenstein*
Robert L. Stevenson	*Strange Case of Dr Jekyll and Mr Hyde and Other Stories*
Jonathan Swift	*Gulliver's Travels*
Antal Szerb	*Journey by Moonlight*
Leo Tolstoy	*Anna Karenina*
Ivan Turgenev	*Fathers and Children*
Mark Twain	*Adventures of Huckleberry Finn*
	The Adventures of Tom Sawyer
Oscar Wilde	*The Picture of Dorian Gray*
Virginia Woolf	*Mrs Dalloway*
Stefan Zweig	*A Game of Chess and Other Stories*

**Order online for a 20% discount at
www.almaclassics.com**